Riches That You Bring

Riches That You Bring

Kevin McGann

authorHOUSE®

AuthorHouse™
1663 Liberty Drive
Bloomington, IN 47403
www.authorhouse.com
Phone: 1-800-839-8640

First published by AuthorHouse 1/26/2010

ISBN: 978-1-4490-6653-6 (e)
ISBN: 978-1-4490-6651-2 (sc)
ISBN: 978-1-4490-6652-9 (hc)

Library of Congress Control Number: 2010900440

Printed in the United States of America
Bloomington, Indiana

This book is printed on acid-free paper.

*To Monica, Mathew,
Jessica, Jake, Daphne,
and Brendan*

*To my parents,
Maria and Charles*

Acknowledgements

Monica, Maria and Charles and their
invaluable help and support, thank you.
Front and back cover design by Kevin McGann.
Author image taken by Kim and Larry Kaufman.

CHAPTER I

The Fundraiser

Grand Ballroom

THOMAS CARLYLE QUICKLY WALKED THROUGH THE REVOLVING door of the luxurious, downtown hotel; he glanced over the foyer, spotted the escalator and headed in its direction. While descending he removed his overcoat and looked in the mirror, "I'm glad I bought this suit," he thought. He noticed his blonde hair was wind-blown and calmed it down with his right hand. He walked off the escalator, stopped at the coat check, and then proceeded to the Grand Ballroom. He stopped and read the sign to the left of the entrance, "First National Ballet Fundraiser." In front of him the doors were closed and he could hear someone speaking inside. He was late. "I hope these doors are at the back," he whispered as he clasped his hand around the door handle and nervously turned to open. He wished he wasn't there and stopped for a moment and thought about leaving. He heard the speaker saying thank you and the audience starting to clap. It was now or never. He took a deep breath, opened the door and walked in.

All the tables were to the left and spread out in a half moon shape around the hall. To the right was a raised platform with a podium on it and a DJ's stereo system and speakers. The space between the tables and the podium was the dance floor and this is where he stood. Somewhere amongst the thirty-five tables and three hundred and fifty people was his empty seat. "How will I ever find it?" he thought. He didn't want to stand were he was nor did he want to go from table to table. As Thomas was contemplating what to do next, a lady had walked onto the podium and introduced the new 'Artistic Director of the First National Ballet, Eric Smythe'. A man in his late-fifties and sporting a traditional black tuxedo was crossing the dance floor to the loud applause of the audience. Eric Smythe stood at the podium, shuffled some papers, and surveyed the tables

1

from right to left. Thomas started to retreat to the back of the room but it was too late.

"Young fellow...young fellow," called Eric in his English accent.

Thomas was so busy trying to make it to the back behind the tables that he didn't hear him.

"Young fellow," he said again and realized Thomas wasn't hearing him. "Please, can someone..." he pointed toward Thomas.

Thomas eventually noticed people at the table closest to him pointing to the front. Thomas turned around and noticed everyone was looking at him. He turned and looked to the front.

"Hello young man. Can I help you find your seat?"

Thomas wanted to say no and crawl under the table, but replied, "uh.... yes...please," his voice shaking. Thomas noticed someone at a far table starting to stand up. He was rescued and decided to walk towards them.

Eric hadn't noticed the girl standing. "Why don't you come up to the podium and we will get this sorted out?"

Thomas changed direction. "There's the door," thought Thomas. "I should bolt." Instead, everyone watched him as he walked to the podium.

Eric stood away from the microphone. "Welcome young man," he said with an outstretched hand.

Thomas shook his hand and he felt a little more at ease.

"What's your name?"

"Thomas Carlyle."

Eric motioned toward the podium, stopped and looked at Thomas. "Maggie Carlyle?" he questioned.

"She's my grandmother."

To Thomas's surprise Eric placed his arms around Thomas and hugged him. "Maggie was a very dear friend. I'm sorry to hear she passed away," he whispered. Eric removed his arms and stood back and looked at Thomas. Eric was fighting back tears as he turned around to the audience. "Please excuse me for a moment ladies and gentlemen." Eric moved away from the microphone and looked at Thomas, "we hadn't talked for a few years and I was on vacation and didn't hear about her passing and funeral till it was too late. She was a lovely lady, I am sorry."

"It was a beautiful service," replied Thomas. He could see the sadness in Eric's eyes. "She spoke very highly of you," said Thomas. He smiled and leaned over and whispered, "Eric Smith".

Eric laughed out loud as he recalled how Margaret used to call him Eric Smith when he was being arrogant; it was her polite way of telling him to stop. How arrogant he was back then he thought. After a while she stopped calling him Eric Smith and one day he asked her why. "There isn't a need anymore," she replied, "now you are truly a dancer and a gentleman." It was her kindness and patience that molded him into the dancer and the man he was today, he owed her everything. He squeezed Thomas's arm, gathered his thoughts, and turned to the audience. "Five minutes ago I was going to read from these," he lifted his hand containing the sheets of paper. He crumpled them up and threw them on the floor, "but I've decided not to because I am going to tell you this story." He looked over at Thomas. "This young fellow is the grandson of the greatest ballerina this company, the world, has ever had. Her presence electrified the stage and her commitment was unprecedented, second to none. When talking with this young man a lifetime of fond memories flashed through my mind." He paused and collected his thoughts. "Most of the information I am passing on to you is second hand so I am going to ask?" Eric looked around at the faces, "Where's Hank Taylor?" he asked. A seventy-eight year old raised his hand in acknowledgement. "There he is! Hank, if I say something incorrect you make sure you put me on the right track." Hank responded with his thumb up. "Fifty years ago Hank was a stage manager, musical director and accountant…not at different times….at the same time." The guests laughed. "The company performed at a playhouse down by the waterfront and Margaret Carlyle performed at this playhouse when she was a young girl. The academy where she danced held their recitals and competitions there and so on. It was at one of these competitions that Margaret was noticed by the director of the American Ballet School of Dance and she was asked to take the examination and eventually enroll. The playhouse helped her with her tuition. Years later, when she started dancing professionally, Margaret would send a portion of her salary to the playhouse. She did so till the day she retired. She was one of the reasons the playhouse was able to grow and become what you all know today as the First National Ballet. But it wasn't just the money; it was also the time she took out of her busy schedule to participate in fundraisers or volunteer her time to teach classes. Let's not forget, she was doing this when she was one of the best in the world. At forty-five she taught ballet at the First National Ballet School and did so for twenty-five years, giving one student a year a full scholarship. She was a kind, generous, loving lady. She never forgot where she came from." He paused and reflected for a moment. "It is her generous sprit that I would like to capture here, not only tonight at our fundraiser, but everyday. Thank you." There was a loud applause and yells of 'Bravo!' Eric turned and squeezed Thomas's shoulder and smiled and whispered 'Thank you." He walked down the three steps and back to his table. Thomas was left alone on the platform.

Rachel

A GIRL IN HER LATE TWENTIES WEARING a black evening gown walked toward Thomas. The gown clung tightly around her perfect figure and her blonde hair was pulled back into a French braid. She stopped in front of him and looked up with sparkling emerald green eyes. She was breathtaking.

"Thomas Carlyle," she said.

"Yes," he replied.

"I believe you are sitting at our table."

Thomas walked down the steps.

"Please, let me escort you to your seat?" She opened up her arm. "My name is Rachel Carter."

"Hello Rachel," said Thomas as he put his arm through hers.

"Hello Thomas," she replied and walked with him to the table.

Rachel introduced the eight people sitting around the table. There was Dr. Gordon and Dr. Mann and their wives, Joanne and Mary. Mr. Levinson and Ms. Cross, who were lawyers, Mr. Collins whom was a close friend of the Carter's, and Jessica Carter, Rachel's mother, who was stunning and could have been mistaken for Rachel's older sister.

"Hello Thomas," smiled Jessica Carter.

"Hello Mrs. Carter."

"Oh please, Jessica."

"Jessica," replied Thomas.

Thomas waited for Rachel to sit down then sat in the vacant spot between her and Mr. Collins.

"Dom Perignon?" asked Mr. Collins.

"Please."

"At fifteen hundred dollars a head we should be getting a bottle each," replied Mr. Collins. "What do you think?" He looked at Thomas as he poured.

"I'll wait and see if they break out the Glenfiddich and cigars after desert," said Thomas with a nervous smile.

Mr. Collins laughed loudly and approved with a nod.

Thomas turned to Rachel and looked into her emerald eyes. "Are you a ballerina?"

Rachel smiled. "No, one of my closest friends became a principal dancer this year and my parents are patrons." She took a sip of her champagne. "I wanted to become a model. I did modeling when I was younger and when I was at university I was able to do some modeling part time, today I just model whenever I can."

"Are you kept busy?"

"Somewhat," she replied, holding back a smile.

"Well I hope it picks up," he said sincerely. "Do you enjoy it?"

"I love it! But someday I would like to do something with children, maybe run a daycare center or children's camp. That's my dream. That's what I went to university for." She looked at him. "What about you?"

As she asked this question the conversations others seemed to be having dissipated. "I work during the day and write in my spare time."

"Really, who do you work for?" inquired Mr. Collins.

"I work for QTech."

"Computers," he nodded a gesture of approval, "Management?"

"No. Distribution center," He felt uncomfortable, not with what he did, but the attention he was receiving.

"I see," said Jessica. "It's a starting point. Many great men have started on the lower rung and worked their way up the ladder of success, some have even gone on to start their own companies and are multimillionaires today."

"I've heard they make great laptops," interjected Mr. Levinson the lawyer.

"The best on the market," replied Thomas with pride.

"I've had mine for a few years now and I've been looking around for a new one. I've done some research and QTech comes highly recommended," continued Mr. Levinson.

"If you decide to buy one I can put you in touch with someone who will get you top of the line with a good discount. I'll give you my phone number before I leave."

"I'd appreciate that," replied Mr. Levinson and thanked him.

Throughout the four courses Mr. Collins made comment about the meal. The soup was cold, not enough salad, the steak was the size of a meatball, and the desert was too rich and so on. His only approval went to the French red wine. Surprisingly all the comments he made, were in the direction of Thomas. Thomas wasn't sure why.

"Your attention ladies and gentlemen, I hope everyone enjoyed the meal. In the next couple of minutes, as is tradition, we will be presenting the Margaret Carlyle Scholarship to an up and coming dancer who has excelled in the areas of ballet, scholastics, and volunteer work; all the fine qualities that Margaret Carlyle possessed. As many of you are aware this award is given out annually at this function. The recipient will be given a scholarship and a plaque with her name. Her name will also be added to the past winners plaque that resides at the First National Ballet School. On behalf of Margaret Carlyle, Thomas Carlyle her grandson, will present the award. After the presentation the bar will be reopened and the music will begin. Throughout the evening we will be stopping the music for special fundraiser events and activities so please give generously. Thomas, if you can come to the podium. Thank you."

Thomas had forgotten about the presentation, he felt inside his pockets and realized his notes were in his overcoat. It was too late to get them now. He stood and walked to the podium. He positioned the microphone took a deep breath and spoke, "It looks as if I am standing between you and the bar." The crowd laughed. He collected his thoughts, thought about his grandmother and spoke from his heart. "As you have heard several times tonight Margaret Carlyle was a kind, wonderful generous woman whom many of you knew either as a ballerina, a teacher, a friend, or a combination of all three. Unfortunately I was too young to ever see my grandmother dance professionally but was fortunate enough to know and meet many of her friends and colleagues who would drop in and visit her and talk about those days. Many of you are here today and I thank you for spending the time with her and creating those memories for me. Margaret Carlyle lived and breathed ballet and her enthusiasm and her passion were contagious." Thomas paused. "I was asked to present the award tonight because she was a very special person; a very kind, caring and loving woman and a very special ballerina. One of the greatest joys my grandmother had was teaching ballet and one of the greatest enjoyments she had and treasured all year was the giving out of her award to one of her students. She loved it." Thomas held up the envelope. "In this envelope is the recipient of the Margaret Carlyle Award. Unless there are any objections I find it fitting that I ask Ms. Penelope Daily, a teacher of twenty five years, a respected member of the First National Ballet, and a dear friend of my grandmother to come up to the podium and present the award not only this year, but every year."

There was a loud standing applause as Penelope Daily, a slight woman with long silvery hair, walked to the podium. She stopped in front of Thomas and gave him a hug and a kiss on the cheek. "Thank you Tommy", she said with tears in her eyes. As she presented the award, Thomas stood far back and off to the right.

Penelope and the recipient walked off the stage and Thomas started back to his table. Someone from behind grabbed his arm. He turned and a watery eyed Penelope kissed him on the cheek, "Thank you, you've made me so very happy," she said with a slight Dutch accent. "You too have Maggie's fine qualities," she kissed him again on the cheek, then smiled and walked away.

Thomas returned to an empty table. He looked around and there was a crowd of men around the bar, Jack was one of them. There were several groups of women heading out to the foyer and he could just make out Jessica. Thomas decided to go outside onto the patio. The late summer air was cool and refreshing.

He walked off the patio and onto a path and into a quaint garden. The light of the old-fashioned lampposts gave off a romantic glow. He stopped and looked up at the multitude of stars in the sky. He continued down the path. Off to his left, nestled in amongst bushes, was a gazebo, two small for a band to play on but large enough for several people to sit in. It was the centerpiece of the garden. He climbed up the two steps, sat down, learned over and looked at the ground and thought about Kate. He hoped her studying was going well; law school took up a lot of her time. It was hard work and expensive; but she was happy and doing well. Still, he wished she could have been here.

Thomas hadn't noticed the figure standing in front of him.

"May I sit down?"

Thomas looked up at Rachel, "Of course."

"Are you sure? It looked like you were deep in thought. Maybe you want to be alone?"

"No, please sit; I would enjoy your company."

Thomas glanced at her body as she turned to sit next to him. She had a perfect figure and full rounded breasts. He wondered what she modeled.

"It's a beautiful night," she suggested. "Late summer and fall are my favorite times of the year, all the color, the bright sunny skies and the cool air."

"Mine too."

"Do you horseback ride?" she asked.

"I have once, no, twice."

"Did you like it?"

"It was fun, although I was a bit sore afterward," Thomas smiled as he remembered the experience. "When you're on the horse the place where you put your feet?"

"Stirrups," said Rachel, helping out.

"Stirrups, they were too high or something I kept bouncing in my saddle. I couldn't walk upright for a week."

She laughed. "That would be painful."

Thomas looked at her. "Do you horseback ride?"

"Almost every weekend," she looked up at the sky. "Tonight would have been perfect, the stars are so beautiful and bright," she leaned back and let out a sigh. "I'm glad we're alone. It finally gives us some time to talk to you without my mother and Mr. Collins listening in."

Thomas smiled approvingly. "Tell me about your modeling? Do you know any famous models?" asked Thomas.

"I would rather talk about your writing?" inquired Rachel as she moved closer to Thomas.

He was about to reply when a couple walked over to them.

"Hello Rachel."

"Hello Mr. and Mrs. Cartwright."

"How's your father?"

"He's doing well."

"Shame he's missing tonight."

"I know, he was supposed to be here but was delayed in Atlanta. He flies back tomorrow morning."

"Oh poor dear," replied Mrs. Cartwright.

Mr. Cartwright looked over, "Thomas."

"Yes". Thomas stood and shook his hand.

"This is my wife Lily and I'm Fred. It's nice to meet you. It was a nice speech and a nice touch with Penelope, you made her night. Not too many young gentlemen left these days. I never knew your grandmother personally but saw her dance many a time, she was..."

"So graceful and elegant," finished Lily Cartwright.

Thomas smiled. "Thank you both. You're very kind."

Rachel realized that the Cartwright's weren't in a hurry to leave and stood and looked at Thomas. "Thomas I would like to go for that walk now," said Rachel.

"Sure," he replied a little puzzled. "Nice meeting you both."

"You too young man," said Fred. "Say hello to your father, Rachel."

"I will."

Rachel put her arm through Thomas's. They left the gazebo and walked in the opposite direction of the patio. Thomas took off his coat and put it around her. She smiled at him and thought about how nice he was. At the end of the garden there were spruce trees and bushes and in the middle a two-seated bench. They sat quietly and both looked up at the full moon while its light fell upon them.

"That's the second most breathtaking sight I've seen tonight," said Thomas not stopping himself in time.

"The second?" questioned Rachel.

Thomas looked at Rachel and noticed a sprinkling of faint freckles on her nose. He quickly changed the subject. "I like your freckles."

Rachel put her hand over her nose. "Oh no, not enough make up."

"What do you mean?"

"I don't like them. I was teased a lot at school."

"I like them," reassured Thomas.

"They were more prominent when I was younger. They've faded over time."

"Well, I like them," said Thomas as he moved her hand away from her face.

She smiled. "I see you've avoided my question."

"You noticed that."

She nodded her head playfully.

There was a long silence.

"The first was this garden." Thomas lied.

"Really?" she replied. She looked at Thomas and asked hesitantly, "Do you have any plans for next Saturday night?"

"No, I don't think so."

"I'm having a party. Would you like to come?"

"Can I say no?"

"Nooo," smiled Rachel.

"Then I guess it's a yes," replied Thomas.

"I have an invitation inside. I'll get it for you." Rachel stood and motioned for Thomas to join her. Before they got back to the patio she gave his coat back, thanked him and said she would meet him back at the table.

As she crossed the dance floor she could still smell his Trussardi cologne on her. She smiled at how wonderful he was.

9

Thomas sat in his seat; there was a scotch and cigar waiting for him.

Mr. Collins was talking to Jessica but broke off the conversation when he saw Thomas sitting. "Glenfiddich and a cigar," grinned Mr. Collins, "compliments of me." He said as he stood.

"Thank you," said Thomas and smiled.

"The drink's for now, cigar is for later.....outside," he touched his glass with Thomas's and patted him on the back. "I know, some people would say that after a meal a Napoleon brandy would be more suited with a cigar," queried Jack as he looked down at Thomas for a response.

"Perhaps, Mr. Collins, that would be the right thing to do, etiquette and all," Thomas replied carefully. "But you look like a man who likes to do what he wants, so you will drink scotch and not worry too much about what others think," Thomas hesitated, "especially when you're paying for it."

Mr. Collins laughed, "You have a good eye for people. You should be a salesman." Then he leaned over and whispered, "Forget these fancy, pretty decorated meals, there's a place I know that serves steaks the size of your arm, fifteen different types of scotch, every brand of beer, and twenty televisions, all with sports. I'd like to take you one day because I know you'll appreciate it"

"Okay, Mr. Collins," replied Thomas as he sipped on his scotch.

"Jack, call me Jack." He smiled at Thomas and walked over and sat next to Jessica and joined in her conversation.

As he walked away Thomas suddenly realized the size of the man. He was at least six feet four and two hundred and sixty pounds, but solid.

Rachel returned and sat next to Thomas.

The disc jockey played Kool & The Gang's 'Celebration' and everyone was getting up to dance. Thomas asked Rachel; he watched her body move to the rhythm and it was hypnotic. After the fourth song they went back to the table. He asked her and Jessica if they wanted a drink. On the way back from the bar he met Jack and Jessica. "Hi Jack, know you'd appreciate another Glenfiddich," and handed him the glass.

"Don't forget we still have to smoke those cigars," said Jack gesturing to his pocket.

"Let me know when you're ready." He turned to Jessica, "Jessica, a rum and coke for you."

"Thank you," she replied with a smile. "We'll be back at the table in a minute."

Thomas left them and went to the table. He put down a Heineken and a glass in front of Rachel's empty seat. He sat down and drank a mouthful of scotch. He looked around the room and watched the people dancing.

"She's gone to powder her nose," answered Jessica as she sat. "Why not go smoke that cigar with Jack; he said he would be out in a minute. I'll wait here for Rachel."

Thomas stood and picked up his scotch. "Thanks, I think I will."

"And in return I'll take a couple of dances when you get back," she teased.

"It would be my pleasure," replied Thomas as he excused himself.

Jessica watched Thomas leave. She liked him, he reminded her of someone she once knew. She quickly looked around for Rachel. She wanted her to hurry back before Thomas returned.

Rebecca

THOMAS WAS GLAD TO GET OUTSIDE AGAIN and feel the cool breeze on his face. He looked around and realized he was alone. Thomas looked back inside and noticed that someone was talking on the microphone. From what he could make out it seemed as if it a fundraising activity was going to take place. Thomas finished his drink and decided to walk to the bench. From there he could be away from the doors but still see Jack come onto the patio. As he got closer he noticed a solitary figure sitting and it sounded as if she was crying. Thomas turned to go.

"Don't go," asked the voice softly.

Thomas turned, "Is everything okay?"

"I'll be fine in a minute." She dried her eyes with a tissue. "Please come over and sit next to me."

Thomas sat and waited for her to regain her composure. "My name's Thomas." She looked up at him; her eyes were blue like the Caribbean Sea.

"Hi," she smiled. "My name's Rebecca."

Her light brown hair was shoulder length and was parted on one side, and her fringe draped over her eyebrow; the moonlight captured her highlights perfectly. Her skin was flawless and looked soft to the touch. She was beautiful.

"Have we met before?" asked Thomas.

"Yes. It was several months ago," she was surprised he remembered.

"Don't tell me," he thought for a few minutes.

"Need help," she teased.

Thomas nodded.

"Month was May."

Thomas was thinking aloud. "Where was I in May?"

She gave him that look of 'need another clue'.

Thomas nodded.

"Twenty-fourth," she teased.

"Keep them coming," replied Thomas and motioned with his hand.

"Saturday night about eight pm…intermission…"

Thomas motioned again with his hand.

She quickly realized something. "You know, you're just teasing me."

Thomas laughed. "Giselle intermission, you were with Mrs. Peterson. It's all come back to me."

"Sure," she replied jokingly and laughed.

"I was with my grandmother in the Patrons Lounge and I was coming back with some drinks and my grandmother turned around and introduced me to Mrs. Peterson and you, Rebecca La Croix. You stayed for a few minutes and had to leave." As he thought back he remembered Rebecca catching him staring at her, at least he thought she had. But tonight there was something about her that was slightly different; he couldn't put his finger on it.

"You do remember," she said and smiled.

"I do, but there was something different about you then?"

"You mean the jeans, sweat top, and no make-up. Please let me explain. I had danced in the matinee that day and had planned on enough time to go home and change. But I was delayed leaving and never made it home. I felt so embarrassed I knew that was why you were staring at me. I wanted to explain to you then; but decided on a hasty retreat instead. When I saw you again I said I would put you straight. You must have thought…"

Thomas cut her off. "It was your hair. You had it up in a ponytail. That's what it was."

She gave a blank look, 'Really, my hair?' She felt relieved "That was it."

It was, partially, Thomas didn't want to tell her that he was staring at her because he thought she was the most beautiful woman he had ever seen. "I've seen you since then," he suggested.

"Yes you have, at your grandmother's funeral." Rebecca looked out in the distance. "Your grandmother was a very special lady. Do you know she taught me from the time I was five to fifteen? I owe her a great deal. She talked about you all the time, even brought pictures in." Rebecca stopped and thought back about those days and smiled.

Thomas noticed how her smile lit up her face.

"You spoke well of her tonight."

"Thank you," replied Thomas. "At Giselle, when you were walking away, my grandmother said to me you would be a principal dancer this year. Are you the new principal dancer I've been hearing about?"

Rebecca humbly replied, "Yes. Penny, she's been instructing me for the last ten years, is as happy as me." Rebecca looked down at her hand and wanted to cry. "Actually, the only other time I've seen her as happy was tonight." She looked up at Thomas. "That was something quite special you did for her."

"Thank you," he replied.

They smiled at each other. There was a long pause.

Rebecca looked up at Thomas. "Would you like to come to my opening night?" asked Rebecca.

"Well, I..."

"I'll buy the ticket.

"I'd..."

"There's a reception afterwards. Please say yes."

Thomas put his hand on his chin and pretended to be thinking. "I think I have plans that night."

"You don't even know the date," responded Rebecca realizing he was being playful again. She lightly pushed his arm from under his chin.

"I wouldn't miss it for the world. I'm honored that you asked. But on one condition, I'll buy the ticket."

"No, please, let me buy the ticket, I'd like to." She smiled and pleaded, "Please."

He agreed.

Someone had opened the patio doors to let the night air in and the sound of someone singing badly inside could be faintly heard.

"What's that?" asked Thomas.

Rebecca laughed. "It's one of our fundraising events. The First National Ballet dancers are approached by guests, who for a hundred dollars can request the dancer to perform a talent that they think they have such as sing, juggle, or they can opt for just a dance with them. Some are good, some not so good. Right now someone has paid to hear Francis Gray sing or should I say, try to sing!" She laughed as she listened.

"Is he singing a George Michael song? It sounds like he's singing 'Faith'"

"Yes he is. He thinks he looks like him."

"Does he?"

She laughed. "I guess so. You'll have to judge for yourself."

"What can you do?"

"Well, I usually accept a dance," and she couldn't believe what she was about to say, "or I can sing?"

"I'd like to hear you sing," replied Thomas.

"What song?"

"I'd like you to choose."

"Okay, I'll choose one especially for you." She looked around and looked back at Thomas.

"Can I ask you something?"

"Anything," replied Thomas.

"Do you believe in fate?"

"No," replied Thomas.

"Why not?"

"I believe our life is in our own hands and we are in control of it."

"So we are responsible for our lives, no one else."

"I believe so." He wondered why she had asked.

Rebecca looked up at the stars and thought. He didn't know about tonight, the award, why she had been crying, about Francis, about her mother and father, and how complicated her life was. She wanted to tell him everything and she knew she may never have the chance again but would he understand? How could she expect him to understand? He hardly knew her but she wanted to confide in him, because she had known him her whole life. She was in love with him.

"It's a beautiful night," interrupted Thomas as he looked up.

She agreed.

"To think how long it has taken the universe to give us this moment."

"I never thought about it that way."

"Rebecca, is that you back there?"

"Yes, Penny," she replied and whispered to Thomas, "I can call her Penny now, rather than Ms. Daily, she insists I do."

Thomas smiled.

"Thomas, you have to put the donation in an envelope," she searched through her bag and pulled one out and a pen. "I'll write my name and the song on it. Here you go." She stopped and held onto the envelope. "Please don't read it."

"I wont, promise."

"Okay," she said. "You need to give this to the DJ and he'll call me up and I'll put the envelope in the basket."

"Rebecca," called out Penny.

"I'll be there in a minute," replied Rebecca. She turned to Thomas, "she needs my help. I'll see you inside." She smiled as she stood up and walked away. The black evening gown was sheer and short. She had slim hips and long lovely legs. She stopped, hesitated, turned around, walked back to Thomas and leaned over and kissed him on the forehead, "Thank you."

Thomas wished she could have stayed for a few more minutes; instead he watched her walk away. He looked up at the moon and wondered why Rebecca had been crying. He didn't like seeing anyone upset, especially her.

As he walked back he thought about her kiss.

"Thomas where have you been, I've been looking for you. Come up to the bar and I'll buy you a drink," ordered Jack.

"I've just got to go talk to the DJ," he replied, "I'll meet you there."

"I'll come with you, the DJ's on the way."

Jack stopped in front of the DJ and talked to a couple. As Thomas waited for the DJ he could see Rachel across the hall; she had her back to him, and was talking to someone. He handed the DJ the envelope and walked down the steps. Jack met him and they walked over to the bar.

"Scotch, Thomas?"

"Thanks Jack."

"Two Glenfiddichs," said Jack to the bartender.

The bartender brought them their drinks and they moved off to the side.

"Play golf?" asked Jack.

"Yes I do," replied Thomas and took a sip of his drink.

"Any good?"

"Okay," replied Thomas. He was a fine golfer but knew enough not to give a fellow golfer the upper hand especially when he knew what the next question was going to be.

"What's your handicap?"

"I didn't have one this summer. I didn't have many chances to play under the circumstances."

"Oh yeah, of course," replied Jack and remembered the funeral. "Sorry."

It was another deception; Thomas had played more this summer than any other. Playing golf had actually helped him take his mind off of the death of his grandmother and the funeral. In fact, he had played twice last week. "What's yours?"

"You know, I haven't been out enough this summer to rank myself," said Jack. "Been busy."

Thomas laughed and Jack joined in.

"I'll give you a call and we'll play one weekend. The loser can pay for lunch."

Thomas couldn't resist. "I like my steak medium and my beer cold Jack."

"You're a cocky S.O.B!" stated Jack and grinned, "And I like that!"

"I knew you would."

Jack looked at the crowded dance floor and looked back at Thomas. "What do you think? Fifty bucks a dance!"

"You're not my type, Jack."

Jack laughed, "the fundraiser event…to dance with one of them….or get them to sing….or whatever it costs a fifty for."

"Thought it was a hundred?"

"No fifty, for the next two hours it's going to cost you a fifty every time you want to dance with Rachel. That's per song."

"But Rachel isn't a ballet dancer?"

"First, it's the dancers then they add people to the list that our well known in the community, you know celebrities, models, television personalities and such. It adds variety, plus helps with the fundraising. They just announced it a few minutes ago."

Thomas realized he had been outside. He was about to ask Jack about Rachel.

"Here you are, I was wondering where you had gotten to," said Rachel looking into his eyes and smiling.

Jack jumped in, "I've just been telling him about the fifty dollars a dance. He was out of the room when they announced it. Drink Rachel?"

"Heineken please Jack."

Jack walked over to the bar.

"Well known in the community," said Thomas. "You must do a lot of volunteer work."

"Yes, I do," she replied and was convinced he had no idea and smiled at him. "When Jack returns can we go back and sit at the table?"

"Okay," replied Thomas.

Jack returned from the bar holding a tray of beers and whiskeys. "Lets head to the table and get this party going."

As they followed Jack, Rachel put her arm through Thomas's.

For the next forty-five minutes Thomas danced with Rachel and her mother. Listened to three dancers sing. He drank and swapped golfing, fishing, and eating stories with Jack. Intermittently he looked around to see if he could spot Rebecca. She was nowhere in sight. Rachel excused herself and walked over to the other side of the hall to speak with one of her friends. Thomas watched her as she walked across the room. He turned and talked to Jack and didn't see Rachel return.

"Thomas," it was Rachel's voice.

Thomas turned around.

"I would like you to meet my close friend."

Thomas looked up at Rebecca La Croix.

"Hi Thomas," Rebecca said softly.

"Hi Rebecca." Thomas stood, Rebecca leaned over, and he kissed her cheek, her skin was soft.

"You two know each other?" asked a surprised Rachel looking a Rebecca.

"We met at the ballet last season, Thomas used to take his grandmother," said Rebecca with a smile. "Did you know Thomas's grandmother taught me for ten years."

"No I didn't."

"I'm what you might say a friend of the family," finished Rebecca.

"Really!" said Rachel and wondered why Rebecca had never told her this before.

The music lowered and the DJ spoke. "Rebecca La Croix to the DJ, Rebecca," the music returned.

"Excuse me?" asked Rebecca.

"Of course," said Thomas standing.

"Don't be too long?" asked Rachel. "Come back and sit with us."

"I'll be back as soon as I've sang."

"Sing! You're singing?" asked a shocked Rachel.

Jessica, who had overheard, looked on with a stunned look not believing what she had heard.

"Yes," smiled Rebecca and walked away.

Both Rachel and Jessica were dumfounded.

Thomas wasn't sure what was going on and asked, "Is she that bad?"

Jessica moved over and sat next to Thomas and explained. "Rebecca's father and mother split when she was a teenager. Her father is a famous opera singer in New York; he is excellent. I saw him once as Rodrigo in Don Carlos and he was unbelievable. Anyway, before the split he used to take her to his shows and when they were together he used to sing to her and with her, they were really close, and she became an exceptional singer. He took her to the ballet when she was very young and got her into the school. Here's the sad part. Her father was having an affair with one of the co-stars and was caught by her mother who threw him out, and he tried for custody but lost. Rebecca didn't want to have anything to do with him; he was devastated and moved to New York. It was in all the society papers! When Rebecca was eighteen her mother remarried and Rebecca moved out. Her mother helped her buy a place and helped her financially, but we've never seen her since then, the humiliation was too much for her, I think she is living in San Francisco. Her father was or I should say is a really nice man. I really liked him and I still find it difficult to believe he did what he did."

"Why?"

"He loved Rebecca so much, she was his life. You couldn't imagine him hurting her like that," she sighed. "He just didn't look like the type; then again what does the type look like."

"What have I done by asking her to sing?" thought Thomas. "Wait a second; I didn't suggest she sing, she offered, something wasn't right."

The music went off and the humdrum of the crowd took over. The DJ spoke, "Ladies and gentlemen to sing for us now is Ms. Rebecca La Croix." There was a sudden silence. People looked to the podium to confirm the DJ was mistaken, he wasn't, and there was a hum of whispering. The DJ offered Rebecca the microphone.

"This song is for someone very special," she handed the microphone back.

She sang, 'Think of Me, from the Phantom of the Opera'. She sang it beautifully, effortlessly and flawlessly. Thomas felt goose bumps on his arms and a wonderful anxiety in his chest. She was exceptional.

When she had finished people shouted 'Brava!' and asked for another. Rebecca graciously curtsied and thanked them and walked off the podium.

It took her fifteen minutes to make it through the crowd. She arrived with Penelope on her arm. Rachel and Jessica both stood and took turns complimenting her and kissing her on the cheek.

Penelope whispered to Thomas. "You must be sent from Heaven, an angel perhaps, only you could have made her sing again."

Thomas had a blank look on his face and said, "Well I really didn't do anything, and we were…."

Penelope didn't hear him and turned to Rebecca and squeezed her hand and whispered in her ear, Thomas couldn't make out the words. Penelope moved over and talked with Jessica and Rachel. Rebecca stood in front of Thomas.

Thomas thanked her with a hug and whispered in her ear. "You know you should sing more often, that was beautiful."

"Thank you Thomas, for you anytime." She squeezed his arm and smiled. "When I get back I'll pay off my dance debt to you, my choice of song though."

"You don't owe me a…"

She cut him off mid sentence, "You paid a hundred that guaranteed you a song, and me, at least one dance." She slyly smiled and moved away from his ear and excused herself and headed for the foyer.

Thomas walked over to Rachel.

"I've never heard her sing before," commented Rachel. "I'd heard she was good."

A slow song came on and Thomas looked at Rachel. "Would you like to dance?"

"I would love to," she replied.

He moved to the dance floor and put one hand around her waist and held her other hand. He could smell the sweetness of her perfume and feel her firm breasts rub up against his chest.

Tonight all she wanted to do was enjoy herself and be a girl named Rachel Carter and he was giving her that opportunity. She knew he would find out sooner than later and that she had to tell him, but not tonight, perhaps tomorrow. Her mother and Jack had promised not to say anything, but everyone else knew.

Rebecca walked out into the foyer and into the bathroom. She checked all the stalls; they were empty. She locked herself in the last one, leaned against the wall and softly cried.

End of the Night

REBECCA EVENTUALLY REJOINED THEM AT THE TABLE. It was getting late and people were starting to leave. Rachel and Jessica had their coats in their arms and were doing the rounds of good-byes. Thomas glanced at Rebecca; there was a distant look on her face.

"Would you like a drink of something?" asked Jack.

"Can I have one of those beers?"

Jack looked down at the ones he'd been stacking on the table all night. "Of course," he poured one into the glass and passed it to her.

Rebecca took a mouthful and swallowed. "You know how long it's been since I've had a beer?" she asked as she stared at the glass.

"About two seconds?" Thomas replied in jest.

She tried to keep a serious face but broke into laughter. Jack and Thomas followed suit.

"I can't even remember the last time I laughed," She looked at Thomas and whispered to him, "but that's all going to change."

Thomas was about to ask her what was going to change when Rachel interrupted.

"It's time for us to go."

"Let me help you with your coat," offered Thomas and stood and helped Jessica, then Rachel.

"Thomas can we drop you anywhere?" asked Jessica.

"Thanks, but I'm staying here tonight. I drove down; there are some things I want to do in town tomorrow. Thanks for the offer."

"Do you have a room?" inquired Jessica.

"Not yet. I asked one of the hotel staff after dinner and he confirmed they have rooms available," reassured Thomas. "I was planning on getting here a little earlier and reserving one."

Jack, using his best English accent, retold Eric trying to get Thomas's attention. They all laughed.

Jessica was searching through her bag. "Here room seventeen ten," she handed Thomas two room keys. "One is for the door the other is for the elevator. Bill was supposed to be back from Atlanta earlier this evening, but won't be coming in till tomorrow, the room is yours."

"Thanks," said Thomas. "As long as I can pay for it!"

"Nonsense," said Jessica and looked at him. "It's prepaid, breakfast is included and there's a free bar. Order what you want and video check out before you leave. Please, enjoy, I feel better knowing someone is going to use it rather than it going to waste."

"Thank you very much," replied Thomas sincerely.

"Time for me to leave too," said Jack pulling his coat check ticket out of his pocket along with two cigars. "Here's one for tonight." He gave one to Thomas and put the other one back.

Thomas offered to walk them up to the lobby and pulled Rebecca out of her seat to join him. Up the escalator and across the lobby they talked about the night. A black stretch limousine pulled up to the front door. Thomas followed Rachel and Jessica outside and walked them to it. He gave each of them a hug and a kiss and waved as the limousine pulled away. It stopped and the door opened.

"Thomas," called Rachel.

Thomas walked over.

"I forgot to give you this," she handed him the invitation. "Don't forget its Saturday and bring a change of clothes. Casual stuff, you know, jeans."

Thomas closed the door and watched the limousine drive away.

"You should have told him Rachel," said Jessica. "You don't want him to find out on his own or from someone else."

"I know. It was so nice just being Rachel. It's not everyday I meet someone who likes me for me. You know we spent so much time talking about my daycare ideas and kid's camps."

"I understand," replied Jessica sympathetically. "But believe me, he should hear it from you first, promise me you'll tell him before the party."

"I promise." She leaned onto her mother's shoulder and her mother put her arm around her. "He is so charming and thoughtful and caring and sexy."

"He is," replied Jessica.

A taxi pulled up and Jack jumped in and rolled down the window and stuck out his head. "Good night Thomas, here's my home number give me a call when you want to play that game of golf. What's your handicap again?"

"Nice try Jack," laughed Thomas. "Goodnight."

He watched the taxi leave. "Guess Taxi Jack can't afford a limousine," thought Thomas. He put the invitation and phone number inside his suit pocket and turned and looked through the window at Rebecca. She was looking at him. He went inside. "Can I have the honor of escorting you back?"

"Yes, young sir. You can," she smiled and put her arm through his and walked.

The music was still playing but there were only a few people dancing. They sat down and sipped their drinks.

"Are you doing anything tomorrow?" asked Thomas.

"No, not really."

"Would you like to walk around town with me?"

"What time?"

"Well, let's see. I'm going to have breakfast in the hotel about ten, go to mass at the cathedral at twelve, then walk around town, say from one onwards. You can meet me at one." He waited. "Or later I don't want to pressure you."

"No, no you're not, I want to meet you. It's just that I haven't been to mass for a long time and would like to go but feel a little…."

"Then meet me after?"

"But I would like to go."

"Okay. Come." He could see she was unsure and nervous. "I'll be with you; you will be okay."

She smiled and thought how nice it would be. "I'll meet you outside the cathedral at eleven forty five."

The DJ's announcement interrupted them. "Ladies and gentlemen these are the last three songs of the evening. We will be slowing it down, thank you for a great night and have a safe drive home."

"I'll take that dance now, Thomas?" asked Rebecca.

They stood and walked onto the dance floor. He placed his hand around her waist, and with his other hand held her hand. She let go and put both her arms around his waist, Thomas responded and put his arms around her shoulders. He looked into her eyes as they swayed to the music. He pulled her close and put his cheek on hers. She slowly put her head on his shoulder. He could feel her warm breath on his neck. She wanted him to hold her forever.

Before the end of the third song Thomas pulled away slightly, Rebecca lifted her head and he looked into her eyes. She was beautiful.

She looked at him, at his lips, and she wanted him to kiss her.

The DJ broke the trance. "Goodnight ladies and gentlemen."

They let go and walked off the dance floor. "How you getting home tonight," asked Thomas.

"Taxi, I live five minutes away."

They left the ballroom and picked up their coats from the coat check. Thomas helped Rebecca put on hers and put his over his arm. They went to the lobby and waited for a cab. One was there almost immediately. They walked outside. Thomas opened the door and waited for her to get in. She kissed him on the cheek and jumped in the cab and closed the door. He watched the cab drive away. In the taxi she smiled and was happy. No matter what happened she would never forget tonight.

Thomas went to his car and grabbed his overnight bag. The room was on the top floor and was in fact a suite: it had two bedrooms, a sitting area with a fireplace, a wet bar and stereo. One of the bedrooms had a bathtub and robes for two. He took a quick shower and put on a bathrobe. He sat in front of the fireplace and thought about the night. He was worried he had entered into a world that he didn't belong in. Maybe he should have never opened that door to the ballroom. Then he would have never have met her. But who was he kidding he was an unpublished writer, who worked in a distribution center. What would she see in him? What could he have that she could possibly want? He had nothing to offer. She had everything.

CHAPTER 2

The Day After

THOMAS ARRIVED AT THE CATHEDRAL AT ELEVEN thirty. He walked across the street to a small park and sat on the wooden bench and waited. The sun was full in the sky and the leaves in the park were green and motionless. It was beautiful. He watched the people walking back and forth and noticed Rebecca standing across the street and called her name and waved. She waved back. Thomas watched as she walked to him. She was wearing light blue jeans and a white-buttoned dress shirt. Her hair was pulled back off her face with a hair clip and her deep blue eyes sparkled in the sunlight. She was beautiful.

"Good morning," she said as she sat next to him and put her jacket on her lap. "Have you been here long?"

"No, I just got here a few minutes ago."

"It's a beautiful day!" she exclaimed.

"I know. Have you seen the color of these trees?" He stared at her as she looked at the trees in the park. "You look great."

"Thank you," she replied and blushed.

"Want to go inside?"

Rebecca held his arm. "Thomas I haven't been to mass for a long time and I'm a little nervous."

Thomas placed his hand on hers, "you'll be fine, come on." They both stood up and Thomas put his arm around her as they crossed the street.

They followed the missal throughout the service and he found the songs in the hymnbook and listened as she sang. She refused to take Communion until she went to confession so Thomas went up alone. On the way out they shook hands with the priest who wished them a nice day.

"Thomas will you come with me again next week?" she asked.

"I would like that. I used to bring my grandmother every Sunday."

"I used to go with my father. We used to sing all the hymns." She smiled to herself as she thought of the fond memories.

Thomas waited a few moments. "Unfortunately I'm tone deaf!" he said and laughed.

"You are pretty awful," she replied and poked him in the side.

"Does your father live around here?"

"No. New York. I haven't talked to him in a very long time. We don't get along."

"What about your mother?"

"She remarried and moved out of the city. I see her once in awhile, either she comes to visit or I go out there. I heard you parents passed away?"

"Yeah, it was a long time ago. I was eighteen. They were on a plane to Europe and it crashed. My grandmother took it the hardest, that was the year she stopped teaching, and she never really recovered."

"I'm sorry."

"That's okay."

They walked in silence for a while.

Rebecca put her arm through his. "Can I ask you a personal question?"

"Of course."

"What was is it like for you? You know, not having your parents?"

"I missed them, I miss them a lot. There's not a day goes by when I don't think of them. I would have loved to have gone fishing with my dad, played golf with him, watched sports or just been able to talk to him. Or gone to church with my mother, or talk with her as she cooked dinner, or have her meet some of my girlfriends. Those things that we take for granted." He stopped and thought for a minute. "You know what I miss most of all?"

Rebecca shook her head.

"Sunday dinners, no matter how busy we were, we always ate Sunday dinners together. We used to talk and laugh. It was a lot of fun."

"It sounds wonderful!"

"It was." He looked over at Rebecca and asked, "How long has it been since you talked to your father?"

"Nine years."

"That's a long time."

"I know, but he hurt me."

Thomas put his arm around her and gave her a squeeze as they approached a young, man playing a sax in the park entrance.

"Hey young lovers how about I play you a love song?" asked the sax man.

"We're just friends," replied Thomas as he removed his arm.

"You make a good couple. How about a song?"

Thomas put five dollars in the hat.

"Okay lovely lady, what will it be?"

"Do you know, 'Unforgettable' by Nat King Cole?" asked Rebecca.

The sax man smiled and started playing.

Thomas whispered in her ear. "Do you know the words?"

She nodded.

"Sing for me?" whispered Thomas.

She looked at him. "Here?"

"Please, for me."

Rebecca sang.

Halfway through the song the sax man stopped and sang with her, he had a deep rich voice that complimented Rebecca's. A small crowd had gathered and clapped when they had finished.

"Thank you," said Rebecca to the sax man.

"Anytime pretty lady," he turned to the people putting money in his hat, "thank you, and thank you."

"That was one of my father's favorites," said Rebecca as they walked onto Main Street and headed south towards the harbor front. They window-shopped along the way.

"It's so beautiful down here at Christmas time, with the lights, and the snow, and the outdoor ice rink with the music playing," said Thomas.

"It is," she replied, "It's so magical."

"We used to come down here and ice skate. North of here, about fifteen minutes," Thomas said as he pointed, "there is an English pub called The Duke, we used to go there for dinner. I'll take you one night, you'd enjoy it?"

"I'd like that," she said.

"Do you golf?"

"I've played but I'm not very good."

"We'll have to go one day and play." Thomas hoped he wasn't being too pushy.

"I'd like that." She was happy at the way the conversation was going.

"Do you know Jack asked me to play?"

"I'd heard," she replied. "Apparently he's really good. He's always telling Penny about his handicap, I think that's what he called it, and last week it was eleven."

"Eleven! Really!" replied Thomas. "I asked him last night he said he didn't have one." Thomas smiled, "I knew he did."

"Oops, sorry Jack."

Thomas laughed and looked at her. "What do you like to do?"

"I like to swim, there's an indoor pool where I live, so I swim quite a bit, and I like to ski, skate, read, I read quite a bit, I like watching old movies, I love watching old movies."

"What kind?"

"Romance, musicals, westerns, mysteries."

"Me too."

They walked and talked for an hour and ended up at the theater where Rebecca performed.

"What's it feel like dancing on stage?" asked Thomas.

She thought for a minute. "Feels like I'm dancing in heaven."

"Do you ever get nervous dancing in front of all those people?"

"I'm always nervous but not a worried type; it's a different kind, more of an excitement, like butterflies. Does that make sense?"

"Yeah."

"Come on I'll take you on a personal, backstage tour," she pulled him by the hand.

She said hello to the security guard at the entrance and she showed him around. The tour ended on the stage.

"Wow!" exclaimed Thomas as he looked out at the empty seats. "I can't even begin to imagine what it would be like if it were full of people."

"Five thousand plus," confirmed Rebecca.

"Will you dance for me?"

"Now?" she asked.

"You don't have to?"

"No, I would like to."

"Will you get in trouble?"

She smiled. "No." She took off her jacket. "Hold this; I'll be back in a minute."

Thomas watched her leave. She looked good in jeans.

She came back wearing ballet slippers tied over her jeans and her hair in a ponytail. "I always keep a pair here." She looked at Thomas. "What ballet?"

Thomas was amazed at her sudden confidence. "What about Romeo and Juliet?"

"One of my favorites," she replied.

"Should I go sit down there?" he pointed to the seats.

"No." She pointed to the side, "there's a chair over there put it on the stage right about here, front and center stage."

He placed the chair down and sat. She left the stage.

Her head poked around the curtain. "Are you ready?"

"Ready."

She danced for thirty minutes and for her finale she stopped in front of him and did fifteen pirouettes. She stood back and curtsied.

Thomas put her coat on the floor, stood, clapped his hands and yelled, "Brava! Brava!" He walked over to her and kissed her hand. "You dance like an angel."

"Thank you." She curtsied. "I'll be back in a minute."

Thomas picked up her jacket and put the chair back. They met in the middle of the stage. She was smiling to herself.

"Can I be in on your secret?" he asked.

"One day."

Outside he helped her put on her jacket. They walked down around the harbor and talked about sports, television shows, movies and music. An hour later they were back at the theater.

"I promised Kate I would be home for dinner."

"What's she like?

"You'd like her; she's a lot of fun, less serious than I am."

"I'm sure I would. I really enjoyed today."

"So did I," replied Thomas.

"Would you like to come over for dinner on Friday? We could go for a swim, listen to some music, and watch some old movies."

"I'd like that. Is there something I can bring?"

"You can bring the movies."

"That's it?'

"That's it, deal?"

"I don't think I could change your mind?"

She smiled and shook her head.

"Deal! Where do you live?"

Rebecca pointed to a block of condominiums across the street and said, "Count twelve floors up and look over to the left corner, that's mine."

He walked with her across the street.

"What's your number?"

"Apartment twelve eleven, the door man will call up and let you in."

"Actually, I meant your phone number."

She smiled and produced a pen and piece of paper from her coat and wrote it down for him and ripped the paper. "Here you go. Can I have yours?"

She wrote as Thomas told her.

"So what time Friday?"

"Around six."

"Six," repeated Thomas

"I had a nice day."

"Me too."

There was an uncertainty in the air.

"Well, I should get going. Thanks for dancing for me." He leaned over and kissed her on the cheek. "I'll see you Friday."

"See you Friday," she said and turned and walked away.

He thought about her as he walked back to the hotel to pick up his car.

"Hi Kate," sorry I'm late.

"It's okay, I'm a little behind."

"How's the studying?"

"Exhausting."

"You should have waited and let me cook," suggested Thomas.

"No, it gives my mind a rest, besides I like cooking for you," she said and smiled.

"I'm just going to take this upstairs," Thomas said, holding up his overnight bag and suit. "I'll just be a minute." Thomas turned to leave.

"A girl called for you," teased Kate.

Thomas stopped and looked at Kate, "Who?"

"Her name was Rachel, she didn't say her last name, I talked to her for a few minutes, and she sounds very nice and seems very interesting. You'll have to tell me about last night," she said with an air of inquisition.

"You lawyers, I'm pleading the Fifth Amendment!" replied Thomas and went upstairs.

Five minutes later he was sitting at the kitchen table and telling Kate about the last twenty-four hours.

"I wish I would have been there. I would have loved to have seen you scampering for the back." She laughed at the thought.

"Very funny, I knew you would get a kick out of that." Thomas stood up.

"Are you interested in either of them?" asked Kate as Thomas cleared the table.

"Both of them are interesting," replied Thomas.

"You know what I mean!" exclaimed Kate.

"Rachel is breathtaking, she could be a world famous model, but looks aside, I really enjoyed talking with her. She wants to open a daycare or kid's camp, which is great. Rebecca's beautiful and graceful. She's a professional ballerina. She's sensitive, fun and compassionate. They're both very rich and…" Thomas hesitated.

"What? What were you going to say?"

Thomas lowered his voice. "Who am I kidding? I work in a warehouse, I'm an unpublished writer, I have twelve hundred dollars in my bank account, actually seven; I spent five last night. I have nothing to offer, nothing."

Kate looked at him and grabbed his hand and made him sit down. "Thomas," she said softly, "if these girls are only worried about your dollar value then you are right, you don't add up to much, but if you want to talk about what's in here," she pointed to his heart, "you're kind, loving, sensitive, caring, thoughtful, compassionate, if you want to talk about all these qualities, then you are the richest man I know." She pointed to his head, "and in here is one bright writer, the novel you've written already shows that, it's terrific, you need to take it to a publisher." Kate paused and backtracked, "we both know that you worked hard to take care of grandma and me and you are still working hard to take care of me. I know you gave up university so that I could go. Then there's my tuition, the bills, and this house. Thomas…"

"Kate everything I've done and everything I do I'm doing for you because I want to and I wouldn't have it any other way."

She knew how much he had sacrificed. "I know."

Thomas gathered his thoughts. "Last night when I walked into that room I felt like one of them and what it was like to be rich and famous and worry free. For that one moment in time, in that room, I felt on equal grounds with them. Today they're still there I'm not. Do you know what I mean? I just don't know what I'm doing or where I'm going. I met Rebecca earlier on today and she lives in a condominium in the city and is a professional ballerina. Rachel invited me to a party Saturday with all her friends. I'm going to be out of place and out of my league! It's not like they are our next door neighbors."

"Thomas, why don't you treat them as if they were the girl next door? Why do you have to put them up there on higher ground? Has either of them asked you to? They both know what you do! Who you are! Yet they're still calling. Why? It seems as if they're accepting you more than you are them?" Kate made eye contact with Thomas. "Thomas this doesn't sound like you. Is there any harm in being friends with these girls? If you don't give them a chance you will never know. Tommy this isn't like you! What are you really afraid of?"

Thomas nervously smiled and looked at Kate. "I don't want to get hurt."

Kate put her arm around him. "Tommy, you can lock yourself in this house and never see either of these girls again? But I will never let that happen. I want you to enjoy yourself, make some new friends. It's time you did more. I'm old enough to look after myself, well not financially," she tried to make him laugh, "but you know what I mean. Thomas you have so much to offer, so much love inside of you, you should share that with someone special." Kate thought and continued, "I wish mom and dad were here they'd be much better at this."

"Kate, if mom and dad were here I would still want to talk to you about this," reassured Thomas, 'thanks for your help." He kissed her on the hand. "I'll take one day at a time and see what happens." He smiled at Kate and she smiled back.

"Oh I meant to tell you before dinner, Rachel said she was out and since she was passing our house on the way home would drop in."

"What time?"

"Around seven-thirty."

Thomas looked at the clock on the wall it was seven twenty five. "I'm going upstairs to get a quick shower, when she arrives can you keep her company till I come down? Unless you have studying?" questioned Thomas.

"No more studying today," said Kate. "Besides I want to meet or should I say cross-examine this breathtaking beauty," teased Kate.

"Lawyers," said Thomas. He kissed Kate on top of her head and went upstairs. The doorbell rang as he closed the bathroom door. Fifteen minutes later Thomas descended the stairs and walked into the living room.

"London and Nice must have been exciting. I've never been to either, I always wanted to go to the French Riviera, see the beaches and the sun tanned…" Kate stopped when she noticed Thomas.

"Hi Thomas," said Rachel. "Your sister's great. We've been having a most informative chat."

"I've promised her inside information anytime she wants," Kate said playfully as she stood.

"And I plan on taking her up on that!" replied Rachel as she got up from her seat.

Kate walked to the closet and picked out her coat. "I need to walk to the store to get some diet coke. I won't be long, see you in about half an hour," and left.

Thomas moved toward Rachel. She was wearing tight fitting gray track pants and a zippered sweatshirt. Her blonde hair was loosely curled and hung down passed her shoulders. She had no make up on. She looked amazing. They sat down.

"Thomas, I came over here because I wanted to give you something, well actually show you, well actually show you something and talk to you about something, well it's the same thing." She was very nervous. She picked up a big brown envelope that had been sitting on the table. "I don't know how or where to begin. I didn't think I would be this nervous."

Thomas put his hand on hers and she looked up at him. "Rachel," he said quietly as he looked into her green eyes. "Why don't you tell me, and then show me."

"Just promise me you will always look at me as Rachel Carter the girl from the fundraiser. Promise me?" she pleaded.

Thomas wasn't sure where she was going with this, "Okay, I promise."

"I'm not a model waiting for her big break?"

"You're not a model?"

"I am, but I am a well known model. I've appeared in national and international magazines and on billboards; I usually model swimsuits and lingerie." She opened the envelope and pulled out four magazines two swimsuit, lingerie, and a woman's magazine. "I want you to see my pictures." She opened up one of the swimsuit issues and placed it on the coffee table.

Thomas looked on. There she was in two full size poses wearing bikinis, as he flipped through, three half-page photographs were she was wearing one pieces; all five were taken on a beach. The lingerie magazine was quickly placed on top. There was a picture of her in a red teddy, a second wearing a white bra and panties with a garter, and the third was a sheer, silk black nightgown with black bra and panties. The cover of the woman's magazine was placed on top; it was a picture of just her smiling face with make up on. Thomas looked up at her at little unsure.

She blurted out. "Do you know what it's like having boys teasing you about your pictures or saying rude comments or just want to go out with you because of who you are or what they think you are; or not going out with you because of those same reasons? Having jealous girlfriends threaten you," she paused. "Last night, after I met you I was so happy that someone was talking to me, Rachel Carter, the unknown. You wanted to be with the unknown, talk to the unknown, be friends with the unknown. I was so happy. I wanted to tell you, but decided not to for my own selfish reasons." She paused. "When I found out you had a sister I knew I had to tell you as soon as possible, I couldn't take the chance that your sister hadn't heard of me, that's why I never told her my last name on the phone. I wanted to be the one who told you, and explain why." Rachel paused, "the pictures are what I do." She glanced at Thomas and looked away when he looked at her.

"Rachel, did you expect me to react differently towards you when I found out who you were?" He brushed her hair away from her eyes. "I'm not like that."

"What do you mean?" asked Rachel.

"Do you think that I would speak to one person any different than another because of who they were or were not? Jack? Your mother? Ms. Daily? The bartender? The DJ? The coat check girl? I see the person for who they are not what they are," stated Thomas."

"I should have told you last night," said Rachel.

"Maybe, especially when you had me believe that you were well known in the community for your charity."

They both laughed.

"Thomas I had my reasons, right or wrong, and I came today to set you straight. I don't want you to think I lied to you intentionally. I'm sorry. I was only hoping…" her words faded.

"Rachel," he whispered.

She turned her head and looked into his eyes, there was a single tear rolling down her cheek and she looked down.

Thomas wiped the tear away. "Rachel, I can't ignore the fact of who you are and I am glad you told me," he raised her chin with his hand and looked into her eyes, "but I can promise you I will always treat you as Rachel Carter the unknown girl from the fundraiser and nothing else. I promise."

Her face broke into a smile.

"Friends?" asked Thomas.

"We'll become best of friends and no more secrets, I promise." She put her arms around him, gave him a squeeze, and let go. She felt a huge burden lift off of her shoulders.

Thomas sorted through the magazines and found the swimsuit issues she had shown him. He opened the page to her pictures. "Where were these taken?"

"These two in Nice, this one in Cannes, these two in St. Tropez?"

"Tell me about it, I never been" said Thomas enthusiastically and closed the magazine.

Rachel talked about the French Riviera and her pictures. Kate returned and brought them each a glass of coke and sat with them. An hour later, Thomas walked Rachel out to her convertible Mustang.

"I'll see you Saturday," said Rachel as she got in her car. She couldn't stop smiling.

"I'm looking forward to it," replied Thomas. He waved goodbye as she drove away. Back in the house Kate was waiting.

"Breathtaking, Thomas? She's absolutely beautiful!" Kate looked at her brother in dismay. "You didn't know who she was?"

"Did you recognize her?"

"As soon as I opened the door."

"If I said her name would you have recognized it?"

"Thomas if you said you met a model named Rachel Carter I would have known for sure."

Thomas was silent.

Kate waited.

Thomas realized what she was waiting for, "relax Kate we're just friends."

Kate looked unconvinced. "She's breathtaking and Rebecca is beautiful, I can't wait to see Rebecca," Kate said. "I'm going upstairs to bed. See you in the morning." She kissed Thomas on the cheek and said good night and went to her room.

Thomas sat in the living room and flipped through the magazines and looked at Rachel's pictures.

CHAPTER 3

Dinner at Rebecca's

"HI THOMAS, COME ON IN. SORRY, I'M running a little late. Follow me into the living room and have a seat. I'll take your bag and coat and put them in the guest room. Do you like Christina Aguilera?"

"Yeah."

"Good," she said. She pressed play and waited to make sure the song, 'Ain't No Other Man' came through the speakers. "Here we go." She looked at Thomas. "I love her voice."

Thomas agreed. "She's got a great voice."

"I'll be back in a few minutes."

Thomas watched as she headed down the hallway with his coat and bag.

She returned five minutes later wearing pink lipstick, eye shadow, and no blush, and had changed into a light pink t-shirt and tight fitted jeans. She looked great.

"Would you like a drink?"

"Sure."

"Beer or wine?"

"Beer, please."

She came back from the kitchen with two Heinekens and poured each into a separate glass and placed them on the coasters on the coffee table. She sat next to Thomas and lifted the glasses and passed one to him and said, "Cheers."

"Cheers" replied Thomas and touched his glass with hers. Thomas sipped his beer and looked down. "I like your coasters," Thomas said, as he picked up the one his glass had been sitting on, "Renoir's Le Moulin De La Galette".

"I bought them up at a store in a small village in the country." She moved closer to Thomas. "There are eight in the set and each of them has a different Renoir painting. Do you like Impressionist artists?"

"I do."

"What do you like about them?"

"I like their technique of using light and similar colors and shapes to capture people and objects." He showed her the one he was holding, she moved closer to him, "see the green leaves, yellow hats, blonde hair, black suits and the ground and faces with yellowish-pink spots and the sunlight through the leaves."

"What else?" She moved closer and looked at him as he looked down at the coaster and spoke.

"See the pyramid shape formed if you connect the three figures. The vertical lines are the people dancing and standing and the trees and the standard lamps. The horizontal lines are the figures in the background, the round lanterns and the white wooden buildings." He looked at her.

"What does it say?" she asked.

"Many things," replied Thomas. "The joys of being young and in love, a social get-together, people enjoying themselves, sunshine, music, voices, flirtation." Thomas looked at her. "What do you see?

"I see love, happiness, a celebration," replied Rebecca. She looked at him inquisitively. "You seem to know a lot? Did you study art?"

"No, I've read some books, been to the art gallery a few times, that's about it. What about you?"

"I've been to the art gallery and read the pamphlets they give you. I only bought these coasters because I liked the pictures."

He smiled and looked around. "I like your condominium!"

"Thanks. Would you like a quick tour"?

"Sure!"

She stood up and Thomas followed her. "At the end of the hallway is the master bedroom, with an en suite, walk in closet and a view of the harbor." She opened the blinds.

"That's spectacular."

"Come on." She pulled Thomas by the hand. "In here is the second bedroom or guest room. Next to which is the den, which is currently being used as a storage area for unopened boxes of memorabilia. I eventually want to unpack them and hang them up and set up a desk and computer over there." They moved to the next room and opened the door. "Here is the main bathroom." She closed the door and held Thomas's hand as they entered the living room. "You're already familiar with this room, in through here is the kitchen and solarium."

"This place is amazing. I love the views."

"Thank you," she replied and looked at him.

"Smells good," indicated Thomas.

"Hope you like lasagna?"

"My favorite dish," replied Thomas.

She secretly knew that and smiled to herself. "If we go through here we're into the dining room."

Thomas noticed the table was attractively set for two.

"I saved the best for last." She let go of his hand and opened the blinds.

"Wow," said Thomas, "this is magnificent!"

Rebecca stood behind Thomas's right shoulder and with her right hand pointed out the landmarks, "there's city hall, Main Street, and you can see the top of the cathedral, and the theater."

He could feel her breasts rubbing against his back and smell her floral perfume. Her breath tickled his neck.

"We're still going to the cathedral on Sunday?" she whispered in his ear.

"Yes," he said and turned, "but it will have to be at nine. I have to leave right after. Is that okay?"

"That's fine. I have some errands to run on Sunday and that will give me more time to complete them."

Thomas was happy that it had worked out. "I'll pick you up at eight thirty."

"Eight-thirty it is." She realized her hand was still resting on his shoulder and moved it and turned to close the blinds. "If we go through here we're back into the living room. She turned a switch and the gas fireplace came on. "You can see it from the living and dining room," she switched it off. "I'll put it back on later." They sat back on the couch.

"This is a beautiful place Rebecca!" said Thomas as he drank his beer.

"Thank you!" she reached over for hers and took a drink. "I thought we could finish these drinks, then go for a swim, and have dinner after. Maybe listen to some music and later on watch some movies. Or are you hungry now?" asked Rebecca.

"No, I like your plan."

"I'll turn off the stove." She stood and went into the kitchen.

"Are there change rooms?" asked Thomas.

"Yes and lockers with keys. It's on the eighteenth floor," echoed her voice from the kitchen. "There shouldn't be many people at this time of night," her voice getting clearer as she walked back into the room and sat down.

They finished their drinks and another.

Thomas changed and waded into the empty pool.

A door opened and out walked Rebecca wearing a navy blue Body Glove bikini. Her nipples were hard, her stomach flat, and her legs were long and lovely. Thomas couldn't help his stare.

Rebecca's question broke the spell. "How's the water?"

"Perfect!" replied Thomas as he swam to the deep end and turned to get a look at her from the back. "Perfect," he repeated.

Rebecca waded in the shallow end, dunked her head, and swam to Thomas. "You're right it is perfect. I'm surprised it's empty; there are usually a couple of people here."

"Does this place have a fitness room?" asked Thomas.

"It's on the ground floor." she replied. "They use one of the rooms for aerobic classes; I usually go Tuesday and Thursday nights. Do you work out?" She could tell he did.

"I run almost every morning, along with sit ups and push ups. I also do weights; I have a bench at home. If I had this I'd be swimming every night. Do you work out here?"

"Here and my dance classes," she replied. "Let's go to the shallow end and we can sit on the steps," suggested Rebecca.

They swam over and both sat on the second to last step, the water just lapping below their chests. Thomas noticed how her bikini complimented her blue eyes.

"So you're a writer?"

Thomas smiled, "I write."

"What have you written?"

"I'll be finishing my second novel in a month or so."

"When did you finish your first?"

"About five months ago?"

"Did you send it to a publisher?"

"No."

"Why didn't you?"

"I guess I write for myself, you know, as a hobby. I just enjoy writing and never really thought about publishing it."

"Can I read it?"

The question took him by surprise. "Do you want to?"

"I would love to!"

Thomas hesitated, "I don't know. Kate's the only person who has read it."

"What did she think?"

"She liked it; she told me I should send it to someone."

"Well I don't want to pressure you and I understand if you don't want me to, I know it's personal."

"Thanks," he appreciated her thoughtfulness. "Do you have any hobbies?"

She laughed, "I love reading. Seriously, remember last week you asked me what I liked to do and I said reading."

"I remember," he said.

An older couple had entered the pool area and where getting into the pool.

"Do you want to go in the hot tub for a few minutes?" Rebecca asked.

"Sure."

Rebecca got out of the water first and walked over and sat in the hot tub. She wanted to watch him walk over. "Thomas, can you press the button on the wall to start it?"

Thomas looked at where she was pointing and pushed the button.

He was perfect.

"Do you cook often?" asked Thomas as he opened the wine.

"Most of the time, I rarely order in and if I dine out it's mostly on the weekends, but that's not too often," answered Rebecca from the kitchen.

She walked in and placed the lasagna and bread on the table. "I hope you're hungry?"

She moved to the CD player and put on the Boston Pops, Debussy's 'Claire de Lune'. Back at the table she served the food as Thomas poured the wine. She lit the candles and turned off the lights.

"It looks delicious. My compliments to the chef!" said Thomas as he raised his wine glass and touched hers.

"Thank you."

They sipped their wine, ate and talked.

"So what have you been doing since last time we met?" asked Rebecca.

"Worked all week. Wrote most nights. Grocery shopped with Kate last night?"

"Do you like where you work?"

"It's a means to an end."

"What would you like to do?"

"If I had a choice?"

She nodded her head and drank her wine.

"I guess write and get paid for it. I think getting paid for something you love would be unbelievable."

"So you want to be a published writer," replied Rebecca teasingly.

Thomas was embarrassed.

"So, you don't have a choice?"

"No, I don't now."

"Why not?"

Thomas was getting uncomfortable, "it's a long story."

Rebecca realized this and changed the topic. "Tell me about your sister."

"You'd like her. She's studying to be a lawyer and in her last year. I'm very proud of her. You'll have to come one night for dinner and meet her. She'd like you."

"I would like that," smiled Rebecca.

"Rachel dropped by last Sunday evening for an hour."

"Really, what for?" asked Rebecca trying not to look worried.

"To say hello, apparently she lives a half hour north of me and dropped in on her way home."

"That was nice of her," replied Rebecca.

"Are you two friends?"

"We see each other at social functions, like the fundraiser, and with us being so close in age we usually sit together, talk and dance. We have the same interests and taste so we get along really well. Day to day we don't see much of each other, she travels a lot because of her job. She asked me to go to France in the summer but I didn't."

"Why not?" asked Thomas.

"I would have liked to have gone but I had some personal reasons."

"Are you going tomorrow night?"

"To Rachel's birthday party?"

Thomas nodded.

"Unfortunately, I have a dinner party that I have to go to. Are you going?"

"Yes," he didn't know it was her birthday he should have read the invitation. He'd have to buy her something tomorrow.

Rebecca was a little more worried.

After dessert they moved into the living room. Rebecca put on the fire and they sat together. The glow of the fire lit the dark room.

"Thanks for dinner it was great."

"My pleasure."

They sipped their wine.

Rebecca stood up and changed the CD to the 'The Style Council', 'You're the Best Thing' came on and she turned to Thomas. "Would you like to dance?" She held out her hand.

Thomas stood, held her hand and followed her around the coffee table. She put her arms over his shoulders and he put his on her waist. As they danced she sang softly in his ear. Thomas asked her to play the song again and again. Each time she sang. They danced to the next three songs on the CD after which she stopped and looked into his pale blue eyes and thanked him and kissed him on the cheek. She let go of him, "I'll get a couple more beers." She left and came back from the kitchen with two and poured them. "Do you want to watch a movie?"

"They're in my bag, I'll go get them."

"Your bag is in the guest room."

Thomas stood and left.

She followed him and stood in the doorway. "I was hoping you might stay the night? Sleep here in the guest room."

"Sure, if you don't mind?"

"No, I would like you to. Would you mind if I put on my pajamas?"

"Go ahead."

"What movies did you bring?"

"I'll show you them after you've changed."

He watched her leave and searched in his bag for the movies. He found them and went into the living room. She returned wearing oversized flannel pajamas. She had washed her face and had put her hair in a ponytail. Thomas thought she looked sexy.

"I like your pajamas."

"They're actually a men's small; they're big and comfortable," she said as she sat down. "Okay, what movies do you have?"

"Well I have 'The Quiet Man', 'To Catch a Thief', and 'Roman Holiday, 'Casablanca' and 'An Affair to Remember'. Which one?"

"I love them all. It's so difficult, 'An Affair to Remember'."

Rebecca sat next to him during, 'An Affair to Remember' and cried at the end. She laid her head on his chest during 'Casablanca' and lay her head on a pillow on his lap and fell asleep after 'The Quiet Man'. He watched her sleeping so peacefully. He stood without waking her and carried her to the bedroom and put her into bed. He removed the elastic from her hair and placed it on the end table. He kissed her on the forehead and said sweet dreams.

He put away the empty beer bottles and the glasses and dessert dishes in the dishwasher. He turned off the lights and fireplace, made sure the front door was locked and went into the guest room.

Lying in bed he thought about Rebecca. She was so kind, compassionate, caring, and so beautiful. He thought about how sexy she looked in jeans, in her bikini, and in her pajamas. He thought about her until he fell asleep.

He woke up at eight o'clock, got washed and dressed and went to the kitchen and made a pot of coffee. He opened the blinds in the solarium and noticed there wasn't a cloud in the sky. He sipped his coffee and looked down at the world below.

Forty minutes later Rebecca walked up behind him. "Sorry I fell asleep, you must think I'm awful?" her hair was wild.

Thomas smiled at it. "I guess my company is like a sleeping pill," he joked.

"Don't say that, you're making me feel bad?"

"I'm joking, it was late, and I was asleep fifteen minutes later."

"Thanks for tidying up. Did you take the elastic out of my hair?"

"I did."

"How did you know to do that?" she asked

"I've taken many a woman to bed," replied Thomas.

She looked unsure.

He laughed. "When my sister was younger she always had them in her hair and when she fell asleep in front of the television I used to take them out of her hair."

"My father did the same for me." She thought for a moment, "it's funny how I just remembered that, come with me." She led him to the master bedroom, opened the drawer, and showed the framed picture of her with her father. "This is the last picture I have of him and me. It was taken at the harbor many summers ago."

Thomas looked at the picture; Rebecca must have been sixteen or seventeen. Her father was a good-sized man. "Why do you keep it in the drawer?"

"Bad memories I guess."

"Was that day one of those bad memories?"

"No. Actually that was one of my fondest."

"Maybe you should only keep the bad ones in the drawer," suggested Thomas.

"You're probably right." She placed it on the end table and closed the draw. She turned to Thomas and caught her image in the mirror, "aaaah, why didn't you say anything about my hair, you're so mean, letting me walk around like this."

"I think it looks sexy!"

"Sexy!" she exclaimed. She slapped his arm. "Do you mind if I get a bath?"

"You get a bath. I'll make you breakfast."

"But you're my guest."

"I wont take no for an answer," replied Thomas. He walked her to her en suite.

"Okay. What do I have in? I have bacon, eggs, bagels, Rice Krispies and fruit."

"What would you like?"

"Rice Krispies and a toasted bagel with pineapple cream cheese."

"And to drink?"

"Orange juice and a tea with milk."

"Enjoy your bath," said Thomas and started to walk away then turned around, "Do you mind if I put the radio on."

"Of course not, there's a television under the kitchen counter that has a radio and a CD player."

He closed the door on the way out and could hear her singing, "Ain't No Other Man," as she ran the bath water.

She came into the solarium wearing a white terry robe; her hair was wet and slicked back. She looked at the food set on the table and stood for a moment and watched Thomas; he was looking out the window at the park below. "Looks great," said Rebecca.

"Thanks," he said as he turned around. "Feeling better?"

She nodded and smiled.

"Have a seat." He pulled out her chair.

"You're so organized."

"Years of practice I guess." He looked around, "This is a bright room and perfect for breakfast time!"

"You know I never use this room. I usually sit in the living room or eat in my bedroom. Rachel noticed that Thomas had put on a CD and Handel's 'Water Music' was softly playing. "You're right though, this is perfect." She looked at him as he ate. "What are you doing today?"

Thomas looked at her. "Well, I need to go shopping."

"I do too! We can go together. If that's okay?"

"I was hoping we would. You see I never read Rachel's invitation and I didn't know it was her birthday and I need to get her a gift. Maybe you could help me pick something out?"

"Okay and you can help me pick out a dress for tonight!"

"Then it's a date, I mean a plan," said Thomas as he corrected himself. "Let's eat up and get going."

"I LIKE WHAT YOU'RE WEARING," SAID THOMAS as they crossed the street.

"Thanks," she said as she put her arm through his, "I'm glad we decided to walk".

"Do you have any suggestions what I can buy Rachel?" asked Thomas. He had this fear that she would be opening these really expensive gifts in front of everyone including his not-so-expensive gift.

"No. She pretty well has everything. I bought her a Versace sweater."

"Oh great," thought Thomas.

"She's probably not expecting you to buy her anything," suggested Rebecca. "But if you feel obliged, I would suggest something not too expensive, but thoughtful."

Thomas looked up to the sky, "Thank you" and turned to Rebecca. "Such as?"

"Perfume."

"Do you know what kind she likes?"

"I do and the best part is that she'll know you would have had to have asked someone to find out her favorite and that means you were thoughtful." Rebecca couldn't believe that she had just said that; but this wasn't about Rachel was it, this was for Thomas. "You can pick it up at the store that I am going to."

Thomas paid for the perfume and followed Rebecca up the escalator to the top floor and walked to the far right hand corner.

"Hello Ms. La Croix, nice to see you again. What are we looking for this morning?" said an attractive lady in her early thirties.

"Hello Janet, I need an outfit for a dinner party I'm going to tonight."

"We had some new designs arrive this week. What color were you interested in?"

"What do think Thomas?" asked Rebecca.

They both turned and looked at Thomas. "With it being fall I would suggest an autumn color, something like beige or light brown, similar to the color you are wearing." He said looking at Rebecca.

"And style?" asked Janet looking at Thomas.

"Because Rebecca has shapely legs I would suggest a dress above the knee, in the event that it's more formal, a pantsuit."

"Excellent," said Janet excitedly. "You have a keen fashion sense! Mr.?"

"Carlyle."

"Mr. Carlyle," said Janet and turned to Rebecca. "I have several items you can try on. I'll be back in a minute." She went off to the back room.

"Come here often Ms. La Croix?" asked Thomas.

"A few times, she usually calls me Becky when I come alone but because I'm with you she has to be formal."

"Has to be?"

"Policy, until you let her know she can call you Thomas it will be Ms. or Mr."

She returned holding several items. "I will put these in change room one. Now will you need my help getting in and out of the garments?"

"No thank you."

"Please follow me," Janet said politely.

They walked through a door into a large room. At one end there was a sofa and coffee table and at the other was a semi-circled wall with full-length angled mirrors. To the right of the mirrors was the change room door. Janet opened the door and hung the outfits inside.

"Can I get either of you a drink, tea, coffee, juice or sparkling water?"

"I'll have water," replied Rebecca.

"Same please," added Thomas.

"I'll be back in a minute Ms. La Croix and Mr. Carlyle." She left.

Thomas looked around the room.

"This room is usually for people who want to try on lingerie," informed Rebecca. "The other change areas aren't as large as this."

She returned with two bottles of water and glasses with ice. "Here you go Mr. Carlyle."

"Please, call me Thomas," he suggested.

"Thank you, Thomas. Becky would you like yours on the table also?"

"That would be fine."

She opened the bottles and poured the water. If you need me there's a button over by the door that will buzz me outside. Otherwise I'll drop by in fifteen minutes or so and see how you're doing. I'll knock once. I'll lock the door behind me so you won't be disturbed." She walked out and they heard the lock click.

"Wow, she's never done this before; she probably thinks you're a fashion designer!"

They both laughed.

"I must admit though you know current fashion." She dropped her coat on the sofa. "I'll try these on."

She came out in a fitted beige dress that was cut above the knee, with a v-shaped neckline and long sleeves. It emphasized her face, neck, chest, waist and when she turned around, her bottom.

"You look stunning!"

"Thank you," she said as she looked in the mirror. "I love it."

She changed into the next dress, which was the same color but below the knee and high neckline.

"Wow that looks good too."

She looked in the mirror. "I quite like this one too." She walked over to the table and had a drink of her water. "I'll try on the pants suit."

The pants were well fitted and straight down, and the jacket was light and single breasted. She took off the jacket to reveal a long sleeve silk cream blouse that you could just see her bra through.

"Classy."

She moved around the mirrors and smiled.

The next pantsuit was a light brown. The pants were wide and it was double breasted.

"I think this is more a business woman's outfit," suggested Thomas.

"It is," she agreed as she looked at it once more. "Well, that's all four," she said and smiled at she looked at Thomas in the mirror. "I am having such a great time." She turned and looked at him, "you're probably ready to go."

"Are you kidding!" replied Thomas and stood and walked over to her. "Not at all, which ones do you like?" asked Thomas.

"Well…you tell me first."

"I liked the first dress and pantsuit you put on."

"I like those too."

"Why don't you try them both on again and take your time so we can have a good look before you make up your mind."

She smiled happily. "Really!"

"Really, go on." He sat back down on the sofa.

A knock at the door, then a click, "How's she doing Thomas?" asked Janet.

"She's down to two. She trying them on again"

"I'll come back in a half hour or so. Need any more water?"

"We're fine thanks."

The door closed and clicked.

She came out in the dress. Thomas stood up and walked over and around her, as he did, he said, "stunning…elegant…graceful…and beautiful!"

She looked in the mirror and moved in a circle so she could see all angles. Thomas moved out of her way and over to the table and picked up his water. She walked over had a sip of her water and looked at Thomas. "Do you mind if I take a few minutes and cool off?" she asked.

"Take all the time you need I'm having fun."

"So am I," she replied with a beautiful smile. She went into the change room and came out in a robe and read Thomas's facial expression. "Yes Thomas, they even supply robes."

"Unbelievable!" he said.

They sat in silence for a minute or two as she drank some water.

"You will have to let me buy you lunch?"

"You don't have to."

She stood up and walked over to the door, opened it and before she closed it, looked at him and said. "I want to and I'm not taking no for an answer, so there," and on those words playfully stuck out her tongue and closed the door behind her.

When she came out in her pantsuit, Thomas stood again and circled her, "classy…sophisticated…delicate…and beautiful!"

She looked at herself in the mirrors. Thomas went back and sat down. She went and changed for the last time and came out holding the two outfits.

"Well Thomas, time to make a decision?"

"As a friend I would have to say either one, they're both beautiful."

"Thomas!" she pleaded. "Okay, if you were my date."

"The dress."

"The dress?"

"Definitely!"

"Can you hold these while I put on my coat?"

Thomas stood up and held the outfits. Rebecca put on her coat and took them off him. She pressed the button.

The door unlocked and opened. "Have you decided?" asked Janet.

"Yes I have."

"Is there anything else you will need Becky?" asked Janet as they walked to the sales counter.

"I wanted to look at some underwear?"

"If you've decided on one of the dresses may I suggest a thong, we have some new ones in, and they are silk and so comfortable and very discreet. I wear them all the time."

"They sound nice."

Thomas was a little uncomfortable. "Listen, I'm going to wait for you outside. Why don't you meet me out front?"

"Okay," she replied and felt bad for embarrassing him.

"Bye Janet."

"Bye Thomas," said Janet. "Will I be seeing you at the Winter Collection show at the Convention Center?"

"Yes, yes you will. I thought it was you. Why didn't you say something earlier?"

"I wasn't sure at first."

"Do you still have the same seat?" Thomas asked.

"Yes I do?" replied Janet.

"I'll make sure to say hello and try not to fall onto your lap. It was my sister's fault anyway. She tripped me on purpose." He leaned over and whispered, "I can blame her since she's not here."

"That was your sister. She's very pretty."

"I'll pass the compliment on Janet, bye for now. Take your time Rebecca," said Thomas and walked away not really too sure of the way out.

"You have a charming boyfriend Becky and handsome," smiled Janet.

"We're only friends," said Rebecca as she looked back at Thomas asking someone for directions.

"You two make a great couple."

Rebecca met Thomas outside and they walked three blocks south to a small, cozy pub.

Rebecca was radiant.

"Two for lunch?" asked the maitre de.

"Yes please," said Thomas.

The waiter sat them down at a table with a view of the street and returned with their drink order. He dropped off a pint of Smithwicks for Thomas and a diet coke for Rebecca.

Thomas looked over the menu and then looked up at Rebecca whose menu was unopened. "Not eating?"

"I already know what I want, fish and chips. They serve the best here."

Thomas closed the menu. "I'll have to try them then but I must warn you I've already had the best fish and chips in the city."

"That sounds like a challenge to my culinary palette and the Cove pub?"

"Remember last week I told you about my favorite pub The Duke, they have the best."

"Ah yes The Duke, maybe one day I will actually see this piece of heaven. They probably serve the best imported draught beer too."

"So you have heard of it," said Thomas as he smiled and drank his beer. "Although this is quite good."

She smiled at him. "Did you know Janet was interested in you?"

"Did she say so?"

"No. I could tell?"

"How?"

"The way she spoke, her body language, the way she looked at you. The fact that she gave us that room! At first I thought she was trying to impress you because she thought you were a designer, looking back, it was because she liked you"

"Likes me!"

"Yes."

"Do you think I should pursue it?"

The question caught Rebecca off guard, "Well, I'm not sure? It's your decision."

"It's my decision?"

"Yes."

"Well let's see, she is attractive, has a nice figure, and very friendly. Would you agree?"

"Yes."

"And you would be comfortable with this?"

"Yes," she lied.

Thomas sat back in his chair giving the impression that he was thinking deeply on the subject.

Rebecca looked on trying not to look interested and sipped on her drink.

Thomas broke into a loud laughter.

"What's so funny?" Rebecca wasn't in good humor.

"I think you may be jealous!" hoped Thomas.

"I am not," insisted Rebecca. She was.

"In any case Rebecca, I am not interested," smiled Thomas.

"Not interested?"

Thomas hesitated. "Janet has a girlfriend! She's a lesbian!" said Thomas as he looked at Rebecca.

She looked at him in disbelief and realized he had been playing her all along. "You new all the time and yet you led me to believe," she looked for the right word, "Otherwise. Why? You!"

"I wanted to see how you would react," smiled Thomas, "jealous and all."

"I was not." She said hitting his arm.

"Okay, I'm teasing. You weren't. Kate and I met Janet and her girlfriend at the fashion show and they were a couple. Kate loves those shows so I take her. I think Janet thought Kate was my date, that's why she was surprised when I told her she was my sister."

The waiter brought their lunch and they ate.

She waited till they were outside to ask, "So what did you think?"

"Not bad, but..."

"Not as good as The Duke?" finished Rebecca.

"One Friday night I'll take you to The Duke and then we can have a vote."

Back at the condominium Rebecca took her shopping bags to her room and Thomas collected his bag from the guest room. He waited for her by the door.

"So we're still going on Sunday?" she said as she walked towards him.

"I'll be here at eight thirty."

Thomas picked up his bag, "I left you the DVDs in case you wanted to watch them."

"Thanks, I would," said Rebecca and smiled. But knew she would wait for him.

"Have a good time tonight. You looked great in that dress."

"Thanks. I will. Say Happy Birthday to Rachel for me."

"Will do, see you Sunday," said Thomas. "I had a great time." He opened the door and walked down the hallway to the elevator.

She wished he had kissed her.

CHAPTER 4

Rachel's Party

THOMAS PULLED ONTO CARTER LANE AND DROVE for fifteen minutes. He reached two large wrought iron gates that were attached to brick walls, which ran for thirty feet on either side. On each wall was a gold plated plaque one read, 'The Carter Estate' and the other, '#1 Carter Lane'. He drove through the open gates. On either side of the road was a line of forty foot oak trees that ran parallel. After ten minutes he veered off to the right and noticed he was on a half circle and could see the mansion off to his left. In the middle of the circled driveway was a beautiful stone water fountain that had statues of fish and dolphins. The water reflected lights of blues and reds. He pulled up in front of the mansion and showed his invitation. The man in the vest looked at his list and instructed him to back up his car and park it over to the right of the mansion in front of the garages. From there he should walk passed the front of the house and follow the posted signs around the back of the mansion to the party. Thomas parked the car and as he walked by the front he noticed that there were several other men in vests valet parking guests' cars on a grass lot to the far left.

He reached the path and followed the arrows to the back of the house and off in the distance could hear the murmur of people getting louder. He continued through an archway of bushes and onto what he considered to be a very large stoned patio bordered by six-foot high bushes. He noticed an opening to the left and walked down the steps and onto the grounds. In the distance there were three enormous canopy tents behind which were huge maple trees circling a large pond. As he walked closer a young lady in a vest instructed him that Tent A was the bar, Tent B was serving food and Tent C was were the music and dancing would take place.

He walked into Tent A. On one side was a long row of tables behind which were fifteen bartenders serving drinks. The interior had some groups of people sitting around tables and chairs. Thomas walked over to a pretty young girl with red hair and asked her for a Heineken. She came back with the beer and offered Thomas a glass, which he politely refused and gave her a smile. She smiled back. He turned around and looked at his watch six thirty. "What to do now?" he thought.

"There's a table in Tent C for gifts," said the red headed girl looking down at the wrapped gift and card.

"Thanks," replied Thomas as he turned to her.

"They're having a live band playing here tonight and a DJ. The band is very good."

"You've heard them play before?" asked Thomas.

"Many times, my husband's the lead singer," she said proudly, "and I am not saying they're good because of that."

"I believe you," said Thomas. "So you couldn't work in the other tent?"

"No, there's no bar service. I was lucky to get this job." She wiped down the table as she spoke. "I don't work for this catering company. Robby, that's my husband, spoke to them and they said okay, otherwise I wouldn't have been allowed on the grounds."

"Really!" He took a sip of his beer. "So what are they called?" he asked with interest.

"Atlas!" she said excitedly.

"Atlas?" asked Thomas.

She leaned over and whispered. "They wanted a universal sounding name."

"I like it," said Thomas.

"So do I," she said and smiled.

"My name's Thomas."

"Hi, I'm Tracy."

"Hi Tracy. What type of songs does Atlas play?"

"Well, tonight they'll be playing those songs that you here at weddings and parties; you know the type of songs to cater to all age groups and the songs that everyone knows."

Thomas shook his head, "yeah, I know."

"But when they play clubs they play their own songs, you know ones they wrote. But he loves Bon Jovi! Actually we both do!" she said excitedly. "They will take requests so if you ask him for a song he'll play it!"

"Okay I will," said Thomas. "What song should I ask for?"

Without hesitation, "Always," said Tracy, "That's our song, He sang it to me on our first date, the night we got engaged and it was our wedding song." She leaned over again, "I'll let you in on a little secret. It's our first wedding anniversary tonight," she let out a half smile. "If you ask him to sing it I'll hear him from here, I may even leave for a minute and sneak a peek."

"It's a shame you had to work to get in here," said Thomas.

"It's okay I'll see him during his breaks. As long as we're together." She smiled a lovely smile and Thomas realized how in love she was. She whispered very softly, "Besides we could use the money. He's promised me the world when he gets his record deal."

"Let me see what I can do for you," said Thomas. He suddenly sensed someone standing behind him waiting to be served. "I'll let you get back to work, nice meeting you," and shook her hand.

"See you later," she replied and turned her attention to the man waiting in line.

Thomas was happy for her and smiled as he left. He walked into Tent C, which was much larger than the previous one and noticed the table with the gifts. He walked over and placed his down. He looked around and at the other end of the tent he noticed the band setting up on the stage. He guessed Robby to be the one with the black, shoulder length hair and in black leather pants testing the microphone. The DJ was set up off to the right. In the middle of the tent was a spacious, wooden dance floor that had been built for the night. Around the dance floor were tables and chairs. With the exception of the band, the DJ, Thomas and a group of five older couples in there fifties, the tent was quite empty.

He decided to take a walk down to the pond, which was more like a small lake. He walked onto the dock and looked down at the speedboat. He looked out onto the pond and could see a small, man-made wooden raft about a quarter of a mile out which he assumed was used for people to swim out to and play and sunbathe on. He walked off the dock and sat off to the right under a large maple tree. As he sipped his beer he wondered if Rachel still swam in the pond or sunbathed on the raft. Then he thought about Rebecca in her bikini and how sexy she was and how beautiful she looked in her dress. He wondered where she was tonight and if she had a date, but concluded she would have said something. He also wondered if there was a reason why she hadn't said anything more about her night; maybe there was nothing to tell. Wherever she was, he hoped she was having fun. He took a sip of his beer and listened to the murmur of the crowd growing and wondered where Rachel was. "She's probably finishing getting ready" he said to himself. He really liked her and couldn't wait to see her. Thomas decided to go back and socialize with some of her guests. He finished his beer and went back to the bar tent.

"Thomas," he heard as he walked in. He looked around. "Thomas over here!" It was Jack waving him over.

"Hi Jack," said Thomas. He was glad to see him.

Jack stood and put his arm around him and gave him a squeeze. "I've been looking for you. Just get here?"

"About twenty minutes ago. I had a walk around."

"Here's your Heineken Thomas," said Tracy, "I'll take that empty back."

"Thanks Tracy."

Jack looked at Tracy walking away and then at Thomas.

"A friend," said Thomas reading Jack's mind.

"Nice friend to have. Come and sit down and meet some of my friends."

He sat down next to Jack.

"This is Tiffany, Giselle and Leanne," said Jack. "Girls this is Thomas."

"Hello," said Thomas.

"Hello," replied the three exceptionally pretty girls.

"From what I understand these are three of Rachel's model friends," whispered Jack. "Have you had a really good look around?"

Thomas followed Jack's eyes around the tent and picked up on what Jack was saying, with the exception of the older guests, a high percentage of the girls were young and very attractive. "Are these all models?" asked Thomas.

Jack laughed. Then whispered, "They're either models or rich kids who can afford to look good."

When Taxi Jack made comments like that Thomas wondered who he really was, not that it really mattered because Thomas actually liked Jack. Yet, there was something about him.

"So, we still on for next Friday?" asked Jack.

"Should we make it a week Saturday so that you can have a chance to improve your eleven handicap!" replied Thomas cheekily.

Jack was caught off guard and choked on his whiskey. It made Thomas laugh out loud.

"How did?" asked Jack wanting to know.

"I have friends," bragged Thomas.

"In low places," stated Jack.

"In the right places," corrected Thomas.

The three girls who had been talking to each other stood up in their micro dresses and excused themselves. Jack and Thomas watched them walk away.

Jack turned to Thomas. "I heard you stopped by and saw Barry Levinson late Wednesday afternoon," mentioned Jack.

"Yes I did. He called me and asked me to pick up a laptop for him. So I dropped one off." He looked at Jack. "How did you know?"

"I ran into him late Thursday. He said the technician had come by and set it up for him," replied Jack.

"Yeah, the warranty he has includes a technician setting him up. He also explains all the bells and whistles."

"He says he really likes it and that you got him a thirty per cent discount."

"Yes", replied Thomas, "I'm glad he likes it."

"He wanted to talk to one of the sales reps at QTech about getting a hundred more for his employees. Wanted me to ask you if you knew anyone he could contact."

"Sure, a good friend of mine is a sales rep I'll give him a call on Monday."

"I'll be seeing Barry tomorrow, I'll let him know," said Jack. "Did you know he's a corporate lawyer?"

"I did."

"That he's the co-owner of that firm?" asked Jack.

"I had an idea," replied Thomas.

"Well he's getting the laptops for the lawyers and paralegals in his firm."

An attendant broke off the conversation. "Please ladies and gentlemen I ask that everyone make their way into Tent C".

Thomas and Jack walked into Tent C and stood in the back. "Familiar territory for you Thomas," said Jack amusing himself by recalling the fundraiser.

"Ha, ha," replied Thomas.

This made Jack laugh loudly.

"Ladies and Gentlemen, if we could have your attention please," said a man in a custom made blue suit. His hair was side parted, short and gray.

"That's Rachel's old man Bill," whispered Jack.

"Thank you. As you know today is my daughters twenty-seventh birthday and you are all here to help us celebrate her special day. Please raise your glasses and help Jessica and I introduce our beautiful daughter Rachel and wish her all the best. No parents could be prouder. To her health, happiness and success."

Rachel walked out from the crowd with her mother on her arm. She walked up to her Dad. She looked incredible.

Everyone sang a chorus of happy birthday and a four-layer cake decorated in white and pink with twenty-seven lit candles was brought and placed in front of her. She blew them out. The crowd cheered. She waited for them to stop and spoke. "I thank you all for being here tonight. It is so wonderful to see so many dear friends and family. Thank you for the presents." She turned to her parent. "Thank you to my parents for throwing me this beautiful party. Again, thank you all for making this day special. But now it is time for everyone to dance, drink, eat and have fun."

"Let's party!" yelled a voice in the crowd. Everyone laughed.

Thomas could only see her smiling face through the crowd as everyone surrounded her. The lights lowered and the DJ said his congratulations and started the music.

The tent was now full of young people on the dance floor and older ones sitting around watching. Jack left Thomas to go speak to an acquaintance. Thomas approached a heavyset girl named Veronica, who was sitting alone and asked her to dance. He danced a couple of songs with her and thanked her. He noticed Jessica and asked her for a dance. After which Jessica introduced him to Bill, who said they would get together later and have a talk, he then excused himself. Thomas left Jessica with a friend and went outside for some fresh air.

"Thomas there you are," said Rachel at the entrance of the tent. "Have you met my friends Tiffany and Leanne?"

"I met them earlier on, hello again."

They smiled back. Rachel took his arm and told her friends she would see them later. She walked away from the entrance and down by the water. She stopped and looked at him. "Thomas I'm so glad you're here!"

"I wouldn't have missed it for the world. Happy Birthday," he said and gave her a kiss. He held her hands and stood back and looked at her. She was wearing a long tight fitting sheer brown dress that showed off all her curves. Her blonde hair was curly and fell past her shoulders. She looked like a super model.

"You look great and I like your dress. Only you could get away with a dress like that."

"Thank you," replied Rachel. She realized she was blushing. "You look very handsome. I'll have to keep an eye on my friends tonight."

"Want to get a drink?" he asked.

"Sure, I haven't had one yet."

As they walked up the steps, she turned and asked him, "Are you enjoying yourself so far?"

"I am. This is great. I've never been to anything like this before."

"You'll have a great time," she said. "Is there anything I can get you? Or anything you need?" she asked.

"No, everything is great." They turned and started to walk. "Besides, it's your birthday I should be taking care of you. Is there anything you need?"

"No, I have everything I need," and squeezed his arm.

Thomas stopped and looked at her. He remembered something, "wait, actually there is something." He told her.

They went to the bar, got a drink and went to the other tent and danced to the DJ's music. Some of her friends joined in and they all danced together. The DJ finished his set and there was a short intermission while the band did some last minute preparations. Rachel excused herself.

The dance floor was empty when Rachel walked in from the far end and up to the front of the stage with Tracy minus the vest. She made Tracy wait and walked onto the stage and talked to Robby. Rachel walked off the stage next to Tracy

"Ready boys?" asked Robby to the band.

"Ready," they replied.

Robby looked excitedly at the crowd. "At the request of the guest of honor, Rachel, for our opening set we will be rocking this party with a set of three 'Bon Jovi' songs. Let's get this party started! Ready boys. One, two, three."

The music started and Rachel danced with Tracy, then pulled Veronica up, and then Thomas. The dance floor was packed as Robby did Jon Bon Jovi justice. On the final song Rachel pulled up a seat for Tracy to sit on next to the steps leading up to the stage. Robby walked down the steps, sat down, looked at Tracy and started to sing 'Always'. Tracy started to cry.

Rachel looked into Thomas's eyes and asked him to dance with her and he did.

Tracy spent the whole night with Robby.

Everyone had a great time.

At one o'clock the party came to an end. Veronica had met a young man from her university days and was sitting at a corner table talking with him. The guy reminded Thomas of Buddy Holly. Jack had gone to the mansion with Bill and Jessica. The band and DJ were taking down their equipment and loading it onto the cube vans. The caterers were starting to clean up.

"Want to go for a walk?" asked Rachel.

"Okay."

"Why don't we go for a walk around the pond?"

"The pond it is," said Thomas.

"Let me tell Veronica."

She came back shortly with a bottle of champagne and two glasses, "let's go."

"Rachel, Thomas," they both turned. It was Tracy calling them and she had Robby with her.

"I wanted to thank you Rachel for what you did, letting me spend the evening with Robby and still getting paid, that was nice," she gave Rachel a hug. She then hugged Thomas and whispered in his ear, "I know you were behind this, thanks," and kissed him softly on the cheek.

"Thank you, Rachel, and congratulations," said Robby. He thanked Thomas and shook his hand.

"You were great," said Thomas to Robby.

"Thanks," replied Robby, "It makes all the difference having that someone special in the crowd." He put his arm around Tracy.

Tracy put her head on his shoulder. "You two make a good couple," said Tracy to Rachel.

Thomas and Rachel looked at each other.

"We're going back to our place to spend some time alone and enjoy our anniversary," Tracy said as Robby moved his arm and held her hand.

"Time to get out of these pants," added Robby.

Everyone laughed.

"I didn't mean it that way."

"They know honey," said Tracy. "Besides, that's my job."

They all laughed again.

"Robby, not to sound odd but those leather pants look great. Who made them?" asked Thomas.

"You're looking right at her!"

"Tracy, you made these."

"And the vest!" added Robby.

"Yeah, I'm studying to be a designer, part time."

Thomas looked at Rachel. "I always wanted to wear leather pants but never had the nerve to get a pair."

"You would look great in them," replied Rachel with a wink.

Tracy looked at Robby, then at Rachel and Thomas. "Thanks again, you made me, us, very happy tonight."

"Here," said Rachel as she handed Tracy the champagne and glasses. "You two have a romantic evening."

"We can't accept this," said Tracy.

"Once Rachel's made up her mind, there's no changing it," interrupted Thomas.

Tracy accepted. "Thank you," she said and hugged Rachel this time and gave her a small kiss on the cheek. She did the same with Thomas.

Robby shook their hands and they watched them leave.

"To the bar," said Rachel. The tent was empty but the beer and champagne was still in the ice filled containers. Rachel picked out a bottle of champagne and two glasses out of the crate.

They walked on the grass and around the left side of the pond. They came to a paved trail that Rachel said went right around the pond.

"Are you cold?" asked Thomas.

"No, I'm fine. I'm still warm from dancing," she replied.

"You and Veronica are close friends then?" asked Thomas.

"We used to be closer. I haven't seen her for a while. That's why I asked her to stay over and go riding with me tomorrow." She looked at Thomas, "she thinks you're great."

They walked quietly for a few minutes.

"What about Rebecca? Are you close?"

"Not really. At social events we are but not everyday." She stopped and thought for a moment. "You know I asked her to go to France with me in the summer. She wasn't dancing and had no summer plans, but she said she couldn't. It had something to do with a personal matter. She never told me what. I thought we might have been closer, you know with neither of us having sisters and always being at the same social functions, but she always keeps her distance. It's like there's something else. I'm not sure what and I can't put my finger on it or explain it, but something. I asked her to come tonight but she couldn't make it because of a dinner party. I wished she would have." Rachel stopped walking. "Well here's the guest house."

Thomas looked away from Rachel and at the house. "This is the guest house?" asked Thomas. "It looks like a Cape Cod beach house."

"It's a replica of the one my grandmother owns in Cape Cod. I love this place. It's peaceful and quiet. I sometimes come here when I want to be alone."

They walked up to the front door and she bent down and reached for the key under a garden gnome. They walked inside and Rachel turned on the light. It was a beautiful, open-concept design. There was a living room area with an entertainment center, a kitchen, a dining room area, a desk and chair with a computer and phone, and a wall of books. Thomas followed Rachel through the kitchen where she put down the bottle and glasses and walked out through the patio doors. There was a large deck that had steps off to the right. Thomas looked out at magnificent view of the pond and trees.

"You can't see the main house from here," noticed Thomas.

"We had it built here for privacy," she smiled. "Come on I'll show you around."

He followed her downstairs to the basement, that was actually a recreation room, there was a full bar, billiard table, poker table, and dartboard. It had rich red carpet, oak paneling, and a brick fireplace with a couple of love seats and armchairs facing it. They walked over to the patio doors and went outside. This deck was longer and wider than the one above and Thomas noticed the steps from the deck above came onto this one.

"Look at this Thomas." Rebecca partially lifted the cover up. "It's a ten-person hot tub. We have this on all year." She put down the cover and grabbed Thomas's hand. "Let me show you upstairs," she said. They went inside and climbed the stairs to the top floor. There were two bedrooms and a bathroom at the front of the house, and a master bedroom with an en suite at the back. The master bedroom had a double bed with a thick down filled duvet on it and several large pillows. Rachel opened two French doors and stepped out onto a large balcony that had two chairs.

"So what do you think Thomas?" asked Rachel.

"This is inspirational!" remarked Thomas.

"Wait till you see the loft." She closed the doors behind them and walked out to the hallway to a smaller set of stairs and ascended. The loft was a small room that had a desk and chair and three bookcases filled with encyclopedias, there were two reclining chairs facing the large round window that viewed the pond. The floor was hardwood with a large Persian rug. There was a small electrical heater by the recliners.

"Now this is inspirational!" exclaimed Thomas.

"I know you're a writer. I thought you might want to come by here on weekends or some weeknights and use it. It's peaceful and quiet. Inspirational! We never use this house, must of our guests stay in the mansion. We have the maids come in and clean it twice a week." She looked at him. "You could come and go as you please, all you would have to do is let the butler know when you would be here and he'd make a notation on his board to make sure there was food and clean sheets."

"Are your parents okay with this?"

"I haven't asked them but I'm sure they would be okay with it. Like I said it never gets used. I was hoping it would help you with your writing. Give you some space of your own. Of course if there was someone visiting they may need to have the use of it although it very rarely happens. As I said, most of our guests stay in the East Wing. That's were Veronica, Jack and a couple of other guests are staying tonight."

"And me," added Thomas.

"I thought you might rather stay here, a kind of trial night, I had the maids clean it up for you. There's food and beer in the kitchen."

"Did you fix this loft up for me?"

"Maybe."

Thomas looked around; he loved it. "And you, where are you sleeping?"

"I was going to stay here. There are two bedrooms. Unless that makes you uncomfortable?"

"No, not at all, but I have to leave early in the morning I go to church every Sunday. I'll be back for lunch."

"That's okay. I thought you might have had a lie in so I promised to go riding with Veronica tomorrow morning before she leaves. She's going after lunch, that'll give us the afternoon alone." She looked at him. "Now, what about other nights?"

"I'd love to. This loft is so perfect and the view is incredible." He looked out of the window and turned to her, "but you need to clear it with your parents first."

"I will."

"Good."

"Now let's go drink the champagne and celebrate!" she stated.

Thomas followed her into the master bedroom where she opened a chest of drawers and pulled out a pair of swimming shorts.

"You can pull the cover off. The button to turn on the hot tub is on the outside wall under the deck stairs. I'll grab the towels, champagne and the glasses," she said as she walked to the door and turned, "I'll be down shortly." She closed the door as she left the room.

Thomas sat in the hot tub and something caught his eye, it was Rachel's silhouette opening the patio doors. Two small floodlights came on. She closed the door and walked over to Thomas. Her curly blonde hair was tied back in a ponytail and she was wearing a yellow Nike bikini that was high cut at the waist. It fit her perfectly in all the right places. She leaned down and placed the champagne bottle and glasses next to Thomas. He noticed her breasts were big and beautiful and that they had a sprinkling of freckles on them. She slipped into the hot tub beside him. Thomas opened the champagne and filled the two glasses and gave one to Rachel.

"What a beautiful night Rachel!" exclaimed Thomas as he looked at the stars in the sky.

"Beautiful," she said as she looked at him. "What a perfect way to end a perfect evening."

CHAPTER 5

8:35 Sunday Morning

"Good morning Robert," said Thomas to the doorman after reading his nametag.

"Good morning sir. Can I help you?"

"Can you phone up to Ms. La Croix and let her know Thomas is here."

"Certainly."

"He picked up the phone and called. "There is no answer, sir. Is she expecting you?"

"Yes, at eight thirty." Thomas looked at his watch to confirm the time.

The doorman looked at his watch. "It is eight thirty five, let me try once more." He dialed again, "no answer."

Thomas stood and thought, "What to do?" He placed a brown envelope on the counter and decided to wait a few minutes. Suddenly there was laughter coming from outside, he recognized the voice and looked out passed the front door and saw Rebecca with another man heading his way. She hadn't noticed him.

"Here she comes," Thomas said to Robert. "She's with another man." Thomas looked around for a place to hide.

"Behind the wall," said Robert, pointing over Thomas's shoulder.

Thomas stood out of sight.

"Good morning Rob," said Rebecca.

"Good morning, Rebecca, Frank," replied Robert.

"Haven't seen you at The Stallion recently?" asked Frank.

"I've been pulling night shifts and double shifts; a wife of one of the doorman had a baby. Hopefully I'll be back there in a couple more weeks."

"Look forward to it," replied Frank.

They moved away from the desk toward the elevator. Thomas moved further back so he would not be seen

"I had a fun time last night," said Rebecca.

"It was a lot of fun. You know I love you," replied Frank.

"I love you too," said Rebecca.

Thomas looked around to see her kiss him on the lips.

"You're okay with this?" asked Rebecca.

"Yes," replied Frank. "Let's go up."

The elevator door opened and Rebecca and Frank walked in. Thomas walked out into the open and noticed she wasn't even wearing the dress he chose but the pantsuit. Rebecca turned around and watched the elevator doors close and caught a glimpse of Thomas.

Thomas turned and headed for the front door.

"Your envelope?" said Robert as he picked it off the counter.

"Throw it away," said Thomas as he walked out.

He walked for twenty minutes and sat on a bench under a tree that blocked him from the sun and the street. There was a light breeze that rustled the leaves in a melancholy, harmony overhead. A young couple pushing a stroller with an infant walked past and out of sight. He looked up through the leaves and could see her condominium. He put his hands over his face. It hurt.

CHAPTER 6

Horseback Riding

"HERE IS YOUR TEA, SIR," SAID THE butler startling Thomas.

"Thank you."

The butler put the tray down on the table closest to where Thomas was standing. "Mr. Carter will be with you shortly. If you need anything please pick up the phone and dial one," he said pointing to a phone on a table. "Would you like me to pour?

"No, I can take care of that," smiled Thomas.

"If there is anything else?" he asked.

"No, that's fine. Thank You."

"Enjoy sir," he said and left.

Thomas poured his tea and looked out the window at the gardens and thought about Rebecca. "You hadn't seen that one coming," he said to his reflection in the glass.

"Sorry to keep you waiting?" said Bill Carter apologetically. He closed the doors and walked over and shook Thomas's hand. "Quite a view?" he asked as he stood next to Thomas and looked out.

"I was admiring your gardens," replied Thomas.

"We have a gardener from England and he's magnificent. You should see what he does to this place in the spring." Bill pointed to a recliner. "Please have a seat?" Bill sat down opposite him.

"I hope you enjoyed yourself last night?" asked Bill.

"I did. Thank you," replied Thomas.

"It's been a long time since I've seen Rachel have so much fun. I don't know if you are aware of this but at one time Rachel and Veronica were best friends, inseparable. Several years ago Rachel stopped spending time with Veronica and more with her model friends. I don't know if you met these so called friends? If you haven't, take it from me they're one dimensional and dumb. I found Veronica better suited, more down to earth, very stable and smart. Besides her father and uncle are business partners of mine and having the two of them, shall I say close, helps us. If you know what I mean?"

Thomas smiled. He knew when to listen.

Bill continued. "In fact the two of them are out riding today. I have a golf game with her father and two of his business associates this afternoon and it's all because they see Rachel and Veronica dancing and having fun and being friends. They're acting like they've never been closer. And whom do you think I have to thank for this? My daughter, you would think so."

Thomas nodded.

"No." He paused, "actually you."

"Me?" asked Thomas surprised.

"Rachel sees you dancing and talking with Veronica. The next minute she is. Rachel likes you. My wife likes you. Veronica and her father like you." He paused for effect. "Veronica's father and his associates look at how his family and my family are getting along and that makes everyone comfortable."

"And you?" thought Thomas.

"As far as I'm concerned," continued Bill as if he read Thomas's mind. "I like the way things are working out and I would like them to continue that way. Do you know what I mean?" asked Bill.

Thomas didn't. "I'm not sure," he replied honestly.

"Since last week my wife has noticed a change in Rachel. I noticed it for the first time last night. My wife and Veronica's father say you're the reason and it's because of your friendship with her." Bill looked up at Thomas. "You two are only friends?" asked Bill.

"Yes Mr. Carter," answered Thomas.

"I believe Rachel removing herself from her modeling friends and having more down to earth friends is a good thing and I believe you are one of those down to earth friends. Would you agree?"

Thomas nodded in agreement.

"Thanks for taking the time to speak with me," said Bill. "Rachel will be back from her ride at twelve-thirty. Rachel and Veronica said that they would have lunch with you in the guest house." He picked up the phone and asked the butler to come in. He looked at Thomas and spoke, "Rachel has asked if you can use the guesthouse on the pond and I have agreed. It's for your use for whatever period of time you need and as often as you like."

"Yes Mr. Carter?" asked the butler.

"Please make sure Mr. Carlyle has a key to the guest house on the pond and that he has a golf cart available for his use when he's here and that all the necessary cleaning and stocking is done as required."

"Yes sir. Is there anything else?" asked the butler.

"Not at this time," replied Bill and watched the butler leave. He looked over at Thomas.

"Thank you Mr. Carter for your hospitality and generosity," said Thomas graciously.

"It's my pleasure, and please, call me Bill." He looked at Thomas. "I have to be honest with you; I am somewhat uncomfortable with this arrangement. I trust you will not compromise my generosity or my daughter's. "

"No sir," replied Thomas.

"Good," said Bill who quickly changed the topic. "So you're a writer?"

"Yes."

"What do you like to write?"

"Fiction."

"I love to read. My preference is mystery." He looked around the room. "There are over two thousand books in here, fiction, non fiction, mystery, romance, and reference, some are first additions. Anytime you want to borrow one help yourself." He pointed. "There is a computer just next to the staircase. You can use it to look up any title, its location and to sign it out. I'm a stickler for organization."

"Thank you," said Thomas, "this room is incredible." He looked around the room at the fifteen-foot walls of shelving filled with books and the accompanying sliding ladders. There were additional books on the second floor, which could be reached by ascending a black, wrought iron circular staircase off to the left. Thomas looked over his right shoulder and out of the window. "The panoramic view is quite magnificent," complimented Thomas.

"This is where I come for my piece of mind," stated Bill and looked at Thomas. "If you ever want your writing critiqued or considered for publication let me know I have some friends in the business."

"Thanks for the offer."

Bill looked at his watch and stood. "Eleven forty five, I have to get going I have a one o'clock tee off. If you like you can stay in here and have a look around or head to the guest house?"

"Thanks, I'll make my way to the guest house," replied Thomas.

"Fine, I'll walk you to the back door and you can follow the path."

Thomas shook Bill's hand and walked out onto the brick patio and followed the path to the guesthouse. There was something unnerving about the conversation and with Bill Carter that unsettled Thomas. He decided not to read too much into it and be thankful for the offer of the guesthouse. The air was refreshing but Thomas was tired and he needed to put his head down for an hour. The image of Rebecca and Frank kept on coming into his mind; she wasn't going to be easy to forget. He arrived at the empty house and went upstairs and lay on the bed. He was asleep minutes later.

"Good afternoon sleepy head," said Rachel softly. She was sitting on the corner of the bed in track pants and a sweater.

"What time is it?" asked Thomas.

"Two thirty! You've been asleep for two hours," exclaimed Rachel.

"Two…why didn't you wake me?"

"Two reasons, first you were sound asleep and looked so peaceful, second, it gave me and Veronica some time to make lunch and talk some more. We've saved some for you. Take a shower and I'll go warm it up. I'll wait for you downstairs," said Rachel breaking into a smile.

"Okay, give me ten minutes." He playfully motioned her to get out of the room.

Fifteen minutes later Thomas walked into the kitchen.

"Go sit outside on the deck, I'll be out in a minute," said Rachel.

Thomas walked outside and sat at a wooden patio table. The sun was warm but a cool breeze blew occasionally across the deck.

"Here you go. I hope you like it?" asked Rachel. "Its homemade chicken noodle soup and a ham and cheese sandwich, we both made the soup from scratch," said Rachel pleased with herself. She took a sip of her diet Pepsi.

Thomas tried the soup. "Wow! This is delicious!" He looked around. "Where is Veronica?"

"She left after lunch. She asked me to say goodbye. She really likes you."

"I like her. She's a nice girl," confirmed Thomas.

In silence she watched him eat. After he finished she picked up his plates and asked him if he wanted a drink with dessert. She took his plates away and came back with a cup of coffee and chocolate chip cookies.

"From scratch?" he asked.

She nodded and smiled. "Do you like them?"

He hesitated, "Not bad."

She gave his bicep a playful squeeze. "Not bad, they're the best in the country".

"Okay, okay they're the best."

She stared at him again.

He had a feeling there was something she wanted to tell him. So he teased. "You know Rachel I think we should sit here a while and enjoy the silence and this lovely day. What do you think?"

"Well, okay." She replied and looked out at the pond.

"Unless there is something you wanted to talk about?" said Thomas.

"No. Nothing in particular," said Rachel realizing that he knew there was and that he was teasing her.

"Are you sure?"

"Positive," she replied still looking at the pond. She finished her Pepsi leaving the ice in the glass.

"Well I guess I won't tell you something I found out this morning," said Thomas as he looked at her.

"There's nothing that you could have heard from the time you left this morning till now that would mildly interest me or that I don't already know!"

"Okay, I guess you're right, a conversation with your dad in his study this morning would be uninteresting or perhaps you already know." As Thomas said this he looked at the pond. "Beautiful day."

"You spoke to my dad in his study? He never lets strangers in there. What did he say?" she asked as she stared at him.

Thomas ignored her stare. "Oh I'm a stranger now!"

"You know what I mean! What did he say?"

"Nothing of interest," he replied. "What a beautiful day!"

"Thomas," she pulled at his arm but he was too strong. She stood up and walked behind him and whispered in his ear, "Thomas, if you don't tell me," she blew in his ear, "then I will have to do something," she licked his ear, "that won't be nice," then lightly kissed his earlobe.

"What's that?" whispered back Thomas.

"This!" she pulled the back of his sweater and poured in the glass of ice and ran inside. Thomas jumped up and opened up the bottom of his sweater to let the ice cubes fall out. He went inside to find her. He heard her breathing in the shower stall in the en suite and slowly walked up and quietly put his hand in the curtain and turned on the cold water.

"I'll get you for this," she yelled and turned off the water and opened the curtain. "Someday when you're not expecting it I'll get you for this." She stood there soaking wet. Her sweater clung to her breasts and her nipples were big and hard. Her hair hung over her face.

Thomas pulled her wet hair aside exposing her sparkling, green eyes. She looked at him and he looked at her.

"I'll get you a towel," he said and turned to go.

"Since I'm wet I might as well get a hot shower. If I throw my clothes over will you hang them over the chair?"

Thomas returned with a towel. Her clothes were on the floor and the shower was running. He picked up the track pants and sweater and hung them over the chair, then her white bra and silk panties. "I'll leave the towel on the floor," he said and looked at the curtain. He could see her silhouette; her hands were over her head washing her hair, her back arched, and her full breasts were extenuated. He could see the outline of her small waist and curvy legs. The steam was filling the room.

She stuck her head around the curtain. "Thanks, I'll only be a minute."

I'll wait for you in the bedroom," said Thomas looking away. He wasn't sure if she had caught him. He turned and walked out the bathroom and decided to go outside onto the balcony. He looked out at the pond. It was peaceful.

"What are you thinking about?" she asked as she stood next to him.

"Nothing," he lied, and turned and faced her. She was in a bathrobe and had her hair brushed back. "We should go in before you catch a cold. Are you going to dry your hair?" he asked.

"I should but I'm tired," she replied.

"Come over here and sit down at the make up table," he pulled her by the hand and she sat down. He left and came back with the hair dyer, plugged it in and started to dry her hair.

"You're very gentle," she whispered. "I think you've done this before."

"Many times."

"Who was the lucky girl?" she teased.

"My sister Kate."

"She's lucky to have a brother like you I wish I had one."

"We're best of friends," explained Thomas. "Like me and you."

"Like me and you," she repeated. She closed her eyes.

"All done," he said.

"That was so wonderful," she said and yawned. "Now I'm tired!"

"Why don't you have a lie down on the bed?"

She pulled him onto the bed. "Lay with me just till I fall asleep."

"Okay," replied Thomas and he lay down next to her.

She moved closer and put her head on his chest and fell asleep soon after. Thomas looked at the ceiling and thought about the hot tub last night and what they talked about. He placed a pillow under her head and left the room.

Rachel woke up and went downstairs. "Here you are," said Rachel entering the recreation room still in her robe. "What time is it?"

"Four," answered Thomas as he sank the black ball. "Do you feel better?"

"I do," she said with a smile. "Thanks." She walked over to him. "Are you staying for dinner?"

"I have to go. I promised Kate I'd be home for six," said Thomas. "I'll have to leave in an hour."

"We never did go horseback riding. Maybe next time?" she asked.

"Next time," he confirmed, "after we've both had a good night sleep."

"I enjoyed last night especially the hot tub. That was a lot of fun," she said smiling.

"It was. It was a great party."

"I'm glad you enjoyed it. Next time you come we'll go swimming," stated Rachel.

"Swimming!" exclaimed Thomas, "In the pond?"

She laughed at him. "No silly, we have an indoor swimming pool connected to the house." She grabbed his arm. "Why don't I take you for a walk and I'll show you around the estate?"

"I would like that."

"Let me get dressed," she said as she walked away, "besides it will give us a chance to talk."

They walked out the front door and around the other side of the pond back to the estate. Rachel was wearing a white sweater, black leggings and Nike running shoes. Her blonde hair was loose and blowing in the breeze.

"Are you interested in what your father and I talked about?"

"Not really."

"No," said Thomas surprised.

Rachel smiled and looked at Thomas out of the corner of her eye, "I saw my dad before he left to go to his golf game. He told me what you two talked about."

"You already knew?" asked Thomas.

"Yes I did. He wanted to meet you and…" she stopped.

"And?" asked Thomas.

"And nothing." Rachel looked straight ahead.

"Rachel!" exclaimed Thomas, "Tell me!"

"Okay, he thinks you would be a good friend for me to have but he's somewhat wary you know the way father's are." She caught herself, "Oh, I'm sorry about the father thing."

"That's okay. I know what you meant. I'm the same way with Kate." He looked over at her, "I got the feeling he was a little uncomfortable."

"Well, he told me he liked you. Besides my mother doesn't have a bad word to say about you and Jack acts as if you and him are best friends. Then there's Veronica, she thinks I should lock you in the guesthouse and never let you go. That reminds me, Veronica has a date with the guy from last night, the one with the black rimmed glasses, looks like Buddy Holly."

"Buddy Holly!" exclaimed Thomas and laughed as he had forgotten all about him.

"Actually his name is Johnny but everyone calls him Buddy, anyway, she really likes him and she's seeing him again on Friday."

"Good for her," said Thomas.

Rachel hesitated, "She was hoping we would meet up with them."

"Friday night?" asked Thomas.

"Yes, Friday night."

"I can't this Friday. I'm playing golf with Jack and after I'm going to his place for dinner," replied Thomas.

"Oh, too bad," said Rachel sadly. "She'll be disappointed too."

"Any other day would be fine?" suggested Thomas, "Saturday?"

"Let me find out," said Rachel. "Do you know when you're coming over again?" asked Rachel.

"I'll have to talk to Kate tonight and try work out a schedule," explained Thomas. "Once I've done that I'll give you a call and check with you." He smiled at her, "I want to make sure you're going to be here."

Rachel smiled. "You should have Kate come with you some time."

"Thanks, I'll mention it to her. Although I fear she will exhaust you with her questions on modeling."

"I love modeling and especially talking about it. I'd look forward to it," she said as she put her arm through his. "You know I talked with Veronica this morning and we're going to look into owning a children's daycare together. We have to find out how to set one up...the legal implications, staffing, location...we're going to set up a meeting with some people over the next couple of weeks and get more details. And we're going to do it on our own."

"That's terrific," said Thomas enthusiastically. "What about modeling?"

"I'll continue with the modeling for now and if later on a decision needs to be made I'll worry about it then. Besides it could take six, twelve, maybe eighteen months to set up a daycare. I'll just have to balance the two."

"You seem excited?" asked Thomas and realized this is what she had been waiting to tell him.

"I am." She stopped walking and looked at Thomas. "I do have one concern."

"What's that?" he asked.

"My parents."

"You haven't told them?"

"You're the first. I'm telling my parents tonight." They started walking again. "I'm a little bit worried about their reaction and was hoping you might be able to help me out on how I should approach them. I'm a little anxious," she said as she squeezed his arm.

"I wouldn't worry, just tell them like you told me and I think you'll find them very supportive," said Thomas confidently.

"You think so?"

"I'm sure of it!" Thomas smiled.

"But I want to do it on my own and that may cause some problems. They'll want to help and get involved. Especially my father, I don't want to hurt their feelings but I really want to do this on my own." She stopped and turned and looked at Thomas. "What do you think I should do?"

"I think you should be direct with them and tell them what you want to do. How you are going to do it and how you feel about it. I'm sure they'll respect that."

She looked unsure.

"Here's a suggestion. Explain to your parents what you and Veronica are planning to do. Stipulate that you want to do it on your own and if you need their help you will ask." Thomas thought for a moment. "Maybe you can set a couple of hours aside, you know, biweekly or monthly, and sit down with them and give them an update. You dad is a businessman he'll appreciate that and so will Veronica's father. Let them know your progress and any roadblocks and ask them for some suggestions. They'll have some good ideas, but ultimately you and Veronica decide if and how you want to use that information. Consider your father and Veronica's father as business advisors, which they will love, and consider your mother more of a personal advisor, the one you talk to about setting up the business. Everyone will feel part of it but ultimately you and Veronica will be in control and in charge." Thomas looked at her. "It's only a suggestion there are probably better ones."

She smiled and softly said, "No, I like that." She put her arm through his and started walking. "I really like that suggestion a lot. Where did you come up with that?"

Thomas laughed. "Kate and I have dinner every Sunday. It gives us time to eat together and talk about different things; I guess sort of a family meeting. We talk about finances, her schedule and school, whatever is on our minds, and basically give each other suggestions as to what we could do or should do. Mostly we just listen to each other." He stopped and thought for a moment. "It's nice to have someone to talk to but its great having someone to listen to you."

She squeezed his arm, "I know it does."

The leaves rustled and the sun started to fade. They walked in silence for several minutes until they came to a clearing and could see the lights of the mansion.

Rachel stopped and pointed. "Can you see the left of the house and the windows of the study?"

"Yes," confirmed Thomas.

"Follow those windows to your left. Can you see the corner of the house?"

"Yes."

"If you look closely you can see a wall jotting out just past the corner and a slight sloping of a roof from the second story of the house. Can you see it?"

"I can."

"That's the glass roof. The pool is in there and there's an outdoor deck on the other side."

"It looks big," suggested Thomas. "Is it?"

"It's a fair size. It has a slide, diving board, there's also a whirlpool and sauna." She pointed off to the left to a rooftop between several trees, "That's the servant quarters, the butler and his wife live there, to the far left is where we have the stables." They began to walk again. "You will see them better as we walk a little closer. The gardener, the maids and stable hands live off the property."

As he listened Thomas noticed there was no tone of snobbery in her voice.

"I hope I'm not sounding like I'm bragging."

"Not at all. Actually, I was just thinking about how you don't sound like that at all."

She kept looking straight ahead. "I just wanted you to be familiar with the surroundings especially since you will be spending time here," she was looking for reassurance.

"I know and I appreciate everything you're doing. I'm really looking forward to coming here," replied Thomas.

She looked at him and smiled. "I'm glad."

They walked around the estate for half an hour. Rachel pointed out the stables. The place she fell off a horse when she was eleven. A trail that took you to a beautiful picnic spot that overlooked the valley. They got back to Thomas's car just after five.

"I'll give you a call when I've talked to Kate," he said as he opened the door, "either tonight or tomorrow night."

"Okay," she said. "I forgot to tell you, I received a call from Tracy earlier, she said her and Robby enjoyed the champagne and had a lovely romantic night and wanted to thank us. She said she would call and let us know when Robby was playing at a local club and would reserve a table for us and some friends."

"Really!"

"I told her that would be great and to call me when she found out. I thought that was nice of her."

"That was," replied Thomas and leaned over and kissed her on the cheek.

She gave him a hug and kissed him back. "I had a great time."

"So did I, thanks for showing me around." He got into his car. "Call me anytime."

"Thanks, I will." She closed the door and stood back.

As he drove away he looked at her in his rear view mirror.

She watched the car till it was out of sight. She turned around and had the happiest of smiles on her face.

DURING DINNER THOMAS TALKED ABOUT THE LAST two days omitting Friday night at Rebecca's and Sunday morning. Kate talked about her studying and how she needed to get into a law firm part time and gain some experience. And how it would help her both before and after the Bar exam. She had submitted resumes but hadn't had any replies to date; she still had a few more to drop off. Thomas told her to be patient and that she would hear back soon. They talked about Thomas spending time at the Carter's and how Kate was looking forward to horseback riding but more importantly talking about modeling with Rachel.

Thomas placed the plates in the dishwasher and walked into the living room with two cups of tea.

Kate watched him as he sat down. She waited a moment, "Thomas, what happened with Rebecca?"

"Happened? What did she know?" thought Thomas. "What do you mean?" he asked.

"Rebecca's been calling all day and she sounds upset. What happened?" She looked at her tea, took a sip and looked at Thomas. "You purposely left out Friday night. Did something happen? Did you have a disagreement?" She stopped and realized she may be too pushy. "I understand if you don't want to talk about it."

Thomas had tried to suppress those events into a dark secret corner of his mind but they wouldn't stay. All day they kept surfacing and haunting him and hurting him. He was only too glad to share them with Kate. He told her about his time with Rebecca and what he witnessed on Sunday morning; the only thing he left out was his name.

"Okay," said Kate. "I'm confused." She thought for a moment. "Do you want her to be more than a friend?"

"What do you mean?" asked Thomas.

"Are you in love with her?"

"In love with her?" questioned Thomas. "No. Why would you think that?"

"It's just the way you speak of her. It's very passionate." Kate said and looked on. "You seem to really like her."

"I'm confused," said Thomas. He put his hands on his head.

"She sounded really upset on the phone. Maybe you need to talk to her?" Kate suggested. "Whatever it is, it has upset her too. She's been calling you all day."

Thomas looked at Kate. "We're supposed to be friends, honesty and trust. She's probably calling to apologize for not telling me."

Kate put her arm around Thomas. "Thomas you're very open and honest, some people need more time." She looked at Thomas. "Have you really given her a chance to explain? You haven't even heard her side of the story and maybe you're jumping to conclusions and it's not like you!" stated Kate. "Thomas, I know that you are upset and maybe you have every reason to be. But I think you need to give her a chance to explain. You said it yourself she's your friend."

"I don't want to talk about it any more, I need to go upstairs and have a lie down." Thomas stood and started for the stairs.

"Rebecca is calling back at eight. You should talk to her."

He walked out the room and up the stairs to his bedroom and closed the door.

At eight o'clock Thomas picked up the ringing phone. "Hello."

"Hello Thomas, its Rebecca. Don't hang up."

Silence.

"Thomas you don't understand what's going on. Please give me a chance to explain. Please."

"Is your explanation going to answer questions I have about your trust, honesty and our friendship?"

"I don't know Thomas, I was wrong, I should have told you but I need to explain some things to you so you will understand..."

Thomas cut her off. "I've been open and honest with you all along and you've had more than enough opportunity to talk to me."

"Please give me a chance now! This isn't easy for me. I wanted to tell you. I was going to explain it all to you this morning."

"Well, now I know."

"Thomas I need to see you and talk to you and explain. Please give me that."

"I'm sorry Rebecca; I can't see you right now."

Rebecca was starting to cry, "Thomas you say you are my friend, why are you treating me this way?"

"Well I guess I can't be trusted either. Goodbye Rebecca."

As he hung up the phone Thomas looked up at Kate standing in the doorway. "Thomas, you didn't even give her a chance?"

Thomas was silent.

"Why not?" she asked and waited.

Thomas remained silent.

"Thomas, this isn't you. You always like to give people the benefit of the doubt. Why are you acting this way towards her? I think you need to listen to what she has to say and try to understand where she is coming from. Friends don't judge friends. Friends are friends through rights and wrongs good times and bad."

"Kate, I guess I don't want to know the whole story. You know, how they met. How she's in love. How he's a nice guy and how I would like him and we could all be friends and hang out together."

"Who's he?"

"George Michael," Thomas laughed a little. "Francis Gray."

"I see." Kate looked long and hard at Thomas, "Thomas do you love her?" asked Kate. Then she stood back and realized something. "Or are you doing this because you are in love with Rachel?"

CHAPTER 7

Jack

"NICE CAR JACK," SAID THOMAS AS THEY drove north in Jack's convertible Cadillac.

"Thanks," replied Jack. "It's quite a drive! Have you ever been behind the wheel of a Cadillac before?"

"Never," said Thomas.

Jack pulled over, "here you take the wheel."

Thomas changed seats, put the car in drive and accelerated onto the highway, "Wow! What a drive!"

"If you're ever looking around for one let me know. I can get you a great deal," said Jack sincerely.

"Thanks for the thought Jack but I don't think I'll be taking you up on that offer anytime soon," replied Thomas.

"Thomas if you think small you'll always be small!" preached Jack. "If you had a choice of any car and price wasn't an issue, what would it be?"

Thomas thought and said, "A metallic blue convertible Aston Martin fully loaded with blue leather interior, six speakers and a CD player". Thomas looked around, "and maybe one of these in silver with black leather and fully loaded. And for when I go skiing, a red Dodge Durango, with cloth interior, again, fully loaded." He looked at Jack. "I believe that would do it."

"That's more like it. Always dream big," said Jack as he smiled back, "and always think big. It's all about confidence and believing in yourself." He patted Thomas on the shoulder, "I must admit you look good behind that wheel."

"So where are we going?" asked Thomas.

"The Devil's Valley," replied Jack. "Have you ever played there before?"

"No. I've heard of it. Isn't it an exclusive private club?"

"That it is!"

"I heard it has a fifty thousand dollar membership?"

"Try seventy-five," answered Jack.

"How long have you been a member?"

"Five years." He looked over at Thomas. "Since you knew my handicap I figured I needed an advantage."

"Jack, I hate to embarrass a man on his home course!" said Thomas confidently.

"You're a cocky little bastard. I can't wait to beat your ass," laughed Jack. "Here let me put on some tunes."

With the top down and the sun shining Thomas and Jack drove to The Devil's Valley.

The Devil's Valley was very exclusive and it portrayed that from the valet attendants to the gold sinks in the bathrooms. They refused caddies and drove the cart to the first tee. Jack turned to Thomas. "Lunch."

"Lunch?" asked Thomas.

"Loser buys lunch at the clubhouse," confirmed Jack. "We won't have time for the Steak House today."

"Deal," said Thomas as they shook. Jack flipped a coin and Thomas won the toss and elected to shoot second.

Thomas looked over the menu and the prices. "Glad you're paying Jack!"

"You play a hell of a game. Where did you learn to play like that?" asked Jack.

"I caddied for a few seasons at The Eagle, after work and on weekends, I became friends with the old guy that owned the place. I used to help him out, you know some painting here and there, cleaning the golf carts, and in return he used to let me play for free. So I played when I could and when I wasn't, I watched," replied Thomas. "The old guy, his name was Marvin, he passed away and his wife ended up selling the place. It was never the same after that. So I started playing the public courses."

The waiter came for their order. "Do you mind if I order for the both of us? The filet mignon is excellent and the baked potatoes are the size of my fist," said Jack as he clenched his hand to the size of a melon.

"Sure Jack," replied Thomas.

"Two filets medium rare and double top shelves, Bob."

"I'll be back with your drinks in a minute Mr. Collins and Mr.?"

"Carlyle, please call me Thomas."

"Okay, I'll be back in a moment."

Bob returned with two double whiskeys, "Here you go Jack, Thomas. Enjoy. Dinner will be fifteen to twenty minutes."

They ate dinner and moved into the lounge that overlooked the eighteenth hole and ordered two more drinks.

"Look its Barry Levinson he's about to chip onto the green," said Jack. "I'll bet you one he takes three strokes to sink the ball."

"I'll take that bet and I'll say two or less and let's make it a five," smiled Thomas.

"Easy money," said Jack.

Barry's chip almost went in; the second shot was just a formality.

Jack looked at Thomas. "Nice call."

Thomas leaned over. "Jack, I'll let you in on a little secret. When I dropped off his laptop we talked about golf and he told me how many times on the eighteenth he's been this close to chipping the ball in for an eagle." said Thomas.

"He told me his score last week and it was horrendous," said Jack.

"You can't win on short game alone," smiled Thomas. "He told me his long game is his weakness."

Jack took out his wallet and gave Thomas five one hundred dollar bills and from the inside of his jacket gave him an envelope.

"What's this Jack?" asked Thomas looking at the five bills.

"You won!" said Jack with a puzzled look. "I always pay my debts."

"Jack, do you have a five dollar bill in your wallet?" asked Thomas.

Jack opened up his wallet, "here you go."

Thomas took the five and gave the five hundred back, "sorry Jack, I meant five dollars."

Jack put the money back in his wallet, "you're lucky you won kid or I would have been looking for the five hundred," said Jack with a stern face that broke into a smile. "Always make sure you clarify your bet first."

"You too," replied Thomas.

They both laughed.

"What's this?" asked Thomas pointing at an envelope with his name on it.

"It's for you," said Jack. "Commission."

"Commission for what?" asked Thomas.

"The laptops, Barry bought a hundred of them. He got a great discount and a great service contract. It ended costing him only four hundred thousand; he saved two. He gave you a one per cent finder's fee on the six," said Jack.

Thomas opened the envelope, inside was a check for six thousand dollars and a note from Barry thanking him. "I can't take this," said Thomas. "I wasn't expecting anything in return I did this as a favor." Thomas took the note, put the check back into the envelope and gave it back to Jack. "I'll keep the note and you can give this back to Barry."

"Thomas, this is business, and in my business we pay people finder's fees. If we don't we get a reputation, a bad reputation. You have no choice but to accept."

Thomas looked a little unsure. "I wouldn't tell anyone."

Jack knew that. "What you did for Barry was the favor! What you did for the firm is business! And what you do with the money is up to you, with one exception, you can't give it back," stated Jack firmly. "Don't take this the wrong way Thomas we still appreciate what you did for us and you taking this money doesn't take away from that." He passed the envelope back to Thomas. "But this business transaction is concluded and we thank you."

Thomas looked at him. "Jack what's all this 'we' and 'in my business'. How do you fit in?"

"I'm the silent partner of Levinson and Associates, so you saved me money too," replied Jack. "At dinner tonight, me and you, we'll have a talk, for now let's enjoy our drinks."

Again Thomas wondered who Taxi Jack really was. "Okay," replied Thomas and took the envelope.

They talked for half an hour about golf, cars and casinos. Jack was talking about Las Vegas when they were interrupted.

"Hello Jack, Thomas," said Barry. "Play today?"

"Sure did," said Jack, "Thomas has a sweet swing."

"Nice chip onto the eighteenth," complimented Thomas.

"Long game still suffering, keep on slicing, luckily the eighteenth is a dog leg," confessed Barry. "Did you get the envelope?"

"Yes," replied Thomas. "Thank you."

"Jack said he was seeing you today. I was scheduled to be in court Monday but last night they opted for an out of court settlement. It freed me up today. Anyway, I wanted to come by and say thank you," he reached out and shook Thomas's hand. "And also give you this." He gave Thomas a larger envelope.

Thomas looked at it and read the name, "Kate Carlyle".

"Kate is your sister?" asked Barry.

"Yes she is."

He sat down. "There is a position opening up in our firm, paralegal, it's lower level entry position, mostly filing, documentation, some time in court and sitting in meetings. Its part time, basically whatever time she has available during the days, nights, and weekends. We give time off to study for the Bar exam and after they pass we hire them on as a lawyer." Barry hesitated then continued, "I'm not going to beat around the bush, I oversee all applications and three met our requirements, Kate was the best candidate. She had the best grade point average of the three and everyone we talked to spoke exceptionally well of her. A select group of lawyers, myself included, made the decision and considered her to be the best candidate. She secured the position on her own merits; the fact that I know you and that she is your sister never factored in. In that envelope is an offer. If she accepts she will have to come in for a set of interviews, which are formalities." He stood up. "I was going to call her on Monday but I heard you were going to be here today so I thought you might like to pass on the good news. Also gives her time to look over the offer on the weekend and get back to me with a decision on Monday."

"I will," said Thomas bewildered. "I'll let her know to call you."

"Thanks," said Barry. "If you will excuse me I have to meet an associate in the dining room. Thanks again Thomas, see you tomorrow Jack." He shook their hands and left.

Thomas looked at Jack, "Did you know about this?"

"This is the first I heard of it. I had nothing to do with it. I know nothing about running a law firm, that's Barry's job. I'm just a partner who cares about the bottom line. But I will tell you this Barry doesn't do favors for anyone especially when it comes to hiring, there's too much at risk. So believe him when he says he screened those applicants. I bet you there were no stones left unturned." Jack smiled, "Business is business." He motioned Thomas to lean over and whispered, "In this room sit some of the richest men in the city, in fact the country. If they're here on a weekday it's all business. If it's after two on a Friday or a weekend then its social slash business."

Thomas looked around the room. All the men were in deep discussions, some were going through documents, and others had their briefcases open on the table. There were only a couple of women.

"Why are there only a few women?" asked Thomas.

"Powerful women do business differently than men. They like to dress up, go for lunches, dinners, and shows. It wouldn't be good business for a woman to beat a man at golf or as you put it, on his home turf. Men have egos and women don't, this gives them an advantage. But don't be fooled, women are just as shrewd as men when it comes to business, if not, shrewder." Jack stopped. "One more drink then we'll head back to my place."

"Where do you live Jack?" asked Thomas.

"At the J.C. Condominium Tower, downtown. I'm leaving my car here overnight in the garage. I'll pick it up tomorrow after I've beaten Barry. We'll get chauffeured home from here," informed Jack, "I'll arrange to have your clubs dropped off at your house."

The name of the condominium tower sounded familiar to Thomas. He must have passed that tower before. As they left the bar Thomas noticed many of the members made a point of going out of their way to say goodbye to Jack. A stretch Rolls Royce pulled up at the front doors of the country club and picked up Jack and Thomas. It had a bar, television, CD and DVD player, and phone.

"This yours Jack?" asked Thomas.

"One of them," smiled Jack. "Same chauffeur though. Let me get you a beer." He gave Thomas one and put on Ray Price's, 'For the Good Times'.

Thomas listened as Jack sang along. When it ended Thomas commented, "That's a sad song, powerful, but sad."

"Sure is!" replied Jack. "It was one of my mother's favorites. She used to sing it all the time." Jack looked over at Thomas. "I guess she was sad. But I like to think about her and that song reminds me of her. That's why I play it a lot." He looked out the window and thought about her then turned to Thomas and changed the subject. "Now me, I like Dean Martin," he put on a CD. "Just sit back enjoy your beer, the ride, the music, and me," Jack sang, along with Dean.

An hour later they passed the theater and pulled into the parking garage of the J.C. Condominium Tower. Thomas now remembered where he had seen that name before it was engraved on the front of Rob the doorman's desk. They walked onto the elevator and Jack inserted a card and pressed the nineteenth floor. On the way up the elevator stopped on the twelfth floor, Thomas's heart was in his mouth, he hadn't spoken to Rebecca since the phone call last Sunday and here he was in her building. A young man walked on and pressed eighteen. The elevator door closed and reopened again on the nineteenth and Thomas and Jack walked off. Ten feet in front was a set of heavy wooden doors. Jack opened one with a key and walked in, Thomas followed behind.

"Welcome to my home in the city Thomas," said Jack.

"Is this floor all yours?" asked Thomas.

"Well all nineteen floors were mine, I just live on the nineteenth," replied Jack, "J.C., Jack Collins"

Thomas never put the two together. He thought back to the fundraiser and Jack getting into the taxi and the comment he made about 'Taxi Jack' and smiled.

"Let me quickly show you around," offered Jack. "To the left we have two bedrooms," he opened one of the doors, "each are a good size and have there own en suite. You can leave your bag in this one it has the best view. Here's the other one. Back here I have a recreation room with a pool table, dartboard and wet bar. Here let me get you a beer." Behind the bar he opened the refrigerator and grabbed two beers and gave one to Thomas. "Down here is the laundry room and if we walk this way we're back at the front door. Let me show you the rest. Here is the dining room. Through here is the kitchen, the living room, and the master bedroom. The master bedroom is the same size as the two other rooms put together and the en suite in here has an oval tub and separate shower. This door here leads into my office."

"Jack this place is incredible," said Thomas in awe.

"I'm glad you like it," replied Jack as they walked into the living room. "Dinner isn't for another couple of hours. I need to make some calls and have a shower and put on some fresh clothes. If you like you can watch the big screen TV, have a lie down, or get a shower. I'm going to be in the room so you have the place to yourself. Help yourself to a drink. There's a bar here in the living room and you know about the one in the recreation room. In case you want to go for a walk here are the keys and the elevator card. The doorman knows you're my guest so you can get back in without disturbing me." Jack looked at his watch and confirmed, "I'll be finished by six thirty. Its just a few minutes passed five," said Jack.

"Thanks, there's enough here to keep me busy," replied Thomas.

Jack went into the master bedroom and Thomas walked into his guest room. It felt weird being seven stories above Rebecca's floor. He missed her and thought about going down to talk to her, but decided against it, instead he had a lie down and fell asleep.

"Thomas," said Jack as he knocked on the door. "Thomas," said Jack again as he opened the door.

"Hi Jack."

"It's six forty five, I thought you might have fell asleep, get a shower and dressed and come on out," ordered Jack.

Thomas walked into the living room at seven, "Jack," he called out.

"In here," replied Jack from the kitchen. "I'm just putting the racks of lamb into the oven. You like lamb?" asked Jack.

"Yes," replied Thomas, "as long as they're not glazed."

"A man after my own heart," commented Jack. "Baked and topped with mint sauce."

Thomas smiled. "You like cooking?"

"I rarely get the chance to these days but when I do, I do," said Jack, happily. "Tonight its lamb, mashed potatoes and carrots."

"Hope you're better at cooking than you are golf," teased Thomas.

"Ha, ha," replied Jack sarcastically. "In case you're wondering why I'm putting in three, Penelope Daily is coming for dinner. Is that okay?"

"Yeah," replied Thomas.

"Here open the wine and pour a couple of glasses," said Jack as he passed the wine and opener. "And not those sample sizes, fill it up."

Thomas pulled out the cork and poured and gave Jack a glass. "Cheers."

"Cheers," replied Thomas.

"Jack, Jack," said a voice from the hallway.

"Penny, I'm in the kitchen with Thomas," shouted Jack.

"Here you are. Hello Thomas," said Penelope. She leaned over and gave him a kiss on the cheek.

"Hello Penelope," replied Thomas.

"Please, call me Penny," she requested. She moved over to Jack, "Hi Jack. How you doing?" and kissed him on the lips.

"Just put the lamb in the oven. They should be ready in an hour. Did you bring dessert?" asked Jack.

"Yes, it's on the hallway table. I'll go and get them." She returned moments later with a baker's box. "I'll put them in the refrigerator." She looked at Thomas, "he loves his chocolate éclairs."

Thomas smiled.

"Let's go in the living room," suggested Jack, "I'll put some music on and we can have a talk."

"How was your golf today?" asked Penny.

"Enjoyed it," replied Thomas, "it's a beautiful course."

"What he is omitting to say is that he really enjoyed beating me," interjected Jack. "He'll have to give me a rematch so I can remove that winning smile off his face." Jack sat down next to Penny on the sofa and Thomas opposite him. All of a sudden Jack became very serious. "Listen Thomas there's something I, actually Penny, needs to talk to you about. I don't like getting involved in these sort of situations, neither does Penny, but when it effects people who you love and their life and careers, then sometimes you have only one choice but to." Jack continued in a more light-hearted tone. "Before I let Penny talk there are some things I would like to share with you. So if you could keep this confidential I would appreciate it."

"Sure Jack, "replied Thomas.

"When I was ten my father left. It wasn't till years later that I found out he took off with another woman and needless to say I never seen him again. My mother was left to take care of my brother and me. She worked a full time job during the week and a part time one on the weekend so she could take care of us and make ends meet. We lived just down the road from here. We were poor, but we were happy, and we had each other. When I was sixteen, my brother was struck by a drunk driver and killed. When I was eighteen, my mother died of cancer. So here I am eighteen with no family and no money. I couldn't even afford to rent the place we lived in. I had little education so I took a job driving a taxi. I soon realized that I was working to make someone else rich. I set my sights and decided that one day I would be the one getting rich. I eventually bought my own taxi company and ran that for a few years. Then I bought another company and then another, I quickly realized that running one company was the same as another. Today I own many companies, I got out of running them I hire people to do that, I just own them. I'm also a silent partner in several big firms, and like I said I don't get involved in the day-to-day business, all I'm interested in is the bottom line, the profit. Today I'm semi-retired from the business of acquisitions; I have a company who does all that," said Jack. "When I was eighteen I had a hundred dollars to my name. Do you know what I'm worth today?" he asked.

Thomas didn't answer. When he waved goodbye to him in the taxi he would have guessed Taxi Jack wasn't worth much. With what he knew now he guessed forty million and that was a high guess.

"Four hundred and fifty million," stated Jack.

"Four hundred and fifty," thought Thomas.

"Why was I so successful? Drive. Determination. Fear. Loneliness. Anger. It all came out from within a boy of eighteen because he was forced into an unpleasant existence. The world owed him and they were going to pay. It had nothing to do with power, fame, and fortune. In fact, I'm low-key about my business, my partnership and my personal life. Seven years ago I had achieved all that I had wanted. So I retired my active participation in businesses and all the day-to-day decision-making and passed them on to a very loyal and long time employee of mine named Ernie Harris. After being semi-retired for six years, I looked around and realized I had nothing in my life. I had no wife or girlfriend, no children; the only friends I had were business associates. I was depressed for a year." He looked over at Penny and grabbed her hand. "I've known Penny for a long time, almost twelve years now, and she was always there for me and helped me get through that tough period in my life. She gave me a purpose and a meaning to my life. She gave me compassion and love. I owe her more than words can say." He kissed her hand and looked at Thomas. "For the last five years Penny and I have been companions."

"Lovers," added Penny.

"Lovers," replied Jack. "Nobody knows about us. Not family or close friends, except you and Rebecca. We enjoy each other's company and we enjoy the times we are together. But we want to keep it private and that hasn't been easy. You haven't been around enough to notice but we never show up together or sit together and we leave separately." Jack leaned over and filled the wine glasses. "Penny has her own place on the sixteenth floor where she lives but she spends most of her time up here with me. We cook and eat dinners together. We go out for meals and on vacations. When people we know bump into us they look at us as a couple of old friends having a drink or a bite to eat. At the fundraiser we danced a few songs and spent some time together but nothing that can be categorized as a romance." Jack stopped and took a drink of his wine and looked at Penny. "The only regret I have is that we didn't find each other sooner, especially since we would have liked to have children." He held Penny's hand again and tears were forming in his eyes.

Penny put her hand on his cheek and wiped a tear away and smiled and looked at Thomas. "I had liked Jack since the first day I met him. You must understand he was a different man then, a little difficult, a little rough around the edges, but he had a kind look in his eyes, similar to yours Thomas. We were both so busy in our own little worlds that we never took the time to share it with anyone. I'll never forget the first time we went out. It was like a big high school football player asking out his first date and he was quite the gentleman." She looked over at Jack. "He's missed out on so many of the good things life has to offer, like me, but in the last six years we've made up for it." She turned and looked deep into Thomas's eyes. "Over the last couple of weeks Jack hasn't stopped talking about you. He has a great deal of respect and admiration for you. What comes so natural to you, is sometimes, so difficult for Jack." She leaned over to Thomas. "Remember when you let me present your grandmothers award?" she asked.

Thomas nodded.

"It was a very kind and unselfish act. You were a gentleman in the truest sense of the word. With that one kind gesture you had made me so very happy. When I was presenting I looked over at Jack and I could see how happy he was for me. You made it possible for me, for us both, to feel that way. Since that night Jack and I have realized how open and honest you are, that you're not judgmental or condescending, and that you respect people for who they are and treat them as an equal. Jack came from a different world, an eye for an eye and two-faced people, but over these last several years he's changed and become more acceptable and trustworthy." Penny stopped and looked at Jack. "We've recently realized that we have done something wrong and would like to change it and make it right."

Jack looked at his wine glass and continued. "When I look back at you and me at eighteen, we were in the same situation, no parents and little money, but yet you turned out completely different than me." He looked at Thomas and asked, "Why do you think that is?"

"I guess I had a sister that I was responsible for and my grandmother," replied Thomas. "I still had some family and they needed me."

"I believe that too," said Jack. "I look at you and I see someone who has both feet on the ground. There is no doubt in my mind that thirty years down the road you wont turn around, like I did, and look at all those things you missed out on. You won't have any regrets. You know why?"

Thomas shook his head.

"When your sister starts working full time I bet you she'll give you the chance at the life she had, university and such, she'll give you back to you what you gave to her. Am I right?" questioned Jack.

Thomas looked at Jack. "She's already said so."

"Penny and I have a friend, actually she's more like a daughter to Penny, and Penny has known her parents, mostly her father, for many years. I met them just before they split up. Her father Henri was a fine gentleman and a loving father, his daughter meant the world to him and he would never do her any harm. He had a soaring career and was well off. His wife on the other hand was unfaithful and had had several affairs.

He eventually caught her one-day and asked that she leave him and his daughter alone and offered her money to go. She wouldn't. Their marriage was basically over. But she was a clever woman. Several months later she had a private investigator take pictures of Henri and his new girlfriend and took him to court seeking divorce and full custody of the daughter. She won and Henri's name was smeared over the papers. He moved a year or so later to protect his daughter from any further embarrassment." Jack looked at his empty glass, stopped talking and went into the kitchen and brought back the opened bottle of wine and filled everyone's glass and sat down. Jack drank his wine then continued, "That was over nine years ago. Only Penny and I know the truth and now you."

"And your grandmother," added Penny.

"My apologies, and your grandmother, rest her soul. Everyone else believes the story in the papers to be true."

Penny concluded. "We keep in touch with Henri and see him from time to time and let him know how his daughter is keeping."

"His daughter?" asked Thomas.

"She doesn't know the truth. Henri had asked us to promise him that we would not tell her or anyone the truth, especially her. Of course she knows we still keep in contact with him because he is still our dear friend," replied Penny.

"But you're telling me?" questioned Thomas.

Penny responded. "It was a promise we should never have agreed to. We were wrong. Worse of all, so was Henri. At the time his daughter didn't want anything to do with him and he felt responsible for the mess he had made of their lives and he thought, we thought, we were doing the right thing." Penny looked over at Jack. "We want to correct this wrong and give her a chance at a relationship with her father."

"So why not tell her now?" asked Thomas.

"We want to, but I want to keep Henri's promise, he was a good friend to me and I value his friendship," replied Penny.

"So why tell me?" asked Thomas.

"We want you to help us?" asked Penny.

"How can I help?" questioned Thomas.

Penny reached over and held his hand, "Henri's daughter is Rebecca."

Thomas felt his heart pounding and thought "of course Rebecca. Why hadn't he realized it sooner?" He looked at them. "I don't think I can help you."

"Thomas I know something has happened between the two of you, I don't know what and I don't need Rebecca to tell me, her body language speaks volumes. But neither Jack, nor I, is here to discuss your personal life, that's between you and her, and not to down play your relationship, but I have greater worries for her. If you would like me to continue I will do so. If you prefer I stop, I will do so. There will be no bad feelings between us," said Penny. "It's your choice?"

Thomas looked down at his wine glass, "I would like to listen to what you have to say." He looked at Penny. "Please continue."

"Thomas, we understand we may be asking a great deal of you and maybe more so if we knew the situation between you two." She sipped her wine. "After her father left Rebecca threw herself into her dancing. She was one of the finest pupils the school has ever seen. She has drive, determination, but also fear, loneliness and anger. It flowed through her and her dancing. Her technique was exceptional and she has won too many awards to count. At the age of twenty-two she became a second soloist, at twenty-four a first soloist, and this year she will become a principal dancer at the company. She will have achieved the greatest goal of a ballerina." Penny stopped and sipped her wine and softly asked. "At the fundraiser, where you the friend she sang for?"

"She said I could pay for a dance or hear her sing. I asked her to sing," explained Thomas. He smiled as he remembered how she had charged him a hundred dollars so that she could get a dance as well.

"I am going to tell you something about that night that no one, not even Jack knows, in fact not even her. After she sang that night she left the room and went to the bathroom. I followed her in moments later and heard her sobbing in the last stall. I closed the door and waited outside and told people a man was mopping the wet floor and to use the other bathroom. When I heard her walking inside I walked in and acted as if I knew nothing. I asked her if she was okay and she said everything was fine although she missed her father. Just like that out of the blue. That was something I never thought I would ever hear her say. Thomas you need to understand that Jack and I were never allowed to mention her father in front of her." Penny drank a mouthful of wine. "No doubt you have heard that since her father left she has never sung in public?"

Thomas nodded his head.

"The following Monday she tells me how she went to the cathedral with you and sang hymns and how she sang with a street musician in the park," Penny looked for confirmation.

"Yes she did. She sang, 'Unforgettable'. She said it was one of her father's favorite songs," replied Thomas quietly.

"This girl for the last nine years has not wanted to know her father, hear her father's name, or sing. Not only is she singing but singing her father's favorite song in the street. I walk into her condominium this week and I see she has a picture of them both on her end table." Penny stopped to collect her thoughts.

"I'm a little confused. Why does that worry you?" asked Thomas.

Jack spoke. "When she dances in three weeks she will have reached the goal of every ballerina but when she looks down at the audience and around at her colleagues she will realize that she will have no family or close friends to share in her joy. The next day she may wake up and wonder what she has done with her life and like myself fall into a deep depression, or worse," answered Jack.

"It could ruin her career and more importantly, her life," added Penny.

"When you're my age and been through what I have and have four hundred million plus you have a bit more salt. Remember Thomas I grew up with no one so I expected nothing. You, you have Kate. Right now she's alone and she's very fragile and vulnerable," said Jack. "Who does she have?"

"What about her mother?" asked Thomas.

"Her mother isn't coming," answered Penny with a laugh. "She's quite out of the picture."

"Rebecca thinks her mother pays for her place and expenses. Her father, as a favor, had asked me to get her the condominium, so she could be in the city and close to work. He has his money come through one of my law firms to make it look as if it's coming from her mother. He pays all her expenses," confided Jack.

Thomas looked at Jack and Penny, then down at his glass and drank his wine. "This is too incredible," he said and looked at them. They watched him and waited. He looked into their eyes and understood their concern for Rebecca. This was about Rebecca, not him, he looked up at them, "How can I help?" he asked.

Penny jumped from her seat and kissed Thomas several times. "I prayed you would!"

Thomas looked at Penny. "So what do I need to do?"

"Let's have some dinner and we can talk about it after we have full stomachs," suggested Penny, she smiled happily at Thomas and danced into the kitchen.

"That lamb was delicious Jack," complimented Thomas as he sat down on the sofa in the living room.

"I'm definitely a meat and potatoes kind of guy and I especially enjoy my lamb," replied Jack.

Penny came in from the kitchen. "That's all the cutlery and plates in the dishwasher. Some coffee perhaps?"

"All the champagne's gone," commented Jack tipping the Bollinger upside down.

"Can I have a Brandy?" asked Thomas.

"Chivas Regal and a cigar," stated Jack.

"If you're smoking cigars out on the balcony," demanded Penny from the kitchen.

"Follow me Thomas. You coming?" asked Jack of Penny.

"Just let me make a coffee and get my cardigan. I'll be out in a minute." She left the room.

Jack poured the drinks at the bar and picked out two cigars from the box, "follow me Thomas." He pulled aside the curtain in the family room and opened the sliding doors. He switched on a light and they walked onto a large and long balcony. "Quite a view from up here! Have a seat." He put the drinks down and gave Thomas a cigar and a box of matches. They drank and smoked in silence.

"Quite night," said Thomas.

"Sure is."

"Jack, when I saw you a couple of weeks ago and you left in a taxi, I thought you were on the lower end of the millionaires club. I don't think it was the taxi alone that brought me to that conclusion, I think after talking to you that night contributed to most of it. The taxi image just confirmed it."

"What do you think now that you know I'm a multi-millionaire?" asked Jack.

"You didn't spend enough money on golf lessons," said Thomas laughing.

Jack laughed.

"I actually gave you a nickname," said Thomas.

"Really! What?"

"Taxi Jack!" replied Thomas and laughed

"Taxi Jack, I like it. You were closer than you thought!" commented Jack. "Why are you telling me?"

"I don't know. Guess to show that I also make mistakes in judging character," replied Thomas.

"You judged me right that night. You knew I was a whiskey drinking, meat and potatoes man," stated Jack as he sucked on his cigar. "Let me ask you a question. What do you think of Bill Carter?" he asked.

"I only met him the one time, besides he's your friend," mentioned Thomas feeling uncomfortable.

"He's a business associate and not a friend," said Jack. "Never mix the two up. So, tell me what you think of him? Be honest."

"Well, there's something about him that I just can't put my finger on. It's difficult to describe," replied Thomas. "He has that look in his eyes."

"Always remember that when you're around him," said Jack. "Be on your guard."

"What are you talking about?" asked Penny as she came outside.

"Bill Carter," answered Jack.

She ignored the topic. "Rachel's very attractive," she said as she sat. "You know I think she's becoming more her old self. For a while there she was becoming a little stuck up," commented Penny. "I know her mother was worried."

"I think she likes Thomas here," teased Jack. "He wasn't too far out of her eyesight at the party."

Thomas blushed. "We're friends," he confirmed. He looked at the both. "Can I ask you two a question?"

"Of course, dear," said Penny.

"How come you want to keep your relationship quiet?" asked Thomas. "I know it's none of my business and you don't have to answer."

Penny looked over at Jack and spoke. "When we first got together Jack was in the news quite a bit. He was a well-known businessman. Anything he did or said ended up in the papers. You could imagine the media if he had been having a relationship. It would be in all the papers and I would be hounded all the time by the press. I didn't want any part of that. I wouldn't have been able to handle it. I asked Jack to keep it private and he promised me he would, and he has."

"I was used to the publicity and I know what reporters can be like, snooping through garbage and looking for love letters. Penny here wasn't comfortable. At the time I believe we made the right decision. But since

I've been semi-retired and Ernie took over, people aren't as interested. We've been talking about making it public. It's really up to Penny," said Jack looking over at Penny and holding her hand.

"Maybe one day," suggested Penny.

Thomas smiled. "Okay, what do you want me to do?" he asked.

Jack leaned over and answered. "Tomorrow we need you to go to Manhattan and talk to Henri and convince him he needs to come here and tell Rebecca the truth."

"That seems easy enough. I'll just go and tell him what you told me. If he doesn't tell her you will," said Thomas.

"Unfortunately Thomas it won't be that easy. As I said we made a promise to Henri. When you talk to him you will have to act as if we never had this conversation and that you don't know the details of what happened. All you need to do is get him up here and the two of them talking, and hope that he tells her himself," replied Penny.

Thomas was taken aback. "How am I going to do that?"

"You have until tomorrow night to think of something," said Jack with a sly smile, "and Thomas, trust me, you will. Just keep in mind what's important, getting him here with her."

Thomas stood up and looked off the balcony and wondered how he was going to do what they asked. He thought about Rebecca and put his hands through his hair. He turned around. "I'll get him up here for Sunday," said Thomas confidently.

"Next Sunday. How will you do that?" asked Penny.

"How indeed?" Jack asked.

"Not next Sunday, this Sunday, and I don't know how," said Thomas. "Jack, you mentioned Manhattan?"

"Tomorrow morning my private jet will fly you to La Guardia. A limousine has been booked for your entire stay and I have made reservations for you at the most luxurious hotel in New York. Henri is performing in Otello at the Opera House; you have a box reserved. You will have to arrange the meeting with Henri yourself," informed Jack. "Before you board the jet I'll give you an envelope that will contain all the information you need."

"You have all this arranged?" asked Thomas.

"We were counting on you," replied Penny.

"If I need to get him on a plane on Sunday?" asked Thomas.

"Call me Saturday night and I'll have the tickets waiting for him at the airport. I'll have one of my limousines pick him up, you tell him its one of yours and I'll make sure the chauffeur asks about you," said Jack.

"Can my sister come with me?" asked Thomas.

"Of course," answered Jack, "I'll arrange for her to be picked up and dropped at the airport tomorrow morning."

"Thanks."

"I will pay for all expenses," stated Jack.

"Okay," agreed Thomas. He thought and looked back and forth at them both. "If there comes a time when I need to tell her about this, I have both of your permissions to tell her everything?"

Penny stood up and walked over to Thomas. "If that time comes, and I hope it does, you have our permission."

"I need to make some phone calls. What time are you leaving in the morning and how long you planning on staying?" asked Jack.

Thomas told him and Jack went inside.

"Thomas," Penny said as she stood close to him. "The week after the fundraiser, at the rehearsals Rebecca danced like I've never seen her dance before, so full of positive energy, love and compassion. The rest of the group stood back and watched in awe. I thought I had seen her dance her best until that week." She held his hand and was about to say something else.

"Jet will be ready for you tomorrow morning. Maybe you should give Kate a call?" asked Jack.

CHAPTER 8

Manhattan

"MY PRIVATE CELL NUMBER IS STORED UNDER Taxi Jack. Call me when you have some news," said Jack as he handed Thomas the cell phone and an envelope.

"Anytime," added Penny.

"Will do," replied Thomas. Thomas smiled as he thought about Jack using his nickname. Thomas boarded the private jet and turned and waved goodbye. He sat down next to Kate.

"Thomas what's going on?" she asked.

"Once we've taken off I'll explain everything," replied Thomas. The plane taxied and took off. Once they reached cruising altitude the flight attendant offered them coffee which they accepted. Thomas turned to Kate and explained everything.

"…And as for you Kate. You're along for the ride. Take some time away from your studying, do some shopping."

"Thomas, are you okay with this?" asked Kate.

"I'm fine."

The flight attendant brought their coffees. Thomas opened the envelope and took out a sheet. As he read over the information he summarized out loud, "Two rooms, two nights and we can check in as soon as we arrive. The tickets for Otello would be waiting for us at the box office and we should get there an hour prior to the start of the show. Jack has suggested several restaurants to dine at with instructions and how to get preferential seating and service. He has also listed two men's stores and five women's each with a persons name next to them." Thomas looked over at Kate. "Jack has traveled to New York before."

Kate nodded.

Thomas looked in the envelope and took out the platinum credit card and one thousand dollars cash. Thomas read out loud the written notation, "Thomas please use the credit card and cash for any expenses occurred.

Make sure you and Kate make time to go shopping and buy some nice clothes, especially for this evening. I have noted the stores to visit and they will take care of you. When ordering at the restaurants, make sure it's the best. Enjoy and thank you, Jack and Penny."

"How much money is there?" Kate asked.

"There are a thousand dollars and a platinum card."

"How expensive is New York?"

"I don't know," replied Thomas as he put the card and cash in his wallet.

Kate smiled. "I'm looking forward to it especially Fifth Avenue."

They landed an hour and a half later and walked into the airport. There was a man in a black suit holding a sign 'Mr. Carlyle'. Thomas approached him and forty-five minutes later they arrived at the hotel. It was a magnificent sight.

Within minutes they were following the bellboy to their tower rooms. The bellboy dropped Kate off first, then Thomas. Thomas thanked him and gave him a twenty.

The suite had a living area with a sofa, chair, big screen television, a stocked wet bar with a refrigerator and a gas fireplace. There was a bedroom with a king size bed, with a robe laid on it, and a walk in closet. The bathroom was marble and it had an oval Jacuzzi tub for two. Around the suite were fresh cut flowers. He decided to go to Kate and see if she was settling in.

"Thomas this is gorgeous," said Kate after she opened the door and let him in, "look at this," she said and took him on a tour. She sat down on the sofa and asked, "So what are we going to do?"

Thomas looked at his watch and said, "It's seven thirty. Why don't we have some breakfast, go shopping on Fifth Avenue and have some lunch?"

"Can I order breakfast to my room?" asked Kate. "I want to have it over here on the table by the window." Kate pointed to the table.

"Fine, call me in an hour," said Thomas, "I'm going to have a sleep."

"How can you sleep!" exclaimed Kate. "I'm going to have a walk around the hotel, find out the best places to shop, then come back and have a nice hot shower and then…."

THEY WALKED OUT OF THE GRAND LOBBY and onto the street.

"Okay, it's ten thirty," said Thomas looking at his watch. "Let's do some shopping." He started walking, "you have to be back at the hotel for three."

"Thomas you're going the wrong way!" said Kate walking the opposite direction. She laughed and waited for him to catch up. "Why three?"

"I booked you an appointment at 'The Spa'. Facial, manicure, pedicure, hair and make up. In between which you get to lie in salt baths," replied Thomas.

"Spa!" said Kate.

"The spa suggested if you take down your outfit for this evening they will help you get dressed."

"Really?" asked Kate surprised.

They started walking and Thomas continued. "Today, we should just concentrate on buying clothes for tonight. We can take tomorrow and Monday to ourselves. If that's okay?" asked Thomas.

"Of course it's okay," replied Kate happily. "Let's go!" She put her arm around Thomas and kissed him on the cheek.

"We have a reservation for dinner at five forty five and need to be at the box office for seven. So I'll meet you in the lobby at five thirty."

They walked along Fifth Avenue and visited the stores that Jack had put on his list. They asked for the people whose names he had provided and were treated with the greatest of attention. They only stopped forty-five minutes for lunch. Thomas walked Kate to the spa and then went to his room. He hung up his black Hugo Boss suit and shirt and put his Dr. Marten Oxfords underneath.

He sat down on the bed. He still needed to think of a way to get Henri to meet with Rebecca. He wasn't any further along when he met Kate in the lobby. "I must say you look absolutely breathtaking."

Kate twirled for him in her Marchesa gown. "Why thank you Thomas," she replied.

"DID YOU ENJOY DINNER?"

"It was delicious. The restaurant was first class."

"It was," replied Thomas.

"I was speaking to a lady in the bathroom and she said that there was a three month waiting list. I couldn't resist and told her we just showed up and got a table within minutes." Kate laughed. "You should have seen her face. Then she turns to me and asks straight out who I was to be getting that kind of treatment."

"What did you say?" asked Thomas.

"I told her that it was none of her concern and to mind her own business," replied Kate.

"Did you?" said Thomas looking a little surprised.

"I was going to," said Kate. "Instead I told her…" She stopped.

Thomas looked at her and he could tell by the tone of her voice that she had said something at his expense. "Okay Kate let me have it. What did you say?"

"I told her that the man sitting with me at the table was one of the most influential men in New York City and that if she didn't know who he was then she obviously wasn't in the right circle of friends."

"You didn't"

"I did"

"And?" asked Thomas.

"That you are the richest man in the country."

"And?"

"Next please," said the ticket lady.

"Saved," said Kate looking at Thomas. "I was only having a little fun besides she was a snob."

The lady handed them the tickets and told them they had an eight-seated box to themselves and access to the exclusive members lounge. They thanked her walked off to the side.

"Kate, I don't know if I feel comfortable with you being a lying lawyer?" asked Thomas dryly.

She made a face at Thomas and said, "Very funny."

"I still don't know how I'm going to meet Henri," said Thomas. "Any crooked suggestions magistrate?" said Thomas smiling.

"This is going to be an ongoing joke all night, isn't it?"

"You know it!" replied Thomas. "Let's go to the stage door and see if I can talk to the doorman, maybe he can pass a note through."

The stage door was packed with fans waiting to catch a glimpse of the stars. They managed to move up to the door and then got the attention of the doorman who told them he wasn't a mail service. Thomas and Kate were moved to one side by a muscular security guard who was escorting out five teenagers.

"If I catch you trying to sneak in here again I'll call the police," said the guard in a deep voice. "Now go home."

"We just wanted to see the show, "answered back one of the girls.

Thomas watched the sad faces walking away.

"Poor things," said Kate.

"We have extra seats," said Thomas.

Kate looked at Thomas and gave him a smile and said "Go on!"

"Hey kids he shouted." The teenagers turned around as Thomas and Kate walked up to them. "How would you like to see the show?"

"Really mister?" replied the same girl.

Fifteen minutes later Thomas walked into the Opera House with his newly adopted children. They were speechless as they walked into the main foyer. Thomas went to the bar and ordered two glasses of champagne and five cokes.

"So what are your names?" asked Kate.

The girl spoke. "My name is Katrina, this is my brother Ethan, this is my best friend Shawna, and this is my friend Bobby, and my brother's friend Michigan."

"How old are you?"

"We're all eighteen, except Ethan and Michigan, they're seventeen."

"You like opera?" asked Kate.

"Yes, we sing in the First Baptist Church of Harlem Choir."

"Choir?" asked Thomas.

"Yes sir. We've never seen an opera before," explained Katrina. "Plus tonight is a special night!"

"Why is that?" asked Kate.

"There is a black man named Rufus Jones singing the lead, Otello, it's his opening night."

"What are your names?" Shawna asked.

"My name is Kate and this is my brother Thomas."

"Thank you for letting us sit with you," said Michigan.

"Shall we go see what are seats are like?" asked Thomas.

"Yes sir," they replied.

"They were friendly and polite," thought Thomas as they walked to the box seats. He picked up seven opera glasses and programs. The five sat down leafing through their programs and looking out through their glasses. The box was to the right of the stage and the view was excellent.

Kate smiled and squeezed his arm, "You're a kind person Thomas."

He smiled back. "Any suggestions on how I'm going to meet Henri?"

"I've been thinking about that and I believe crooked people would say you're doing it the hard way?" suggested Kate.

"What do you mean?" asked Thomas.

"Why wait outside by the stage door with the common folk? Use your influence!" said Kate. She whispered. "Sometimes a little grease goes along way."

They watched the opera and were mesmerized. Rufus and Henri were unbelievable.

During the intermission they went and bought some more drinks. Thomas excused himself and spoke to the usher.

"How did it go?" Kate asked.

"He's going to get the note to Henri," said Thomas.

"How will you know if he got it or not?" asked Kate.

"In the note I asked Henri to give me a sign," smiled Thomas. "You'll have to wait and see."

As the curtain fell to end the show the kids stood up and applauded the loudest. They joined in the calls of 'Bravo!' There were three curtain calls and on the last one Rufus Jones came from behind the curtain and spoke to the audience.

"I would like to thank you all for coming to my debut tonight." He looked down at the front row, "My mother and my brother thank you for being part of this special night with me," he looked up at the audience, "and you, the audience, thank you. As many of you know I was raised right her in Harlem and tonight I am very honored to have five special guests here, tonight from the First Baptist Church of Harlem Choir, they are Katrina, Shawna, Ethan, Bobby and Michigan, can you shine the light up there," said Rufus pointing to their box. The teenagers were shocked.

"Stand up and wave," said Thomas.

The teenagers stood and waved and the two girls blew Rufus a kiss.

The light returned to Rufus who said, "Thank you," bowed and blew a kiss back. He looked at the crowd thanked them, bowed and went behind the curtain. The crowd applauded and the house lights came on.

Kate turned to Thomas, "Subtle sign."

"I thought you would appreciate it," said Thomas. On the way out he gave the usher the other half of the five hundred.

Outside Kate looked at the teenagers. "Are you going to be okay getting home?

"We'll be okay," said Katrina. "Do you live in New York Kate?"

"No. Why?"

"Never mind," said Katrina.

"She was hoping you would take us again," said Shawna.

"You know what Katrina why don't you give me your address and I'll see what I can do," said Thomas.

"Okay," replied Katrina. "Can we have yours?" she asked, "so we can send you a thank you note."

The rest of the teenagers agreed.

They swapped addresses and said goodbye.

"Where to now?" asked Kate.

"The hotel lobby bar," said Thomas. "I have an hour to come up with something."

They walked into the hotel and went up to the front desk and asked for their keys.

The receptionist noticed the program in Kate's hand, "Did you enjoy the opera?" he asked.

"Immensely," replied Kate

"Our manager is the biggest opera fan," he said.

"Really, is he here?" asked Thomas.

"Yes he is."

"May I speak to him?"

Thomas spoke to the manager in private. They returned and he walked them to the lounge and sat them in a partially secluded table. He left and spoke with the waitress and returned shortly after. "I will make sure your guest is brought over to your table upon his arrival. When you leave for your room, the waitress will inform me and the food and drink you have ordered will be delivered to your room shortly after. Is there anything else I can do for you Mr. Carlyle?" asked the manager.

"No. Thank you, you have been most helpful," replied Thomas.

The manager left and the waitress brought a bottle of Dom Perignon in a bucket of ice and three glasses to the table. She placed them down and departed.

"What did you say to him?" asked Kate.

"I promised him that Henri La Croix would sing tonight and he would get his picture taken with him," replied Thomas.

"How are you going to pull that off?" asked Kate.

"I'm not sure," said Thomas.

"But why get the manager involved?" asked Kate.

"He is the senior manager and working tomorrow and Monday afternoon and I may need a favor from him or one of the other managers. Its called making friends," said Thomas. "Or as Jack would say business is business."

"If you pull this one off I'll…" Kate was cut off.

"You'll what?" interrupted Thomas.

"I'll sing after he does," said Kate confidently.

"You're on! But you sing to him, right after he does," confirmed Thomas.

"Agreed!" said Kate shaking his hand. "I've finally got you Thomas. When you lose we shop all Sunday and Monday! In women stores only! You call me Ms. Carlyle and you carry my bags!"

"But you sing one of your favorite songs, a Carrie Underwood song!"

"You can even pick the song!" replied Kate full of confidence.

"Agreed," said Thomas letting go of her hand.

The waitress appeared and asked if they would like the champagne opened and poured. As they drank Kate smiled behind her glass at Thomas.

"Enjoy it while you can," he said, "because I will be later on."

The manager brought Henri La Croix to the table. "I wanted you to know what an honor it is to have you here tonight," said the manager, "if there is anything you need please don't hesitate to ask for me."

"Thank you," replied Henri.

The manager left and Henri sat down and asked, "Thomas Carlyle?"

"Yes and this is my sister Kate," replied Thomas. Thomas was now convinced he had met Henri before. "Would you like some champagne?"

"Please," said Henri.

Thomas poured a glass and filled theirs up.

"You sang beautifully tonight," complimented Kate.

"Thank you," replied Henri nervously. "You're friends of Rebecca?"

"Yes," replied Thomas.

"Is she okay?" inquired Henri. "By your note you said she was but I am worried that there is something the matter."

"Yes and no," replied Thomas.

"Pardon me for my directness but please tell me," begged Henri.

Thomas told Henri what Jack and Penny had told him.

"How could they do this? Are you friends of Jack and Penny?" asked Henri a little upset.

"Yes. I am," said Thomas.

"They shouldn't have told you. I had asked them for their word," said Henri, a little more upset.

"They didn't tell me," said Thomas softly.

"If not, then who?" asked Henri. "They are the only ones that know," he said confidently.

"Unfortunately they are not the only ones who knew," replied Thomas. "Henri, I met you nine years ago. Do you remember me?"

"No."

"I didn't remember you either until I saw the picture of you and Rebecca taken in the summer at the harbor front, you had a beard," stated Thomas.

"And?" asked Henri.

"Do you remember Maggie Carlyle? She danced at the First National Ballet?" asked Thomas.

"Of course. She was a friend of Penny's, and mine," he replied. "I heard she had passed away in the summer."

"Yes she did. We are her grandchildren," said Thomas.

"Oh, I am so sorry. I didn't realize, please forgive me, my deepest sympathies," apologized Henri. "She was a fine lady."

"Thank you," said Thomas. He hesitated a moment and spoke. "One night you came to my grandmother's house with Penny and spoke to them both and revealed to them what I have just revealed to you. I was in the house that day. Do you remember my grandmother introducing me when you walked in? I was doing my homework in the kitchen," said Thomas trying to refresh his memory.

"Yes I do, vaguely," concurred Henri.

Thomas turned to Kate. "The upstairs was being decorated and I had to do homework downstairs. You tried to talk low but I heard you all talking. It was only by chance that I saw the photograph of the two of you that I made the connection," explained Thomas. "Jack and Penny only confirmed my suspicions after I had approached them."

Henri thought for a while. "You are right I do remember that night and meeting you. I can't remember the conversation. But how did you know about my financial arrangement with Jack."

Thomas sipped his champagne and thought "good question." He put his drink down and spoke. "When I confronted Jack and Penny with what I knew they just filled in the blanks. It's important that you must realize that I knew most of it anyway; Jack and Penny had no option but to tell me everything. If they didn't, I told them I would tell Rebecca. So, they agreed."

"So why are you telling me this?" asked Henri.

Thomas relayed what Jack and Penny had told him about Rebecca.

Henri looked at Thomas. "I understand what you are saying and you are right to be concerned, many people in the business put themselves into their work, so much so that their life is work, there needs to be a balance but when there is no balance." He stopped and looked at Thomas. "What should I do?"

"Can I suggest we finish these drinks then go to my room and talk so we can have some privacy," suggested Thomas as he looked around. "I believe you are drawing attention."

"Yes," said Henri looking around. "I believe you are right. Hopefully they haven't taken our serious conversation in the wrong way."

"I've been looking around and most of them are just realizing who you are," said Kate. "I wouldn't be concerned but we should go to the room."

"Henri, I have a suggestion, my sister and the people here would be honored to hear you sing and I believe if you do so you would remove any doubts."

"That is an excellent suggestion," replied Henri.

"Let me check with the manager and see if it's okay," said Thomas and stood up and went to the front desk.

Thomas returned. "He said he would be overjoyed if you would sing here in the lounge. He asked if he could have his picture taken with you first and several taken of you while you perform?" asked Thomas.

"Of course," replied Henri.

Thomas motioned the manager over.

"This is quite an honor Mr. La Croix," said the manager as he stood next to him, the bellboy took his picture. "Thank you," he said and shook his hand. He turned to the people in the lounge, "attention, attention please. As many of you have already noticed we are graced with one of the greatest opera baritones of our time, Mr. Henri La Croix, and he has graciously accepted an offer to sing one song for us tonight."

Henri spoke. "This song is dedicated to this beautiful and delicate creature sitting next to me, Kate." He sang Rossini's 'Largo al Factotum'. The bellboy took pictures and the manager cried. Everyone clapped and shouted 'Bravo!' after he had finished. He said, "thank you," and bowed.

Thomas waited for the clapping to subside and stood. "Ladies and gentlemen it is an old tradition in our family that when a man sings to a lady, she in return must sing to him, please let me introduce my sister, Kate Carlyle, and she will be singing Carrie Underwood's, 'Last Name'.

Kate was shocked. She didn't think he would follow through with it, and not only that, she had expected him to a least pick one of her love songs, not one about a girl getting drunk in Vegas and getting married to a man she'd just met. She gave Thomas a horrified look as he helped her stand. He sat down and smiled at Kate. Everyone looked at her. They waited. There was no way out. She looked at Henri and said, "For Henri." She sang Carrie Underwood's 'Last Name' and the bellboy took pictures. Once she finished everyone clapped and Henri stood and gave her a kiss on the hand. Thomas contained his laughter and stood and shouted "Brava!"

They finished their drinks and went to Thomas's suite, the food arrived shortly afterwards, "compliments of the manager," said the hotel waiter. He set up the food and drinks on the table and took the tip from Thomas on the way out.

"Can you leave tomorrow and meet Rebecca and tell her everything that has happened?" asked Thomas.

"I can. But why must I tell her?" asked Henri.

"To me it's quite simple. If you go and start a relationship with her and she finds this information later on you will lose her again, but this time for ever," said Thomas.

"I see what you mean. What happens if I tell her and she sends me away?" he asked.

"You won't be any better off than you are today with the exception that the burden you have been carrying around all these years will be lifted."

"You're right! In my heart I know you're right, but in my mind I'm worried. Can I ask you a question?"

"Yes."

"What happens if I don't tell her?"

"When I arrive back Monday night I will tell her." He looked at Henri, "I can't keep this secret from a dear friend of mine and still call myself her friend. I have no promise to keep with you or Jack or Penny, but I do with her. You may not like the position I have taken with you but to be honest I don't care."

Henri looked down, then over at Kate and back at Thomas. "You are a decent man for giving me this opportunity, you could have told her, yet you have come here and faced me and gave me an opportunity. I appreciate you being so candid," said Henri. He looked at Thomas and rubbed his chin. "Tell me are you in love with my daughter?"

Kate looked at Thomas.

"She is in love with another."

"That was not my question."

"I am her friend."

Henri looked at Thomas for a while. "Then you are a good friend and she is lucky to have you, I thank you."

"You must make me one promise Henri."

"Anything Thomas."

"You must not let her know that I was here or that Jack and Penny know of this."

"I believe that is best for all involved and it is a promise I shall keep."

"Thank you. Let's eat and plan tomorrow," said Thomas.

They talked for another forty-five minutes. At one thirty Thomas walked Henri down to the lobby and outside to his limousine. They said goodbye and Henri hugged Thomas and thanked him again. Thomas watched him leave and walked back to his suite and sat next to Kate.

"Thomas why are you doing this?" asked Kate.

"What do you mean?"

"You know what I mean," said Kate softly.

"She has a chance of being with her father."

"Is that the only reason?"

"It is," replied Thomas.

Kate decided to change the topic. "You would make a good lawyer too."

"What do you mean?"

"I don't believe that you overheard Henri's conversation," suggested Kate.

"I won't answer that question on the grounds I may incriminate myself," replied Thomas, "besides he wants to tell her."

"How do you know that?"

"No one was putting a gun to his head. He could have told me to tell her and left. He didn't. He must have known that if I told her I would be responsible for the outcome."

"I hope everything works out for them," said Kate.

"It can't be any worse than it is today," replied Thomas.

"I guess not." Kate looked at him. "Thomas, do you love her?"

Thomas smiled and changed the topic. "By the way nice singing," he said and laughed.

She let it go and didn't press him on the subject. "I'll get you back for that one day."

"You haven't yet! Besides you sang it great. I would never have embarrassed you if I didn't think you could carry a note. Besides I really like that song," said Thomas. He broke out into laughter. "Not only did you have to sing after him, but to him, I'm impressed." He laughed louder.

"Go ahead and laugh. I'm still going to pay you back one day."

"Oh, I'm shaking!" replied Thomas and laughed even louder.

She laughed with him. "Okay, okay. So what are our plans for tomorrow?"

"There's a church around the corner. Let's go at nine, come back and have breakfast in the room. I want to give you your surprise before we go shopping."

"Surprise! What surprise?" asked Kate.

"Good night Kate." He stood up. "I'll walk you to your door."

Kate opened the door to her suite and before she closed it turned to Thomas. "Any hints?"

"Goodnight Kate." He closed her door.

When he got back in the room Thomas called Jack and told him what had happened. He hung up the phone and got ready for bed. He wasn't happy about lying to Henri or threatening him with telling Rebecca but he believed it was for the best. He thought about Rebecca and wondered what she was doing at this very moment. He decided she was probably sleeping and thought about her in her pajamas. Then he remembered her falling asleep on his chest and picking her up and carrying her into her room. He remembered how beautiful she looked and how soft her skin was to touch. He remembered how much it hurt seeing her with Francis. He wondered why he was doing this, but he already knew the answer. He had known the answer for quite some time. He eventually fell asleep.

The next morning Thomas ate breakfast in Kate's room. She had the curtains and the windows open and a gentle breeze blew in.

"There's a patio through there," said Kate as she pointed towards the doors.

Thomas looked through the sheers and could see the silhouette of the railings.

"It's a lovely view," said Kate. She glanced at the envelope resting on the bed. "Thomas I can't keep my eyes off that envelope you brought with you. What's in it?"

Thomas stood and picked up the envelope. "Come and sit with me on the sofa?" asked Thomas.

Kate followed him and sat down.

"On Friday, after I had played golf with Jack, Barry Levinson dropped by our table," said Thomas.

"The man who you got the laptop for?" asked Kate.

"The same, he gave me this envelope," continued Thomas, "he said he was going to courier it to you on Monday but knew he was going to see me and asked if I would hand it to you."

"What is it?" asked Kate.

"Do you remember what law firm he works for?" asked Thomas.

"Levinson and Associates!" stated Kate.

"Are they well known?" Thomas asked.

"Thomas, they are one of the best law firms in the country," explained Kate, "and one of the most respected. They have some of the biggest accounts. I was going to drop off my resume there this week."

Thomas gave Kate the envelope and she opened it. "Thomas it's an offer for a position as a paralegal," said Kate excitedly, she reviewed the document and read out loud the key points, "they're offering me a part time placement, whatever time I have available during the week, some night and weekends, minimal fifteen hours. Once I pass the Bar exam they will hire me on as a lawyer, salary to be discussed, but no less than one hundred and twenty five thousand. Depending on my placement in the Bar exam there will be a signing bonus. The minimal is twenty thousand and up to fifty. Am I dreaming?" she asked.

Thomas pinched her arm.

"Ouch. Why you? That's two I owe you," she stopped and looked up at him. "You had something to do with this?"

"I would like to say I did, but I didn't. I went down to drop off his laptop and thought while I was there I would drop off your resume to Human Resources, actually I gave it to Barry's administrative assistant and she said she would pass it on for me."

"Really?"

"Barry was very specific on why they chose you; he said it was because you were the best of the three applicants. Apparently a group of lawyers, including Barry, reviewed the three potential candidates, they thought you were the best and chose you. They were very thorough on their research; they even spoke with your professors. He said it was in there," said Thomas pointing.

Kate flipped through the paperwork and read. "There's a letter here explaining why he chose me and basically says what you just told me," confirmed Kate. She put her hand on her head and broke down and cried. She leaned over and put her head on Thomas. "This is one of the happiest days of my life."

Thomas held her. "I think it may get a little better."

Kate wiped her eyes and looked at Thomas. "How?"

"Remember when I gave Jack the contact name and number for Barry?" asked Thomas.

Kate nodded.

"Barry ended up buying a hundred units and gave me a one percent finder's fee. At first I said I wouldn't accept," said Thomas.

"Thomas those companies have reputations," said Kate looking at Thomas.

"That's what they said. So they gave me six thousand dollars. I'm keeping one thousand aside but the other five is for you to buy some clothes for your new job."

"Really!" said Kate excitedly.

Thomas was happy for her.

"But Thomas you shouldn't spend all this money on me there must be things you would like to buy."

"Kate the money is yours and I want my sister looking her best. Please take it?" He squeezed her hand. "Besides I want to see the smile on your face when you're going from store to store trying on clothes. Nothing would make me happier."

She smiled again and started to cry. "Thank you Thomas." She kissed him on the cheek.

"Barry asked that you call him tomorrow to let him know your decision. If you accept he will arrange the interviews this week, it's just a formality," said Thomas.

The cell phone rang. Thomas picked it up. "Hello," and waited for a reply. "Hi Jack," Thomas listened for five minutes. "So he arrived and was dropped off at the cathedral and met her. Thanks Jack, let me know when you hear anything else. By the way, is there any way Kate can get in touch with Barry," Thomas listened, "he is. I'll put her on." Thomas covered the mouthpiece as he passed the phone to Kate, "Barry is with Jack."

Kate gained her composure. "Good morning, Mr. Levinson," she said and listened. "Yes I did it's a very generous offer," she replied and listened. "I accept," answered Kate. Kate listened and reconfirmed, "Tuesday at four. That's fine." She listened again. "Oh, okay. Thank you. I'll put Thomas back on." She passed the phone to Thomas.

"Barry!" said Thomas, "Jack, it's you." Thomas listened and said, "Goodbye." He looked at Kate.

"Five thousand dollars to spend on clothes for accepting the offer," said Kate.

"Jack said to put it on his card and Barry will reimburse him. Looks like you have ten thousand dollars to spend on clothes," said Thomas smiling.

Kate spoke softly, "Thomas I owe all this to you."

"I didn't get you the job," said Thomas.

"Not the job. The opportunity," smiled Kate.

Thomas smiled back. "You deserve it Kate you've worked hard."

"I'm the luckiest sister! Never leave me alone in this world?" asked Kate.

"Never," replied Thomas. He held her for a few moments and pulled away and looked into her eyes. "Do you ever feel guilty?"

Kate hesitated and replied, "A little, you sacrificed so much for me. I know you don't like your job and you wanted to go to university. You've missed out on so many things for me."

"Kate, I never want you to feel guilty. I haven't missed out on anything. I've only postponed them. Right?" said Thomas.

"You would give me the chance to take care of you and pay for you to go to university?" asked Kate.

"If the offer still stands?" asked Thomas.

"Always," replied Kate.

"And if down the road I decide on another path and refuse your offer you will be comfortable knowing that you gave me the opportunity?" asked Thomas.

"Certainly!" said Kate, "all I want is for you to have no regrets and be happy."

"No more guilt then," said Thomas.

"None," replied Kate.

Thomas yawned. "Well I think I'll have a lie down."

"Nice try. Fifth Avenue waits!" exclaimed Kate.

Thomas laughed. "Look out Fifth here comes Kate."

"Very funny," replied Kate and stood up. "Seriously, let's go."

They left the room and in the lobby Thomas stopped by to talk with the manager.

Six hours later they returned to the hotel. Kate's suite had bags and boxes everywhere, "...and I still have three thousand left to spend tomorrow," said Kate.

"I'm sure you won't have a problem," replied Thomas.

"You will have to thank Jack for giving us the names of the people in the store, they were definitely an asset," said Kate. "What time do we have to leave tomorrow?"

"Whenever you want, the jet is on standby, all I have to do is give them a call."

"Can we leave when its night so we can see the lights of New York?" asked Kate.

"That's a great idea. In fact the later we leave tomorrow the better. We can miss the rush hour traffic."

"What are we doing tonight?" asked Kate.

"I thought we could go out and get something to eat. One of the restaurants on Jack's list is supposed to be fantastic. We couldn't go there last night because of the show."

"I'll leave it all in you capable hands."

"When we come back you can give me a fashion show and call it an early night," said Thomas. "How does that sound?"

"Perfect," replied Kate.

THE RING OF THE CELL PHONE WOKE Thomas, "Hello," he said. "Hi Jack," he replied. Thomas listened and suddenly sat up in bed. "Thanks Jack, talk to you when I get back". He looked at the clock it was eight. He had been sound asleep for ten hours. "I must have been tired," he said. He called in sick to work. He walked over to the sofa and sat down still half asleep and put on some music. There was a knock at the door. "Who is it?"

"Henri."

Thomas opened the door, "Good morning."

"Did I wake you?" he asked apologetically.

"No, I was already up."

"Here's a coffee and a muffin, I stopped off at the deli and picked one up for us. Is your sister still here?" Henri asked as he looked around.

"Next door," replied Thomas, "she won't be awake for another hour she's resting up for her second day of shopping."

"I'm glad you're still here, I wanted to come by and thank you from the bottom of my heart. I am reunited with my daughter and I thank you." He kissed Thomas on both cheeks. "A debt I am afraid which has no adequate payment," said Henri and kissed Thomas once more on each cheek and gave him a squeeze.

"Would you like to tell me what happened?" asked Thomas.

"That's why I'm here," smiled Henri, "I am so very happy. Your limousine picked me up, by the way your driver asked how you were enjoying New York, and drove me to the cathedral. I went in late and spotted her close to the back so I sat behind her and waited till they asked you to shake hands as an offering of peace. She turned and when she realized who it was, she gave me the biggest smile and hug. I moved around and sat next to her. After church we walked to her place and we talked on the way. I told her about New York and she told me about her ballet. After we got to her place she made us something to eat. Shortly after, I told her everything. She got upset and ran to her room crying. I thought that was it. I went to her room and asked if she wanted me to go. She said no and I closed her door and waited in the living room. She came out of her room and ran to me crying. She said, "Daddy I've missed you, don't go", and held me. I held her for what seemed like hours. I also cried. We agreed that the past was the past and to start off slow. We had dinner and she drove me to the airport. Before I left she said she was coming to New York this Friday for a week. I am so very happy!"

"I'm so glad it all worked out," said Thomas. He was relieved.

Henri cried. "I have my little Becky back."

Thomas put his arm around Henri and comforted him.

Henri stopped. "No more tears, there has been too many tears." He looked at Thomas and spoke with conviction. "I owe you my life and I ask myself what can I give a man who has everything?" He said as he looked at Thomas and around the room.

"You owe me nothing," replied Thomas. "I'm happy for you both."

"You are humble as well," said Henri. "I hope Rebecca realizes what a good friend she has in you. This reminds me. She asked why I decided to come and see her, now, after all these years. I told her it was time she knew the truth and that I couldn't carry the burden and the guilt anymore and that I missed her and wanted to be a part of her life."

"Thank you," said Thomas.

"Is there anything I can do for you that can match the magnitude of your kindness and thoughtfulness?" asked Henri. "Anything?"

"Actually there are a couple of things. Let me get dressed and I can explain to you on the way down to the lobby." Thomas stood and went into the bedroom.

Thomas picked up three envelopes from the front desk and sat down with Henri on one of the sofas. "If you are uncomfortable with this please let me know?"

"I will," replied Henri.

"I would like you to call Ms. Brown at the number in the envelope, she runs the First Baptist Church of Harlem Choir, and arrange to meet with her and the five children listed next Sunday and give them this envelope. If you could spend an hour of your time with them I would be grateful." He gave Henri the envelope.

"I would be honored. Can I ask what is in the envelope?"

"Under Ms. Browns name I have reserved eight sets of tickets, one set per matinee per month. They're all paid for all she has to do is go to the box office and show some identification. I've listed the operas and the dates on the sheet," said Thomas looking at Henri. "If you could let them know that this is from your company and not me," requested Thomas.

"Okay," said Henri. "You are a kind and a curious person Thomas."

Thomas gave the second envelope to Henri. "This contains pictures of you with the manager and pictures of you singing. The manager has put some notes on each of them and asked if you would write the notation on the picture and sign them."

Henri wrote and signed the pictures and put them back inside the envelope.

"That's it," said Thomas. "Consider us even."

"For the time being," replied Henri. "Thank you."

"Nice meeting you and hopefully I will see you soon," suggested Thomas.

"You can count on it," smiled Henri. "I plan on visiting Rebecca regularly."

They both stood and Thomas shook his hand. Henri gave him a hug and whispered, "Thank you from the bottom of my heart."

Thomas went upstairs and called Jack's cell and spoke with Penny. He told her the good news. At nine o'clock they flew over New York City and looked down at the lights. Kate turned to Thomas, "This is the best weekend I've ever had. I wont forget this, ever," and smiled. "Me, Rebecca, Henri, the teenagers, you're something special."

"It's only time and money," replied Thomas.

"Money you no longer have," pointed out Kate.

"I wasn't expecting it in the first place," acknowledged Thomas.

Kate looked out the window. "I thought it was funny seeing the hotel manager instructing the bell boy as he was putting up the signed picture of him and Henri." She said and laughed.

"You want to hear something funnier?" asked Thomas.

She turned to Thomas. "Sure!"

He looked at her. "I signed your picture and name and told him you were a famous actress and you were playing on Broadway next month in a new production."

"You're not serious!"

"The manager said he was sorry he didn't get his picture with you as well. He's hanging your picture right next to Henri's."

"Thomas!" shouted Kate and punched him in the arm. "You're a rotten scoundrel."

Thomas looked at her and laughed.

"That's three I owe you!" said Kate.

Jack's limousine picked them up at the airport and dropped them off at home. Thomas realized that he would be going into work tomorrow and unloading skids of computers. For a long time he despised his job but this was the first time he actually regretted going in. He wished he could quit. He realized it was time to make some changes in his own life.

CHAPTER 9

Frank

"HELLO FRANCIS."

"Thomas?"

"Yes it is."

"I'll buzz you in," replied Francis, "just walk the three flights of stairs there's only one door at the end, that's mine."

The buzzer sounded and Thomas opened the door and started climbing the steps.

He had received a call from Francis on Thursday asking, actually pleading, to meet him for a drink, dinner and a talk. Thomas didn't really want to but when Frank asked what he had done, Thomas realized nothing and agreed to meet him at his place Saturday afternoon.

"Thomas, how are you?" asked Francis as he shook Thomas's hand.

"Good Francis. How are you?"

"Please, call me Frank," he replied. "I'm doing fine, I'm so glad you decided to come. Don't be standing outside come in, come in. Here let me take your coat."

Frank hung up the jacket on a brass hook in the hallway. "Come into the living room. I'm making a Martini would you like one?"

"Okay."

"Make yourself comfortable I'll get the drinks," he left the room.

Thomas sat down and looked around the room. It was very clean and attractively decorated.

Frank returned and noticed Thomas looking around. "It's not much; they call it a one bedroom bachelor apartment. There's this room, the kitchen, a den, a bedroom and a bathroom."

"I like it," replied Thomas. "It's cozy."

"Well it's perfect for me and I love the location. Why don't we go outside on the balcony and I'll show you what I mean."

Thomas followed him out.

Frank put the drinks on the table and looked out onto the road. "I love this time of the day. When the sun is shining and people are walking back and forth."

Thomas stood next to him and looked down at the street and the people.

Frank pointed to his left. "If you look down the street, you can just see the small stores; there's a grocery store, pharmacy and video store. A little further past they have on outdoor farmers market every Saturday that sells fresh vegetables. In the opposite direction," he said pointing to his right, "there are bars and pubs and a couple of dance clubs." He looked at Thomas. "If you like, I can take you for a walk before dinner?"

"I would like that," replied Thomas.

"In the meantime sit down, have a drink, and enjoy the sun," said Frank pointing to the patio chair. He sat after Thomas had. "Do you like retrospective music? You know eighties music?"

"Yeah, I do."

"Mind if I put some on?"

"No, please do."

"This is a mixed CD it has Erasure, Frankie Goes to Hollywood, Depeche Mode, The Cult." He turned on the portable CD player and played the music. "One of the clubs down the road has 'Saturday Retro Nights', they play all this type of music. They ask people to come on the stage and take off the singers and give a prize to the best. There not professional people, just people in the club. If you look too good you get booed off the stage. If you're interested you should stick around. It's a lot of fun." He watched Thomas take a drink. "How's the Martini?"

"Excellent," replied Thomas. "Lots of practice?"

"I worked part time in a lounge bar, one of those trendy places. It even had a lounge lizard, you know one of those guys that played the piano and sang upbeat Dean Martin and Frank Sinatra songs. It attracted the after work crowd and because of the atmosphere people ordered lots of Martini's, Manhattan's, and Rusty Nails. I had a great time working there," said Frank. He thought back. "Everyone thought I looked like George Michael, they even called me GM. Did you hear me singing at the fundraiser?" he asked.

"I remember you singing." Thomas recalled him singing while he was sitting with Rebecca outside. It seemed like a lifetime ago.

"Unfortunately its not one of those occasions where people remember you because you sound good." asked Frank

Thomas smiled. "You're like me, tone deaf."

"You weren't supposed to agree with me," laughed Frank.

Frank talked about his parents who lived east of the city and how his father owned three garages and how his mother, who had retired this year, had worked in a department store. He explained how he fell in love with dancing while on a school trip to see the Nutcracker. He was seven. He told Thomas that he started taking dance lessons when he was eight and how his parents, mostly his mother, had supported him. "My mother took me to my first lessons. My father played sports when he was younger, hockey, football, track and field, and he had his dreams set on me following in his footsteps. He envisioned himself going out to my games and cheering me on and bragging to his friends and people at his work. Instead he sits in a theater with a buttoned up shirt and listens to people yelling 'Bravo!' and throwing roses on the stage. He never talks to anyone about me. Luckily I have a younger brother who took a great interest in sports, football actually, so it helped me out." Frank thought and continued, "You know when my father talks about my brother Ted and his athleticism there is so much pride in his voice and you can see it on his face; with me he never does he always has this fear that I'll walk in one day with a boyfriend and announce that I'm a homosexual." Frank laughed and sipped his drink. "My mother on the other hand loves watching me, she's never missed me dance yet. Sometimes she'll come and watch me rehearse with Rebecca and a couple of the other dances and bring a pack lunch for us all. At first I was horrified, but everyone thought it was great, and I realized that she just wanted to be a part of my life. And she does make the best lunches. I have a sister who's the middle child, let me see Ted's almost eighteen, Stephanie is twenty-three. She's studying to be a veterinarian; she's a very gentle loving person. She loves people and loves animals. Ted is probably going to get an athletic scholarship. He also promised my dad he would get his business degree and take over the family business. Something else my father wanted me to do." Frank took a big gulp of his drink. "I love dance, I don't know what I would have done if I had had two left feet." Frank smiled and looked over at Thomas.

"You just have to give people time, they'll come around eventually."

"I know and I wait patiently." Frank looked at Thomas as he took a sip of his drink. "Rebecca was right."

"About what?"

"She said I would like you."

Thomas came here disliking the person Frank Gray. He no longer did. Thomas lifted up his glass to Frank, "friends."

"Friends," replied Frank and let out a sigh of relief. "I'm so glad. I was so nervous. I had this image of me opening the door and you punching me on the nose." He had his hand on his chest as he spoke. "Okay! Enough! Let me bring out the pitcher of Martini."

As they drank, Thomas talked about his parents, Kate, his work and his writing. After they emptied the pitcher they left the apartment and went for a walk.

"What do you call this area?" asked Thomas.

"They call it The Village. They wanted to recreate a village type atmosphere with low-rise apartments, stores, markets and pubs. I think they did a good job," commented Frank.

"I like it, it does have a great atmosphere," acknowledged Thomas. As they walked Thomas noticed that Frank knew everyone.

The stores they entered were small and the owners were the ones who served the customers. When they picked up the bacon, Thomas was introduced to Gary the butcher. When they picked up the eggs and bread at the grocery store, he met Steve. At 'Thom & Gerry Florist' he met Thom and Gerry. They walked around the market and bought some fruit and walked back to Frank's.

"Let me drop this stuff off and fill out the card for Mrs. Waters," said Frank.

They went upstairs and Thomas listened to Frank put away the items in the kitchen and watched him fill out the card and put it with the flowers. On the first floor they stopped at a door and dropped them off. They walked outside and Frank explained. "Mr. Water's is going to see his wife at the hospital later, she broke her hip, he usually has a nap in the afternoon before heading back to see her. They're a sweet couple and great landlords." Outside they stood on the sidewalk. "Okay why don't we go down to the Stallion and have a drink and some dinner," said Frank. "Do you like pub food?"

Thomas nodded approvingly.

"And English beer," he added. "They pour a good pint of Tenants and have the best fish and chips in the city," stated Frank, looking at Thomas for a reaction.

Thomas laughed. "The best fish and chips!"

Frank laughed, "Rebecca told me to say that. This place actually has the best roast beef, mashed potatoes and Yorkshire pudding in the city and their sticky toffee pudding is to die for."

Along the way a couple was approaching holding hands. As they got closer they recognized Frank. "Frank, how are you? Long time no see? Give me a hug," said the man with the long brown hair. He hugged and kissed Frank on the cheek. "You remember Blair?"

"Of course. Hi Blair," said Frank and gave him a hug and kiss on the cheek.

"Hi Frank," replied Blair.

Frank turned to Thomas, "Greg, Blair, this is a friend of Rebecca's and mine, Thomas."

"Hi Greg, Blair," Thomas wasn't sure what to do so he decided to wait and see.

"Hi Thomas," said Greg and shook Thomas's hand.

"Hi Thomas," said Blair who also shook his hand.

Greg turned to Frank. "Where are you going?"

"The Stallion for dinner," replied Frank. "What are you two up to?"

"We're going to the Bistro," replied Greg.

"Fancy place. Is there a special occasion?" asked Frank.

"Third year anniversary," they replied together as they squeezed each other's hand.

"We're all meeting at The Bear tonight for drinks; everyone is going to be there. You should try and make it," said Greg.

"I'll try," replied Frank.

"We'll be there about nine and we're going to The Saddle afterwards for the 'Retro Night'. So come over and help us celebrate."

"Sounds like fun, I'll try," replied Frank.

"Thomas you're welcome too," added Blair.

"Thanks," said Thomas.

They said goodbye and continued down the street. A few minutes later they walked into The Stallion and sat in an isolated corner booth and ordered two Tenants and two roast beef dinners. During dinner Frank talked about Greg and Blair and how they were in the stage production of West Side Story and how they played parts in the Jets gang and could dance and sing wonderfully. Frank had known Greg since he moved to The Village five years ago.

They ate dessert and drank their coffee. Frank leaned back and stared at Thomas, "If you don't mind I would like to talk to you about me and Rebecca?"

"Okay," replied Thomas unsure as to whether or not he wanted to hear what he had to say.

"At first I thought about telling you as soon as you walked in my place but decided it would be better if we got to know each other first and I'm glad I waited," said Frank.

"Me too."

"Thomas I'm not too sure what you know?" inquired Frank.

"All I know is what I saw and heard in the foyer. Rebecca saying she loved you and you two kissing. Rebecca was still in her clothes from the night before saying she had a great night and me standing in the foyer looking like Humphrey Bogart as he read the note at the train station in the movie Casablanca," replied Thomas. He realized he was sounding a bit melodramatic and laughed.

Frank laughed with him.

"I'm glad we're enjoying my misery," said Thomas.

"Thomas, why are you miserable?" asked Frank.

"She betrayed our friendship."

"Anything else?"

"I guess I was hoping she would have been more open and honest with me."

Frank leaned forward. "This conversation we are going to have is probably not going to answer those questions and I believe you will need to speak with her. But I will try to clear up the circumstances around the events that you have witnessed and hopefully shed some light."

"Okay," replied Thomas.

"Before I start please remember that Rebecca wanted to tell you this herself."

"I understand," confirmed Thomas.

"You are right I do love Rebecca and she loves me. We've known each other for a very long time and this season we'll be dancing together, I will be her partner. We have a great friendship. She has helped me and I have helped her through difficult times. Not only the day-to-day but inside the world of ballet. I'm referring to the training, the steps, and the pressure. We have the highest respect for one another. I compare our love to the love one has for a sister or a brother or a dance partner." Frank stopped and looked at Thomas. "You don't look convinced. Okay." Frank thought, "Let's go back to what you had seen. I've explained why she said she loved me. The kiss between us was one of friendship. The clothes, okay, the dinner party was at Penelope Daily's. She lives in the same condominium tower on the sixteenth floor. We both stayed over. You've been to Rebecca's place; well Penny's is almost the same accept she has three bedrooms. Rebecca and I slept in separate rooms."

"Why didn't she just go home?" asked Thomas.

"Penny and I were up talking about a problem I'm having with one of my routines, it didn't involve Rebecca, it was late and she fell asleep. Penny told her to go and lie down in the room. Penny followed her in and covered her with the sheets. Penny and I talked into the early hours and she invited me to stay. That morning we left Penny asleep and got up and went for a walk and a cup of coffee. We didn't want to wake her up."

"Why were you both going upstairs?" asked Thomas.

"We were going back to Rebecca's apartment."

Thomas smiled and thought, "at last."

"Thomas you're still not getting it. All night Rebecca talked about you. How you went swimming, ate dinner, had a romantic dance, watched old movies, went shopping for the afternoon, she was on cloud nine. I haven't seen her happy in a very long time, in fact, since I've known her. That night she asked if we could break off the 'so called' relationship. I agreed. We should never have done what we did in the first place. It was all a charade. But she was trying to help me out. That Sunday morning she was so happy because she was going to tell you and I was going to help her explain. That's the reason she said she loved me and kissed me." Frank stopped for a moment and noticed Thomas was still confused and continued to clarify, "I see Rebecca as a beautiful person and a very good friend and I love her because of whom she is. But when I look at her all I see is a female and a dance partner. I am not, nor ever will be, physically attracted to her," he looked into Thomas's eyes. "Thomas I'm homosexual."

Thomas felt like he had been hit with a baseball bat.

"Rumors started to fly in the media about my homosexuality. My father called me up and asked me, and I quote, 'If I was a fairy?' I told him no and made up a lie and said I was dating Rebecca. I spoke to Rebecca and told her what I had said and she suggested that we keep the role-playing going until I was comfortable confronting my parents and the media. After which we could break up and I would 'come out of the closet' as the term goes." Frank got the attention of the waiter. "Crown Royal and seven," he looked at Thomas.

"Same," replied Thomas, "and make them doubles."

Frank waited for the waiter to drop off the drinks, took a sip and continued. "For the last six months we've been acting out this make-believe relationship. She goes to my parents place and we act as if we are dating. We're together quite a bit anyway so it was easy enough."

"But I never heard about anything in the papers about you and Rebecca or people talking about you as being a couple. Then again I'm not one for reading the society page," confirmed Thomas.

"No, you're right. People aren't interested in two people who are dating, but a homosexual, that's news."

"But today homosexuality is more in the open than it has ever been?" asked Thomas.

"I'm not worried about the public or the media. It's my family, actually my father, hearing him say 'I told you he would end up becoming a great, big puff'. Good old dad." He looked at Thomas nervously and drank. "For quite some time I've been celibate. I'm very choosy about the man I want to be with and I guess it all comes down to the fact that I want to be in love. All my life I've had a difficult time looking at myself in the mirror and being Catholic makes me feel hypocritical. So here I have my father, my lifestyle, and my faith all pulling me in different directions." Frank stopped. "What Rebecca and I were doing was postponing the inevitable." He smiled to himself. "Enough about me this is about Rebecca." He sipped his drink and looked at Thomas. "So you see you were wrong. She wanted to tell you everything herself. I really think you need to meet with her and talk."

"Does Rebecca know that we were meeting?" asked Thomas.

"I told her I would try and talk to you. She will probably call me this week and find out what happened. Maybe I should have her call you? She'll be back from New York on Friday."

Thomas took a drink and looked up at Frank. "Do you mind if I talk to her first when she gets back?"

"Not at all," replied Frank. "After talking with you I realized some things about myself. It's funny when you talk to someone how much clearer things get." He paused. "My faith is my faith and my lifestyle is my lifestyle and no one can interfere with them or take them away." He smiled nervously, "The media will find out eventually but they can find out on their own. I know I have to tell my family before it goes public. I worry mostly about my dad." He stopped and nervously smiled at Thomas. He stood up and excused himself and went to the bathroom.

While he was gone an image came to Thomas of Frank in the last stall sobbing. He felt sorry for him

Frank returned and they drank their drinks.

"Frank, what time do we have to meet your friends at The Bear?" asked Thomas.

Frank smiled, he was glad he was staying. "They said around nine, we could head over there now and save some seats, it's just across the road."

They both stood. "Where's the club?" asked Thomas.

"Down the road."

"You don't mind if I crash for the night?"

"The sofa is a pullout bed and it's yours," Frank said. "I was hoping you would stick around."

They finished their drinks and went to The Bear.

On the way Frank asked, "When are you going to call Rebecca?"

"Friday," replied Thomas.

Frank put his arm around Thomas as they crossed the street. "Good."

They walked into The Bear and Thomas sat down and Frank stood over him. "What should we have to drink?"

"Something that describes our new found friendship," replied Thomas.

"I know the perfect drink," said Frank. He stood up and went behind the bar and started to mix a drink. He came back holding a pitcher and two cocktail glasses and poured. "This is my own creation, it's smooth and strong; I call it a Careless Whisper. Appropriate don't you think?"

"Very!" said Thomas. He took a sip, "It tastes good."

"I'm glad you like it." He put the pitcher down and sat next to him in the booth.

"Do they always let you go behind the bar?" asked Thomas.

"They should, I'm a silent partner but don't mention that to my friends tonight, they don't know. I always make sure we run a tab and that twenty five percent is taken off the total. The other owner Stuart, he's the one behind the bar, he runs the place and he tells them that the discount is because they're regulars here. I find it works out better this way," explained Frank. "I only go behind the bar to make Martini's for my friends and because I make the best," said Frank with a smile.

"They are good," replied Thomas and looked around. "Why are these places named after animals?" he asked.

Frank laughed. "The Bear is not referring to the animal. It's a man. If you notice the picture under the name it's a man with a beard. A bear is a particular type of homosexual; big sized men, with belly's, hairy chests and backs, and beards and mustaches. Look at Stuart he's a bear," said Frank.

Thomas looked over at him again. "I see what you mean." Thomas didn't need to ask what The Stallion referred to.

"Does my homosexuality bother you?" asked Frank.

"No," replied Thomas. "Does my heterosexuality bother you?"

They both laughed.

The place started to fill and Thom and Gerry joined Frank and Thomas, they were a couple, Gary, Steve, Greg and Blair, Phil the lawyer and his friend Josh, Miguel the designer, Pat the engineer and Lawrence the teacher. Thomas drank and listened for a while, he eventually joined in on the conversations.

"Miguel, I like your biker's jacket," complimented Thomas.

"Thanks," replied Miguel looking at it. "I design and make them. This one is Franks." He looked up at Thomas. "What I do is wear them for a week or so, to soften them up and give them that lived in look, there's nothing worse than a wrinkle free biker's jacket. I wore this tonight so Frank can take it home." He leaned over and whispered to Thomas. "It's good marketing too."

Thomas smiled approvingly. "What happens if the size is too small for you?" he asked.

"I get one of the girls to wear it," replied Miguel.

"If I were to give you a size could you make me one for a friend?"

"Sure!"

"How long would it take?"

"For a friend of Franks, Friday, with a good discount. What size?"

"A woman's medium," said Frank interrupting. "Right?"

"Right," confirmed Thomas.

"The women's design is similar to the men's but a little less brass and softer leather and classier," explained Miguel. "They look marvelous."

"Do you want me to pay you now or give you a deposit?" asked Thomas.

"Like I said you're a friend of Franks, you can pay on delivery," said Miguel.

Frank whispered a question to Thomas, "Did you know that Miguel and several of the others are in The Valley Choir?"

"What's that?" asked Thomas.

"Tell him you'll order the jacket on one condition, they sing."

Thomas looked away from Frank and over to Miguel. "Miguel, I've been speaking to my legal aid here and he suggests that before I place that order The Valley Choir should sing a song, you know, to seal the deal," suggested Thomas.

"Your legal aid will do anything to hear us sing and I mean anything," replied Miguel smiling over at Frank. He looked at Thomas. "Deal." He looked down the table, "okay, it's that time."

Miguel, Thom, Gerry, Lawrence, Blair, and Greg stood up and arranged themselves off to one side.

"Any particular request?" asked Greg looking at Thomas.

"What do you know?" asked Thomas.

"Shout them out," said Greg, "we'll tell you if we know it or not."

"As Time Goes By."

Once they started harmonizing, the bar stereo and televisions were turned off and everyone went quiet. They were amazing.

Everyone clapped loudly when they finished.

"How Deep is Your Love," requested Frank. He looked over at Thomas and whispered, "they sing this and Yesterday beautifully."

They took people's request from around the bar and sang for thirty minutes. Pitchers of beer started arriving at the table from thankful patrons. They stopped singing and had a drink.

"Frank they are really good!" said Thomas.

"They sing at the hospital, usually the cancer and children's wards, and nursing homes. Last year Miguel lost his nephew to leukemia. While his nephew was in hospital Miguel and the group used to go in and cheer him up by singing his favorite songs. That's how it started. His nephew was a great kid and he loved to sing. After he passed away they decided to keep on singing in his memory. They go almost every Sunday afternoon and during the Christmas holidays. In fact tomorrow they're going in to see Mrs. Water's," explained Frank.

Twenty minutes later the group stood up again and the place went quiet. Greg spoke, "We are going to sing four more songs. We will take two requests from this table, Frank and Thomas, and two from the bar," people in the bar put up their hands, "the young lady in the black dress and the man with the black hair leaning on the bar. Ladies first, what will it be?"

They sang, 'Can't Hurry Love' for the lady, 'Green, Green, Grass of Home' for the man, and 'Yesterday' for Frank.

"Okay Thomas. What's it going to be?" asked Greg.

"'You're the Best Thing,'" replied Thomas.

As they sang he thought about Rebecca.

THEY ARRIVED AT THE NIGHTCLUB AT TEN thirty and walked passed the line up and straight in. Greg had reserved a table close to the dance floor but far enough so people could talk. There were bottles of champagne chilling in buckets. They all sat down except Greg who remained standing and started to open a bottle of champagne, as he did he spoke, "I would like to thank you all for being here and helping Blair and I celebrate our third year anniversary. From this point on the remainder of the night is on us. After the champagne is gone feel free to order what you like from the bar we have a tab. Again thank you and enjoy." He popped open the champagne and filled the glasses.

Lawrence stood and spoke for several minutes describing how Greg and Blair met and how they made such a wonderful couple, he finished his speech by asking everyone to lift their glasses and toast Greg and Blair and wish them all the best and future happiness. "To Greg and Blair."

Everyone replied, "To Greg and Blair," and drank.

Thomas looked over at Frank and caught something in his eyes. Was it sadness or perhaps loneliness or was he thinking about his family and how different their reaction would be to this kind of celebration. Frank caught Thomas's stare and quickly smiled and stood up. He looked at Greg and Blair and congratulated them on their union, commitment and happiness.

They all stood one by one and offered their congratulations and best wishes.

Miguel leaned over the table and said, "If anyone asks for these two empty chairs don't let them have them, I have two friends arriving shortly." He then whispered. "You'll be expected to say something."

Thomas didn't know what to say and decided to keep it simple and say, "All the best," and sit down, but as he rose he recalled a poem of John Donne's called 'The Good Morrow'. He recited it perfectly for Greg and Blair. They all clapped.

"Thomas that was a beautiful recital of John Donne and quite appropriate," said Blair as he stood and looked at Thomas, then the group. "Thank you all for sharing this special time with me and the man I love." Blair leaned and kissed Greg full on the mouth.

The table, with the exception of Thomas, cheered Blair on. Thomas was feeling a little uncomfortable. Was it because he had been caught off guard by the unexpected action? Surely he wasn't expecting any couple to turn around to him and notify him that they were about to kiss so that he could prepare himself. Was it because they were kissing? He thought hard. No, he was a firm believer that you should openly show affection for the one you love. Was it because it was two men and he was heterosexual? Was that it? What about his religious beliefs, they must definitely play a role? He wasn't too sure but one thing was for certain they were in love, they were happy and that was all that mattered. The chanting stopped when the kiss did and the conversation around the table resumed. Thomas drank his champagne and watched Blair, Greg, Thom and Gerry stand up and go to the dance floor and watched them dancing, laughing, and having fun. He suddenly came to a realization that the worst feeling a human being could have was to be on a planet with over six billion others and feel alone. He looked over at Frank and felt sorry for him. He had only just understood what he must have been going through.

"This is one of my all time favorite songs," said Frank.

"Want to dance?" asked Thomas.

"Are you okay with it?" asked Frank.

"I've danced with friends before at a club. I don't see any difference," smiled Thomas.

"I'll make sure no one tries to cut in," joked Frank.

They danced to Talk Talk's 'It's My Life'. Halfway through the song Thomas spoke. "Isn't it ironic that you like this song?"

"That's the reason I like it so much," commented Frank.

They danced two more songs and sat down. Miguel's friends had arrived.

"Hi Thomas."

"Janet. How are you?" asked Thomas.

"I'm doing well. I wouldn't expect to find you here?" she asked as she leaned over and brushed her cheek with his.

"I'm a friend of Franks," replied Thomas and gave her a smile.

"Do you remember my girlfriend from the show, Betty?" asked Janet.

"I remember her. But I didn't remember her name. Hello Betty," said Thomas.

"Hello Thomas," she replied and shook his hand.

"Is Rebecca here?" asked Janet.

"No," replied Thomas. "She's in New York."

"That's right. She was in the store a few days ago buying an outfit for New York. I was surprised not to see you with her?"

Thomas was silent.

She continued. "Last time she told me how much fun it was having you around and how she was going to beg you to come with her again." She looked at Thomas.

"I've been really busy," said Thomas.

"She only tried two outfits on and ended up asking me to pick one. She looked so miserable. I asked her how she was. She said she was fine and that she was seeing her father this week and hadn't seen him for some time. I said you should be happy then. She forced a smile. I don't think she was there more than twenty minutes." Janet took a sip of her drink. "She wasn't herself. When I saw her walking away and compared it to the last time she was with you I knew there was something upsetting her. Is she okay?"

"I don't know. I haven't seen her for a while. You would have to ask Frank," Thomas suggested.

"You haven't seen her for a while," repeated Janet. "Maybe that's it."

Thomas quickly changed the subject. "When I went with her she thought you were trying to pick me up."

Janet laughed. "I was only being playful. I thought she knew."

"She didn't."

"Really!"

"I had some fun with her for a while, before I told her," said Thomas.

"Did you like her in the dress?" asked Janet.

"I thought she looked beautiful!"

"I think you two make a good couple."

"We're just friends."

Greg and Blair were getting up again to dance and pulled Thomas up with them. Janet, Betty and Miguel followed them. Throughout the night they had people go on the stage to lip-synching and dance to various artists, Frank did George Michael and Thom and Gerry did Erasure. Thomas was dancing with Frank and Miguel when Billy Idol's "Rebel Yell' came on. Thomas unbuttoned his shirt and started pumping his arm and singing with the sneer like Billy Idol. Miguel whispered to Frank, who headed toward the disc jockey while Miguel took Thomas back to the table, "It's time," he said.

"Time for what?" asked Thomas.

"Billy Idol to hit the stage," said Miguel. Miguel took off Thomas's shirt and put on the biker's jacket. He looked at Janet, "Janet, we need to do something with the hair." Janet took out her brush and gel and fixed Thomas's blonde hair.

The music died and a voice came over the speakers, it was Frank's, "ladies and gentlemen, tonight flown in from England via New York for a special guest appearance, the one, the only, Billy Idol."

"That's you," said Miguel.

"Here," Janet gave him a shot of tequila.

Thomas drank it and headed for the stage. Billy Idol's 'Rebel Yell' started again and Thomas imitated him to almost perfection. After he'd finished and walked off the stage he could hear the group chanting, 'Billy, Billy' and from that point on he would always be known to them as Billy. They chanted once more when he went on the stage for his runner up prize of a bottle of wine, which he gave to Blair and Greg. He gave the three phone numbers to Frank.

Thomas and Frank were the first to leave the nightclub. They all gave Thomas a hug goodbye and told him they would see him soon.

Janet whispered in Thomas's ear, "I hope you work it out with Rebecca, you two looked good together."

"I hope so too," replied Thomas and gave her a kiss on the cheek.

As Frank and Thomas walked away the group chanted, "Billy, Billy, Billy."

Thomas turned and smiled and gave them one more Billy Idol pose. Out on the street they staggered to Frank's place.

Frank pulled out the sofa bed and gave Thomas some blankets. "I usually sleep in on Sundays and make some breakfast and go to church at noon over at St. Theresa's, you're welcome to join me?"

"I'll stick around and leave after church," said Thomas as he took off the jacket and passed it to Frank. "I'll need to borrow a shirt."

Frank laughed, "I'll give you one in the morning."

"Your friends are great," complimented Thomas.

"Thanks. They like you too," replied Frank. "Have a good sleep."

"Goodnight."

"Goodnight."

Thomas woke before Frank and made himself a coffee. He put on his pants and sat outside on the balcony. He thought about Rebecca in New York. He was happy it was working out with her and her father. Then he thought about him and Rebecca and what he had done and what she must have thought of him.

Half an hour later Frank walked onto the balcony and passed a shirt to Thomas, "Here you go." He looked down on the street and turned to Thomas, "Come inside and I'll make some breakfast."

Thomas followed him into the kitchen and sat down and listened to Frank talk about dance, as he cooked. They sat and ate a plate of bacon and eggs and left and went to mass. On the way back Frank confided in Thomas. "I need to talk to my parents."

Thomas nodded in silence.

"Sooner than later," he said and half smiled. "That'll be fun."

Thomas noticed the worried look in his eyes. They walked back to Frank's house and stopped by Thomas's car.

"Thomas, last night you were right, it is my life," stated Frank. "It's time I started living it."

"Frank, if you like I can go with you to your parents and offer you some support. I don't want to interfere in any way but if you need me, I'll be there."

"You would?"

"Yeah, if you want me to."

"Thanks, I feared going alone. I'll give you a call." Frank stopped and thought. "Do you think Rebecca would come as well?" asked Frank.

"I think you already know the answer to that," said Thomas.

"Yeah, I do."

Frank gave Thomas a hug. "You're going to talk to Rebecca?"

"Friday night."

"Good, make sure you do, you two have a lot to talk about." He looked at Thomas and said with sincerity, "thanks again."

"Call me," said Thomas as he got into the car. He started it and lowered the window. "Thanks for the invite, I had a great time, we'll do it again soon."

"You can count on it." As he started to drive Frank pumped his arm back and forth and chanted, "Billy, Billy, Billy."

Chapter 10

Abuse

Thomas parked his car and walked to the path to the guesthouse. A young man in a two-piece blue suit slowed down as he approached and stopped him. "Thomas?" asked the man.

"Yes," replied Thomas a little confused.

"I'm Mathew York, the lawyer that's helping Rachel and Veronica open up the daycare."

"I know the name, Rachel's mentioned you," remembered Thomas. "How's everything going?"

"Slow," replied Mathew. "I came by to give them the information on the municipal and federal by-laws."

"Red tape," suggested Thomas.

Mathew nodded his head. "Yeah."

"Well I'm sure once they get passed the bureaucracy it will speed up," assured Thomas.

"Definitely," replied Mathew. "Are you here to do some writing?"

"Yeah. Is Rachel in the guest house?"

"She is."

"I'll see you again," said Thomas shaking his hand.

"Good luck," said Mathew not too sure what else to say to someone who writes.

"Thanks," replied Thomas.

Thomas walked to the house and was ascending the stairs when he met Rachel coming down dressed in jeans and a vest.

"Thomas," she screamed and gave him a hug, "I missed you. What's this coming on a Wednesday rather than Tuesday?"

"I had a busy weekend," he replied.

"You look tired?"

"I am it's been busy at work." He looked up at her and noticed her hair and touched it. "Wet," he said.

"I just got out of the shower," she replied.

"You always look so fresh and smell so good," he commented. "I passed Mathew, he stopped and said hello."

"He's a nice guy." She grabbed Thomas's hand. "Come downstairs to the kitchen. Have you had dinner? I'll make you my famous ham and cheese sandwich," she said.

"That would be great," replied Thomas. They went down to the kitchen and he watched in silence as Rachel made the sandwich.

She put it in front of him and watched him eat. "Remember when I asked you if you could come out with me and Veronica and Buddy, and you were busy, well Veronica asked Mathew to come and he said yes and we had so much fun. I went out with him again last weekend." She waited for his reaction.

"Did you have fun?"

"Yes, he took me for dinner and we went for a drink."

"You like him then?"

"He seems really nice."

"Seems?"

"Thomas, I've only been on one date."

"You look happy," suggested Thomas.

"I am, but that's because you're here, I haven't seen you since Thursday."

"How is he with you being a model?" asked Thomas.

"He's great. He's very understanding," replied Rachel. "Like you." She looked anxiously at Thomas.

Thomas noticed it. "What's the problem?"

Rachel spoke cautiously. "I want you to meet him and let me know what you think. It's important to me that you like him. Your friendship is important to me."

"Why don't you arrange something this Saturday," suggested Thomas.

"Tracy called me yesterday and said Atlas was playing in a club in the city, I'm sure she said the date was this Saturday, I have it written down," said Rachel excitedly.

"Saturday it is," said Thomas.

"Yeah," she screamed and kissed him on the cheek. "I'll call Mathew. Veronica and Buddy, you can ask Kate and I'll let you know the details tomorrow," she stood up and was walking away.

"Where are you going?" asked Thomas.

"To call people. Make plans," replied Rachel. "Nothing like the present."

Thomas smiled and shook his head. "I'm going up to your house to return a book I borrowed from your father's study," said Thomas standing.

"I'll see you up there in fifteen minutes or so," replied Rachel as she disappeared upstairs.

Thomas walked to the house and went in through the back door. He entered the study, signed the book back in on the computer and walked over to the shelf and returned it to its original place.

"You have a nerve."

Thomas turned and looked at Bill Carter he was furious. "You said I could borrow your books," replied Thomas.

"Not the books you idiot, I'm talking about you fucking my daughter in my guesthouse," replied Bill as he walked towards Thomas. He stopped and stared inches away from Thomas's eyes.

Thomas could smell booze. "What are you talking about?" asked Thomas.

"I was suspicious of you when I first met you, no money, working in a two bit warehouse. I thought to myself this guy is on the game. So I humored my wife and Jack and said I'd agree to what Rachel wanted but I said I'll be keeping a close eye on you. Then I hear from the servants that you've been fucking my daughter in my guesthouse. Everyone said you would be a good friend for my daughter but I was right all you were interested in was poking my daughter's rich pussy in hopes of getting a windfall. I knew you were too good to be true. You fucking bastard," screamed Bill.

"I don't know what you're talking about," said Thomas.

"Thirty minutes ago a staff member came by and told me he could hear you and that slut fucking in the hot tub," screamed Bill. Bill's forehead tapped Thomas's nose.

"Bill, what's going on? Who are you calling a slut? And why do you have members of our staff spying on our guests," asked Jessica as she walked in.

"Jessica I have no idea what he's talking about," pleaded Thomas to Jessica.

"You don't speak to my wife with that filthy mouth," screamed Bill.

Bill head-butted Thomas above the right eye, an inch slit opened, and the blood poured. Thomas wasn't expecting it and his knees weakened.

With his arms he leveraged himself against the bookshelf. Jessica shouted at Bill to stop and ran out to get help.

"Time to taste some rich mans fists," said Bill as he punched Thomas to the ground. "Get up!"

Jessica returned to witness Bill punching and kicking Thomas. "Bill stop!" she screamed and ran over to him, he turned and pushed her to the ground.

Bill turned and looked down at Thomas and kicked him repeatedly. Bill suddenly felt a strong hand on his shoulder turning him around. A fist the size of a melon swiped across Bill's face and the distinctive cracking of Bill's nose filled the air. Bill staggered back and fell and over the sofa. Jack had knocked him out. He turned and helped Thomas up.

"Is he okay?" asked Jessica.

"I need to get him to a hospital. He'll need to be looked at. He's going to need some stitches. I'll take him in my car." Jack leaned Thomas on his shoulder. "Call the hospital and let them know I'm coming," said Jack, "and get rid of that piece of shit you call your husband."

"What's happening?" asked Rachel as she walked up behind her mother and Jack. Her mother turned and she noticed Thomas, his face covered in blood, leaning on Jack. "Thomas!" she screamed. "What happened? Thomas!" she cried. She ran and got a towel from the bathroom and met them outside.

Jack walked Thomas to his car and put him in the passenger side, he looked at Jessica and Rachel, "call his sister and tell her the hospital. I'll call you later on your cell phone. I suggest that you two stay somewhere safer tonight."

Thomas was dazed and held the towel over his cut. They went to emergency and were seen to straight away. While Thomas was getting stitched up Jack went outside and called Jessica to find out what had happened. After getting the details he went back and waited outside.

"Are you a family member?" asked the doctor.

"No. A close friend of the family," replied Jack.

"I'm his sister," interrupted Kate as she walked up to them. "How is he?"

"He's stable. He has fifteen stitches above his right eyebrow, some bruised ribs, and bruising on his hands, arms and legs. He has a mild concussion. I've given him a mild sedative for the pain and I want to keep him in overnight just as a precaution," explained the doctor. "This man was beaten. Would you like me to call the police?"

Kate looked at Jack. "What happened?"

"Doctor, can we have a minute?" asked Jack.

"Take several. We'll be moving him into room three twelve. You can visit him there."

Jack walked Kate to the waiting room and explained to her what had just happened. He also told her about Jessica and Bill. Kate listened and walked over with Jack to the doctor and told him that they would talk to Thomas.

"I will still have to put it in his file no matter what the decision is," explained the doctor.

"That's fine," said Kate.

"Okay," replied the doctor. "We've moved him upstairs."

They walked into the semi private room and over to its only occupant. Kate looked at him and cried. Jack, after seeing his swollen right eye, the stitches, and bruises, wished he had punched Bill a few more times. He moved an armchair next to the bed for Kate. She sat and picked up his bruised hand and kissed it.

"Can I get you a cup of coffee?" asked Jack.

"Please Jack. Do you think they'll let me sleep in that bed tonight?" asked Kate.

"Sure they will," said Jack. "I'll take care of it."

Jack called Jessica and told her about Thomas's condition and hung up, he then called Penny. He spoke to the nurse and picked up two cups of coffee.

"Thomas has the room to himself and you have the use of the bed for as long as he's here," said Jack.

"Jack, he could have killed him," said Kate.

"I know," said Jack as he put his hand on her shoulder and thought, "Bill's finished." Jack sat with Kate until eleven. He got up kissed Kate on the head and said he and Penny would be back tomorrow morning. At midnight Kate lay in the empty bed and looked over at Thomas. He hadn't moved all night and his breathing was so light.

"Kate, Kate is that you?" asked Thomas.

She woke up and was disorientated for a minute. She turned around and looked at Thomas he was awake. She jumped out of bed and went to his side.

"How are you?" she asked.

"Thirsty."

"Let me call the nurse," said Kate and pressed the button.

"Where am I?"

"In hospital," answered Kate.

The nurse came in. "How are you Thomas?" she asked.

"Thirsty."

"Good, I'll get you some water," said the nurse.

"My head and body aches," said Thomas

"I'll get you a mild sedative it will take the pain away and let you sleep," she replied.

The nurse left and Thomas closed his eyes. He opened them when she returned. "Take these two pills and drink some water, slowly," she warned.

Thomas stopped drinking and closed his eyes.

The nurse looked at Kate and said, "You should let him sleep. I'll leave the water in case he wants more; make sure he drinks it slowly." She walked out of the room. It was three when Kate lay on the bed and slowly fell back asleep.

Thomas still hadn't woken when Rachel came in the room.

"What do you think you're doing? Get out? Haven't you done enough?" said Kate in a stern voice trying to hold back the tears.

"I'm so sorry Kate. I didn't mean for any of this to happen. I feel so bad don't send me away, please!" begged Rachel.

"Get out? Get out or I'll throw you out!" said Kate in a more determined voice.

"Kate," whispered Thomas.

"Thomas," said Kate. "How are you?"

"Kate, come closer," whispered Thomas. "I know your upset but she is my friend. She had nothing to do with it. Don't blame her."

Kate cried and spoke in between sobs, "I know…. I'm just frightened."

"Rachel's your friend too," said Thomas trying to smile, "ouch." He waited and then spoke again. "I love you. I'll always be here for you. I'm not going anywhere."

Thomas closed his eyes. Kate turned and looked at Rachel who was sobbing and walked over and put her arms around her.

Ten minutes later Jessica came in and looked at Thomas and cried. "It's my fault," she said.

"Jessica," said Kate, "it's not your fault."

Jessica turned and looked at Kate, "many times I've looked in the mirror and seen my face like Thomas's and have never done a thing to stop it from happening again. If I would have, maybe this would never have happened." She started to cry again.

Kate held her, "it's not your fault. It's not your fault. Come and be with Thomas." She sat Jessica in her seat. "He likes it when you hold his hand."

Jessica held his hand and looked at the bruises. She knew her marriage with Bill was over. She looked at Rachel who was sitting at the end of the bed.

"Did you know?" asked Jessica.

"About dad?" Rachel asked. "About the abuse?"

"Yes," replied Jessica.

"When I heard the yelling it reminded me of bad dreams that I used to have when I was younger, but now I realize they weren't dreams. I remember you were never around for days after those dreams and I wanted to tell you about them so you could make them go away. I went to dad and he told me they were just bad dreams. I understand looking at Thomas why you weren't around and that they weren't dreams."

"I didn't want you to be a part of it. I was scared that if you knew he might hurt you. I should have made him leave." She looked at Thomas, "this time".

Rachel walked over and stood behind her mother. Her mother lifted her hand on her shoulder and Rachel held it. "Maybe we can spend some time together like we used to. Go horseback riding?" asked Rachel.

"Can I go as well?" asked Thomas.

They both looked at him. "How long have you been awake?" Jessica asked.

"Long enough," replied Thomas.

"How are you feeling?" asked Rachel.

"Thirsty," said Thomas. Rachel held the water to his mouth. He drank some and stopped. "Can one of you get the nurse?" asked Thomas.

"I'll go," said Jessica. She stood and walked out.

"I don't think I can make it Saturday," said Thomas trying to smile.

"It's okay I got the wrong date, it's a week Saturday," replied Rachel.

"Then I'll be there," said Thomas and winked with his left eye.

Rachel couldn't hold back the tears and cried over Thomas's chest, "It's my fault!"

"Rachel," whispered Thomas, "it's not your fault. Never blame yourself." He couldn't lift his hand to comfort her. "Rachel, look at me, look at me." She looked up. "I need you to be here, friends, remember like brother and sister."

She smiled.

"Come closer. Closer," said Thomas.

She leaned over close to his mouth.

"I can see right down your top," said Thomas.

She put her hand over her shirt and playfully hit his arm, "some brother," she said.

"Ouch," said Thomas.

"Sorry," she kissed it better.

"How are you doing?" asked the nurse.

"My eyesight is fine," said Thomas and looked over at Rachel.

Rachel shook her head and smiled.

"Actually I wondered if I can have some more of those pills?" asked Thomas.

"The doctor will be here in ten minutes or so, he's making his rounds. Can you wait till then?" suggested the nurse.

"That'll mean I have to listen to this blonde bore me with talk about her super sex life," said Thomas.

"Thomas!" said Rachel embarrassed.

"You should be so lucky to have such a beautiful woman at your bedside," said the nurse in Rachel's defense.

"He calls that a sense of humor," said Rachel. She looked over at Thomas, "I'm taking the flowers and fruit basket back."

The nurse was still shaking her head on the way out.

"Thomas I'll get you for that," said Rachel.

"Kate's first in line with three," replied Thomas, "you're next."

The doctor walked in and Rachel and Kate left. "Good morning Thomas I'm Doctor Reed I treated you last night and I'm here to have a look at you." He pulled the curtains around the bed and examined Thomas. "You're doing fine; the swelling will go down over the next day or two. The bruising will take a little longer. Make an appointment to see your family doctor in a week to ten days so he can examine your stitches. Later on this morning you should get out of bed, go to the bathroom and for a walk. I'll be back tomorrow, same time. I'll probably release you then. Take the week off. If you need a note for work I'll give you one tomorrow."

"Can I have some pills for the pain?" asked Thomas.

The doctor pulled back the curtain. "I'll have the nurse give you some and let her know that anytime you need them you can have them. Remind me to give you a prescription tomorrow," said the doctor. The doctor looked at Thomas and spoke quietly, "Thomas I asked your sister if she wanted to press charges and she suggested that you should make that decision. Would you like to press charges?" asked the doctor.

Thomas looked at Rachel and Jessica outside. "No."

"Are you sure?" asked the doctor.

"Yes," said Thomas. His life is ruined anyway thought Thomas.

"Okay. I'll see you same time tomorrow."

"Thank you Dr. Reed."

The doctor opened the door and said to the people outside, "he's all yours."

Kate came in alone and closed the door, "What did he say?"

"Later on I need to get out of bed and go for a walk and to take the pills when I need them. He said I should be released tomorrow and to take the week off work and relax," summarized Thomas.

"That's good news," said Kate.

The nurse came in with the pills and some cold water.

Kate went outside and gave them the update.

After the nurse left Penny and Jack came in.

"Oh poor Thomas," said Penny. She walked over and put some flowers and chocolates on the side table. "Feeling better?" she asked.

"Much better," replied Thomas. He looked at Jack and spoke, "thanks Jack. I owe you one."

"Forget it. We'll talk about it later. You just get well," said Jack. "I'm going to go outside and give you two some time alone. By the way Thomas if you want you can use my rustic cabin up north for the weekend, week, whatever. You can have it all to yourself or invite a friend."

"Thanks Jack I just might take you up on that offer," said Thomas. He watched Jack close the door and turned and looked at Penny.

"Thomas, I know we thanked you last week over the phone, but I wanted to thank you again in person. You should come by for dinner next weekend, once you're better, and we can talk some more," said Penny.

"I look forward to it," replied Thomas and hesitated, "I was going to call Rebecca this Friday and see if she wanted to get together and talk. We need to talk," he stopped for a moment. "Did you know about Frank and what they were doing?" asked Thomas.

"Yes," said Penny. She talked slowly, "I thought it best that one of them told you. The last thing that needed was another person involved," smiled Penny. "Since you didn't want to give Rebecca a chance she asked Frank.

Rebecca tells me lots of things, not always in her speech, sometimes in her body language. Besides, who would you rather hear from, them or me?" She touched his face. "You should call her."

"I will. I was hoping to look a little better when I see her." He looked down at his hand. "I don't want her to see me like this!"

"In you, Rebecca sees what's in here first," she pointed to his heart, "in here second," she pointed to his temple, "and what comes out of here," she put her finger on his lips." Penny smiled.

"Thanks Penny," said Thomas, "I'll see you a week Friday for dinner!"

"Week Friday," said Penny. She leaned over and kissed him on the cheek and went outside. Thomas could see her crying in Jack's arms.

Thomas closed his eyes for a moment and fell asleep. He awoke a few hours later and looked at Jessica sitting forward in the seat softly crying. He lifted his hand and played with her hair. She looked over at him and he gently brushed his fingers over her cheek, "an attractive woman like you deserves to be caressed," said Thomas softly.

Jessica smiled. "Rachel and Kate have just gone down for some lunch."

"Good. You can help me out of my bed and we can go for a walk around the ward. I'll be the envy of all the patients," said Thomas. He slowly moved his legs over to the side of the bed Jessica was sitting on and she helped him stand. She picked up a robe from the end of the bed and put it on him. "Let me go to the bathroom first," he slowly walked to the bathroom and closed the door behind him. He had forgotten he hadn't seen himself in the mirror yet and was shocked by his reflection. He quickly composed himself and used the bathroom. He put his arm through Jessica's and walked out the room and down the hall. They stopped at the refrigerator and got some water and walked some more. Thomas noticed the television room was empty and decided to stop there for a rest.

Jessica helped him sit down then sat next to him. "Thomas when I first met you at the fundraiser you reminded me so much of Bill when he was young - charming, charismatic, independent, proud, confident, but also very caring and sensitive. The difference between Bill and you is that you see all the good in people and treat everything equal. Bill is very judgmental and jumps to conclusions, usually the wrong ones." As she spoke she looked at the finger that once occupied her wedding ring. "I first met Bill when I was twenty and he was twenty-five. I fell in love with him when we first met. He didn't have much money at that time but he worked hard and became a millionaire before he was thirty-five. He was very ambitious and very smart. We had Rachel when I was twenty-five." She stopped looking at her finger and looked up at Thomas. "He first hit me when Rachel was five. For a few years after he continued to hit me, once in a while, you know a slap or two, here and there. After, he was always sorry and would buy me flowers or jewelry. He was very jealous and used to get so angry if a man talked to me or even looked at me. I could tell just by the look in his eyes that I was going to get it when I got home, especially when he'd been drinking. You slut, smack! Whore, smack! He beat me for the first time when Rachel was eleven; the slapping was replaced with clenched fists. The next day when he was sober he apologized and took me away to our cottage. I thought it was the pressure of the job. But he had a problem and when he started drinking, he had two. Up until Rachel was eighteen nobody knew about the beatings, they weren't that often and I had learned to protect myself. One day Jack came over and saw my face healing from a beating I'd taken a few days earlier. He went straight to Bill and threatened to kill him if he touched me again. Jack told me to call the police and throw him out. I didn't listen. He beat me after Jack left and has occasionally beaten me since. I moved out of our room five years ago. Bill travels more these days. I know he has a girlfriend and uses hookers. But I didn't mind it's kept his attention and fists off of me for the last few years. I wanted to have more children, give Rachel a brother and a sister, but for obvious reasons we didn't. Rachel always asked me why. She thought I was selfish and I think she despised me for it. I came from a family of three sisters and two brothers and would have loved her to have what I had. Over the last year Rachel distanced herself from us, especially me. She changed and became a spoilt, confused girl. I was worried she was going to leave me. She never knew what was going on and it really affected her indirectly. I used to put on a performance with Bill when we were in public and especially around Rachel but over the last several years I dropped it. Rachel realized I had stopped loving her father and she started to take his side. She was even spending more time with him. Don't get me wrong she always loved me." Jessica paused. "I never wanted her to become spoilt; I sent her to public schools and was careful with her. She didn't get her first car till she was twenty. Bill, to get back at me, bought her horses and built her the stable. But he didn't notice the change in her. I did, I noticed the change in her personality and that she was becoming someone else. She became more confused. After the fundraiser I was going to tell her the truth about Bill and me. Then she met you and just like that she became the old Rachel." Jessica stopped and sipped her water and continued. "Over the last few weeks I've noticed the transformation back to her old self. We were starting to be close again and I didn't realize how this was infuriating Bill. Did you know he tried to stop you from coming to her party? That evening I talked with Jack and told him everything. He threatened Bill, not only with force, something far more severe, money or should I say lack of it. Jack told Bill that he and his associates would withdraw all their money from everything they were partners in. It would have financially crippled Bill. When Bill spoke to you that morning and said you could stay it was because Jack and I had told him earlier that morning that he had to. He didn't want you anywhere near her or our house. You know he even took away the joy of me telling Rachel," Jessica stopped and looked at Thomas. "Jack and I knew that you being around Rachel would help her and that she would be safe. Bill was drinking more and I could see that look in his eyes and the tone in his voice when he spoke to her. I should have told Rachel a long time ago. I should have left him a long time ago."

"Why didn't you leave him? Was it the money?" asked Thomas.

Jessica had a surprised look on her face and laughed. "All that money is mine. The estates, the house, the cottage, they're all mine. My net worth is over a hundred million and Bill can't touch it. My father never liked Bill and would only let me marry him if I signed a prenuptial. My father wanted the six children to run his business after he died, no spouses involved in the business at all, so he made us all equal partners and applied the condition that it was only transferable to direct offspring. My two brothers and sister run the business today. Even the estates I own are under my name and my direct offspring, Rachel. Bill signed the contracts, but he knew he could use my influence and contacts to succeed in his own ambitions, plus he knew I had liquid assets and would be receiving profits from the family business. With the help of my connections Bill has done well for himself. In fact Bill would have to give me my share of his fifteen million. When I die Rachel gets everything I own. Did you know she's made three quarters of a million from her modeling and gave it all to me? I give her an allowance each week. She's so responsible and trustworthy." She stopped for a moment. "Funny, when I think back, if it were up to me I would have married Bill without my fathers contracts; credit to Bill he married me with them." She looked at her finger again. "To answer your question I was in love with him. But not anymore," Jessica stopped talking and took several drinks of water and began again. "Bill was having the guest house spied on by the servants who were there to clean it and stock the cupboards, you know, report the goings on, anything unusual, stains on the sheets, that sort of stuff. Late yesterday afternoon one of the servants was cleaning the guesthouse grounds and said they saw Rachel talking to someone in the kitchen. Several minutes later the servant went in to ask if he could have a drink, only the kitchen was empty, so he went back to work down by the side of the house. Ten minutes later he heard the sliding door open and Rachel and a male enter the hot tub and having sex. Half an hour later he reports his findings to Bill in the study. What had actually happened, was that Rachel had been talking to Mathew, Veronica and Buddy in the kitchen. Mathew and Rachel went outside on the porch to say goodbye. Veronica and Buddy go down to the recreation room and are getting hot and bothered. Rachel comes in and goes upstairs to get a shower. She is notorious for taking long showers. She told me she wanted to look nice for you. Anyway Veronica hears the shower go on and knows Rachel will be in there for a while and with the noise of the shower she knows she wouldn't hear them. Veronica and Buddy get naked, get into the hot tub and have sex. They hear the shower go off and go back into the house. A half an hour later the servant is telling Bill in the study what he heard. Bill looks out the window and sees you coming from the direction of the guesthouse with a book in your hand. He thinks it was you and Rachel in the hot tub and you know the rest." She stopped and was about to cry but gained her composure, "not to take anything away from what he did to you but I believe if he had seen Rachel approaching and confronted her in the study he would have beaten her. She is so fragile." Jessica put her head down and cried.

Thomas put his arms around her and waited till she finished. "What's next?" he asked.

"You, Kate, Jack and Penny know everything and let me tell you it's not easy for me. I'm a very private and proud woman."

"I understand," comforted Thomas.

"Tomorrow morning I'm going to take Rachel away for the weekend and tell her everything. She only knows pieces. I don't know how she's going to respond. Jack and his lawyer are going over to see Bill tomorrow to end their business relationship with him. We're going to give Bill some breaks, let him keep his fifteen million, a million in cash, his car and personal items. All he has to do is sign a contract that says he will move out of the city, leave me and Rachel alone, and can't come back or try to get more money from me before, during or after our divorce. He will also have to admit to the beatings. Rachel will have to decide if she wants to visit him or not, I wouldn't stop her, but she would need a chaperone," said Jessica. "He has until noon on Sunday to be out of the house."

"Will he sign?" asked Thomas.

"If he doesn't he would be a fool. He's not expecting what we're giving him and he'll know he will be getting more than he should. Plus the fact that he's not being charged by me," replied Jessica. "This will suit him fine. Our marriage has been over for along time. He can go live with his girlfriend Suzy."

"I can't help but feel responsible for this," expressed Thomas.

"Thomas don't," said Jessica sympathetically. "Honestly I can't take the chance anymore especially with Rachel." Jessica hesitated, "he could have seriously injured you, even killed you. You are still within your rights to press charges and sue him?"

"No."

"No?" questioned Jessica. "You could make a small fortune fast."

"No."

"Why not?" asked Jessica.

"Correct me if I'm wrong. If I press charges, your life and Rachel's would be in the newspapers, and the media would hound you throughout the trial. Isn't that why you are paying Bill off?"

"Yes," replied Jessica.

"I wouldn't want you two to go through that, no amount of money is worth that. Rachel's my friend, and so are you."

"Thanks Thomas," she said and sat in silence. She changed the topic. "Rachel told me that your eyesight was okay." Jessica laughed.

The laughing subsided and the mentioning of Rachel's name by Jessica had reminded him of something. "Jessica, I thought Bill had confused me with Rachel and Mathew having sex because he was leaving when I got there."

"No, not Rachel, she's very particular about certain things. Besides she loves you," replied Jessica.

"Here you two are!" said Kate with Rachel standing behind her.

"Thomas they dropped off your lunch in the room and mother I brought you a sandwich and tea," said Rachel.

"Well let's have lunch," said Thomas to Jessica as he stood up awkwardly. He walked with her help back to his room.

They talked all afternoon.

Kate and Thomas told them about New York City. In fact they talked about it so much they talked Jessica into taking Rachel there for a few days.

"Make sure you stay in the same hotel as we did, you will see the famous face of one Kate Carlyle gracing its walls, and make sure you talk to Richard the manager and make a point to ask if she stayed there," said Thomas.

"Thomas I still owe you for that," said Kate.

"I'll make sure we do," said Rachel.

Thomas was released the next morning and Kate drove him home.

"I'm glad you're okay. You look much better than you did last night," said Kate.

"You must be behind in school?" asked Thomas.

"I'll catch up. I start work Monday and Barry's asked me to come in Saturday afternoon to meet some people. I'm looking forward to it," said Kate.

"Jack offered me his cabin for the week," said Thomas.

"You should go!" said Kate, "you have the week off."

"Did you want to come up Saturday after work?" asked Thomas.

"Thanks for the offer but I would get more studying done here at home," replied Kate.

"I thought you wouldn't but I wanted to ask," said Thomas. "I think I'll go up for the week, put my feet up and relax in Jack's rustic cabin."

CHAPTER 11

Rustic Cabin

THOMAS WATCHED JACK'S CHAUFFEUR DRIVE AWAY AS he picked up his bag off the ground. He could have driven but Jack insisted he relax in the back seat of his Bentley. He turned and looked at the so-called rustic cabin. It was a spectacular log cabin and Thomas guessed it to be twenty five hundred square feet. He walked up the wooden steps onto the large porch. There were several patio chairs and end tables and a two-seated chair swing to the far left. The patio continued around the corner on the right. Thomas found the key under the front door mat and opened the door and walked into the main room. It had a magnificent five feet by five feet open fireplace. Above the fireplace were a shield and two crossed swords. Taking up the majority of the room were two large sofas, a portion of a tree's trunk that had been treated and now had legs and played the role of a coffee table, an armchair, an end table, and a rifle lamp, "must have been a gift," thought Thomas. The Indian rug partially covered the hardwood floor. In the far left corner was a wooden bar and stools. To the right was a dining table and chairs and by the kitchen was a breakfast bar. Thomas walked towards the right of the bar and into a large room that had big windows and looked out a stunning view of the lake. There was a boathouse and a dock. The sofa and two recliners faced out towards the lake. There was a pool table at the back of the room and against the far wall was a rising staircase. To his left was the stereo system and to the right a big screen television. Thomas noticed that there were two doors leading out to a deck, he opened one and looked out. There was a barbecue, patio table and chairs, and a hot tub. The six steps were the length of the deck and took you down to a manicured garden. At the back of the garden were steps leading to the lake. Thomas closed the door and walked past the pool table to the hallway. The door on the left was a bathroom and the right was the laundry room. He walked further and opened the door on the left. It was a long room with two big bay windows. The double bed was against the wall on the right. There was an end table with a phone on it and a chest of drawers with a mirror. There was a television and a shelf stacked with books. He walked inside the room and opened the door on the left and looked at a full size bathroom. Behind two doors on the right was a closet. He walked to the windows looked out at the lake. He walked back and noticed the thick beige carpet. He closed the door and walked down the hallway. He stopped and opened the double doors on his left and looked into an incredible master bedroom. There was a four-poster king size bed, two end tables, a tallboy, and chest of drawers. The room was carpeted with a thick white carpet. Against the far wall were three, five foot mirrored doors behind which, Thomas assumed, was the closet. He walked in the room and opened the door to his left it was a stunning ceramic tiled en suite. There was a two-man tub, shower stall and a large mirror and two sinks. He looked out the window above the tub at the trees. He exited the room and continued down the hallway. He turned and walked into the door on his right. It was the same room as the first. He put his bags on the bed and took his laptop out and put it on the desk. There was no office and he thought that maybe Jack didn't work up here. He unpacked his bag and lay on the bed and looked at his watch and read ten o'clock. He picked up the phone and called Rebecca, "if she agrees to come, I'll call Jack and make sure its okay, besides he said I could bring a guest," The phone rang unanswered. He tried again thirty minutes later, and another thirty minutes, still no answer. He decided he would try later on and closed his eyes and slept for a couple of hours. He woke and spent the afternoon sitting on the deck looking out at the lake and thinking about Rebecca.

The sun was starting to set and Thomas was getting hungry, he decided to barbecue something while there was still daylight.

Jack's retired next-door neighbor Jim Smith had left a note in the kitchen. It told Thomas that he had stacked the refrigerator, freezer, cupboards, and the bar. That the fireplace was ready and all he had to do was light the newspaper. Jimmy had signed his name, left his phone number, and said to call him if he needed anything. Thomas read aloud, "PS I've left two T-bone steaks defrosting in the refrigerator, the barbecue is gas and just need to be turned on and lit." Thomas repeated. "Two? Maybe he's stopping by for dinner?" Thomas went onto the deck and lit the barbecue. He walked back into the main room and went behind the bar and pulled out a Heineken from the refrigerator. He put it on the bar and was looking for an opener. He hadn't noticed the figure standing in the doorway. He found one and opened the bottle.

"I knocked. You must have been outside. So I came in," she said.

He looked up. "Rebecca," he said softly.

She stood there, her small suitcase beside her. "I hope you don't mind me intruding. I called your house and spoke to Kate. Then I called Jack. Now I'm here. I had to see you."

"I called you, you weren't home," said Thomas.

"I was on my way here," replied Rebecca. "Why did you call?"

He walked from behind the bar and toward her. "I needed to talk to you," replied Thomas.

"Over the phone?" she asked cautiously.

He stopped in front of her. "I was going to ask you if you wanted to join me."

There was an uncomfortable silence.

"I've missed you," said Thomas.

Rebecca fought back the tears, "I've missed you!"

"I'm so sorry. Can you forgive me?" asked Thomas.

"Thomas, I should have been honest with you up front. You shouldn't have found out that way. I was wrong. It is me that should be asking to be forgiven?"

Thomas looked at her beautiful face. "I'm sorry."

"I'm sorry too," replied Rebecca. "I'm making you a promise right now, from this point on I will have no secrets and by the end of the night you will know everything."

"Okay," replied Thomas with a smile. He looked over at the lake. "This afternoon I sat and looked out on the lake and have done a lot of thinking. I really need to talk to you too." He looked into her eyes, "I've missed you."

"I've missed you!" The tears started to fall.

He reached over and held her in his arms. He loved the way she felt, the smell of her hair, her perfume. He could feel her soft skin on his cheek. He felt her tears and pulled his face away. He lifted her chin up and looked her in the eyes, "no more tears," he smiled and wiped them away.

"They're not tears of sadness," she said and gave him that radiant smile.

Thomas smiled back. "Good," replied Thomas.

"Let me put my bag and coat in the bedroom. I'll be back in a minute," she said.

"I'll be out on the deck," said Thomas.

"Okay," she replied and looked at his stitches, "I heard what happened." She reached up and gently kissed them, "kissing it better," she explained. She smiled, turned and walked away. He watched her walk down the hallway.

She came out on the deck wearing a pair of jeans and a thick beige sweater, and her hair up in a ponytail. She walked to the first step and sat down. Thomas grabbed the beers and gave her one and sat down on the fourth step and turned and looked up at her. The sun was setting on her face and the light breeze blew a few strands of her hair about. She looked gorgeous.

She looked down at Thomas. "What are you thinking about?"

"How beautiful you look?" Thomas replied.

She smiled. "Can we go for a walk?"

"Sure."

"What about the barbecue?"

"I can turn it off," he said as he stood.

They walked down the steps and onto the garden and Thomas listened as she spoke. "I need to be completely honest with you and as you know I haven't been so far, but there is more." She had a happy tone in her voice. "Your grandmother used to talk to our class about you all the time. It was Thomas did this and Thomas did that. She used to show photographs of you and your sister. When she instructed me alone I would always ask after you. She would talk about you and bring in photo albums and show me pictures. I even remember you coming in and picking her up. I guess I was young and had a crush on you," she stopped and collected her thoughts. "After your grandmother left and Penny took over, she used to talk to your grandmother frequently and Penny told me everything that happened, about your parent's death and you taking over as man of the house and taking care of your grandmother and your sister. I know that your parents had no life insurance and hadn't left you any money and how you took over your grandmother's mortgage. How you had to work and couldn't attend university and so on." She stopped and looked at him. "I never got to see any more pictures of you, I must have been sixteen, but throughout these last ten years I heard about you through Penny. Last year, by chance, I had heard that your grandmother was going to the ballet and specifically ones that I was performing in." She looked at Thomas. "Last May was no accident," she stopped as they walked down the steps to the beach area, and continued. "I wanted to see you and meet you. You already know this part of the story, I was so late that I never had time to change and ended up wearing jeans, that is when I caught you staring at me. I wanted to look so nice for you and here I am looking awful. I was horrified! I wanted to crawl under something and hide. When I saw you at your grandmother's funeral on the way home I concocted a plan and told Penny." They walked off the beach and onto the dock. "I asked Penny if you could present the award. I thought if you were presenting something on behalf of your grandmother you would certainly come. It almost backfired when Kate agreed to attend. Then for whatever reason Kate called Penny and told her she couldn't make it and that you would be presenting. I was so happy. I made sure you were at our table and sitting next to me. I had some anxious moments when you showed up late. I stood up to bring you to your seat but Eric called you to the podium. Then after the presentation you were standing there, I wanted to come up and bring you back to our table but I was nervous and scared. As it turns out stunning Rachel walks up with her sexy dress, fitted on a perfect body and she's all smiles as she escorts you back to the table and sits you in her absent father's seat. That night I'm outside and start thinking about everything. You've done the most wonderful thing, you let Penny present the award and she's so happy, I'm role-playing being Frank's girlfriend and he's happy, and you're laughing and dancing with Rachel and she's happy. I'm so miserable. Everything went wrong, nothing had gone to plan, and I started to cry. Then you appear." She stopped as they reached the end of the dock and they looked at the setting sun and its final rays making the water glisten. She looked at Thomas. "I have never sung for anyone since my father left, never. Many people have asked me, including Penny, but the pain was too deep. When you asked me, I did it because you wanted me to and I wanted to sing for you. That's the reason I picked that song. I wanted you to 'think of me'. From that point on I made one decision, I was going to take control of my life and be responsible for my own actions. What was it you said? 'You believe our life is in our own hands and we are in control of it'." She hesitated, "that night before I sang, I told Frank that the dinner party was the last time we would be role playing as a couple. After I sang, I came back and sat with you alongside Rachel because I wanted to be with you and for you to notice me. Later after we danced and you agreed to meet me the following day I was so happy. I wanted to tell you about Frank then but decided it was too soon. I know I've had many opportunities since then but convinced myself that after the dinner party it would be over anyway and nothing had actually happened, and once I told you that you would understand. Looking back I should have said something to you sooner. That night at the dinner party I had decided I wanted to tell you on Sunday morning and I talked to Frank and he agreed to be with me when I did. Unfortunately it was too late."

"Rebecca I…" started Thomas.

She put her finger on his lips. "Please, let me finish."

"Okay."

"After I sang I went into the stall in the bathroom and cried. I met Penny and I told her how I missed my father," she hesitated and looked into Thomas's eyes and softly brushed her hand on his cheek, "and that I loved you." She smiled at Thomas. "I love you, and I've loved you for a very long time. I know you so well. I know all there is to know about you. I love you." She removed her hand from his lips and he held it.

He looked into her eyes and softly said, "I love the way you wear your hair, your blue eyes, your soft skin, your radiant smile, your beautiful body and long legs. I love your sincerity and your sensitivity. I love the way you make me feel. I love the way you sing, the way you dance, the way you dress. The way you love old movies and the way we talk and laugh and dance. I love shopping with you, talking with you, and laughing with you. I love you completely," said Thomas. "I love you."

"And Rachel?" asked Rebecca.

"We're friends, good friends, nothing more."

"Oh Thomas, I love you so much!" exclaimed Rebecca.

They held each other tightly.

"I'm so sorry," said Rebecca.

"I'm so sorry I've kept us apart," said Thomas.

They looked into each other's eyes; their lips came together in a short, gentle kiss. Their love was unified. They separated, looked into each other's eyes, and then came together in a long, passionate kiss. They kissed till the sunset and the night stars appeared.

They held hands and walked back to the cabin.

"I have a secret too."

"You do?" asked Rebecca.

"You know my grandmother and Penny always spoke of you, so I know quite a lot about you. Penny used to bring pictures of you to show my grandmother and talk about how much you had grown." He stopped and looked at her. "That time we met in May I was staring at you because I thought you were the most beautiful person I had ever seen. I was hoping you were going to be at the fundraiser," revealed Thomas.

"Do you think your grandmother and Penny arranged this?" asked Rebecca.

"I wonder," said Thomas.

They walked onto the garden Thomas stopped and turned and looked at Rebecca, the light of the cabin was enough to make her eyes sparkle. He held her hand and spoke. "Rebecca, I'm not too sure how to say this any other way so I'll just ask," he hesitated.

"Ask," she said.

"What happens when we are together in public?" asked Thomas. "You being who you are and me being who I am?"

She moved closely to him. "Thomas I knew what you did before we ever met. If you stay in the same job till you die I will always be proud of you and love you. You are my love and you have qualities that no one will ever match. My love for you is stronger than anyone's words." She kissed him softly on the cheek. She looked into his eyes. "Thomas is there something else?"

"This afternoon I was out on the deck and looking out at the lake and I asked myself what I was doing here? And thought this is crazy."

"What is?"

"Rebecca, I'm socializing with people who have millions of dollars. They lend me their houses; I eat their food and spend their money. Take this weekend for example I got a ride up here in a Bentley, have this cabin, and there's bottles of Bollinger in the refrigerator. I drive to work in a beat up second hand car and work in a warehouse, come home to a sixteen hundred square foot house and work out my pennies," replied Thomas.

"And?" asked Rebecca.

"I'm in over my head. What happens when people move on?" asked Thomas.

"What?" Rebecca asked. "What do you mean?"

Thomas continued, "I'm always going to be me."

"I love you," said Rebecca.

Thomas smiled, "I like hearing that."

"Thomas, if Jack, Jessica or Rachel gave you a million dollars would you take it?"

"No."

"If you told them what you told me and they said, here take this million we want you to be comfortable around us and be one of us. Would you take it?"

"No."

"If you had an opportunity of making money from one of them would you?"

"No." replied Thomas.

"Why not?" Rebecca asked.

"Because I consider them my friends," replied Thomas.

"So by turning around what you are saying you think they are using you and they are really not your friends?" asked Rebecca.

"No. I don't know. I'm confused. I know they like me because of what I am, but what I am doesn't make me money."

"No Thomas it doesn't make you money it makes you friends and it makes you who you are," said Rebecca. "I know Jack has told you his life story. Did you know that Jessica's father sent her to public school and brought her up learning to respect people and value money, he had her working on the ground floor making minimal wage, and Jessica did the same with Rachel. Here's something else, Jack said that Jessica's father was one of the most respected businessmen. He ate lunch with his employees, played golf with them, and he even had picnics on his estate for them and their families. Jessica's father and Jack are new money. Do you know what that means Thomas? They weren't born into it they made it on their own. If you think they are not your friends then you are blind."

"I know they are."

"Then what is it?" asked Rebecca.

"I hate my job," said Thomas.

"That's it. All that to come to this," said Rebecca and laughed.

"You think that's funny," said Thomas smiling.

"I do," she laughed some more.

"Why?" Thomas asked.

"You are confused. If you don't like something and it makes you unhappy then quit!" stated Rebecca. "Do something that will make you happy."

"Rebecca I have a few hundred dollars in my account, I have Kate, her education, the mortgage and bills," said Thomas.

"Thomas why don't we go back to the house and get another couple of beers and put on the steaks and tell me what you've been up to and I can tell you what I've been up to. Then once we're all caught up lets talk about how we can help you out. Okay?"

"Okay," he replied. "It feels good to have someone to confide in." Thomas said and kissed her. "I love you."

"That's another reason why I love you because you tell me the way you feel." She kissed him back.

Thomas kissed her again and picked her up and laid her down on the grass.

They kissed.

They eventually made it to the deck and made dinner. During the meal Thomas talked about Rachel's birthday party, the Sunday afternoon at Rachel's guesthouse, playing golf with Jack and having dinner at his place, Kate's job, going out with Frank and his friends, the fight and Jessica being abused. He intentionally missed out Manhattan and the topics leading up to it because of the promise he made to Penny and Jack. Thomas felt very awkward about it though. He knew they had agreed to him telling Rebecca when warranted and that time was now but he wanted to hear how it went first.

"So 'Billy Idols' been busy?" asked Rebecca.

"Don't you start with that!" said Thomas.

"I wish I had seen you!"

"I wish you were there," he said and smiled. "I'll give you a personal performance."

"Promise?"

"Promise," replied Thomas. "So what have you been doing?"

"Well I cried a lot, rehearsed and exercised more than I should have, did some reading and read one piece in particular that was very exceptional. My father came from out of the blue and visited me. He spent the day and night with me before flying back to New York. We talked and cried a lot and we came to terms with everything that had happened. We're taking it slow but I'm glad we're together. I missed him a lot. Actually I went to New York last week and he's going to come back up in a few weeks." She looked up at Thomas. "If I would have known what had happened to you I would have flown back sooner."

"I know," said Thomas.

"Thank you," said Rebecca.

"For what?" Thomas asked.

"You know."

Thomas decided to change the subject. "What did you do in New York?"

She smiled slyly at him. "I'm glad you asked. While I was there my father had invited the members of the First Baptist Church of Harlem Choir for a tour of the Opera House and held a class on the stage with Rufus Jones. At the end of the class Rufus asked the kids how they liked the opera last Saturday night and the teenagers talked about how much they enjoyed it. Then one of the girls stands up and tells this amazing story of how they tried to sneak in, got caught and thrown out, and how a brother and sister named Thomas and Kate let them sit with them in their private box and how she had wished they were going to be here because she had a letter she wanted to give to him. My father said he would make sure that they got the letter and took it off her. My father then gave them opera tickets compliments of the Opera House. The same girl puts up her hand, I think her name was Katrina, and she said you mean compliments of Thomas and Kate don't you. My father looked over at me and I gave him an interested look. So he told them how Thomas Carlyle had asked him to present the tickets and set up a class with them. I thought to myself Thomas in New York and meeting my father. That's a coincidence or was it?" she asked.

"I took Kate there as a surprise. I told her about her job offer and took her shopping and to the Opera," said Thomas nervously. "The teenagers were so upset."

"And you met my father how?" she asked.

"Good question. It was actually by coincidence we bumped into each other at the hotel and I found out he was your father. One thing led to another and he agreed to give them the tickets, as a favor, nice man," said Thomas. "Another drink?"

"No thanks," she replied.

"I need one," he said and quickly stood up and walked inside to the bar and opened a beer. Rebecca followed him in.

"You met him on what day and gave him the tickets when and where?" she inquired.

"I think Monday. Yes Monday."

"It was just a coincidence that he flew out on the Sunday to see me and bumped into you on the Monday," she said.

"Yes it was, he actually said that he'd just got back from seeing you," said Thomas.

"Thomas! Tell me the whole story." She walked closer to him and Thomas walked backward till his back was up against the wall. "I love you," she said and kissed him. "Now tell me!"

"Okay, okay, No more torture," he teased.

"Torture is it," she kissed him again and again and again.

"I'll tell you, I'll tell you," he said, "let's go back outside and sit on the steps."

He told her everything.

"Did you really see my father at your grandmother's?" she asked.

"Yes. I recognized him in the picture of you and him."

"Did you hear him talking to them that night?" she asked.

"He told Penny and my grandmother that night at my house," said Thomas.

"Then you heard him?" she asked.

"After your father left, I went into the living room and my grandmother said to me that your father was in a bad situation. From what Penny and my grandmother had said and a few words I had picked up that night while they were talking I made an assumption and told him that I overheard him that night. So to answer your question, no I didn't hear him. I had headphones on and was listening to music. I would never eavesdrop on my grandmother. When I told Penny about my assumption she laughed because I was actually right."

"I see," said Rebecca.

"Rebecca, Penny did tell me that you said you missed your father. She conveniently missed out the part about how you were in love with me; it must have slipped her mind." He looked over at her.

"Must have," she replied.

"Rebecca, the reason I did what I did was for you and because I love you. I would do anything for you."

"Thomas you have made me so happy." She kissed him.

"We will have to tell Jack and Penny that you know," said Thomas.

"We will. I'm your date for dinner am I not?" asked Rebecca.

"Dinner?" asked Thomas.

"Dinner at Penny's? Friday?" she asked.

"I had forgotten. I'm going with someone," said Thomas in a serious voice.

"You are," said Rebecca sadly.

Thomas laughed.

"Why you," she stood in front of him and pushed him on the deck. He pulled her on top of him. They kissed. She was very happy. She had the man she loved and her father.

She stopped kissing him and looked into his eyes. "Thomas," she whispered, "Tell me what do you want?"

"If I had a choice?" he asked.

"If you had a choice and no financial worries?" she asked. "I know I've asked you this before I just want to hear it again."

"I would be a writer, I enjoy writing so much," he replied. "You know the enjoyment and excitement you feel when you dance, that's how I feel when I write."

She rolled off and looked at him, with her one hand resting on his chest and the other holding up her head and spoke gently. "When your sister is working full time can't you leave your job and write? I'm sure she would want to do that for you?"

"She's already offered," revealed Thomas. "But she wont be full time for at least another eight months," he replied. "I don't think I'll last that long."

"I have almost eighty thousand dollars in a savings account you can have that!" said Rebecca. "In fact I want you to have it!"

"I couldn't take your money," he said.

"Why not?" she asked.

"It's your money, and Kate wouldn't be comfortable with the idea either," said Thomas.

"Ask Jack for an interest free loan?"

"It's called a handout!" said Thomas.

She corrected him. "It's called a hand up."

"I couldn't face looking at Jack knowing I owed him money, besides, I would rather borrow from you," he said.

"You wouldn't have to."

"I know," replied Thomas.

"Thomas let me help you," she pleaded. "If it were up to me you could have the money. I want to help you. I want you to be happy."

"I know you do and I appreciate it but I don't feel comfortable."

"What about this?" Rebecca asked as she sat up excitedly. "If you like I'll be your business partner and I'll invest eighty thousand dollars in you. I'll send your work off to publishers and you write," she said proud of herself.

Thomas thought. "Can we put something in writing, like a business contract that indicated it was your money and that the money we made went to paying off the loan and anything over would be split equally."

She looked at Thomas. "If you want."

"Maybe we can register as a company and write something up legally."

"Thomas, whatever you want."

Thomas smiled. "Okay." He hugged her. "Thank you."

She kissed him. "So what are you going to do?"

"I'll go in on Monday and quit," he confirmed and smiled. "I'll have to sit down with you and go through our monthly payments."

"Okay," she replied.

"And you should come to the house and you should meet Kate. You haven't met her yet," Thomas realized. "Kate! I'll have to tell her."

"You should," replied Rebecca.

"We should," confirmed Thomas.

"We should." She smiled. "I'm so happy for you!" she said and lied down and put her head on his chest.

He put his arm around her, "I'm happy too. I guess I'll have to let you read my novel?"

"I already have!" she exclaimed.

"What? How?"

"That exceptional piece of work was yours. You left it with the doorman that Sunday and he gave it to me. I think you told him to throw it out but he's a friend of mine and kept it and gave it to me," she said.

"What did you think?" asked Thomas.

"I loved it. I read it three times and cried each time," replied Rebecca and looked up at Thomas. "We should send it off to a publisher this week."

He agreed. "I'll have to put together a sample package because they won't accept an unsolicited manuscript."

"We should look into it," confirmed Rebecca. "Maybe Kate will help us put together a business contract. We could put together a rough outline and show it to her."

He smiled at her. "I love you."

"I love you. Tomorrow night why don't we celebrate? I'll cook dinner."

"That sounds wonderful," said Thomas.

They kissed and went inside.

"TONIGHT IS MUSICAL NIGHT, FIRST 'GIGI', THEN 'Seven Brides for Seven Brothers', 'West Side Story', and 'Singin' in the Rain'. But before I press play let me go put my pajamas on."

He watched her happily dance out of the room.

They lay together on the sofa and watched the first two; Rebecca fell asleep at the beginning of 'West Side Story'. Thomas carried her to her bed. He locked all the doors and turned off all the lights and went to his bed. He slept soundly for the first time in what seemed like a lifetime.

In the morning he was woken by the sound of a knock at the bedroom door.

"Can I come in?" asked Rebecca.

"Come in," replied Thomas.

Rebecca walked in with a breakfast tray and placed it on the bed, "good morning," she said and kissed him. "I fell asleep on you again."

Thomas nodded. "I don't mind. I was tired too. What do we have here?"

"We have Kellogg's Corn Flakes, bagel and cream cheese, tea and orange juice. You sit up and I'll put the tray on top of you. Let me move these drinks onto the table and I'll lie next to you and put my cereal on the bed."

Thomas watched her.

"What should we do today?" she asked.

"I don't know. What time do you want to have dinner?" he asked.

"Seven"

"To prepare?"

"Start at five thirty," she replied. She thought for a moment. "Let's go for a picnic."

"A picnic, perfect," agreed Thomas.

They ate breakfast and got ready and met in the kitchen. They picked out cheese, cold cuts, fruit, yogurt, cookies, bread and crackers and put them on the counter. "What are we going to put this in?" asked Rebecca.

"I know," said Thomas and walked down the hallway. He came back with a wicker picnic basket. "I saw it yesterday in the laundry room."

"It doesn't look like it's been used. Let me open it up," said Rebecca. "It has all the plates, cutlery, cups and napkins. I know what we're missing," she said as she walked over to the bar.

Thomas filled the basket.

"A bottle of red wine," said Rebecca and placed it in the designated spot and closed the basket, "done."

They drove in Rebecca's BMW and stopped off at small towns along the way and looked in the antique shops, bookshops and craft shops. They pulled into the state park and drove to a secluded spot. Rebecca spread out a blanket under a large tree and sat down and took off her shoes and put them next to her handbag. She lay down and watched Thomas carrying the picnic basket. "I like you in jeans," she said.

Thomas looked at her brown hair blowing in the breeze; she looked so beautiful and sexy. He put the picnic basket down on the blanket and walked back to the car.

"There's a portable CD player in the trunk and some CD's bring those back," she said.

Thomas closed the trunk and placed them on the blanket next to her and lay down. She turned and looked at him and they kissed for a long period of time.

"Will you dance for me again," he asked.

"Okay," she said and sat up and placed a CD in the player. "Let me get in place first and then put on the music," she looked around the grass and made sure it was clear of obstacles. She took off her socks and sweater and threw them to Thomas. She got in position and said to him, "Okay play the music."

In her jeans and t-shirt she danced gracefully to Tchaikovsky's 'Swan Lake'. Thomas was hypnotized. After she finished she curtsied. Thomas clapped and went up to her and offered her a dandelion, which she graciously accepted with a bow of the head.

"I love watching you dance," said Thomas. "You dance like an angel."

"Thomas, come around me here," said Rebecca positioning Thomas behind her, "I will turn my body clockwise and when I slow down to stop, you stop me by holding my waist, the trick is that I need to be facing the audience. Mr. Blanket and Ms. Basket are the audience."

Thomas tried and finally got it right on the fifth time. On the sixth he stopped her facing him on purpose and kissed her. She wrapped her legs around him and he carried her to the blanket were he lay down on top of her. They kissed passionately. Thomas's hand went slowly up and down the side of her body. He stopped kissing her and smiled.

"Thomas, I have something for you," said Rebecca. She turned off the music reached into her handbag and pulled out a paperback.

Thomas rolled off of her and looked at the paperback and read it out loud, "'100 Best-Loved Poems' edited by 'Philip Smith'." He gave her a kiss on the lips. "Thank you."

"I picked it up at the last book store," said Rebecca, "there's an inscription inside."

Thomas turned to the front page:

"Thomas,
With all my love,"
Rebecca.

"Read something for me?" she asked.

"Okay," replied Thomas as he sat up.

He reviewed the table of contents as Rebecca put on her sweater and socks and lay close to him.

He read Lord Byron's, 'She Walks in Beauty'. He knew the poem well and looked over at her as he read. When he finished he said, "That's you."

She smiled. "Please, read some more?"

Thomas read several.

She pulled him on top and kissed him, then pulled and asked, "Thomas will you read some of your novel to me one day?"

"If you would like me to?"

"I would!"

"I will."

She looked into his eyes and whispered, "I love you. I love you with all my heart and soul." She kissed him in the beautiful sunshine, with the leaves rustling and the breeze blowing. It was as if they were the only two people in the world.

"THOMAS PUT ON SOME MUSIC, THE CD's are next to the stereo, and open a bottle of champagne," said Rebecca's voice from her bedroom.

Thomas poured two glasses and placed them on the tree-trunk coffee table. He lit the fireplace and put on a CD. He sat down on the sofa and looked at the glowing fire.

She walked in the room wearing her hair in a French braid and the dress that Thomas had picked out. She walked up to Thomas, "Do you still like it?"

"Stunning! You look absolutely beautiful!" exclaimed Thomas, as he looked her over. "Dance with me?" he asked.

They danced to, 'You're the Best Thing."

"I love this song," said Rebecca.

"Me too," replied Thomas.

"I think this is our song," they said at the same time and laughed and kissed.

The next song came on and while they danced Thomas looked at her and asked. "Did you go back and get this dress for me?"

"Go back?" asked Rebecca confused.

"You were wearing the pantsuit?"

She looked at Thomas. "The night I went to the dinner party with Frank I wore the suit?"

"You didn't buy the dress…" Thomas was cut off.

"Thomas, did you think I only bought the pantsuit?" She could tell by his look that he did. "Thomas I bought the pantsuit for that night and the dress for when we I went out with you. This is the first chance I've had to wear it."

"That's why Janet asked me if I liked the dress," said Thomas.

"Yes, and I bought the underwear too," she said with a teasing smile. "They're pure white. I'm wearing them as we speak."

An image of Rebecca in her white thong ran through Thomas's mind.

"Thomas when you saw me that Sunday morning in the pantsuit and not the dress you must have thought I was horrible?" she asked.

"I did. I have been a fool," he concluded, "such a fool."

She held him tightly and they danced.

"Would you rather eat in front of the fire?" whispered Thomas.

"That would be romantic. Let me move the cutlery and napkins over," she suggested and started away.

"No, you sit down and have some champagne. I'll move them."

She sat down and picked up the glass of champagne and watched him walk there and back. Thomas put the items on the coffee table and looked at her.

"What are you thinking about?" he asked as he sat down.

"Nothing. I was just watching you," she replied and smiled.

"A toast," said Thomas, "to the most beautiful girl in the world."

"To the handsomest man in the world."

They touched their glasses and took a sip.

"Dinner is warming in the oven, we can have it whenever we are ready," she said.

"Let's wait a while," said Thomas. "I'm enjoying this."

"Me too." She hesitated and spoke, "Thomas I've never been in a serious relationship before? I mean I've had boyfriends." She gave a nervous look. "I've never been in love before. I love you, I know it, I feel it in my heart and in my soul and I want to give you all of me in here," she put her hand on her chest. She continued slowly, "and all of me." She looked into Thomas's eyes. "I want to make love to you, but…." she hesitated, "Thomas, in this day and age this is going to sound very old fashioned but I made a promise to myself that I would wait till I was married to give myself to the man I am going to spend my life with, to you. But being around you isn't making it easy for me to keep that promise and I feel that one day I may break it. But until that day I don't want you to think I don't love you."

Thomas looked at her and took her hand. "I will never think that. I love you and I want you to keep that promise. You're worth the wait and if a time comes for us to break it, then…"

Her face illuminated. "Oh Thomas!"

He held her and they kissed.

They ate dinner in front of the crackling fire, drank champagne, slow danced and talked all night. They were as happy as any couple in love could be. The fire had turned to hot ash by the time they stood to go to bed. Thomas locked the door, turned off the light and walked with her down the hallway. Outside her bedroom door she turned and kissed him, "I'll see you in the morning my love."

"The morning."

Thomas closed the door and went into the bathroom and brushed his teeth. He looked at his stitches, the swelling had gone down and there was a light shade of yellow around the area. His hands and body still had the signs of bruising but the stiffness was completely gone. He thought about Rebecca's body and imagined her undressing. He wondered what she looked like in her underwear and in the nude. He closed the bathroom door and undressed. He wanted to make love to her but she was worth waiting an eternity for.

The next morning Thomas woke up and got dressed and went into the kitchen and cleaned up. He made some coffee and heard Rebecca's bath being run. He went to her door and called in. "Can I bring you something?"

"No, I'll be out in fifteen minutes."

As he left he could hear her singing 'You're the Best Thing' and smiled. He walked to the kitchen and poured some coffee and went out on the deck and decided to the walk to the end. He thought about her leaving tomorrow and being at the cabin alone. In one way he would be able to concentrate on finishing his second novel, on the other hand he would not see her. Everything was happening so fast. He wondered how often she wanted to see him.

"Good Morning," she said and kissed him. "You're deep in thought!"

"Good morning. Sleep well?" he asked.

"Somewhat restless," she replied.

"Same."

"So, what were you thinking about?" she asked.

"Us."

"Really. Good or bad?"

"You're leaving tomorrow," he stated.

"Yes."

Thomas looked out at the water. It was a cool day and the sky was cloudy.

"Thomas, are you worried about what happens next?" she asked, and looked into his eyes.

"I'm not worried, a little unsure."

"I'm the same."

"I need to tell Kate what's going on."

"I know."

"I would like us both to be there."

"We should."

"Rebecca it's important to me that you two get to know one another."

"Thomas, I want to get to know her and spend some time with her and become friends. What should we do?" she asked.

"I want her to know how we feel about each other and what our plans are."

"What are our plans?" she asked.

"That's what I was just thinking about. Everything is happening so fast," he replied.

"Too fast?" she asked.

"No. I'm just not sure about what's next," he replied and put his arm around her. They both looked out.

"Thomas I know I have to leave tomorrow and in my heart I know I love you and you love me and that I'll be seeing you on Friday night. I know I will be dancing on air all week." She turned and looked at him, "but when I come home at night you won't be there and I'll be alone and I will miss you. I'm trying not to be selfish."

"Be selfish for a minute and tell me."

Rebecca smiled. "I would want you to come home with me tomorrow and stay at my place for the week. You could write during the day when I'm out. We could have dinner together. Maybe you could meet me for lunch sometimes. And when you need to work at night you tell me. I would leave you alone. Maybe you could arrange to write when I'm at my workout classes. Free nights we could watch television or go to a movie or for a swim."

"What happens after the week?" asked Thomas.

"I don't know. Can we take it a week at a time? All I want to do is be with you! If I had it my way I would have you there forever."

"I want to be with you too." He looked and drowned in her deep blue eyes. "I'll leave with you tomorrow," he said.

"Really!" She kissed him and smiled.

He smiled back at her. "When do you want to tell Penny and Jack?"

"Friday night. Penny will know before then. She knows I'm up here this weekend and when she sees how happy I am on Monday she'll have an idea what went on and she'll tell Jack. We'll confirm it with them Friday," said Rebecca. "What about Rachel?"

Thomas had completely forgotten about Rachel. This weekend she was finding out the truth about her father and he wondered how she would take it and how they were doing. "You know I had forgotten about her. Rachel was going to find out this weekend about her father and I was going to give her a call in the middle of the week to see how they were doing. They probably need some time together. You've reminded me, this Saturday I promised to go out with Rachel to a bar to see a group playing."

"On a date?" asked Rebecca.

"That came out wrong. Rachel and Mathew, Veronica and Buddy, are going. Rachel asked Kate and me to go. I was going to ask Frank to go as well." He looked at Rebecca, "I wasn't sure about us." He smiled and asked, "Would you like to go with me on Saturday? You would make me the happiest and most envied man in the world?"

She put her arms around him and kissed him, "I would love to."

They kissed.

"I'll ask Frank tomorrow."

"I need to talk to Rachel about us but I would like you to be there?" asked Thomas.

"I will," she replied. "She's another person I need to talk to. She tried her best to be my friend and I've been avoiding her, especially these last few weeks. I've acted like she was the plague. I think I was jealous of her spending so much time with you. I thought you might have liked her."

"Rebecca, we're just friends and Rachel wants to be your friend too, that's why she asked you to go to France with her."

"I know," replied Rebecca. She looked into his eyes. "Thomas, where have you always wanted to visit?" she asked.

"Nice, France, replied Thomas."

"Your grandmother and Penny used to tell me how you always wanted to go there and how you said that one day when you had the money you would. That's where Rachel was going. After I saw you at the funeral I told you how I planned with Penny to have you come to the fundraiser. I also dreamed that if everything worked out between us that one day we would go to Nice together. That's why I didn't want to go with Rachel. I couldn't tell her the real reason or about you. Is that crazy? It's crazy. I'm crazy. I sound like a stalker."

"You're not a stalker," said Thomas and comforted her. "Crazy? Yes!"

"Why you," said Rebecca and hit him on the arm.

Thomas smiled. "Why don't we leave here this afternoon and go to my house and have dinner, compliments of Kate's cooking, we can talk to her and bring her up to speed on everything that has happened. We can ask her about the business contract and get some advice. If you want you can stay the night and that way you get to spend some time with Kate and see where I live and where I write. Then tomorrow morning we'll go to your place where I will stay for the rest of the week.

"What about Rachel?"

"Tuesday or Wednesday we can see Rachel, Friday, Penny and Jack and Saturday we'll all go out and see Atlas. How does that sound?"

"I love it. I love you."

"Love you."

"Let's get some breakfast and we can call Kate and Jack," said Rebecca.

They started back to the cabin. Rebecca suddenly stopped.

"Did you say the group was Atlas?" asked Rebecca.

"Yes."

"My friend's boyfriend plays in that band," said Rebecca.

"Are you sure? This is the same group that played Rachel's birthday," confirmed Thomas.

"I know! I helped them get the show."

"Really!

"Tracy used to go to ballet school with me and we're old friends. She was a talented ballerina and we were in the same troupe but she quit. She wanted to spend more time with her boyfriend, apparently the band toured a lot and she didn't get to see him, so she left so she could be with him. He told her to keep on dancing but she didn't listen to him."

"She quit?" asked Thomas.

"She said she loved him and he loved her. She told me he didn't want her to give up her dream. She said she was unhappy and had other dreams."

"What did you think?"

"At the time I told her she was insane and that one day he could leave her and she would have nothing. She told me I was so wrapped up in my ballet and my life that I couldn't really understand how she felt and to talk to her about it again when I was in love." Rebecca thought for moment. "I guess she was right."

"So you still talk to her?" asked Thomas.

"Yes, she calls when she's in town. They've been on tour for a year so I hadn't talked to her in a while. When I heard she was back I called and told her about the party and that Rachel wanted to have a band. She was hoping I would be there, she said she had some good news. I told her I had a dinner party and couldn't make it and we would get together soon. It will be good to see her again and find out what she's been up to," said Rebecca. "Was the band good?"

"They were great."

"I'm glad. I always hoped she was doing well and things worked out for her."

"I'm sure they are." Thomas said and left it at that.

They went to the cabin and had breakfast and made the phone calls. They cleaned up the cabin and packed up the car.

Outside the cabin Rebecca walked over to Thomas and kissed him, "I'm so in love with you."

He smiled and kissed her back, "I love you."

They got in the car and drove down the dirt road.

"How's your dancing going?" asked Thomas.

"Good. I'll be busy over the next couple of weeks. Did I tell you my father is coming to my opening night?"

"You said he was coming to see you in a couple of weeks, that's wonderful that he'll be there."

"He'll be sitting next to you." She looked over at him. "He asked if he could, he really likes you and Kate," stated Rebecca. "Make sure I don't forget to give you the letters. They're actually addressed to you and Kate so I'll wait till we get to your house and you can both read them, I'm sure she would like to read them with you."

At noon they stopped at a small turn of the century church and went to mass. They had lunch in a quaint country inn and drove a long, scenic route back to Thomas's house. They talked and laughed all the way. It was as if they had known each other all their lives and in a sense, they had.

CHAPTER 12

Marquise

THEY STOOD OUTSIDE THOMAS'S FRONT DOOR. REBECCA was nervous. "What happens if she doesn't like me?" asked Rebecca.

"She will, be your self. On second thought," said Thomas and smiled.

Rebecca smiled back. "I'll get you for that." She squeezed his hand.

They walked through the door. Kate wasn't in the kitchen or the living room. Thomas called her.

"I'm up here I'll be down in a minute," she answered.

"Let's have a seat in the living room," said Thomas.

Rebecca walked into the small room. "This is just as I had imagined it, I can picture your grandmother and Penny sitting here and gossiping." She sat down on the sofa.

"I'll make some tea," said Thomas and went into the kitchen.

Thomas could see Rebecca stand up and walk over to the several pictures displayed in a wall unit. She looked at the one of Thomas and Kate, another of Thomas, Kate and their grandmother, another one of Thomas, Kate and their parents, one of their grandmother and Penny, and pictures of people whom Rebecca didn't know.

"Hello. You must be Rebecca?" asked Kate.

"Hello Kate. I am, nice to meet you."

"That one of me and Thomas was taken at a fashion show he took me to," said Kate politely.

"Is that the time he tripped onto the girl's lap?" asked Rebecca.

"Yes it was," replied Kate laughing. "How did you know?"

"He met that girl by accident in town, her name's Janet and she works at a store I shop at and she recognized him."

"You know what's really funny is that I tripped him on purpose!"

"Really? On purpose?" asked Rebecca.

"Of course! He's always embarrassing me in public and playing practical jokes. So it was payback."

"I know what you mean," confirmed Rebecca. "Thomas tripping onto Janet's lap, I would have liked to have seen that."

"I see you two have met," said Thomas as he walked in with two cups of tea.

"Yes, we've been talking about your next trip at the fashion show," replied Kate.

"I realize now would be a good time to start bribing Kate to stop her from telling too much," said Thomas. He put the two cups down, "this one is Rebecca's and this one is Kate's. I'll be back in a minute."

They both sat down.

"I heard you start work tomorrow?"

"Yes. I went in on Saturday afternoon and met some people. Barry's great, in fact they all are. I'm going in Monday morning for a few hours." She picked up her tea. "You're a ballet dancer?"

"Yes."

"Is it as demanding and disciplined as they say it is?" asked Kate.

"More so, but when you enjoy what you do, it's not. You going to law school and now working, that must be a challenge?"

"It will be. It'll take up most of my free time but I love it and I wouldn't give it up for the world."

Thomas sat down next to Rebecca and opposite Kate. Kate leaned over and looked at Thomas. "Your eye looks better. When do you need to see the doctor?"

"Next week. I need to make an appointment," he replied. Thomas looked at Rebecca and smiled and looked at Kate. "Kate how long will dinner be?"

She looked at her watch, "the roast beef won't be ready for another hour, and I still need to make the mashed potatoes. Is that okay? You're here earlier than I thought," she confessed.

"That's fine. I, we, need to talk to you. That's why we're early."

Kate sipped on her tea and listened for thirty minutes as Thomas and Rebecca explained both side of their stories and told her they were in love. When they finished Kate looked back and forth at them both, her eyes stopped on Thomas. "Have you felt this way all this time?" she asked.

"Yes."

"I thought so!" She looked at them both and leaned over and gave Thomas a kiss on the cheek, then Rebecca. "I'm so happy for you both," she said and smiled. Her eyes watered. It was good to see her brother so happy.

"Kate there is something else you need to know," said Thomas.

"You sound serious Thomas?" asked Kate.

"I don't mean to, I'm just anxious," replied Thomas. "I'm quitting work on Monday."

"What!" exclaimed Kate.

"Let me explain. Over the last few months I've started to hate my job, I wake up and go into work unhappy. You're almost finished school and you have a job lined up. I know you said you would help me out once you started working full time job but I can't wait any longer," explained Thomas. "I want to write full time."

"How will we? I?" mumbled Kate.

"Kate, Rebecca and I are going to start a company. Rebecca is going into a partnership with me and she's going to invest eighty thousand dollars. That will pay for all our on going expenses. We still need to work out the details and figure out what that means but we thought we could do that tonight. The money you make from work is all yours and if you run short we will help you out," Thomas could see that Kate was upset and stopped talking.

"Thomas I wanted to help you!" stated Kate. "You said I could."

"Kate, how can you help me out today?"

Kate was getting more upset. "I can't."

"Would you rather me wait?" asked Thomas. "I would if you want me to."

"Of course not!" said Kate she started to cry.

"Kate the money is a business investment. Once Thomas starts making some income, we're planning on paying it off. If you like you can help us with that when you start working full time," suggested Rebecca.

"I need to put on the potatoes," Kate stood up and walked out the room and into the kitchen. They could hear her crying.

"I should go talk to her," said Thomas starting to get up.

Rebecca held him down. "Let me go." Rebecca stood and went into the kitchen. Thomas could hear them.

"Kate, I don't want you to be upset. I want us to be friends and get along. I offered the money to Thomas, no loan, and no contract. He said no. He wouldn't take it unless we started a business. You know him better than I do and how proud he is. He's been so worried about how you would react. He cares about you a great deal. Maybe we should have all talked about it together and come to a decision rather than us telling you what we had decided. I guess we got carried away. All I want is for Thomas to be happy. I know you want that too." She waited a moment. "You've read his novel. What did you think?"

"I loved it. I told him to send it out to publishers but he wouldn't," replied Kate.

"Kate before he can move forward with this he needs to have your blessing," stated Rebecca.

"I want him to be happy. He's done so much for me and I wanted to help him out," said Kate.

"Why don't we go back in the room and talk about it and come up with a suggestion that we all agree on?" asked Rebecca.

"Okay," replied Kate.

They walked into the room and Thomas stood. Kate walked into his arms. "I can't believe I'm acting this way. You have the opportunity to write full time. Someone who is going to help you out financially and support you and believes in you, and all I think about is, me. After all you've done for me. I should be happy for you and supporting you and telling you to go for it." Kate cried, "I'm worried I'm losing you."

Rebecca whispered to Thomas, "I'll make some tea," and picked up the cups and went into the kitchen.

"I'll always be here. You will never lose me," said Thomas as he held Kate closely.

"I'm sorry Thomas I want you to be happy. I'm actually surprised you lasted this long in that job; you have so much more potential. You should do what you've planned. I want you to. You are an excellent writer," said Kate as she pulled away from Thomas. "She seems great."

"Rebecca said we should all talk about it and come up with an arrangement we all accept. She's right we should have done that at the offset," said Thomas.

Rebecca came in the room with the three cups of tea and sugar and milk on a tray. Thomas and Kate stared at her.

She noticed them staring. "What's wrong?" she asked.

Thomas helped her with the tray and put it on the coffee table. "My grandmother used that tray all the time, neither myself or Kate has used it since she died."

"Oh, I'm so sorry!" exclaimed Rebecca.

"Don't worry about it," said Kate and smiled. "We should have never stopped using it, my grandmother would have wanted us to; it has some fond memories. I'm glad you did."

"Let me serve," offered Rebecca feeling a little better. She added the milk and sugar and passed around the cups. "What should we do?" she asked.

Thomas answered, "I think I should write, Rebecca takes care of the publishers, and Kate should be our lawyer."

"Really?" asked Kate.

"We were going to ask you to set up the contract for us," replied Rebecca.

"The only question is the finances?" asked Thomas.

"You've always taken care of them and its Rebecca's investment," said Kate.

"Then Rebecca and I will do the finances and the last day of each month we all meet and review them," said Thomas.

"Is that okay?" asked Rebecca.

"That's okay with me," said Kate.

"Kate, can you put together a contract that we can all review and sign?

"I can!" replied Kate.

"Rebecca researches publishers and sends my first novel out."

"Will do!"

"And I will finish my second novel."

"Are there any other plans for the company?" asked Kate.

"Well, I thought we should concentrate on getting my work published first. Then we could look at helping other local writers. Maybe set up a web site and sell them online as E-books. I think we have lots of options but first things first."

"What should I put in the contract?" asked Kate.

"That we three are owners of company 'X'. That all profits will first go to pay back the eighty thousand and anything above and beyond with be split. Fifty per cent for Rebecca and twenty-five each for Kate, and me" answered Thomas.

"Wait a minute. I'm not going for that," replied Rebecca, "fifty for you and twenty five for me and Kate."

"Twenty five is too much for me," replied Kate.

"Okay, okay," said Thomas, "twenty-five percent each and twenty-five percent back in the company. Agreed?"

"Agreed," they both replied.

"You'll need to name the company and register it," explained Kate.

"Why don't we think about it and let's say…" Rebecca looked at the clock, "…at ten o'clock we put forward our ideas and vote on the best one."

They all agreed.

Kate stood up. "I need to put on the vegetables."

"Can I help?" asked Rebecca.

"You sit here and take it easy," replied Kate.

"I would like to help," said Rebecca.

"I could use a hand," smiled Kate.

They went into the kitchen and Thomas was left alone and said, "I guess I'll watch some television." He turned on the television. From the kitchen he could hear them talking and laughing. Thomas was happy they were getting along.

"That was delicious," said Thomas.

"It was," agreed Rebecca. "Kate how did you like New York?" she asked.

Kate looked at Thomas.

"She knows," confirmed Thomas.

Kate smiled. "I had a wonderful time there. The hotel was beautiful and the shopping was magnificent. I loved the Opera; your father is an amazing singer."

"Did you know Kate sings quite well too?" asked Thomas as he looked at Rebecca.

"I didn't know," replied Rebecca.

"He's teasing you. Let me tell you what kind of person you're in love with," said Kate. She told her every detail.

Rebecca laughed, "You sang 'Last Name' to my father."

Thomas joined in with Rebecca and laughed.

"I'm glad you two find it so funny," said Kate smiling. "So here we are leaving and guess whose picture they are putting on the wall next to your father's? Mine!"

Thomas interrupted. "I told the hotel manager that she was a famous singer and dancer on Broadway. I secretly signed her name on the picture and they put it on the wall next to your father's."

They all laughed.

"The letters! Let me go and get them," remembered Rebecca. She went to the hall and looked in her bag. She came back with three. "Who wants to read them?"

"Thomas can," said Kate.

Thomas took the envelopes and opened one. It was a card and read:

Dear Thomas and Kate,

Thank you for letting us in to see Otello. We are all grateful for your kind generosity. We've put one of the programs and our tickets in our display case in the church hall where we practice so that we will always have one good copy. We leave the others out so that people can read them. We put a thank you note next to them with both your names. I have enclosed a picture so you can see what I'm talking about. I have also included a picture of the five of us. When you are back in New York City I hope you will come visit us and see us practice. Please write and send us a picture of you and Kate. Maybe one day we can come and visit you. Your friends, Katrina, Shawna, Bobby, Ethan, Michigan.

They looked at the pictures.

"We'll put these in the wall unit," said Kate.

Thomas opened the next envelope.

Dear Thomas and Kate,

We have just come back from buying this card with Rebecca. I knew she was going to see you shortly and we wanted to thank you both again. Henri La Croix spent the afternoon showing us around the Opera House and later on Rufus Jones joined us and we spent an hour practicing on the stage with him and Mr. La Croix. We were all very excited and nervous. They have agreed to set up a class one Sunday a month and someone from the company will take us through a practice.

At the end of the day Mr. La Croix gave us our surprise. We cried when we found out we had been given tickets to see an opera a month. Mr. La Croix had tried to say it was the company but I spoke up, we all know it was you and Kate that set up the meeting and got us the tickets. Mr. La Croix explained to us that you wanted to remain anonymous. I asked why because you were our friend. Rebecca explained the whole story. We like her a lot too. Rebecca bought a Polaroid camera and took some pictures of us and we have included them. We are in our Sunday best. We will write to you often. Thank you, Katrina, Shawna, Bobby, Ethan, Michigan.

They looked at the five smiling faces. The girls were wearing dresses and the boys were in dress pants, shirt and ties. There were other pictures with Rufus and Henri and one with their teacher and one with the Rebecca. The last one was with all of them.

Thomas opened the final envelope it was a note:

Dear Thomas and Kate,

My name is Ms. Lydia Brown and I teach the children their lessons. I wanted to send you a short note and thank you for your generosity. Unfortunately it's so much easier for these children to get mixed up with gangs, drugs, violence and the wrong side of the law. Your kind gesture has given them an inspiration to aspire above all that. I can see the difference in their faces, in the way they talk and when they sing.

Myself, and the piano player Leroy 'Lenny' Johnson will be chaperoning the children to the shows. We have one ticket over so each month we will be treating a mother of one of the children to a show. I hope one day we will meet so that I can thank you in person. You are always welcome to visit and look forward to meeting you. Rebecca was wonderful with the children. The children took a picture of me and Lenny and I have included it. God bless, Lydia Brown.

They looked at the picture.

"That was thoughtful," said Thomas

"It was," added Kate.

"You should have seen the look on their faces," added Rebecca.

"Here," said Kate taking the pictures, letters, and envelopes, "I'll put them over here," and placed them in the wall unit. "There," she said and left and went into the kitchen.

Thomas stood up and put his arms around Rebecca and gave her a kiss. "So what did you tell them?"

"That you thought I was in love with someone else and how much I loved you," she replied and kissed him.

From the corner of his eyes Thomas saw Kate walking in and walking out. He shouted after her and she walked back in.

"Kate, you and Rebecca sit down and have a chat. I'll clean up," ordered Thomas. He pushed them onto the sofa. "Why don't you show her around? Rebecca is sleeping in my room tonight." He looked over at Rebecca. "You can drop your bag in there."

Kate gave Thomas a surprised look.

"Yes you heard me right Kate. She's sleeping in my room tonight. Better put on some earplugs because we are going to be doing the dirty dance all night long. You know what I mean?" As Thomas said this he thrust his pelvis forward and made it into somewhat of a dance. "Do you have a problem with that?" He emphasized the word 'that' with a big thrust.

They both looked at each other and laughed.

"Do you really know what you are getting yourself into?" asked Kate.

"I'm starting to wonder," replied Rebecca. She watched Thomas as he walked away and accentuated his wiggle.

He turned his head around, "can't help but look!"

"More in disgust," replied Kate.

"You have potatoes mashed into your jeans," added Rebecca.

"Where?" Thomas asked as he stretched back to look.

They both laughed at him and stood up and walked out of the living room.

Thomas took a little longer than usual to clean the kitchen so that they could have some time to be alone and talk. The phone rang and he picked it up.

"Hello."

"Hello. Thomas?"

"Rachel?"

"Yes, it's so good to hear your voice. How are you?"

"I'm okay."

"How's your eye?"

"The swellings gone down and there's a slight bruising around the stitches. But I'm in no pain and I'm doing fine so don't you worry. How was New York?"

"We had a great time. We shopped in all the stores on Fifth Avenue and bought loads of clothes. We did some sightseeing. We went to the Spa. I took my mother to a show. The hotel was beautiful. We only got back a couple of hours ago. I was just with my mother and Jack in the kitchen and he's been telling us what happened with my father and our lawyers."

"How is she doing?"

"Okay. She told me everything. She also told me that you, Kate, Jack and Penny know."

"Yes, but only because of what happened to me."

"I know."

She sounded sad. "So, are you okay?"

"A little confused, but I'm okay. My dad signed the documents and packed up his stuff and left, just like that. He didn't even leave a note saying goodbye."

"You have to give him time. He's a little confused too. Your mother said you can see him when you like."

"Yes, but that will be quite some time." She hesitated, "I need to talk to you. Are you comfortable coming up to the house?"

"Yes, of course."

"Why don't you come up on Thursday? Jack's going to be here and he needs to talk to you too, it has something to do with my father, and he wants my mother and me to listen in as well. Is that okay?"

"Of course it is."

"I'll let Jack know before he goes."

"Thomas I need to talk to you about a few things and I have some news."

"Really, I'm curious!"

"We'll talk Thursday."

"Okay Thursday. I'll see you then. Oh, I almost forgot, they had your picture up in the hotel."

"What?" Thomas yelled.

"Remember you said to look for Rebecca's father and Kate's picture on the wall, well we did and found them. There was also a picture of you. It had 'Country's Richest Man, Thomas Carlyle'. Remember Kate said we would be in for a surprise."

"That Kate, I'll get her for that," said Thomas.

"My mother and I thought it was great. We went and asked for the manager so that we could tell him we knew the people on the wall. Well, it seems that the bellboy and the doorman had already recognized me and told the manager, so when he came out to speak to us he asked if he could take a picture with me and put it up. Its right next to yours," said Rachel. "I took a picture of it and I'll show you on Thursday. Oh, before I forget my mother said to say hello."

"Tell your mother I said hello and I'll see her on Thursday."

"Bye."

"Bye Rachel."

Thomas hung up and went upstairs; they were sitting on his bed. He sat next to Kate and put her arm around her, "Are you ready to do some explaining?"

"For what?" Kate asked a little confused.

"Picture! Wall! Hotel! New York!" said Thomas.

Kate bolted for her room. Thomas chased her and Rebecca followed behind. Kate was hiding under her blankets on her bed. He pulled the blankets off her head. Her hair was covering her face and she was trying not to laugh.

"You think you are so funny? You think you've outsmarted me?" asked Thomas.

"What? What?" Rebecca asked.

"You tell her Kate. It's your moment."

Kate moved her hair from her face and looked at Rebecca. "In New York I asked the manager at the hotel to take a picture of Thomas, he took one of him in his hotel restaurant drinking champagne, I told him he was the 'Country's Richest Man'. I wrote that on the picture and signed his name." Kate laughed out loud and put the blanket over her head.

Rebecca laughed louder.

"You two keep laughing, I'll be in my room sulking," said Thomas. Before he left he turned and looked at the bed, "Kate I'm going to get you good for this." He looked over at Rebecca, "and you for laughing so hard."

Kate stopped laughing and threw the blankets off her face. "No. Please Thomas, no."

He walked out the room. Rebecca had a puzzled look.

Kate turned to Rebecca. "When he says he's going to get us good, he's going to get us good. Wait and see!" warned Kate.

They looked at the door and each other and started laughing.

"I like your room," said Rebecca to Thomas's back.

He turned around from his desk and looked at her and called her over.

She closed the door and walked to him. He put his arms around her waist and his head on her chest. She gently played with his hair. He pulled her on his lap. She wrapped her legs around him and the chair. He kissed her neck, her cheek, her ear and her lips. She pulled herself tighter against him. He could feel her breasts on his chest. He picked her up, placed her on the bed and lay on top of her. Again he kissed her cheek, her ear, her neck, her shoulder and her lips. She was breathing heavy. He gently let his hand roam the side of her body and squeezed her thigh. He gently moved his hand up the side of her body and lightly brushed her breast. She breathed heavier. She didn't want him to stop. Thomas suddenly rolled off her and stood up.

"You'll be sleeping in this bed tonight," said Thomas.

She realized what he had done. "You, you." She gave him a malevolent look and threw a pillow at him.

He smiled at her. "Who is laughing now?" He exaggerated his laugh as he walked toward the door. "I warned you."

"That is so cruel I'll get you for that," she jumped out of bed and chased him down the stairs. He jumped on the sofa and she jumped on him. She pinned his arms down and sat on his pelvis. "If that's the kind of games you play, then beware, because now I'm a player too." She kissed him and laid her head on his chest. She could hear his heart beating. "I love you."

"I love you."

She lifted her head and looked at him and softly asked, "Don't ever leave me?"

"I won't."

"Promise me?"

"I promise."

She kissed him on the nose and moved off him and sat on the floor. "So who told you about the picture?"

"Rachel, she called before."

"How is she?"

"She's okay. A little confused. She says she wants to talk to me. She also said Jack needed to talk to me about her father and wanted Rachel and her mother there as well," said Thomas.

"That's strange. Did she say why?" asked Rebecca.

"She didn't know. She said her father had signed all the paperwork and had moved out. She was upset that he didn't leave a note saying goodbye," explained Thomas.

"I feel sorry for her. When are you going up?"

"Thursday night. I thought we would both go?"

"Do you think that's a good idea?"

"You don't?"

"I would feel out of place."

"I don't want you to be uncomfortable."

Kate interrupted them. "Have you thought of some names?" asked Kate as she walked into the room in a nightgown and robe. "I have some paper and pens."

"How are we going to do this?" asked Rebecca.

"I thought we could each right down three names and then put them all together in a list so that we have nine in total. We make three copies of the list and we each go through a list marking the company names one to nine, one being the best. Then we combine the three lists and add them up. The two company names with the lowest points are put together and we decide the best," suggested Kate. "The company is going to publish novels on line. So we'll probably want to keep that in mind."

"That's fine," said Thomas his thoughts still on the previous conversation.

"I like it," replied Rebecca.

Kate handed out the paper and pencils and sat around the coffee table with Rebecca. Thomas remained on the sofa and leaned over the coffee table. They went through the process and each came up with three names and combined them and voted.

"Okay we have the final two. Thomas's 'KRT Publishers' and my 'E-Publishers.'"

They went back and forth for few minutes with no decision. Then Thomas made a suggestion, "Why don't we have each person explain how they came up with the name and it may help us come to a decision."

They all agreed.

"I'll go first," said Thomas. 'KRT' simply means Kate, Rebecca, and Thomas. Kate."

"I thought about the type of publishing, electronic, E-Publishing," said "Kate."

"Okay let's see if we can make a decision?" asked Thomas.

They talked for a few more minutes.

Then Rebecca just said it aloud. "What about 'Carlyle Publishing'?" She wrote it on the piece of paper, "The 'e' can be capitalized like this." She showed them what she had written, 'CarlylE-Publishing'.

"I like it, I really like it!" said Kate.

They both looked at Thomas. "I love it! 'Carlyle Publishing' it is. Let's have a celebration drink, teas all around." He stood and walked to the kitchen.

Rebecca followed him in. "Can I help?"

"You can get the milk out the refrigerator."

"Thomas, is everything okay?"

He shook his head, "not really."

"Tell me what's wrong?"

"I thought we agreed on both of us going?" he asked.

"I thought maybe you wanted to go alone under the circumstances," she replied.

"I want you to be there with me."

"I'll go," she said and smiled.

"You will?"

"I wanted to make sure you wanted me to go and you do and I love you all the more for that," she kissed him and walked out the kitchen.

"What about helping me making the tea?"

She stuck her head in the kitchen and said, "I only wanted to know what was on your mind," and blew him a kiss, "I always want to be with you." She smiled. "I'm going to put on my pajamas I'll be down in a minute."

As they drank their tea Kate and Rebecca made plans to go shopping Wednesday night and talked about the latest fashions. Thomas listened.

"Well, it's getting late," said Kate standing, "please excuse me I have an early morning." She looked over at Rebecca, "it was pleasure meeting you, goodnight. Goodnight Thomas," she said and went to bed.

Rebecca watched her leave. "I like your sister, she's different than you, she's nice," said Rebecca. She gave Thomas a look out of the side of her eye and laughed. "You know I'm joking. You're nice too," she moved over and sat on his lap. She looked into his eyes and ran her fingers through his thick hair. She put her head on his shoulder and Thomas put his arms around her. "You feel so good," she whispered, "and so warm." She fell asleep.

She woke up the next morning in Thomas's bed and lay there awhile looking at the posters of the French Riviera. She got out of bed and went into the bathroom and cleaned her teeth. She went downstairs and looked at Thomas sleeping peacefully on the pull out sofa bed. She quietly got under the sheets and lay next to him. She fell asleep and awoke with Thomas's arms around her. She felt him kiss the back of her head.

"You're lovely and warm," said Thomas.

"And you are lovely to cuddle," replied Rebecca.

"What time do we need to leave?" asked Thomas.

"Nine. I'll get up now and take a shower. Has Kate left?" she asked.

"Yes, you have the upstairs to yourself," said Thomas as he held her close. "I'll go up when you've finished. Do you want something to eat?"

"Can we pick up a coffee and bagel on the way?"

"That's a good idea."

She turned and kissed him on the lips and got out of bed. Thomas watched her walk upstairs.

SHE CLOSED THE CONDOMINIUM DOOR BEHIND HER. "I have a surprise for you. Follow me." She took Thomas into the guest bedroom where he put down his bags and coat. "Now close your eyes and walk behind me. Here, hold my hand." They crossed the hallway. Rebecca opened the door and walked in with Thomas trailing. "Okay, you can open them."

Thomas looked around. The room that was once full of boxes now had a desk and chair, sofa and posters of Nice and Cannes.

"Come sit down," she pulled Thomas in and sat him down. "There's a cordless phone, a modem under the desk so you can get onto the Internet, a color printer, paper, pens, pencils, and a dictionary," explained Rebecca. "How does the chair feel?"

"Very comfortable," he replied.

"You can also sit on the sofa. That's comfortable too. I put some posters up. Over here I framed the front page of the novel you gave me. I like what you wrote on it. She read it out loud:

Dear Rebecca,
When I asked you for a song you sang,
When I asked you to dance you danced.
Thank you. Your friend always,
Thomas Carlyle.

"That's so sweet." She looked at him and smiled. "You have a good size window for light," she said as she opened the blinds.

"You did this for me?" he asked.

"Do you like it?" she asked looking for approval.

"I do...I do. When did you do all this?"

"Friday."

"Friday?" asked Thomas.

"I arrived home just after eight. I emptied all the boxes and cleaned up the room. Then I went and did some furniture shopping. The room was finished by three," said Rebecca proudly. She looked at Thomas. "Your thinking what I would have done if it hadn't worked out?"

Thomas nodded.

She sat on the sofa. "It wasn't that big of a gamble. I already knew what you had done for my father and for me. You did that even before knowing the truth about Frank and me. You could have tried to convince me that you did it out of friendship but I wouldn't have believed you. Your actions speak volumes. Thomas, I'm tired of waiting for things to happen to me, I'm tired of relying on other people's help to get me what I want, I'm tired of being in love with you and not being with you. You've helped me so much. On Friday at the cabin, do you think if you had said that we can be friends I would have put my hands in the air and said okay? Not a chance! I had driven up there to tell you everything. I wanted you to know how I felt and that I was in love with you. You needed to know and I wanted to tell you and show you." She walked over to Thomas and knelt down in front of him and whispered, "You are the only person I have ever loved and will ever love, and I will continue to love you till the day I die. I want you to always hear me say it and believe it." She paused, "Thomas I've been alone and lonely for such a long time but those few weeks we didn't talk and I didn't see you were the loneliest. I was devastated. I have never cried so much. Then you go and do something so wonderful and make me realize maybe all isn't lost." She looked up at him, "I love you and want to be with you and grow old with you."

Thomas looked in her beautiful blue eyes and spoke in a low voice, "you sing for me, you dance for me, you help me, and you support me. Now you do this room for me. I love you. I love who you are." He stood up and pulled her up and hugged her. "I will always love you, and no other, till the day I die."

They kissed for a while.

Rebecca pulled away, "I should get going." She kissed him again. "Let me get my bag from my bedroom I'll be back in a minute."

Thomas sat and twirled the seat around and stopped facing the desk. He noticed a framed picture laying flat and picked it up. It was a recent picture of Rebecca, just her face, taken outdoors. Thomas read what was written on the picture in pen 'Love Rebecca'.

"I didn't want you to see that, I meant to take it away," said Rebecca walking towards Thomas.

"Why? Is it for me?"

Rebecca blushed. "It was for you but I changed my mind and thought it was too forward."

"Too forward would be a picture of you naked," replied Thomas. "Can I have it?"

She nodded yes.

He opened the frame's flap and put it on the desk. "There, you will be with me always."

She smiled. "It was taken by my father outside in the small park by the building. I'm glad you like it," she said and smiled. "I'll be back by six. Help yourself to the kitchen." She hesitated. "Thomas, I want you to consider this your place too."

"I will," he smiled and kissed her.

"By the way don't make dinner! I'll pick up some Chinese food on the way home."

"That sounds great."

"I'll be thinking of you," she said and kissed him.

He watched her walk out the room and then heard the front door open, close and lock. He looked at her picture and smiled. He brought in his laptop, plugged it in and started typing. The words flowed.

There was a banging on the door. Thomas looked at his watch and realized the time. He walked out the room and unlocked the door. Standing there was Rebecca holding two bags of Chinese food and her workout bag. Thomas took the bags of food and Rebecca put down her bag and closed the door.

"With both your hands occupied I now have you just were I want you," she said putting her arms around his waist and kissing his lips.

"How was your day?"

"I was dancing on air," she replied as she let go and stood on her toes and lifted her arms up and tilted her head to one side. She turned around and looked at him and laughed and relaxed. "How was your day?"

Thomas put the bags down. "I was tap dancing on that keyboard," and positioned his hands above his chest in a typewriting pose, moved his fingers up and down, and tilted his head to one side. He turned and looked at her.

She laughed. "Very funny!"

They sat in the solarium and ate. Thomas told her that he had written all day and figured another four to six weeks and he would be finished. Rebecca talked about her class and how a sister of one of the dancers had fell on the weekend and broken her leg. After they finished they went for a long walk around the harbor front and held hands and talked. They stopped in a coffee shop and ordered hot chocolates and continued their walk.

"You should come and watch my rehearsal one day?" asked Rebecca.

"I would like that," replied Thomas.

"Friday morning I'm rehearsing with Frank. Come down and we could all go for lunch," suggested Rebecca.

"I will. What time?"

"Eleven till twelve."

They walked back to the condominium and Rebecca took a bath. Thomas lied on her bed and read a magazine article on Peter Gabriel. She came out of the en suite wearing a terry robe and towel around her head and lay next to him.

"Is it a good article?" she asked.

"Yeah, I like him. I have his solo albums and the ones when he sang lead with Genesis."

"He sang with Genesis?"

"He did, back in the seventies. I have a couple of their discs with me, 'Selling England by The Pound' and 'The Lamb Lies Down on Broadway'. I listen to them when I write." Thomas sat up. "A few years back there was this guy at work, we were paired together to unload the trucks and he was always playing this music and I asked him one day who it was and he told me. He got me hooked on them. He was a great guy and a good friend but he moved out west. He bought me these CDs before he left."

"That was thoughtful."

"Yeah it was," replied Thomas. "Do you want to hear one? It's progressive rock."

"I'll listen to them while I do my nails and get my clothes ready for tomorrow."

Thomas left and came back with the CD player and put on 'The Lamb Lies Down on Broadway." Thomas went to his room and got his accounting book and sat at the dining room table and looked it over. Rebecca walked in an hour later wearing a short pink nightgown and matching silk robe. Her hair was pulled back with a clip. She looked incredibly sexy.

"No pajamas?" asked Thomas.

"I don't wear them all the time and I never get to wear these sets. This one, shall we say, hides the least," teased Rebecca. She crouched down at the coffee table and purposely let the nightgown fall to the side so Thomas could see her inner thigh. She pulled out a pad and paper from the bottom drawer and slowly stood. Thomas looked at her long lovely legs as she walked over to him. She stood behind him and put her arms around him and whispered in his ear. "I'm not wearing underwear either," she said and licked his ear. She kissed him on the neck and smiled as she sat down next to him.

"Getting me back for last night?" asked Thomas.

"This is just the beginning!" she purred, and licked her lips. "Unless?"

"Unless what?"

"Let's talk figures."

"Figures?" questioned Thomas.

She smiled. "Let's do it!"

"Do what?"

"Let's do the finances." She laughed.

"Oh. Okay," he opened up his book. She had him good.

"I liked the CDs."

"You did."

"It was different than what I'm used to but I liked them. I really liked the one that starts off with the grand piano."

"Firth of Fifth," replied Thomas. "That's a great song."

"Is that what it's called? Can I take that CD with me tomorrow so that I can listen to it when I'm doing my stretching and warm ups. It has so much emotion. I just love it!"

"Of course you can."

She smiled and looked down at Thomas's book.

"Okay, let's talk finances. Not taking any other income into account, the eighty thousand will cover the monthly out goings and expenses for almost three years. On top of that you keep your own money and Kate keeps hers and I have two hundred dollars salary a week."

"Thomas that's not much. You should have put more down. You must have had more money to yourself when you worked?" asked Rebecca.

"Rebecca there were times I had no money for a couple of weeks. Even when I did it wasn't much. I gave most of it to Kate. She needed it more than I did. I managed to save some here and there and put some aside to play golf. If I need more I'll ask you and Kate for a raise," he said and smiled. "Why how much do you have each week?"

Rebecca was silent.

"I'm sorry, I shouldn't have asked that's your personal business, forgive me," said Thomas and changed the subject. "I figure if Kate works at least fifteen hours she'll clear several hundred dollars a week which should be more than enough for her. She bought enough clothes in New York to last her to the spring. I almost forgot I still have the seven hundred dollars in savings that I haven't included. We can use that for a celebration if things work out."

"Thomas stop!" yelled Rebecca.

He had been looking down at his book and working out numbers as he was speaking. He looked up at Rebecca and realized she was crying. "What's wrong?"

She got up and went to the bedroom and closed the door. He could hear her crying. Thomas didn't know what to do. He walked up to her door and knocked. "Are you okay?"

"I'll be fine in a minute," replied Rebecca. "I'll see you in the morning."

"Okay, I'll give you some time alone," he said and walked away from her door confused. He picked up his book and papers and turned off the lights and went into his room and shut the door. He turned off the light and lay on the bed and wondered what was wrong.

Twenty minutes later he heard footsteps passing his door. The lights in the living room went on and shone under his door. There was a knock.

"Come in," said Thomas.

Rebecca opened the door, "Thomas can you please come into the living room so we can talk." She walked away.

Thomas got out of bed and went into the living room. She was sitting at the dining room table with a folder in front of her. He sat next to her.

"First," she said, "I'm sorry I told you to be quiet. Please say you'll forgive me."

"I do. It's okay," replied Thomas.

"It's not okay, I was wrong."

He smiled and said, "I forgive you."

She smiled back and spoke, "you made me realize something. But first I want to explain this folder," she opened it, "this is my finances and net worth. I want you to take it and read through it," she closed it and slid it to him. "But for now I want to give you a summary." She took a deep breath and started, "this condominium is mine and it's worth five hundred and seventy five thousand dollars. My father bought this for me, until last week I thought my mother was responsible. My father sent me money to live on; again I thought it was my mother. I had so much over each month Jack offered to have someone set up an investment portfolio, which I did and I have over two hundred thousand dollars in investments. My BMW is paid for. With my salary and the money that I keep from my father I clear easily two thousand a week. Some of it I save, which today is the eighty thousand and the investments, and the rest, I spend. There are two reasons I am telling you this, the first is I want you to know my financial status and the second, I want the eighty thousand dollars to be our money or our company's money, whatever, as long as you agree you wont repay it back to me. I feel like we have a prenuptial agreement for our relationship and I don't want that. Thomas if I had it my way you could have as much of my money as you needed. I love you and I want to help you. I know if you were in my shoes you would be saying the same to me. So I want the repayment off the contract." Thomas was looking down at the table. "Thomas, please look at me. The reason I agreed to do the finances with you and send your work to the publishers is so I could be with you and be a part of your dream. It's the same as you watching me rehearse or perform or asking me to dance or about my day," she held his hand. "Am I making any sense?" she asked.

Thomas looked down at the folder again and spoke quietly, "you are." He waited a moment. "If I say no to what you're asking?"

"I would go ahead with what we had agreed to the only difference being you would know how I feel," replied Rebecca. "Thomas," she said calmly, "I want it to be ours."

"Rebecca, I need some time to think?" he stood up and helped her up. "I want you to know that I love you for what you're doing, not just the money, but for being honest with me and talking to me. The more I'm with you the more I love you." He held her and kissed her. "Are you going to bed?" he asked.

"Yes."

"I'll see you in the morning," he said and started to walk away, he stopped and turned and asked, "If we were married?"

"Everything we have is ours. That's what I believe," expressed Rebecca. "And you?

Thomas nodded, "the same."

She watched him turn and walk away. She sat down and wondered if she had done the right thing but she felt awkward loaning the man she loved money.

Very early that morning Thomas came into her room and watched her while she slept. She looked so peaceful. He kissed her cheek.

"Thomas," she said still half asleep. She lifted up the blankets, "lie next to me and hold me." He got under the blankets and she rested her head on his chest and fell back asleep. Thomas hadn't slept well that night and fell asleep. Rebecca started to stir and woke Thomas up.

They looked into each other's eyes.

"Rebecca, I love you and I want to spend the rest of my life with you. So, everything you have, I have, we have, is ours," he leaned over and kissed her on the lips and moved back and looked into her eyes.

"Oh Thomas I want to spend the rest of my life with you," she pulled him close and held him tightly and whispered, "I love you more than anything in this world. Thank you."

Rebecca walked around the condominium looking for Thomas and realized he was out. She went into her room, lay down and wondered where he was. The front door opened.

"Thomas," she called.

"It's me. Where are you?"

"In my room," she replied.

He walked in and jumped on the bed and gave her a passionate kiss. "Take a bath and put on something sexy we have reservations for eight. I thought we would go out and celebrate," he gave her a quick kiss. "I'm going to get a shower and get dressed," and rolled off the bed and headed out the door.

Rebecca got out the bath and stood naked in front of the mirror. She dried her hair leaving it side parted and loose to her shoulders. She put on her black bra and matching thong underwear and a short, black, spaghetti strapped dress that was straight up and down. She looked at herself in the mirror and was pleased with her New York purchase. She put on her lipstick, blush, and eye make up and went into the bedroom and put on her shoes and picked up the matching handbag. She walked back into the en suite and she sprayed herself with perfume before throwing it and her lipstick into the handbag. She stood back and looked at herself one last time. She had bought this outfit for such an occasion and was happy with it. She walked down the hall and into the living room and stopped and looked at Thomas. He was wearing a black two-piece suit with a tie. "You look very handsome," she commented as she walked over to him.

"Wow," responded Thomas.

"Thank you."

"You look beautiful." He put his arm around her.

"So where are we going?" asked Rebecca.

"We are going for dinner up town to La Petite Maison."

"Very chic," she replied.

THEY ORDERED CHAMPAGNE AND THOMAS MADE A toast. "Rebecca, you are talented, beautiful, smart and sexy. To our happiness, health, and love. To us."

"To us," replied Rebecca. She was radiant.

They danced to the pianist's renditions of famous love songs. On the way back to the table Thomas stopped by and made a request.

They sat down and talked. The waiter filled up the champagne glasses and the piano played, 'You're the Best Thing."

"Did you request this?" asked Rebecca.

"Yes I did," replied Thomas.

"Dance with me?" she asked.

"First I need an answer from you," said Thomas as he stood in front of her and went down on one knee and opened the small blue velvet box. "Rebecca make me the happiest man alive and give me the pleasure of your hand in marriage?" asked Thomas looking up into her eyes.

Rebecca was taken by surprise. Everything seemed to be happening in slow motion. She looked deep into his eyes and from the bottom of her heart said, "I love you and I will love you forever. It will make me the happiest woman alive to be your wife." They both stood and kissed. Neither of them had realized that the pianist had stopped playing, the waiters stopped serving and the patrons stopped eating and dancing, they were all watching them and clapped when she accepted.

Thomas took the one-carat marquise diamond ring out of the box and put it on her finger. Rebecca stretched out her arm and admired. She thought she was dreaming.

"For the two newly engaged couple let me start that song over," said the pianist.

While Thomas and Rebecca danced, Rebecca cried tears of joy. Thomas told her from the bottom of his heart he would love her for as long as he lived. They agreed that this would be their wedding song, their song. They danced the evening away.

Once inside the front door she held his hand and walked him into the living room. She sat down next to him and looked at him. "Thomas I think I'm dreaming?"

"If you are, don't wake up," he said and leaned over and kissed her.

She pushed him back and put her leg over him and sat on his lap and stared straight into his eyes. She kissed him. "Mrs. Rebecca Carlyle. I like the way that sounds. You know people are going to ask us the date?"

"I wanted you to pick the date," suggested Thomas.

"One minute." She stood and went into the kitchen and came back with a wall calendar and opened it up on the coffee table, "one, three, six, twelve months?"

"Not twelve too long," he replied.

"Not one," replied Rebecca, "too soon."

"Six isn't bad," suggested Thomas.

"But three is perfect!" exclaimed Rebecca. "January!" she looked at Thomas.

"January, it is!" agreed Thomas.

"What date?" she asked.

"What's your lucky number?"

"Seventeen!" She looked at the calendar. "It falls on a Saturday," she said excitedly.

"January seventeenth it is!" smiled Thomas. "Now what kind of wedding do you want?"

"Small. Family and close friends," replied Rebecca.

"Where?"

"Here at the cathedral and have a reception, maybe at the 'La Petite Maison' we could hire it for the day, that place is beautiful. Or we could get married on a Caribbean island like St. John's, St. Thomas, or Tortola. We could fly guests down. What do you think?"

"They both sound great," replied Thomas.

"I guess we need to know how many we are inviting," she said, "then decide."

"One minute." She came back with a pen and paper.

They quickly put a list together.

"Approximately twenty-five and up to fifty," estimated Rebecca. "So we can do either. You know what I just thought; we need to tell Kate and my father."

"She's coming here to meet you to go shopping we can tell her then," said Thomas.

"I'll phone my father tomorrow afternoon," said Rebecca. "Penny and Jack?"

"Tomorrow, tell Penny that you want her and Jack to drop by and see you for a few minutes, after you've finished shopping." suggested Thomas.

"I will. But I'll have to leave my ring here tomorrow," said Rebecca, and put on a sad face.

"I'll keep it company," said Thomas.

She smiled, "okay."

"We can tell Rachel and Jessica Thursday night and Frank Friday at lunch," said Thomas.

Rebecca sat back and asked, "What about Kate living alone out there in the house?"

"I don't know. I told her I would never leave her alone," recalled Thomas.

"Listen why don't we talk to her tomorrow," suggested Rebecca.

"That's a good idea."

"I'm so excited. I love you."

KATE AND THOMAS WERE IN THE LIVING room when Rebecca walked in through the front door.

"Hello Kate.

"Hello Thomas," she walked over and gave him a kiss.

"Kate was just admiring your place. I showed her around."

"I love it. You have a great location. This would be perfect for me. School is down the road and I can see the law firm I work for from the dining room window. Thomas we should sell the house and buy one of these," said Kate.

"They have a pool upstairs and downstairs they run fitness classes Tuesday and Thursday," added Rebecca. "I'll show you on the way out. We should get going."

Kate agreed and she stood up.

"Kate one second," said Thomas. He whispered to Rebecca who left the room and returned moments later smiling. "There's something we need to tell you."

"Is everything okay?" asked Kate.

"Everything is okay," he stood and lifted up Rebecca's left hand to Kate, "we're engaged."

Kate was silent. They waited for her to absorb the words and what she was looking at. "Wow! Thomas, Rebecca, I'm so happy for you both. Let me have a look at it."

"I thought you would be shocked and tell me it was too soon," stated Thomas.

"Thomas it's a surprise but not a shock. You're both responsible, mature adults, not teenagers. I can see how in love you are," replied Kate. "When is the date?"

"Guess?" asked Rebecca.

"Since you got engaged so quickly I don't think you will wait so long to get married, so I'll say before Christmas."

"Close," said Thomas.

"January seventeenth," answered Rebecca.

Kate walked over to Rebecca and gave her a hug and a kiss on the cheek, "future sister in-law." She kissed Thomas and gave him a long hug.

Thomas held her hand and spoke, "Kate, I need to ask you something."

"Ask," said Kate

"After we're married I will be living here." He felt as if the words were hanging in the air.

"I guess so," said Kate.

"I'm worried about you living in grandmother's house alone," said Thomas.

"Thomas, it's our house, let's sell it and split the money," said Kate.

"Are you sure?" asked Thomas.

"Thomas the only reason I haven't suggested selling it before is because I thought you didn't want to."

"But I thought you didn't want to."

"I would have sold it after she died. Without her, it's only a house," she looked around the room. "Maybe I can rent something like this in the city that way we can still be close and see each other."

"That would be perfect," said Rebecca.

"Let me look into the value of our house and what's available in the city," said Thomas.

"I want you to know how happy I am for you both and that I support you a hundred percent." Kate looked at them both and smiled. "Now, future sister-in-law, let's go shopping."

They both kissed Thomas on either cheek.

"Have fun," he said as he closed the door behind them.

"Hello Thomas," said Jack, "your eye is looking a lot better." They shook hands.

"It feels better," replied Thomas.

"Hello Thomas," said Penny kissing him on the cheek, "you look much better."

"Thanks. Rebecca and Kate are on the way up they were out shopping. Come in and sit down. Can I get you a drink?"

"Black coffee, no sugar," replied Jack.

"Same," said Penny.

"I'll be back in a minute," said Thomas and walked out to the kitchen and put the electric kettle on. He walked back into the living room.

"If you're available next week, can we squeeze in another game of golf?" asked Jack.

"Any day next week is fine let me know," said Thomas.

"I'll see what's available and talk to you Friday," confirmed Jack.

"Okay," said Thomas. "Jack, are there condominiums up for sale in this building?"

"There are three. I'm selling one; it's a one bedroom with a den on the sixteenth floor and has a great view. I used to use it for clients visiting from out of town. I have no use for it any more and I already own too many. I'm putting it on the market on Monday. Why?"

"I know someone who is looking in the area and I said I would ask around," replied Thomas. "Do you mind if I ask what the asking price is?"

"Four hundred and fifty thousand," replied Jack.

"It's a beautiful place," expressed Penny. "You should have a look at it. It's hardly been used."

Jack pulled out his keys and took one off and gave it to Thomas. "Here, take a look, you can give me the key back on Friday."

"Sixteen ten," informed Penny.

The door opened and in walked Rebecca and Kate with handfuls of bags.

"How was it?" asked Thomas.

"We had a lot of fun," said Kate from the front door.

"A lot of fun!" added Rebecca.

Kate walked in the room first. Jack and Penny stood and gave her a kiss and asked her how she was doing.

"I heard you've already impressed them down at the firm," said Jack.

Kate smiled shyly.

Rebecca walked in and kissed them both. Everyone sat down except Rebecca and Thomas. "Thomas and I have some news."

Penny looked at Jack and back at Rebecca, "Thomas and I, we are engaged to be married January seventeenth."

Penny jumped out of her seat and yelled, "Yes" and ran over to Rebecca and gave her a hug and kissed her face.

Jack stood and walked over to Thomas and shook his hand, "she's a fine lady and you're a fine man, congratulations." He pulled Thomas to him and gave him a hug. Jack walked over to Rebecca and congratulated and kissed her.

"Thomas," said Penny, "I've prayed for you both and your happiness." She hugged and kissed him. "Your grandmother would be so happy."

Penny sat down on the sofa next to Rebecca and Kate. They started to talk about the wedding.

"I'll make those coffees," said Thomas.

"I'll come with you," said Jack and followed him into the kitchen. "That's great news Thomas. I know I'm not your father but I'm as happy and proud of you as any father would be."

"Thanks Jack."

Thomas reheated the water and put the coffee into the cups.

"Listen, you going to be there tomorrow night."

"Rachel's house?" asked Thomas.

"Yeah."

"I am. Rachel said that you needed to talk to me," confirmed Thomas.

"Not me, Jessica's lawyer! You need to be there at seven."

"Her lawyer? I thought it was Bill's lawyer?"

"Tomorrow it will be Jessica's lawyer, Jessica, Rachel, and us. We'll be listening to something to do with Bill. That's all we know. My lawyer is ninety nine percent sure he thinks it has to be something to do with Bill assaulting you," said Jack.

Thomas was confused, "Jack in lay man terms."

"Jessica gave Bill such a great deal when he signed the contract that we never thought about him trying to make a settlement with you," explained Bill.

"An out of court settlement?" asked Thomas.

"More like a never go to court settlement," replied Jack.

"I won't accept. I've told you that," said Thomas.

"It doesn't always work like that," said Jack.

"What do you mean?"

"What are you two talking about?" asked Rebecca.

Jack and Thomas looked at each other.

"Jack was reminding me about tomorrow night. We have to be there at seven," replied Thomas.

"Okay. Let me take a couple of cups in," said Rebecca picking up two, "come back inside."

Jack and Thomas picked up the remaining cups and followed Rebecca into the room.

"Thomas, Kate's going to stay here tonight. It will save her driving home late in the dark."

"Great," replied Thomas.

I thought Penny ran your rehearsals?" asked Thomas, as they walked out the restaurant and onto the street.

"No, it's usually Eric," replied Frank, "Penny helps us more one on one."

"She's busy between the school and the First National Ballet and her first responsibility is the school," added Rebecca. "Eric is the artistic director."

They crossed the street and walked into a park. Rebecca asked if they could sit on one of the benches for a few minutes. She sat between Thomas and Frank

"Before I forget thanks for lunch," said Frank.

"My pleasure," replied Thomas.

"Frank, I have some wonderful news," stated Rebecca.

"What is it?" asked Frank.

"I thought you may have noticed at lunch," she said as she waved her left hand in front of his eyes.

"Rebecca!" exclaimed Frank. "Thomas!"

"We got engaged Tuesday evening," blurted out Rebecca excitedly.

"That's great news. I'm happy for you both," he said as he kissed and held her. He then looked at her and spoke, "I should have known something was up. You had a glow about you all week. Does Penny know?" he asked then answered his own question, "of course she does. I saw her earlier on and she asked if I had spoken with you and she had this look in her eye."

"We told Penny, Jack and Kate yesterday. I haven't been able to get in touch with my father yet. We've been missing each other's calls so I left him a message on his voice mail with a time for him to call me this afternoon. I'm so excited," expressed Rebecca.

"I'm so happy for you, both," he looked at Thomas and shook his hands, "you are a lucky man, she's a treasure," he said letting go of Thomas's hand and looking at Rebecca, "and you, take care of Billy, he's a good man." He looked back and forth at them both, "I'm so happy for both of you."

Rebecca smiled, "we're happy," and looked at Thomas who smiled back.

"I'd say you two were destined for each other," continued Frank. "When's the big day?"

"January seventeenth," replied Rebecca holding Thomas's hand.

"Not much time wasted!" he said and smiled.

"Are you surprised?" asked Rebecca.

"Surprised, a little, but I think you are doing the right thing." He looked at Thomas and said, "It's your life and life's too short."

They stood and started to walk.

"I was going to ask if you two would like to come with me to my parents Sunday afternoon for an early dinner?" asked Frank.

"Of course, what time?" asked Rebecca.

"Say two o'clock," replied Frank.

"Why don't we pick you up and we can go together?" asked Thomas.

"Good," Frank replied and hesitated. "Rebecca I'm going over there to tell my family that I'm homosexual."

Rebecca looked at Thomas and back at Frank.

"Thomas has already offered to come with me. I wanted to warn you and make sure you were okay with that. I didn't want to put you in an uncomfortable position. I wanted to ask you myself, not Thomas," explained Frank.

"You never told me till now that you were going to say anything," said Rebecca.

"Thomas and I had talked about it last time we met and I've been putting it off these last few weeks. I didn't want to tell you till I had a definite date plus you both had other things going on." He stopped and slowly spoke, "Rebecca, I should have told them a long time ago. I look at you two moving ahead with your lives and making plans. I'm living a lie." Frank stopped and looked at them both. "I wish I were in love."

Rebecca and Thomas realized how lucky they were to have each other and how lonely he was.

CHAPTER 13

Kate's Condominium

THOMAS OPENED THE DOOR TO SIXTEEN TEN. Rebecca walked in and Thomas followed. The ceramic tiled foyer was spacious and had two mirrored doors that when opened exposed a closet. They walked down the ceramic hallway to the right. The first door was a full bathroom, the next was a roomy den with a large window, and it was furnished with an executive table, a cabinet and chairs, all in cherry wood. The last door was the laundry room. They retraced their steps, passed the foyer and walked into the kitchen, which was open and had a bleached wood table with four chairs, black appliances, a speckled gray counter top and an island. They walked through another doorway into a dining room; it contained a long oak table, six chairs, a buffet and hutch. Rebecca turned on the light and a beautiful chandelier lit up the room. She turned off the light and pressed another button that opened the blinds. They walked out into the living room, which had a full size white sofa and love seat, and black end tables. There was an entertainment center with a thirty-six inch plasma television. They walked out of the living room into the hallway. The front door was to their right so they went left. They opened two French doors and walked into the master bedroom. It had a four-poster king size bed, end tables, chest of drawers and cabinet, all in bleached oak, and a walk in closet and en suite with an oval tub. It had windows all around. Thomas looked out at the harbor front and realized this was a corner suite.

Rebecca sat on the bed. "Thomas this is beautiful. This would be perfect for her!"

"It would. It has the den. It's modern and has a lot of space. She would love it," replied Thomas.

"How much is your place worth?" asked Rebecca.

"Around three hundred and fifty," replied Thomas. "If we paid off everything we owed, including the agent, we'd be left with two fifty. If Kate bought this, the remaining two hundred we could mortgage and could pay until she started working full time." Thomas looked around. "There maybe more expenses, like furnishing the place. Maybe she'd want some of this stuff and we could buy it from Jack."

"Thomas, I'm not too sure about her taste, but this furniture is beautiful and looks new," replied Rebecca.

"I know."

Thomas was thinking about something.

"What is it?" Rebecca asked.

"We would have to get close to the asking price for the house to pull this off," replied Thomas. "I'm sure Jack would hold it for us."

"Of course he would and he may give us a better deal," suggested Rebecca.

"You know he would," replied Thomas.

"I know Thomas, I don't want to take advantage of them either, but they are our friends," implied Rebecca.

"I wonder sometimes if I'm too proud?" asked Thomas.

Rebecca stood and walked over and put her arms around him. "No Thomas you're not. You value their friendship and don't want to take advantage of them." She gave him a kiss on the lips and held him close. "If Kate lived here she would be close to us, to work, to school, and she would be safe. I know you would feel better. Sell the house and buy this for her."

"I should," said Thomas.

They arrived at the Carter Estate ten minutes before seven. Jack came out to meet them. "They're waiting for you in the study."

Thomas, Rebecca and Jack walked in and Thomas noticed all the bookshelves were empty. The room had a very somber atmosphere. Rachel and Jessica were sitting on one couch and gave half smiles. A man in a suit was sitting behind a desk that had been set up for the occasion. Rebecca sat down. Thomas walked over and said hello to Rachel and Jessica and gave them each a kiss on the cheek. They didn't seem to be themselves.

He whispered to Rachel, "I can see down your top from here."

Rachel snickered and swiped at him.

He whispered into Jessica's ear. "You must be the younger sister."

Jessica couldn't hold back her smile

"Better," he thought.

Jack introduced Thomas to the suit at the desk. "This is Mrs. Carter's lawyer Sidney Goldstein."

Sidney waited for Thomas to sit. "Let me begin, by making sure everyone is present before proceeding." He looked up as he said each of their names. "Jessica. Rachel. Jack. Thomas." He looked at Rebecca. "Who are you?"

"She's with me," replied Thomas.

"Any objections Jessica?" asked Sidney.

Jessica shook her head.

"Your name please?" asked Sidney.

"Rebecca La Croix," she replied

Sidney wrote it down and looked up. "At this time I ask you all to leave, except Mr. Carlyle," requested Sidney.

Everyone stood to leave the room, Thomas told Rebecca to stay.

"I will have to ask the young lady to leave," said Sidney.

"I prefer she stays," said Thomas.

"It's okay Sidney," said Jessica.

Sidney watched them leave. He stood up and walked around the desk and pulled up a chair in front of Thomas and Rebecca and shook their hands and said hello. "Thomas, do you have any idea why we are meeting?"

"No," replied Thomas.

"Let me start off by saying this is an informal meeting but its nature is very serious. Let me cut to the chase. You are aware of the state of affairs that took place two weekends ago between Mr. and Mrs. Carter, actually between their lawyers?"

"We are," replied Thomas.

"Good," replied Sidney. "Mr. Carter agreed to all the conditions and signed all documents. It was really an offer he couldn't refuse. We believe that Mr. Carter's lawyer will be approaching you in the near future."

"Why?" Thomas asked.

"We believe to offer you a settlement for the physical and mental damages he caused you. We could say 'a never go to court settlement'. If you were to accept his offer he would ask you to sign papers in which you would agree not to press charges nor take him to court." Sidney gave a brief smile. "There are two reasons for our meeting. First I am here purely to protect the interests of Mrs. Carter, and secondly, to make sure that the meeting between you and Mr. Carter's lawyer never takes place."

"You're telling me you're trying to beat him to the punch?" asked Thomas.

"You could say that."

"If you are here representing Jessica, why is she outside?"

"Thomas, this is a very delicate matter and of great importance to Jessica and Rachel. I told her and Jack it would be in her best interests that she let me take care of the, shall we say, negotiations and to keep personalities out of it. That's what they pay me for."

"Business is business," stated Thomas.

"Precisely!" exclaimed Sidney.

"Okay," said Thomas.

"Mrs. Carter would like you to sign a document tonight that you and any medical records due to your injuries can be used in a court of law to testify against Mr. Carter's violence towards you should it be deemed necessary."

"Okay," said Thomas wondering where the document was to sign.

"After which a deposit of one million dollars will be put into an account of your choosing."

"What!" exclaimed Thomas and looked over at Rebecca, then Sidney. "Did you say a million dollars?"

Sidney realized they should have offered more. "Yes."

"Unbelievable," said Thomas. He looked over at Rebecca. "Sidney, can we be left alone?" asked Thomas.

Sidney stood and walked away with a worried look on his face.

"Sidney, can you do me a favor?" asked Thomas.

"Sure."

"Ask Jessica if she can have Rachel come in with some soft drinks?" asked Thomas. "Rachel," clarified Thomas.

"Not a problem," replied Sidney and walked out and closed the door.

Thomas looked at Rebecca and asked her, "What's going on?"

"I don't know!" she replied.

"What do you think?"

Rebecca looked at him. "It's a lot of money."

"A lot of money," he echoed. He stood up and walked up to the window and looked out. Rebecca followed him and stood behind him. "Rebecca, I can walk out of here a millionaire or I can walk out of here with fifty dollars in my account."

"I thought you had seven?" she teased.

"I paid for the engagement meal," he said.

Rebecca laughed. Thomas joined in.

"Rebecca, I could walk out of here a wealthy man."

"Thomas," she whispered, "I believe you walked in here a very wealthy man and I know you will do what's right in your heart." She kissed him on the cheek. "That's one of the reasons why I love you."

"What about Kate?" he asked, "We could buy her that condominium."

"We don't need the money to buy her the condominium," she replied. She hesitated. "Remember when Kate wrote that line on your picture in New York, 'Country's Richest Man'?"

Thomas looked at her. "Yes."

"It had nothing to do with money! That's the reason she loves you. That's why I love you. You will never let us down."

Thomas smiled.

The door opened and Rachel walked in with three cokes and sat them on the table. Thomas walked over to her and gave her a hug and a kiss on the cheek. She hugged Rebecca awkwardly. They all sat down.

"How's Mathew?" asked Thomas.

"He's great. I saw him yesterday," she replied. "What have you two been up to?" she asked.

"Funny you should ask," replied Thomas.

"Why?" Rachel asked.

"Rebecca and I are engaged to be married on January seventeenth," said Thomas.

"Is this another one of your jokes?"

He looked at Rebecca. "Rebecca, I know you've been waiting patiently, show her."

Rebecca modeled the ring.

"Rebecca, I'm so happy for you," said Rachel. She gave Rebecca a hug and a kiss on the cheek. She leaned over and kissed Thomas. "I'm so happy for you too. This is so sudden."

"Rachel, I have an interesting story to tell you and there are so many things that I need to explain. Maybe we can talk?" asked Rebecca.

"After this, come up to my room and we can talk," said Rachel excitedly. "I love your ring. You can tell me about the wedding."

"That being said, let's get this over with," said Thomas and stood up and walked to the doors and opened them. "Why don't you all come in?"

Once in the study Thomas asked them to sit down and he sat on the table. "Okay, can someone beside Sidney explain to me what is going on?" asked Thomas. "Jessica?"

Jessica spoke nervously. "We think Bill is going to put in a good offer and we wanted to talk to you first. If Bill reneged on his contract with me your testimony could be crucial to my defense. You see I have no witnesses or medical reports. I needed you to sign an agreement outlining the events and to say that you would testify in court. I need to be protected from Bill for the rest of my life and you may not always be here. What if something was to happen to you or I never see you again it's as good as you signing Bills documents. I'm not very good when it comes to these things I just wanted to make sure you were taken care of. I will give you anything, anything, for your signature." She put her hand over her eyes and cried. Rachel comforted her.

"Jack?" asked Thomas.

"Bill is going to offer you a lot of money. I was protecting Jessica's interests and yours," replied Jack.

"Rachel, what did you think about all this?" asked Thomas.

"I told them that they should leave you alone and that you would never take any money from my father or us," replied Rachel. "I told them that you would sign anything for us."

"Sidney, answer this question. If I were going to formally charge Mr. Carter how much money could I potentially win, out of court?"

Sidney looked at Jack, who nodded his head, then spoke. "You have a strong case, witnesses, medical report and he could have killed you. He could receive a jail sentence. If not, the publicity alone would kill him financially. We believe he would have probably settled out of court for two million."

"So Sidney, Mr. and Mrs. Carter, in business terms, are protecting their interests?" asked Thomas.

"In a manner of speaking, yes," he replied.

Thomas looked at Sidney, Jessica, Jack and then Rachel, who smiled at him. He put his eyes on Rebecca who looked at him so proudly and mouthed, "Love you," and smiled. "I need a few minutes alone?" asked Thomas.

"We'll leave!" suggested Sidney.

"No," said Thomas, "I need some air. Give me ten minutes."

Thomas went outside and walked over to the fountain and thought about the situation. He came back in the room thirty minutes later. They were all sitting very quietly, it was as if no one had moved or spoken since he left. Talking to Rebecca later he would find out that Jessica and Jack had agreed that they had handled it very wrong and that Thomas was a friend and they should have approached him as one. Sidney disagreed and told them this was the best way to handle these situations, he had been through many of these before, and seen them go awry. The rest of the time they were silent.

Thomas stood in front of them and spoke. "I took a long walk and thought about what was going on here and I took Sidney's advice and thought about this rationally rather than personally and have come to a decision based on that." He looked down at Jessica and Rachel. "I understand your situation and what Mr. Carter is trying to do. It must be very difficult times for you two and I feel a great pain and sorrow for you both. Jessica, I understand your predicament and what you must be experiencing right now and its time to get this over and move on with your life." He looked over at Jack. "Then there's Jack. I must say I am proud of his loyalty and friendship. He understands that Jessica had a great deal to lose, were I had nothing, only to gain financially. So why not help out his friend Jessica and at the same time his friend Thomas, and screw Bill, business is business," he smiled at Jack and Jack smiled back. "There is still the issue of my compensation, which means I still have to make a decision."

There was a long silence.

Sidney asked the question that everyone wanted to know the answer to. "What is your decision?"

Thomas sat back on the desk. "I'll get to that momentarily," replied Thomas and looked at Jessica. "Jessica did I tell you that Kate and me are selling our house?" asked Thomas.

"No. I didn't know," replied Jessica.

"You wouldn't know of any condominiums that are for sale in the city?" asked Thomas. "You see I'm looking at buying one for Kate."

Jessica looked at him confused. "No, I don't know much about real estate."

"Sidney, do you?"

"I live an hour out of town. I don't know the area," he replied.

"Jack?" asked Thomas.

"Actually, there's one going up for sale on Monday, right in the city, down from where I live," he replied.

"The house we're selling is worth about three hundred and fifty, by the time we pay off outstanding debts, we'll have two hundred and fifty left over. My sister is going to use that two hundred and fifty to buy a condominium in the city. I'm not too sure what the prices are in town?" asked Thomas.

"The owner is trying to get rid of it and is selling it at below market value, in fact, two hundred and thirty. That would include all the furniture, and an underground parking spot. The extra twenty could be used for any miscellaneous expenses or to replace any unwanted furniture."

"I need to let Kate see the condominium and would need time to sell the house. Would there be a problem with the owner putting it on hold if I have a definite answer, let's say Friday?" asked Thomas.

"Not at all, he's so desperate he would help you sell your house," replied Jack.

"Kate will be so happy," smiled Thomas. "You know, now I'm happy."

Sidney and Jessica were confused.

"Mr. Carlyle I wonder if we could get back to the business at hand and your decision?" asked Sidney.

Jack already knew that it was over. Everyone was going to get what he or she wanted except Bill Carter. Jack would have to explain everything to Jessica and Sidney, but for now the offer would have to be updated with the dollar figure removed. Thomas never wanted their money; after all, they were friends. He had helped them out and took care of his sister. From that point on, Thomas was the son that Jack would have wanted.

"Rachel, my cola has gone warm, why don't you, me and Rebecca go into the kitchen and get some more and go up to your room. We can leave Jack and Jessica with Sidney to write up the new offer and Jessica can bring it up to the room and I can sign it there," suggested Thomas.

The three all stood and walked to the door. Rebecca put her arm around him and whispered, "Jack's going to want to adopt you," and kissed him on the earlobe.

"I know," replied Thomas.

They walked out the room.

REBECCA AND THOMAS SAT ON THE FOUR-POSTED king size bed and waited for Kate's response.

"I love it. It's beautiful. It's perfect. It's got a breathtaking view," said Kate.

"What about the furnishings?" Thomas asked.

"Is the furniture included?" she asked.

"Whatever you want."

"You know I was really looking at the space and imagining it without the furniture. Can we look around so I can look once more?" begged Kate. They looked around the condominium three more times and stopped in the kitchen. "Are all these counter top appliances, dishes, and pots included?" asked Kate as she opened the cupboards.

"Everything," replied Thomas.

"Kate, all the furniture and appliances are top of the line. These dishes are Mikasa and the ones in the dining room are Royal Doulton," added Rebecca.

"I don't think I would get rid of anything, maybe bring some of grandmother's pieces, but nothing more," she said. "Rebecca what do you think?" she asked.

"It's beautiful, it's modern, it has lots of space, is a perfect size and it has a den. It's perfect," replied Rebecca.

"Thomas?" Kate asked.

"What Rebecca said," he replied, "it's close to work, school and us. It's safe. You would be insane not to take it."

"Can we afford it?" she asked.

"Do you want it?" asked Rebecca.

"I do. I do. But I don't want to be disappointed if we can't afford it," she replied.

"Come and sit around the table," said Thomas.

He opened the envelope that Jack had given him and read through it.

"What's that?" asked Kate.

Thomas continued looking through the documents and looked up at her. "It's a surprise."

"Surprise?" asked Kate looking at Thomas, then Rebecca.

"Last night we went to Penny's for dinner. Jack talked to us while Penny was getting ready and told us that he was going to buy our house for Penny," explained Rebecca.

"Why?"

"She likes it and always has. She had told Jack how she liked the location and how cozy it was and how she liked having a garden to grow flowers and vegetables. Apparently she used to garden with your grandmother."

"I remember she did, but I never thought anything of it," said Kate.

"Jack said the cottage is too far for her to travel on weekends so he's going to buy our house for her and surprise her tonight."

"I'm so glad," said Kate. "Especially having someone like Penny taking the house."

"So what has he offered?" asked Rebecca.

"Four hundred thousand for the house," stated Thomas.

"I thought you said it was almost three fifty?" asked Kate.

"I was guessing. There are several quotes in here from agents indicating the worth of the house and they range from three fifty to four, he gave us top price. On this page it indicates the price we've been offered minus the price for this condominium and minus what we owe, we will be left with a check for seventy thousand," explained Thomas.

"You're getting this for two hundred and thirty. Is there something wrong with it?" asked Kate.

Thomas explained to Kate what happened on Thursday night.

"One million!" she repeated.

"I didn't want to tell you over the phone. I thought I would wait till today and surprise you with this," replied Thomas.

She looked around the kitchen, "I want to live here."

Thomas looked at them both. "So what are we going to do with the money?"

"Thomas you keep it," said Kate.

Thomas looked at Rebecca and Kate, and then asked Kate a question, "Did you write up the contract?"

"I did. I was going to show you after we had dinner."

"Kate, if you take twenty. Would that cover your expenses and bills for the next year?" asked Thomas

"Thomas that's more than enough, I could probably pay my bills off with the money I'm making now and have enough over to buy whatever clothes I needed. It's probably too much," she insisted.

"Okay you take twenty. So now we are left with fifty thousand," said Thomas and looked at Rebecca, "now that Kate is taken care of that leaves the question of the fifty thousand."

"Thomas, I told you before, it's our money whether it's in a bank or our company, whatever," replied Rebecca.

"Rebecca how much would you say it will cost for our wedding?" asked Thomas.

Rebecca went silent.

"What is it?" he asked.

Rebecca spoke softly. "Thomas, I wanted to ask you at dinner tonight. I guess I'll ask you now. When I spoke to my father yesterday I told you how happy he was for us both and how he liked you. He asked if he could pay for the wedding. I said I would let him know."

Thomas looked at Rebecca, then Kate, and then Rebecca, "What do you want?"

"I want him to. It would make me so happy," she replied.

"Rebecca, all I want is for you to be happy. If you're happy then I'm happy so call him and tell him he can pay for the wedding."

"Oh Thomas!" She sat on his knee and kissed him.

"Maybe I should leave," joked Kate.

Thomas and Rebecca smiled.

"So, I can't give away this fifty thousand," stated Thomas.

"Put it in your bank account," said Kate.

Thomas thought. "Here's what I'm going to do. Put the fifty thousand into the company. That's twenty-five each for Kate and me. Rebecca you put twenty-five in. That's seventy five thousand."

Rebecca interrupted. "No Thomas I…"

Thomas put his finger on her lips. "Rebecca!" said Thomas in a stern tone. "We will go to the bank and set up a joint account for the remaining fifty five thousand." He removed his finger and kissed her. "We'll need money for our honeymoon."

"Thomas I like it when you get upset with me," she kissed his neck and his ear.

"This time I am leaving," Kate walked out the room.

Thomas kissed Rebecca passionately for a moment and stopped and looked at her. "Are you okay with that?"

"Yes and I can't wait for our honeymoon," she replied. "By the way, last night in the condominium because it was so warm I slept in the nude."

"You did!"

"On top of my bed," she whispered and purred in his ear.

"No, you didn't. You're teasing me," he said and looked at her. "You did!"

"And in the middle of the night I was thirsty so I got up and walked to the kitchen and had a glass of water. It was cool and I drank it fast and some spilled on my breast and ran down my body. I put the glass down and went into your room and kissed you on the cheek goodnight. If you had woken up you would have caught me, naked and wet. I went back to my bed and lay down with the door wide open. If you would have woken up first and came into my room you would have seen me, completely naked."

"Really?" asked Thomas.

"No," said Rebecca and laughed at him and ran out the room.

Thomas chased her and caught up to her in the den.

Kate was sitting on the chair behind the desk. "To be in love," she said.

Thomas noticed the time. "You only have an hour and a half to shop. Is that enough time?" asked Thomas

Rebecca looked at Kate and they both laughed. "Is that enough time? Men!" she said.

Kate stood up and walked to Thomas. "You're always thinking about us." She kissed him. "Thanks Thomas I love the place. When can I move in?"

"I'll go talk to Jack while you two shop. Do you have any other questions?"

"No. If we can drop the signed documents off before I go tonight I could thank him then," said Kate.

"Alright," said Thomas. He walked Kate and Rebecca outside and waved goodbye. He went back inside and took the elevator up to Jack's.

Chapter 14

Children

"How do I look?" asked Kate.

Thomas looked away from the television and at Kate in brown pants, with a cropped white shirt and a black leather jacket.

"Sexy!" said Thomas turning off the television.

"Wait till you see your fiancée," she said and smiled. "Want a beer?"

"Sure."

Kate walked into the kitchen as Rebecca walked into the room. She was wearing fitted brown suede pants that hung on her hips, a cream-colored shirt that seductively revealed her bra and opened teasingly above her navel. She was carrying a matching suede waist length jacket. Kate walked back into the room. "See, he never gawked at me like that. Thomas close you mouth."

"You're only my sister. This woman here," he stood and walked over to Rebecca and put his arms around her exposed mid section, "is my goddess," and kissed her on the lips.

"Kate, please pour that cold beer over his head and cool him down. He's getting out of control," said Rebecca.

"And embarrassing," added Kate.

"You two are lucky that I'm not sporting my leather pants tonight because I would have to fight the girls off," said Thomas turning around and wiggling his behind as he walked back to the sofa.

They were both laughing. "You don't even have leather pants," said Kate.

"If I did!" stated Thomas.

"If you did would you wear them?" asked Rebecca.

"You know I would."

"So if I go out tomorrow and buy you a pair you will wear them for me when we go out?" she asked.

"Most definitely," he replied.

Kate looked over at Rebecca. "No way would he wear them."

Thomas stood up. "Ladies beware, I warned you about fighting the girls off." He went into his makeshift bedroom, the den, to get ready.

Kate and Rebecca were drinking their beer when Thomas walked out wearing a pair of black leather pants and a white cotton shirt.

"No way," said Kate.

"Wow! Thomas you look sexy," said Rebecca. "Really hot!"

"Thomas, you do look good in them," added Kate.

"Please ladies, please." Thomas put a CD into the player and located a song and put on pause. He moved the coffee table out of the way and put his back to the girls and using the CD remote pressed play. The Doors 'L.A. Woman' started. When the drums and bass began Thomas moved his bum with the beat. As the guitar kicked in he moved his head and with all the instruments he moved his body. He used the remote as a microphone and sang the first verse and drowned out Jim Morrison's voice.

"Thomas, what are you doing?" asked Rebecca laughing. She looked at Kate who gave an unsure look. They both laughed.

He finished the first verse with a scream of "Whoa! Come on!" and danced around, back and forth with the music, still with his back to them.

"Whoa," screamed Rebecca and clapped.

Kate just laughed and put her hand over her face.

As the tempo slowed Thomas stopped and just moved his hips and sang the second verse.

Rebecca continued to clap and Kate joined in. Rebecca leaned over and patted his bum.

He finished the second verse with an "Oh yeah!" The music went faster and he continued his dance back and forth, still with his back to them.

"Whoa!" screamed Rebecca. "Turn around."

"Turn around," said Kate getting into it.

They continued to clap.

The tempo slowed down and Thomas turned around.

Rebecca and Kate screamed.

Thomas went down on one knee and looked at Kate and sang, "I see your hair is burnin', hills are filled with fire," then looked at Rebecca and sang, "If they say I never loved you, you know they are a liar." The tempo picked up again and he stood up and sang the rest of the verse to them, thrusting his hips back and forth with the music.

They screamed louder.

The verse ended and the tempo slowed down and Thomas walked over to Kate and took her beer had a drink then put it on the table and pointed at her. He moved over to Rebecca and took her beer, had a drink, put it on the table and gave her a wink. They both looked at each other and laughed as he moved in front of them.

Thomas started to sing. "Mr. Mojo Risin'," and repeated the words of the song several times. He looked down at them. "Come on girls you know the words stand up."

They stood and joined in and sang into the remote. "Mr. Mojo Risin'," they repeated it again and again and faster and faster.

"Keep on singing," said Thomas as he started singing and repeating the phrase, "risin', risin'," over and over. Then he screamed the end of the verse, "Whoa! Yeah! Risin'! ...Oh...Yeah!"

The girls stopped and looked at him. Thomas had taken off and started dancing to the music. They danced with him. Thomas dropped to his knees as he sang the next verse. Rebecca danced in front of him moving her firm stomach in front of his face. Thomas ended the verse with a scream of "Whoa! Come on!" and kissed Rebecca's stomach with an open mouth. He stood up and danced with them. They all sang the last verse together, the music faded.

"Forget being a writer we should take you to Vegas," said Kate.

"Or my room!" whispered Rebecca. "That was hot!"

"Wait till you see what I've got planned for you on our wedding night," said Thomas with a cunning smile.

"Oh really!" said Rebecca. She walked up to him and gave him a sexy open mouth kiss and put her arms around him. "I have to tell you that turned me on."

Thomas smiled, "I thought it might."

"Okay you two, separate or I get the hose," said Kate separating them. She looked at Thomas. "I must admit that was a lot of fun." She was glad to see her brother so happy.

"I'm delighted Penny is going to keep some of grandma's furniture," said Kate as she looked out the taxicab window.

"Me too," replied Thomas.

"Jack told me I have a large storage unit in the basement," said Kate.

"They're a good size," confirmed Rebecca.

"Good, I think I'll need it," confessed Kate. "Jack said he is going to be dropping off the spare keys tomorrow morning. I'll go home tomorrow and bring some clothes and personal stuff back. Maybe one weekend we can book a small van and you can help me move some of the bigger items?"

"On a Saturday?" asked Rebecca.

"I was thinking a Saturday would be best, then I can go back Sunday and clean the place up and have one final look around," said Kate. "I need to buy some new sheets and a comforter for the bed. Maybe I can do that tomorrow afternoon." She looked at Thomas. "I'm thinking about moving in tomorrow?"

"You should," replied Thomas.

"Just pick up what you need from the house," added Rebecca.

"I think I will. And tomorrow night I will update the contract in my new den," she smiled at the thought. "Then we can sign it and on Monday I can register the company."

"Once we're registered, I'll set up a bank account in the company's name and get each of us a bank card and call American Express and apply for a small business credit card," said Rebecca.

The taxi pulled up in front of 'The Cat Club'. Thomas paid the cab driver and caught up with the girls who had bypassed the line and were talking with the bouncer. Thomas read the neon sign "Appearing Tonight Atlas." The bouncer verified their names on his VIP list and let them in. They were directed upstairs to a reserved table. They were the first ones to arrive and sat at the table and ordered drinks. Kate excused herself and went to the bathroom.

"You look very sexy tonight," whispered Thomas in Rebecca's ear.

"Thank you," she replied with a smile.

"Thomas?" said a voice from behind.

Thomas turned around, "Tracy! How are you?" He stood and gave her a kiss on the cheek and a hug. Rebecca stared.

"Rebecca!" cried Tracy. "How I've missed seeing you. We have so much to catch up on?" They hugged for a while and separated.

Rebecca looked at Thomas and Tracy. "You know each other?" she asked.

"We met at Rachel's birthday party. This was the guy I was talking to you about, you know, the one that got me out of work, with pay I may add," replied Tracy.

"I remember you telling me, it never dawned on me that you were talking about Thomas?" said Rebecca looking at Thomas dumbfounded.

Tracy turned to Thomas. "I was telling her all about you."

"You said he was Rachel's boyfriend?" asked Rebecca looking at Tracy.

"He is. They make such a good couple and they were having such a good time," she noticed something in his eyes and hesitated. "You are Rachel's boyfriend?"

"No. Rachel and I are very good friends. I'm engaged to Rebecca."

"This is the guy you were telling me about? The one you are in love with!" asked Tracy.

Rebecca smiled. "Yes, the one I am in love with."

"I never thought that your Thomas was my Thomas. I never realized we were talking about the same person. That's too weird." She turned to Thomas, "I'm sorry I jumped to the conclusion about you and Rachel."

"It's okay," replied Thomas.

She turned to Rebecca, "let me see the ring. Oh it's gorgeous! I'm so happy for you." She hugged her and said, "He's a great guy."

She turned and hugged Thomas, "You take care of her. She's one in a billion."

"I know and I will," confirmed Thomas. He let go of Tracy and put his arm around Rebecca. "How was your anniversary?"

Tracy looked at them both and gave a smile. "We drank that bottle of champagne, fooled around and didn't get to sleep till seven."

"Anniversary?" questioned Rebecca.

Thomas and Tracy looked at each other and then at Rebecca. "I forgot, you don't know. This is what I wanted to tell you at the party. Robby and I were married in Vegas last year," said Tracy.

"Congratulations!" screamed Rebecca. "Tell me all the details."

"Well, we had been on the road for eight months and we were in Vegas and they got a gig for a week so we decided right then and there to get married. It was so great. He proposed to me on stage and after the show we went to the Graceland Chapel and were married by an Elvis impersonator that night. It was so much fun. I'll come by one night and show you the pictures and you can tell me about your wedding plans."

"I'm so happy for you, congratulations, you look like you're on cloud nine," said Rebecca.

"I am. Robby's is going to come up after the second set, we have another surprise," said Tracy excitedly.

"What is it?" asked Rebecca.

"You'll have to wait," said Tracy.

Rebecca looked at her curiously, "okay."

"Did you get lost?" asked Thomas as he smiled at Kate approaching.

"No, I met someone from work and was talking to him for a few minutes," replied Kate.

"Kate this is Tracy. Tracy this is my sister Kate. Tracy's husband is the lead singer," explained Thomas.

"I can't wait to hear him," said Kate.

"I love the leather pants," said Thomas to Tracy and gave her a smile.

"Thank you," replied Tracy and blushed.

"You made these!" said Rebecca and Kate at the same time.

"They look great on him," said Rebecca. She mouthed the word, "Wow!" to Tracy. "I didn't know you designed clothes."

"I know there's so much to tell you. I started making Robby's clothes while on tour; you know to give me something to do. Then I started to make them for the band. I'm going to go to college part time; Robby's going to help me out."

"You will have to let me give you something for them," said Thomas.

"No way!" replied Tracy. "These are a gift."

"You're very talented," complimented Rebecca. "I love them."

"Me too," said Kate.

"Looks like you have some new customers," said Thomas.

Kate and Tracy talked about her designs.

Rebecca looked at Thomas and whispered. "So you are the romantic Tracy was talking about. I should have known," said Rebecca. "But she threw me off when she said he was Rachel's boyfriend. I was actually relieved that Rachel had a boyfriend. I thought you would be left alone, I guess I was wrong." She kissed him on the lips. "Why didn't you tell me about Tracy?"

"You didn't know she was married or about designing clothes and she wanted to surprise you. I didn't want to ruin it for her," replied Thomas.

"Hello everyone," said Rachel. She walked over to Thomas and Rachel. "You are a lucky woman Rebecca!" She smiled and gave her a hug and a kiss and turned and did the same to Thomas. "And you are a lucky man!" She said hello to Kate and Tracy and kissed them on the cheek and asked Tracy about Robby.

Rebecca picked up the bottle of beer and glass of rum and coke from the table and handed the beer to Thomas. She looked at Rachel in her light blue dress, her perfect figure and green eyes and blonde hair. "She is beautiful," said Rebecca looking at Thomas.

"She is attractive," agreed Thomas.

She looked back over at Rachel. "Thomas, she has beautiful features, a great body, intelligent and personable." She looked back at Thomas. "Did you ever want to be with her?" she asked nervously.

Thomas brushed his hand on her cheek and looked deeply into her blue eyes. "I have the most beautiful and complete woman on this earth, I fell in love with you the first time we met." He leaned over and kissed her on the cheek.

"Thomas, never leave me!" Rebecca whispered.

"I never will. I'll always be here," replied Thomas.

"Promise me, again?" she asked.

"I promise," he replied and kissed her. She squeezed his hand tightly and smiled.

Frank, Greg, Blair, Miguel, Janet and Betty arrived thirty minutes later. They congratulated Thomas and Rebecca on their engagement and Miguel talked about Thomas's lip-synching to Billy Idol, apparently he had been the talk of The Village and people were asking when he was returning from New York.

They all laughed.

The waitress brought over several bottles of champagne in ice buckets and placed them around the table. She opened a couple and filled everyone a glass. Kate stood and spoke, "To Thomas, the best brother and friend a sister could have and to his beautiful, talented fiancée Rebecca, who I am honored to call my sister-in-law. Congratulations on your engagement and wishing you future happiness, health and wealth. To Thomas and Rebecca!"

"Thomas and Rebecca," they all echoed.

They drank champagne, talked, and laughed. Atlas came on to play their first set and they watched and listened to the first few songs.

Thomas danced with Rebecca and was hypnotized as he watched her move to the beat; she looked beautiful and was incredibly sexy. He danced with Kate and thanked her for the champagne and the wonderful toast. As he danced with Rachel he noticed how many men were looking at her; several men had already come to the table to ask her for a dance which she politely, and oddly, refused. Almost every woman recognized her and stopped her to talk about modeling. Thomas was impressed how professionally she handled it. When they got back to the table Kate, Rebecca, and Frank left to go dance.

"Thomas, are you still coming horseback riding?" asked Rachel.

"Whenever you want me to," he replied. "I was waiting to see how things were working out for you at home."

"Rebecca had told me you quit your job and are writing full time."

"Yeah, it was time to take a chance."

"So you don't need the guesthouse any more?"

"Well..."

She cut him off. "I wanted to let you know that you were still welcome. I don't want what happened that night with my father to keep you away. You can both come over," she said.

"Rachel, I was just waiting for the invite. I wanted to give you and your mother some time. Just let me know. If Rebecca's busy I'll come alone," he said in a comforting tone.

"That makes me feel better. I was afraid you may not want to," she stopped and thought. "Rebecca really opened up to me last week. I didn't know she felt that way about you. I hope we can be better friends."

"I know she wants to be," replied Thomas.

"Remember I was telling you both that I have a photo shoot?" she asked.

"Yeah."

"Well the shoot is on Palm Beach in Aruba and it's for the last Thursday and Friday in November. I was planning on flying down there Wednesday afternoon and flying back Sunday night. My mother said she would speak with Jack and ask if we can use his plane. Can you and Rebecca come?"

"It's okay with me. We would have to check with Rebecca."

"I'll ask her when she comes back. I was going to ask Kate and Frank. Veronica and Buddy have already accepted. My mother's coming and she was thinking about asking Jack and Penny. She could really use the break and it would do her some good to get away and relax on a beach."

"I think you're right," replied Thomas. "What about Mathew?"

"We're just friends. He's really sweet and kind. I guess I like him as a friend. I really need some time to myself especially right now," replied Rachel.

"I understand," sympathized Thomas. "What about your daycare?"

"We're still pursuing that. It's not as easy as I thought, a lot of red tape, and with the current events I've been preoccupied. Mathew helped us to get started and gave us an overview of what we needed to do and he was very helpful but he suggested that we look into hiring a lawyer that is an expert in the field and has connections. I thought about hiring someone from one of Jack's firms so I talked to him and he has suggested a couple of names. Veronica is still keen and so am I but we have to be patient. Hopefully this time next year we'll have our grand opening."

"I'm sure you will," smiled Thomas. "I look forward to it."

Rachel smiled at Thomas and looked at him in a way that Thomas couldn't describe.

"What are you two talking about?" asked Kate.

"Aruba!" said Thomas.

"Aruba!" said Kate and Rebecca.

"I was telling Thomas about the photo shoot in Aruba the last week in November. I want you guys to come down with me from Wednesday to Sunday. Say you can make it?" begged Rachel.

"Thomas?" asked Rebecca.

"I'll be finished the novel and my proof reads," replied Thomas. "I wasn't sure about you?"

"Let me think. I dance the Saturday before and have the last week of November off and we start the Nutcracker rehearsal in early December," concluded Rebecca. "Let me check with Frank when he gets back."

"Kate?" asked Rachel.

"School is okay. Work may be a problem. I'll have to ask? I'll let you know Monday," answered Kate.

"Frank, do we have the last week in November off and the first week in December?"

"Yes. Why?" he asked.

Rebecca looked at Thomas and Rachel, "I guess we're going." She smiled. "I can't wait! Aruba!"

"Aruba!" said Frank.

"The last week in November, I have a shoot, Wednesday to Sunday in Aruba. Can you make it?" asked Rachel.

"I'll be there," replied Frank without hesitation.

"There's one condition and it's my mother's, she's picking up the tab, all expenses paid," Rachel looked over at Thomas, "no exceptions."

They talked excitedly about Aruba.

After the second set Robby and Tracy joined them upstairs and Tracy made the announcement, she was pregnant.

"THOMAS CAN WE GO FOR A WALK?" asked Rebecca as they walked to the bottom of the cathedral steps. "It's a lovely Sunday morning."

"Okay," replied Thomas as he looked at his watch. "We have a few hours before we have to pick up Frank. Should we get the car and take a drive to the city park."

"I'd like that," she confirmed.

They crossed the road and walked to the car. Twenty minutes later as they parked, the clouds were breaking up and the sun's rays were starting to peak through. There was a cool breeze coming at them as they walked the asphalt path. They passed a family on bicycles and Rebecca smiled at the two small children as they peddled by. They passed an old man and lady walking their dog and said good morning. They walked in silence for ten minutes. Thomas knew something was on her mind.

Rebecca eventually spoke. "Tracy looks so happy," she said.

"Yes. I thought they both did," replied Thomas.

"They did. Imagine arriving in Vegas and deciding to get married," said Rebecca. "Just like that!"

"That's love. Besides, eight months on the road is a true test of conviction."

"I know but now she's pregnant. What happens if he doesn't succeed? What happens when he's on the road and she's at home? She'll be all alone?" asked Rebecca.

Thomas stopped and looked at her. "Rebecca, Robby told me that they were going to tour for a few more months then they were coming back to the city and he was going to do some local bars and clubs. He said he wanted to be with her and take care of her and the baby. They said he was going to work part time during the day and do some shows at night. Her mother said they could stay in her basement till his musical career could pay the bills and she would babysit while she attended college. Sounds like they have it all worked out, besides as long as they're happy and they're together." He stopped speaking for a moment and looked at her. "Rebecca this isn't about them is it? It's about us. Are you worried about us? That I won't succeed?" asked Thomas.

"Oh no Thomas not at all," replied Rebecca. "I know you will." She put her arm through his and her head on his shoulder as they walked.

They walked over to a bench and sat down. "Rebecca, what's on your mind?"

"When I look at Tracy, she's been married for a year; she's made love for at least a year. Now she's pregnant and is going to have a baby," replied Rebecca. "She has done all that but sacrificed her life and ambitions."

She stopped and looked at Thomas the tears were starting to form in her eyes.

"Rebecca," Thomas said softly, "people start their lives on one path and often they come to forks along the way and have to make decisions. Sometimes these decisions seem to be dramatic, more like a right turn. Tracy wanted to be with Robby more than her dancing," Thomas paused, "are you having a hard time with her decisions?" asked Thomas.

"No Thomas. I actually respect her decisions and her courage," replied Rebecca.

"We'll be married in a few months and we'll be together. Do you want to get married earlier? Is it making love?" asked Thomas as he searched for the answer.

"Thomas, when I marry you it will be the happiest day of my life and I would marry you today. But I want to wait and plan our wedding and give our family and friends the opportunity to be a part of the celebration. I also want to go through the excitement of picking a dress and doing a guest list and sending out the invitations." She hesitated and spoke quietly, "I won't lie to you Thomas I want to make love to you so badly, yet when I look at how close our wedding date is I know I can wait. I don't know what I would do if it were later?"

"Rebecca I'm confused! Is it you and your ballet?" asked Thomas.

"Yes."

"Rebecca I would never ask you to leave ballet. I know how hard you've trained and disciplined yourself. I can't think of a reason I would ever ask you to leave?" questioned Thomas.

"I know you would never put me in that position," she confirmed.

"No I wouldn't."

She looked at Thomas and a tear came down her cheek. "Thomas we never talked about children."

"No," he replied and wiped the tear off her face. "We can try to plan them so that you only miss a season or two. They give you time off; ballerinas do have children. Don't they? Your position would still be there, right?" he asked.

"They do and I know all that."

Thomas was confused. "Then why are you tormenting yourself over this. Are you scared you may not be able to have any?" he asked. "We could always adopt?"

"It's not that!" Her tears flowed. "Thomas I was so caught up in my love for you and what I wanted that I overlooked something that you may want, children." She looked up at Thomas. "Thomas I'm so sorry. I'm not worried about not being able to have children or adopting. I've been worried about how you will respond when I tell you I don't want to have children, ever." Rebecca cried.

"Rebecca, why not?"

She looked up at Thomas. "What are the reasons you want children?" she asked.

Thomas thought. "I want us to grow as man and wife and eventually as a family. I want to see our children grow up and be little ballerinas or writers or football players. I want to have birthday parties, drop them off at school and see them playing with their friends. Rebecca, there are so many reasons," replied Thomas.

"Thomas I love you and want to marry you and live with you forever," she said. "I know you want children. I love children. I just don't want any."

"Why don't you want any?" He asked again." "I still don't understand.

"Thomas I've been alone for so long. I have no brothers or sisters. I've had no father for the last nine years and a mother who lied to me. I don't want to put anyone through what I went through."

"Rebecca it would be different for us. You are making a decision based on other people's lives and decisions," said Thomas.

"No Thomas, I'm making a decision based on my life!" she said in a strong voice. "What about Frank? What about his parents? He won't confront them with the truth."

"That was Frank's choice. Don't blame his parents for something they are unaware of," said Thomas in an angry voice. "If he speaks to his parents and they shut the door on him and tell him he is no longer their son then you can condemn them and I would agree with you. But don't pass judgment until all the facts are revealed." Thomas took a moment and spoke in a calmer tone. "You and I can make a difference. Rebecca I love you so much. I see so much love in you. You are so kind and gentle and you have so much to give." Thomas smiled. "You know I always imagined you with little Rebecca practicing ballet movements in our living room. Yes, I do want children." He hesitated and talked slowly. "Rebecca, there is just as many good parents out there as there are bad parents. There are so many children who live happy lives."

"What about you?" she asked.

Thomas thought she was being unfair but she was very upset. "You don't think I hated my parents for leaving me alone. You don't think I blamed them. I was mad at them for a long time. But looking back, I had a wonderful relationship with my grandmother. I have a great sister. It made me who I am today. I also got to meet you," he said.

"Thomas you told me you didn't believe in fate," said Rebecca.

"Rebecca I don't. I had the choice to be angry with my parents and be bitter all my life and walk around with a chip on my shoulder; or I could do something positive with my life. It wasn't my parent's decision to leave us and I know that in my heart that before they died Kate and I were the last thoughts they had on this earth and I know they would be worried for us."

"Thomas I don't want to lose you because of the way I'm talking. I like children, I really do, I like being around them. I just don't know if I'd be a good mother. I just don't know. I don't know what I want? Before I met you I definitely didn't want any children but I don't want to say I do now because I don't know if I'm saying that because I'm scared of losing you."

Thomas held her closely and kissed the top of her head. "Rebecca I love you with all my heart and I will always love you. I can't wait to marry you on January seventeenth. Let's take it one step at a time. We've told each other how we feel. I promise you I will never pressure you into having children or hold that against you if you decide not to. You're confused and I understand that. The answer will come to you one day, maybe not today or tomorrow, but one day, and whatever that answer is, I'll respect and honor it even if it means no children."

"Thomas you will stay with me no matter what I decide?" she asked.

"I will," he replied. He wiped the tears from her face. "How long has this been bothering you for?"

"I never gave it too much thought until last night when I saw how happy you were for Tracy and Robby and hearing you talk about how much you loved kids and wanting your own. Then Rachel joined in and started talking about children and how she couldn't wait to have them. I sat there and said nothing, Kate noticed. I think she could tell by my silence what I was thinking. I don't want you to marry me under false pretenses Thomas?"

"Rebecca, make me a promise?

"Okay," she replied.

"For the next three months you will concentrate on your dancing and planning the wedding. Promise me?"

She smiled. "I promise."

"Don't worry. Let's take one day at a time."

She smiled, "Okay." She looked at Thomas and put her head on his shoulder and sobbed. "I was so worried?"

"You shouldn't have. We can get through anything?" He stroked her hair. "I guess I jumped to conclusions and was a little insensitive."

"You didn't know. Don't blame yourself."

"I never want you to worry about talking to me?"

"I'm not, that's one of the qualities I love about you!" She looked up at him." I was scared you wouldn't want to marry me." Tears formed in her eyes.

"Never think that," he said. Thomas lightened up the conversation. "Oh I see! You're trying to get out of it are you? Well it's not going to be that easy!" stated Thomas with a smile.

She knew what he was doing. "Oh Thomas," she said and kissed him.

"How about we take next weekend to ourselves?"

"I would like that."

"Friday I'll take you to The Duke and we can talk about the wedding and decide on where we are going to have the ceremony and reception."

"Then on Saturday we can look for invitations and put together a list of who we're are inviting and what we have to do," she said enthusiastically.

"Saturday night we can go for a swim and watch some old movies."

"I'll make lasagna."

"Then Sunday after mass we can come here again for a walk."

"That sounds wonderful."

They kissed and walked slowly back to the car. They passed the family riding on their bicycles and Rebecca smiled at the two youngsters as they went by.

"Mommy, that pretty lady smiled at me again," said the youngest.

FRANK SAT NERVOUSLY IN THE BACK OF the car. Thomas tried to make conversation with him but he was getting little response.

They pulled into the driveway of a pretty two-story home in the suburbs.

"I'm going to tell them after dinner," said Frank as he rang the doorbell.

"Frank we're both here for you," replied Rebecca.

The front door opened and Frank's mother Eileen and sister, Stephanie, greeted them. Frank introduced Thomas.

They closed the door behind them. Frank's father was walking down the stairs.

"Rebecca, how are you?" he said and gave her a hug.

"I'm fine John," and gave him a kiss on the cheek.

He shook Frank's hand, "Frank."

"Dad this is my friend Thomas," said Frank.

Thomas said, "Hello".

"Come in and have a seat," suggested Eileen.

They followed her into the living room. Frank sat on one end of the sofa, Rebecca in the middle and Thomas at the other end. John sat in the recliner and Stephanie carried in a chair from the dining room and sat on the floor. Eileen asked what they would like to drink and went to the kitchen.

"Thomas, are you a ballet dancer?" asked Stephanie.

Thomas smiled, "No I'm not."

"What do you do?" she asked.

"I write."

"For a newspaper?"

"No, I write novels."

"That's great. Are any published?"

"Not yet. I just sent my first novel out to the publishers," replied Thomas. "I'm just finishing my second."

"How exciting! I love reading," said Stephanie.

"He's very good," replied Rebecca. "His first novel is amazing. You'll cry at the end, guaranteed," added Rebecca.

"Can I read it?" she asked. "It would be so exciting to read a potential best seller."

"Stephanie," said Frank. "Don't put him on the spot!"

"I don't mind," said Thomas. "Write down your address and I'll forward a copy."

"Make sure you don't make copies and pass them around," warned Frank.

"I wouldn't. I promise."

"Here are the coffees," said Eileen as she put the tray on the table. "I haven't added milk or sugar." She sat down on the chair and looked at Thomas. "So Thomas, how do you know Frank and Rebecca?" asked Eileen.

"My grandmother use to teach Rebecca when she was younger and Rebecca's new teacher Penelope Daily and my grandmother were old friends, so we were introduced. I met Frank through Rebecca. Frank and I have got to know each other over the last few weeks and we've become good friends," replied Thomas.

"Don't you think they make such a good couple?" she asked.

"Yes, they dance well together," replied Thomas as he avoided the real question. He was amazed how well he was answering without faulting and by the look on Rebecca's face she was too. Frank on the other hand looked very nervous.

Eileen looked at Frank. "So Frank, you said you had something to tell us.

"Well," said Frank nervously then he went quiet and sat there.

"He wanted to ask you to come to my 'opening night' next week. It's on Wednesday. It's my debut as a principal dancer and he thought you may want to come down and watch us, him," explained Rebecca and redirected the conversation.

"Oh that would be wonderful!" said Eileen.

"Me too?" asked Stephanie.

"Of course! John and Ted also," replied Rebecca. "We've booked a hall after the show. Family, friends, special patrons and fellow dancers are all invited to attend."

"Oh it sounds great! What should I wear?" asked Stephanie.

"I would suggest something elegant."

"Like," she looked for more help.

"Something you would wear if you were going on a date to an expensive restaurant," replied Rebecca, "and you wanted to make an impression."

"I know just the dress," said Stephanie excitedly.

John sat there and said nothing. The door opened and in walked Ted. He was six foot two and at least two hundred and fifty pounds. His dad stood up proudly and introduced him to Thomas.

"How did your training go, son?" asked John.

"Good," replied Ted.

"He's going to be MVP this year Thomas, fifteen quarter back sacks, six fumble recoveries, and four interceptions, two for touchdowns," gloated John. "This year we should be hearing from the top colleges."

"Dad," said Ted embarrassed.

"We've been waiting for you," said Eileen to Ted. "Please sit around the dining room table and I'll get dinner."

They sat around the table and Stephanie told Ted about the opening night and reception.

"That sound's great Frank, I'm looking forward to it. Congratulations Rebecca," said Ted.

"I thought you had practice Wednesday nights?" asked John.

"I do. But I'll miss it," replied Ted.

"If you miss practices you'll be letting the team down," replied John.

"Dad, it's not as if I don't have a good reason," "he said and looked over at his older brother.

"You should go to practice," stated John.

"Ted, it's okay if you have practice, I understand. Your football is important," said Frank.

"You see Ted, even your brother understands," said John glaring at Ted.

The table went silent. Stephanie broke it with a question to Rebecca. "Maybe after dinner we could go upstairs and I could show you the dress?"

"I would like that," replied Rebecca.

They ate dinner and everyone spoke except for John. Thomas came to realize he wasn't looking forward to the after dinner conversation with him.

The table was cleared and the coffee was to be served in the living room. Rebecca went upstairs for a few minutes with Stephanie while the coffee was brewing and Ted spoke with Thomas and Frank. Eileen brought in the coffee and the girls joined shortly after. Ted stood up to excuse himself.

"Ted can you have a seat? I have an announcement to make and it's for the whole family," asked Frank.

"Sure Frank. Is everything okay you look a little pale," noted Ted.

"I'm fine," Frank replied.

"Frank, don't be nervous. Stephanie and I already know," stated Eileen.

"You do," said Frank confused.

"It's obvious. You and Rebecca are engaged. She's wearing a ring," replied Eileen.

Rebecca looked down at her finger; she had meant to take it off outside. Thomas looked at it as well; he had forgotten to remind her.

Frank was numb. "No mother it's not that," replied Frank, "I'm not engaged to Rebecca."

"Someone else is engaged to your girlfriend?" asked Stephanie.

"If you stop asking questions I can explain," he said loudly, and got their attention. "Rebecca and I are only friends. She was going along with being my girlfriend to help me and to protect me."

"Help you and protect you from what?" asked Eileen.

"Mom, Dad, Stephanie, Ted," he looked at them as he said their names. "I'm homosexual and have been for the last ten years."

The room was silent and they stared at Frank.

"Do you have a boyfriend?" asked Stephanie.

Frank let out a slight smile but before he could answer.

"Of course he does he's sitting right there," said John pointing at Thomas. "He said they had been going out and had become good friends. It's the faggot poet."

"Frank you brought your boyfriend here, into our house, to tell us?" asked Eileen.

"Mom, Thomas is not gay. He's engaged to Rebecca," replied Frank.

"Oh, so now he's going out with her. That's convenient!" said John in a loud and sarcastic tone. "I want you two love birds out of my house. You too missy," said John standing. "Don't bother coming here again." He looked at his wife. "Eileen, I told you that ballet was going to turn him into a fruitcake."

Frank spoke up. "I'm sorry. I don't want to intrude but there are some things I would like you to hear. All I'm asking is ten minutes of your time. After I finish I will leave and you don't ever have to see me again. I'm begging you!"

"I don't want to hear what you have to say," said John as he stood up and went to the kitchen.

The other three remained.

"I'm not here asking you to condemn me only to accept me." He looked at his mother, "as your son." He looked at Ted and Stephanie, "as your brother." They sat and listened as Frank talked for fifteen minutes about him and Rebecca, and Rebecca and Thomas, and the media.

Eileen looked at Thomas. "So you're not gay?"

"No I'm not," replied Thomas.

"So you and Rebecca are engaged?" asked Stephanie.

"Our wedding date is January seventeenth," replied Rebecca.

"So Frank, these are your friends?" asked Ted.

"Yes, my good friends," he replied proudly. "I was afraid to face you alone. I told them what I needed to do and they offered me their support."

"Thomas, you're not gay. It must be weird being with him and his friends then?" asked Ted.

"Since we are all being honest Ted, I'm not a hundred percent comfortable around homosexuals but that's because I'm heterosexual. A homosexual probably feels the same way around a group of heterosexuals. To me it all comes down to respecting one another. I would go out with them again because I enjoy their company and they enjoy mine, and because I respect them and they respect me. Frank wouldn't invite me to something he thought I might find offensive," Thomas looked at Frank.

Frank continued. "Ted when you play college football you will have homosexuals playing on your team. Are you going to look beyond that and evaluate them on their talents as a football player?"

"I don't know," replied Ted. "I hope I would."

"I'm not here to wave the homosexual flag. All I want is for my family to understand me, stand by me and support me. To know that I am gay and to look past that and to see me for what I am in here." Frank pointed at his heart. "I love you all. Please don't hold my homosexuality against me and push me away." Frank stopped speaking and stood. "Thanks for listening." He looked toward the kitchen. "Dad I know you've been listening. All I ever wanted from you was for you to be as proud of me as you are of Ted." He looked at Ted and whispered. "Sorry Ted."

Ted looked up with a sad look of agreement.

"Ted," Frank said, "I'm very proud of you. I never stop talking about my younger brother who's going to college on a football scholarship and one day going to play professionally. You know I'll be there for your finals." He looked over at Stephanie, "or my sister the veterinarian." He walked and crouched in front of his mother, "I would miss not seeing you walking in at lunch times with sandwiches for everyone." He kissed her on the cheek.

Frank, Rebecca and Thomas walked to the front door and walked out. They closed the door behind them and started down the driveway to the car.

The front door opened and they turned.

"Frank wait," said Stephanie. Stephanie and Eileen came out and closed the door behind them.

"Stephanie! Mom!" said Frank.

Stephanie and Eileen walked to Frank and hugged him. They started to cry.

Thomas walked to the sidewalk and Rebecca followed. "Let's go for a walk and give them some time alone," said Thomas.

They walked down the street and behind them they could hear them tell each other how much they loved one another.

Thomas held Rebecca's hand as they slowly walked around the block. Thirty minutes later they walked up to the driveway. They were all laughing.

"I told them to go inside but they wanted to see you both," said Frank in better spirits.

"We just wanted to say goodnight," said Eileen.

"Goodnight," said Rebecca and kissed Eileen on the cheek.

"Goodnight," said Stephanie to Rebecca and Thomas and kissed them on the cheek. She whispered, "Thank you," to both of them.

Eileen grabbed Rebecca and Thomas and pulled them in for a big squeeze. "Thank you! Thank you! Thank you!" She pulled away and looked at them. "You two are angels." She turned to Frank, "I'll see you Wednesday for lunch," and kissed him.

Stephanie kissed Frank. "Maybe I can come down one night this week and we can go for a drink with your friends, somewhere local."

"I would like that," replied Frank.

"I'll call you."

Eileen and Stephanie walked back to the house arm in arm.

Frank pulled them both together and hugged them, "I love you two. You don't believe what a weight this is off of my shoulders." He kissed them both on the top of their heads. "I wasn't expecting any of them to ever want to see me again and all I can say is thank you."

They dropped Frank off at home a different man. He had a wonderful smile on his face and they laughed as he sang, 'It's My Life'. They waved goodbye and drove away."

Rebecca looked at Thomas. "I have to agree with Frank. I was surprised that they came outside."

"Families," replied Thomas. "They're all different and yet they're all the same."

"I guess blood is thicker than water," commented Rebecca.

The phone was ringing when they opened the door and Rebecca caught it in time. Thomas went into his room and sat on the bed to take off his shoes. He looked at himself in the mirror.

Rebecca walked in. "Here you are?"

"Do I look gay?" he asked her.

She broke out laughing. "I had to stop myself from laughing when he said that you were his boyfriend."

Thomas laughed. "I know it caught me by complete surprise." He looked at her. "You didn't answer the question?"

"No one looks gay?" she replied and laughed. "But maybe I should find out for sure." She walked over to him and pushed him on the bed and straddled him. She leaned down and kissed him and caressed him. "Definitely not," she answered as she felt his rising response.

They kissed for a while and stopped when the doorbell rang.

"That's Kate," said Rebecca, "she called before and wants us to sign the contract." Rebecca rolled off Thomas and opened the front door.

"Hello Kate, come in."

"Hello Rebecca."

"Like a tea?"

"Please. Where's my brother?"

"In the room," replied Rebecca.

"Hello lazy bones." She walked over to Thomas and lay next to him on the bed. "What's up?"

Thomas laughed. "I'll tell you later," he replied. "Actually Rebecca can."

"I had fun last night," said Kate.

"It was a lot of fun."

Kate looked toward the door and heard Rebecca in the kitchen and turned to Thomas. "There's something we need to talk about when we are alone."

Thomas over exaggerated her look to the door and the listening for Rebecca.

Kate punched him in the arm, "You're so funny!"

"Is it about Rebecca watching me talking about having children?"

"How did you know?" she asked.

"Rebecca caught you looking at her last night when everyone, except her, was going on about having children."

"Was I that obvious?"

"I guess so," replied Thomas copying the look to the door and the listening.

"Stop it you!"

He laughed.

"She doesn't want children?" she asked.

"No."

"You said you would never marry anyone that didn't want to have children,"

"I know I did."

"She's very special," she replied.

"She is." He turned on his side. "So what have you been up to?"

"I went to the house today and got a lot of my clothes. One, maybe two trips and I'll have it all over here. Are you going tomorrow night?"

"Yes. We both are? Are you coming with us?"

"Not tomorrow, I can't. I have three boxes on my bedroom floor. Can you bring those back? Then I'll only have one more trip."

"I'll get them before we leave."

"By the way I booked the van for Saturday at seven. I need to be in work by twelve. Is that okay?"

"That's fine."

"Should I bring the tea in here or are we having it in one of the other rooms?" asked Rebecca standing in the doorway.

"Let's have it in the solarium," suggested Thomas.

They drank the tea and signed the five copies of the contract.

"I'll have one of the senior lawyers quickly review it tomorrow and if he says its okay I'll go ahead and register the company on Tuesday," explained Kate.

She finished her tea quickly and said she had to go upstairs to unpack some clothes and prepare for her first night in her new place.

"Did you get the sheets and duvet?" asked Rebecca.

"I made it to the store thirty minutes before closing. Do you want to come up and have a look at them?" she asked.

Rebecca followed her upstairs and Thomas went into his room and had a lie down and fell asleep.

"Okay Thomas. You can ride Thunder. She's a timid horse and easy to control. I'll go into the stall and saddle her up."

Thomas watched as Rachel, dressed in riding boots, tight riding pants and a woolen sweater, opened the stall and saddled the horse. She went to the next stall and saddled up the second horse. He read the name above out loud, "Lightning."

"That's her name. She's my horse and she's fast," replied Rachel.

"You remember I'm not very good," explained Thomas.

"Don't worry. Thunder will take care of you. You go at the pace you feel most comfortable. We'll be following a trail and going through some open fields. If I gallop through a field I'll wait for you on the other side. Okay?"

"Okay," replied Thomas somewhat more at ease.

They pulled the horses out of the stable, mounted them and walked to the grass. They followed the trail and came to the first open field. Lightening galloped out of sight. Thunder slowly trotted. When Rachel returned, Thomas was halfway across the field.

"Thomas if you give her a light kick with your heel she'll go quicker and if it's too fast pull gently on the reigns and she'll slow down into a trot. She's not a fast horse," said Rachel.

Thomas gave the horse a light kick and the horse went into a slow gallop. When he got to the other side of the field he pulled on the reigns and the horse slowed into a trot, then a walk.

"That's it," encouraged Rachel. She led him through the trail in the dense woods and out into another field. She galloped away and Thomas kicked Thunder into a slow gallop. He could see Rachel in the distance. They rode for an hour through woods and fields until they came to a clearing. Rachel dismounted and walked over to Thomas and helped him. She tied the horses to a tree and lead Thomas by the hand down a steep incline. At the bottom there was a folded blanket and a picnic basket. She let go of Thomas's hand and opened up the blanket and lay it on the grass. She sat and motioned for Thomas to sit next to her. Thomas looked down at the valley below and could see a small river running through it.

"This is the most peaceful place on earth. I come here a lot on my own." She said as she looked down on the valley then over at Thomas. "You are the first person I've ever brought here. Isn't the sunset beautiful?"

Thomas looked to the west and agreed. He turned and looked at Rachel. She had her eyes closed and the sun was on her face. He could see the freckles on her nose. Her blonde hair blew in the light breeze. She was leaning back on her hands with her back arched and her breasts full. "So what really happened between you and Mathew?"

She opened her eyes and looked at Thomas. "The same old thing," she replied.

"What's that?"

"He had a difficult time dealing with people in public. He got frustrated with people approaching me, men asking for my number and staring at me. He tried to ignore it but it was too much."

"He didn't seem like that to me," replied Thomas.

Rachel laughed. "Nothing gets by you. I liked him as a friend, nothing more, he wanted more." She changed the topic. "It's too bad Rebecca and Kate couldn't come. You said Tracy was meeting Rebecca for dinner?"

"Yeah, Tracy's leaving this weekend and she wanted to see Rebecca before she left. She's bringing over pictures of the wedding and the tour. Rebecca's making her dinner and Tracy is staying the night. Kate is working tonight, she's been busy moving her stuff into the condominium amongst a hundred other things she has on the go. She told me she was heading straight to bed when she gets home."

"How does she like her place?"

"She loves it?"

"So where are you staying?"

"I'm staying between the two, last night at Rebecca's and tonight at Kate's. I do my writing at Rebecca's during the day."

"So why not just stay at Rebecca's?"

"Then we would have to tell people we were living together. Neither of us wants that right now."

Rachel looked at him. "Are you hungry?" she asked.

"I am."

She stood up and carried over the picnic basket and opened it up. She gave him a sandwich and a coke and opened a big bag of potato chips. "You're probably wondering, how I got these here?"

"It crossed my mind."

She pointed behind Thomas to a group of trees, "behind those trees is a path that goes west, down to the valley below and if you go the other way it leads back to our house. I came out here before you arrived and dropped it off."

"Do you own all this land?"

"Add a mile on the other side of the valley and work your way back to the house and add that distance in the other direction. If you look to the west you can see a small road in the distance, to the east, where that fence is, that's our property boundaries. It's a big rectangle. I've seen deer, foxes, rabbits and eagles on the property."

"It's beautiful."

"It is," she took a bite of her sandwich and looked at Thomas. "Have you made any wedding plans yet?"

"No, this weekend."

"January seventeenth. The engagement and wedding is so sudden."

"I guess."

"Have you talked about children?"

"We have."

"When I get married I want to be completely selfish and spend the first three years with my husband, then I want to have children."

"How many do you want?"

"I was thinking three or four."

"Really!"

"Why? What about you?"

"I guess three or four."

"What about Rebecca?"

"She's not sure?"

"About how many?"

Thomas was uncomfortable with the conversation. So he answered, "Yes," and thought zero is a number.

"I can't wait to have children and take them pony riding, swimming, to school and arranging birthday parties." She hesitated and let out a light laugh. "All I have to do is get the right man."

"Don't you mean find?"

She smiled and looked at him. "Thomas I've already found him. I just haven't had enough courage to walk up to him and tell him. I may have missed my opportunity."

"Do I know him?"

"I believe you've met him?"

"Was he at your party?"

"He was."

"He was?" Thomas asked, and thought who it could be.

She interrupted his train of thought. "No more hints. I'm not going to tell you who he is; I am allowed to have some secrets. But I will tell you he's a lot like you."

"Then you have good taste," said Thomas smiling. He took a bite of his sandwich. "You make the best sandwiches."

"Thank you. Wait till you taste dessert," she teased.

Thomas ate another sandwich and they watched the sunset. "This is your special place," stated Thomas.

"It's one of them. But it's my favorite. In the summer I can sunbathe here in private and in the fall I can ride here and look at the sunset and the stars."

"What about the winter?"

"For the winter I have another place."

"Do I get to see that?"

"Maybe I'll show you in the winter."

"Is this the place you were going to bring me to Sunday afternoon after your party?"

"Yes."

"I can't believe this is the first time we've been able to go riding since then."

"I know. So much has happened." She looked at the sun sinking out of sight. "Maybe we should head back to the house?"

"I thought we were going to watch the stars?"

"Do you want to?"

"Do you?"

"I do." She stood up. "Let me clean up and we can lie down. We'll see who spots the first one."

"What about your dessert?"

She talked as she packed up the picnic basket. "That's in the refrigerator at the house. We can have that when we get back."

As they lay on the blanket Thomas tried his best to locate the first star.

Rachel looked deep in her heart for some answers.

"THOMAS, NOT ONE OF YOUR BETTER ROUNDS," said Jack as they stood by the bar and took the drinks from the bar tender. "Did you let me win?"

"No Jack. I'm a little preoccupied," said Thomas.

"Why don't we sit in our usual spot and watch the people screw up on eighteen," said Jack as he led the way to the table. They sat down and Jack looked at Thomas, "Is there anything I can help you with?"

"I don't think so."

"Do you want me to listen? I'm good at that," replied Jack sipping his Crown Royal.

"I'd like that," said Thomas collecting his thoughts. "It's very easy to summarize but difficult to resolve."

"Okay. Shoot."

"Rebecca doesn't want to have children and I do. I trust my instincts and they tell me as time passes she will change her mind. I told her I loved her and would marry her no matter what she decided."

"You are worried that she may never change her mind?" asked Jack.

"Right now that's a great possibility," said Thomas.

"Why do you say that?"

"Her friend Tracy is pregnant and Kate and Rachel have both said they want to have children. They don't even think twice about it and they all want more than one. Rebecca seems so detached from it all."

"Would you have gotten engaged to her if she had told you this before hand?"

"Yes," said Thomas, "I love her more than anything else on this earth."

"Well, it's important that you know how you feel and also to know what you want." He sipped his drink. "Do you want to be with her forever?"

"I do."

"Forever is enough time for someone to change their mind," said Jack. "Are you willing to wait that long for the woman you love?"

"I am"

"I think you're on the right track Thomas. Trust your instincts on this one and let nature sort this one out for you." Jack smiled, "it's out of your hands."

Thomas agreed with a nod. "Thanks Jack."

"I always wanted children. Looking back I probably could have done some things differently. Not that I have regrets. I'm happy with what I've done with my life. But sometimes I think about what it would have been like."

"You're never too old to have children," commented Thomas.

Jack looked at him.

"I meant adopt."

"Adopt?"

"Jack, there are so many unwanted children living in foster homes and third world countries around the world. You could be giving someone a chance at a better life."

"I've never thought about it like that," he said and looked at Thomas. "This may sound crazy but you're the closest I have to a son. I know I haven't known you that long. That's why it's sounds crazy. I guess it's because you are everything I ever wanted in a son. Your parents would be proud of you."

"Thanks Jack," replied Thomas. "You know there was no one else I would have talked to about this, except you."

CHAPTER 15

Wedding Plans

"How do I look?" asked Rebecca as she walked into the living room.

"You look absolutely stunning," replied Thomas.

"So do you," she replied and kissed him. "The only problem is that I don't know what jacket to wear. Most of my jackets are a bit too dressy."

"One second," said Thomas. He left the room and came back with a box, "this is for you. I've had it under the bed for a couple of weeks and was waiting for an opportunity."

Rebecca opened the box and pulled out the black leather biker's jacket, "you got this for me. Thomas it's beautiful." She put it on and went to the mirror in the hallway. "Thomas I love it and it fits perfect." She ran back in and put her arms around him and kissed him.

"I'm glad you like it."

"I love it!"

"Frank's friend Miguel is in the leather business and made it especially for you. He said that it's one of a kind, there's not two the same, just like you."

"You are so sweet. I've been to his store; he has beautiful clothes, especially his jackets and dresses. I've been meaning to buy one from him. This is very special. Thank you."

"You look great in it," complimented Thomas and gave her a kiss. He put on his coat and they left.

They sat in a secluded booth at The Duke. Thomas ordered a Carlsberg and Rebecca a white wine. They both ordered fish and chips.

"You know a lot of people here," stated Rebecca.

"Yeah, well I used to come here a lot."

"Not so much any more?" asked Rebecca.

"Not as much. I didn't come at all when my grandmother took ill. I've been here a few times since her funeral. I tried to stay home with Kate and keep her company; unfortunately I didn't realize I was driving her crazy.

She finally told me to go out or she was going to either throw me out or move out."

Rebecca laughed and looked around. "I like it here. It has a nice atmosphere and the people seem friendly. I like all the pictures of John Wayne."

"The guy that owns the place is a John Wayne fanatic, that's why he called it The Duke." Thomas couldn't resist. "He also makes the best fish and chips."

Rebecca laughed at his attempt. "We will have to see about that," replied Rebecca. "I never got a chance to ask? How's Rachel doing?"

"She's doing well. She wanted to know if you would like to go shopping with her for some clothes for Aruba."

"Did she say when?"

"She said she would call you."

"I heard they have Jack's plane and they've booked a beautiful deluxe hotel on Palm Beach. Everyone is going, Rachel, Jessica, Veronica, Buddy, Kate, Frank, Jack and Penny."

"We're going to have so much fun. What time do we leave?" asked Thomas.

"We're flying out on Wednesday at one thirty and we'll get there around dinner time. We fly back Sunday evening and arrive around eleven."

"I can't wait to be with you, the beach, the waves and the sunset."

"I can't either. I'll have to buy some new bikinis and dresses."

"Any excuse to shop!"

"You're catching on." She said and looked at Thomas. "When I was with Tracy, don't get me wrong I like her and she's great company, but I wished you were there. It's not as much fun when you're not there. I missed you. I know we need to have some time on our own and with different people. But still…I was wondering how you felt?"

"Rebecca, we spend enough time apart during the day. I don't think we need to spend more time away at night. At Rachel's I kept turning around to ask you what you thought or to say something that you would find funny and I realized you weren't there to answer. It was like a part of me was missing. I like having you with me. I wanted to say something to you but I didn't want you to feel as if I were crowding you."

"I want you to." She held his hand. "I would like to go shopping with Rachel but I know it won't be as much fun as going with you. Well maybe I shouldn't say it quite like that that's a little unfair to her; it's a different kind of fun. What I am saying is that I would like to go shopping and buy some bikinis and dresses with you then go with her and pick out a few surprise items. I have so much fun when we are together. I guess I want us to go shopping and buy some things together, as a couple."

"I understand I feel the same way too."

"I love you." She leaned over and kissed him. "Tomorrow we'll go shopping for invitations and clothes for Aruba."

They started to kiss until a polite throat clearing from the waiter got their attention. He dropped off their food and left.

"Looks good" she replied and smiled.

They ate quietly and Rebecca put her knife and fork on the empty plate. "Can we talk about the wedding?"

"First things first. What did you think about The Duke's fish and chips?"

"I thought they were equivalent to the Cove and therefore I conclude they are both as good as the other."

"In that case I have the winning vote and I pick The Duke."

"No, that's unfair. I want to vote for the Cove.

"It's too late!"

Rebecca gave him a frown and a playful pout. She then leaned over and whispered, "If you change your vote I'll let you undress me and put on my night shirt."

Thomas looked away and yawned as if he was bored.

She continued. "I don't plan on wearing anything under my night shirt." She licked his ear.

Thomas gave her a somewhat uninterested glance.

"I'll let you take advantage of me." She licked her lips.

"Okay, okay."

"It's too late. You had your chance and you blew it?"

"Really," replied Thomas. "You mean you blew it!"

"What do you mean? I blew it!"

"Tonight I was going to pick you up and carry you to your bed and kiss you on your ear," he touched her ear with his finger. "Then your cheek," he moved his finger to her cheek. "Then your lips." he put his finger on her lips and she kissed them. "Then I would kiss your cute chin and your neck. I would undo your top button and kiss and unbutton my way down to your navel. I would then open up your shirt and undo your bra at the front and kiss and suck on your hard nipples. You would moan gently. I would move my hand down to your knee and run my hand up the inside of your leg and stop between you thighs and rub gently. You would let out a loud moan. I would undo your jeans, slowly, and slide my hand down underneath your cotton panties, past your pubic mound and rub softly. You would moan louder and faster and move your pelvis in rhythm with my hand. I would insert my finger deep inside you and you would let out a light scream. Then I would kiss my way past your navel and down your body, kissing your legs as I remove your pants and underwear. I would then place my tongue on your toes and lick my way up your calf, inside your thighs. You would open your legs wide and I…" Thomas got the waitresses attention, "another round please." He looked at Rebecca and smiled.

"That was cruel! Unkind! Unfair!" pouted Rebecca.

"It gives you something to think about till our wedding night."

"You never finished?"

"I know. To be continued," he smiled slyly, "on our wedding night."

"Thomas, I'll get you for this."

"Promises, promises," he replied.

The waitress put down the drinks.

"Now what about our wedding?" he asked.

"I'm back and forth. One part of me thinks we should have it here and book the cathedral and the restaurant. On the other hand I think of going to a beautiful island and getting married outdoors with sea, the sun and sand. Then I think we should do something totally outrageous like Tracy and get married in Las Vegas. What do you think?" asked Rebecca.

"I like all three. Whatever you want?"

"I like them all too. We need to decide tonight and get the invitations out this week," replied Rebecca.

"I know," said Thomas. "I would rather go to Las Vegas one weekend in the summer and do some gambling and go swimming, see the shows and renew our vows at one of those crazy ceremonies."

"I feel the same, Vegas is out. So now we either have it here or on an island. Why don't we talk about getting married on an island?" suggested Rebecca.

"Okay, which ones did you like?"

"I like the Virgin Islands, St. Thomas, St. John, and Tortola. All three have beautiful resorts on them. We could fly to one for a long weekend. Similar to what we are doing with Aruba," she stopped and repeated, "like Aruba." She looked up at Thomas. "If we go to one of these islands we're going to have everyone there all the time."

"Not necessarily. Guests will fly out on the Sunday or Monday and we will have the following week to ourselves."

"That's true." She thought for a moment. "If we stay here and have our wedding and reception, we can stay in a beautiful suite at a local hotel and fly out on the Sunday to an island; that would be very romantic. Or we could fly to an exotic location with all our friends and family and have our ceremony outside and reception in a beautiful hotel and stay in a beautiful suite." She became frustrated, "both of them are romantic."

"Both of them sound beautiful," replied Thomas holding her hand.

"We should at least pick an island."

"I agree."

"They're all beautiful," she stated. "St. John."

"St. John it is!"

"There is a luxurious resort on the island and the more I think about it the more I think we should have our wedding here and spend our honeymoon there."

"I agree," replied Thomas with a smile. "Tomorrow we should get some brochures and magazines and look on the Internet and find out what accommodations the resort offers and pick the one we like best and book it."

"Perfect," she said. "The more I think about it the more I like this idea the best." She looked at Thomas, "I love you."

"I love you."

They finished their drinks and went to a nightclub three blocks away.

"This place plays all the latest music. It's one on the best dance clubs around," said Rebecca as they walked in.

Thomas got two beers and walked over to Rebecca to the edge of the dance floor and watched the crowd dance to the music. A song by 'Christina Aguilera' came on.

"I love this song. Dance with me?" asked Rebecca pulling Thomas onto the dance floor.

They danced all night.

"I LIKE THIS ONE THE BEST," SAID Rebecca pointing out the white invitation with the pink highlight, "it has the rings, the cross, and the flowers. It's gorgeous."

"I can have them ready by the end of the week," replied the salesman.

"That would be great," replied Rebecca.

He took down all their personal information and Rebecca said she would call him Monday with the location of the wedding and reception.

"Tomorrow we can talk to the priest and ask him about the date," said Rebecca to Thomas, as they walked out the store. She stopped. "We need to visit the restaurant and book that."

"We can do that after we finish shopping," suggested Thomas.

"I'm so excited," she replied.

They went into a travel agent and picked up some brochures and then into a bookstore and bought some travel magazines and travel books.

"There are so many thoughts going through my mind, dresses, tuxedos, flowers, limousines. We are making that list tonight? Right!"

"We are," confirmed Thomas.

They began walking and stopped at Bikini Village. Rebecca picked out several bikinis and tried each of them on for Thomas.

"I like them all," replied Thomas. "The bikini was made for your body."

"I'm taking a total of four. So I need you to pick two today. When I go with Rachel I'll pick the other two."

"But I like all four. This isn't easy," said Thomas. He thought for a moment. "The dark blue one and the floral."

She leaned over and whispered in Thomas's ear. "If you're a good boy I might give you a private showing later on." She blew in his ear.

She tried on three dresses and bought them all. On the way home they stopped in 'La Petite Maison' and booked the restaurant for the day and evening.

They dropped off the bags at the condominium and went for a swim.

"It didn't take us long to move this morning," said Rebecca.

Thomas looked on as Rebecca prepared the lasagna. "No it didn't. It was kind of sad leaving the house but I'm glad Penny bought it. At least we can go by once in a while," said Thomas.

"Thomas I was thinking, why don't you move in with me? Kate lives upstairs. It seems foolish you living between both places. What do you think?"

"What about people talking?"

"To be quite honest I don't really care about what people say and secondly we are engaged." She gave Thomas a long look. "Why? Are you worried?"

"Not really. It's just that when you say you're living together people assume you are sleeping together," replied Thomas.

"Let them assume." She walked over to Thomas. "It's your choice. I just think its silly going back and forth."

"I know."

They made a wedding list and a list of invitees while the lasagna cooked.

"Twenty six," confirmed Rebecca.

"Have you thought about a maid of honor?"

"I thought about Penny and having Kate and Rachel as bridesmaids. What about a best man?"

"I was thinking about Jack. I could have Frank as an usher?"

"I think they would like that. This all sounds so nice."

"When should we ask them?"

"Let's wait till we have all the particulars finalized. Then we can ask them and send off the invitations. Maybe in Aruba," suggested Rebecca.

"That's a great idea."

As they ate dinner they looked through the holiday brochures, the travel magazines and books, and went online. They agreed on the resort and the accommodations and decided to book it with a travel agent in the morning.

"Caneel Bay, it looks so romantic, the clear blue water and white sandy beaches and the villa is right on the beach. Just think, when we are there, I'll be Mrs. Rebecca Carlyle. I wish it were tomorrow."

"It will be here soon." Thomas put his arm around her. "Are you nervous about Wednesday?"

"No, I've been practicing for this day all my life. I was ready months ago. You are coming to my dress rehearsal on Tuesday?"

"I am."

"You know I also dance on Friday evening," said Rebecca in a low voice.

"You do?" said Thomas trying to act surprised.

"You don't have to come," said Rebecca.

"Good, because I have something important to do," replied Thomas.

"You do? What?" asked Rebecca.

"I'll show you." He stood up and went to his room and came back with an envelope. "Here you open it."

"What's this?" Rebecca opened the envelope and screamed with joy. "You bought tickets to all my performances."

"I wouldn't miss one for the world," he replied.

"I'm in the Nutcracker five times!" she cried.

"I have tickets for all five," he said and smiled. "I bought front row so I could have a good view of you."

"Oh Thomas I love you for this," she said and put her head on his chest.

"I even bought a couple of extra tickets for some of the shows in case Kate, Rachel, or Jessica wanted to go."

AFTER MASS THEY WENT INTO THE RECTORY to speak with the priest.

"Father Brendan will be with you in a moment, please take a seat. Would you like some coffee?"

"No thank you," they both replied.

They sat in silence looking around the reception area nervously.

"Rebecca and Thomas please come in," said Father Brendan.

"What can I do for you today?" asked the priest.

"We would like to get married," replied Thomas.

"Both Catholics?" he asked.

"Yes," they replied.

"Where is my calendar?" he searched around his table and found a book. "Here it is. So what date?"

"January seventeenth," replied Rebecca.

"A year January seventeenth," replied the priest flipping through his book.

"This January," replied Rebecca.

The priest closed his book and looked at them. "We require a year in advance," replied Father Brendan. "January is only three months. You also have to take a marriage course."

"We hoped we could take the course sometime over the next three months," explained Thomas.

"How long have you been together?" he asked.

"A couple of months," replied Rebecca.

"I can't marry you this soon under these circumstances," replied the priest.

They went silent.

"You must understand it is your best interests that we are looking out for," he confirmed.

"Father we love each other," said Thomas.

"I'm sure you do. Every couple that comes in here says that they are in love and forty percent of their marriages end in divorce, a sad statistic in this day and age."

"Father, Thomas and I may have only been together for a couple of months but we have known each other for a very long time. Please let me explain?" asked Rebecca.

"Please do," replied the priest.

For half an hour she did.

"I'm not denying that you two are in love. We have a certain criteria that we follow. I'm sure you can understand my position?" he asked.

"Father, are you saying you won't marry us?" asked Thomas.

"I'm not saying that. I'm saying I can't marry you that soon," replied the priest.

Thomas stood up. "Thank you father but we will be getting married on that day, if not by you, then by a justice of the peace."

"Thomas, please sit. We may be able to do something earlier than a year let me look through the calendar," said Father Brendan.

"Father, Thomas and I are firm on the date. Unless you are looking at January seventeenth you are wasting your time," said Rebecca in a firm voice.

The priest looked at them both. "Give me one reason why I should marry you sooner, besides the love that you have for one another," inquired the father.

Thomas looked at Rebecca and Rebecca at Thomas.

"Father, I have saved myself my whole life to give myself to the man I love on my wedding night. The Catholic Church taught me that and its something I hold dear to my heart. I now ask the church to trust me when I tell them that come January seventeenth this man will wed me and I will make love to him whether married in a catholic or non-catholic ceremony. I am asking, begging you, to let us marry in January in this cathedral."

The priest looked at Thomas, "if you were living together in sin." Then over at Rebecca, "or Rebecca you were pregnant, we would be pushing you to get married as soon as possible. Why don't we set up an appointment for this week?" he asked. He looked through his calendar, "Wednesday evening at eight."

"Sorry father I dance that night?"

"You dance. May I ask what type of dancing?"

"I dance ballet for the First National Ballet."

"Very good," he looked at Thomas. "Are you a dancer too?"

"No. I'm a writer."

"You write stories?"

"Yes, I do."

He looked at Rebecca. "What evening is best for you?"

"Either Monday or Thursday."

He looked in his calendar. "Okay, Thursday at eight, after seven o'clock mass." One more thing, he looked through his calendar. "January seventeenth at three o'clock, is that okay?"

Their faces lit up. "Thank you Father!"

"You will have to take the marriage course before then. It will probably be on a weekend, I will give you a list of dates and times on Thursday," he stood up and showed them to the door.

They thanked him again and left. Outside they kissed.

They drove to the park and went for a walk. Rebecca took her list out of her handbag. "We have booked the church and the reception. We need to reserve some rooms at the hotel across the street. I'll call with the information for the invitations. We need to book a couple of limousines and we are going to the travel agent tomorrow instead of today. We are going to talk to the bridal party this weekend. Dresses, tuxedos and flowers we still have to do. As well as pick the courses, champagne, and wine for the reception. And finally, decide on the music and the wedding cake." She looked and smiled at Thomas. "I'm so excited."

"I can tell."

As she put her list away the same family passed on their bicycles. "Hello pretty lady," said the youngest and smiled.

"Hello," replied Rebecca and smiled back as she watched them peddle away.

CHAPTER 16

Swan Lake

THOMAS SAT IN THE FRONT ROW. To his left was Henri, who had arrived from New York only a few hours earlier, and to his right was Kate. Next to Kate were Rachel, Jessica and Jack. Next to Henri were Eileen, Stephanie and Ted, and John's empty seat.

Thomas had stopped by earlier on to see how Rebecca was doing. He kissed her and told her how proud he was.

"Did she look nervous?" asked Kate.

"No," replied Thomas. "She looked very comfortable. I think I'm more nervous."

"She will be wonderful," comforted Henri.

The lights dimmed, the conductor appeared, the music started and the curtains rose and the ballet began. Rebecca danced like an angel. Her routines were graceful and flawless. It was like being in a dream. Thomas smiled as he watched her move across the floor. After the first ten minutes his nerves had settled and he enjoyed the performance. At the end of the first intermission the audience applauded loudly.

"Thomas she is dancing on air," said Kate as she stood.

"I've never seen her dance with so much energy and passion," added Jessica. "Her routine has been flawless and they compliment each other magnificently. Frank lifts and carries her without any strain whatsoever," continued Jessica looking at Eileen.

"They dance divinely together. I'm proud of both of them," said Eileen.

They went out to the lounge and Jack and Rachel came back with a tray of glasses filled with champagne. They all took a glass. Ted walked over and spoke with Thomas.

"I wanted you to know, well, I just wanted to thank you for standing up for Frank and being there for him."

Thomas smiled and looked at Ted and gave him the silence to talk.

Ted continued. "I went with Stephanie to see him last Wednesday and I'm glad I did. You know he's coming to my championship game Sunday."

"I didn't but I knew he would," replied Thomas.

"I wanted to ask you and Rebecca to come and watch, that's if you wanted to, I understand if you are busy," mumbled Ted.

"What time?"

"Two o'clock kick off."

"We'll be there. Thanks for asking."

Ted looked at his glass nervously. "There was something Frank said at the house that stuck in my mind, about my father always gloating about me and ignoring Frank. I used to love all that attention and I used to look at Frank and inside I thought I have something he would never have, my father's respect. Now that I think about it I'm so ashamed of my father and more so of myself for thinking that way. Frank's always been there for me. Did you know he's never missed any of my games?"

"No I didn't."

"This is the first time I've watched him dance, I'm not one for ballet, but I should have been there for him. Even when he used to come over and visit we always talked about football and me, never about him or his dance. He always brags about me to everyone. I've never talk about him; I was too embarrassed to say that my brother was a ballet dancer." He stopped and looked at Thomas. "My father never wants to see Frank again. I tried talking to him but he doesn't want to listen." He looked sadly at his glass. "What do you think?"

Thomas looked at Ted. "Unfortunately Ted everything that can be said has been said. Your father needs time, maybe a couple of days, weeks, months or years. It could be never."

"You think it will be never?"

"No, I think your father will come around one day soon. You need to be patient and let him come to terms with this in his own time. The worst thing you can do is to push him into a corner. And don't be so hard on yourself. Frank will be so happy when he finds out you're here."

"Hello Thomas," interrupted Stephanie.

"Thanks Thomas, I'll see you later," said Ted as he left and stood next to his mother.

"Thomas I wanted to tell you I finished reading your novel." She stopped and was waiting for him to ask.

"Okay," said Thomas, "I'll take the bait. What did you think?"

"I loved it. I cried and cried and cried. Have you heard back from any publishers?"

"Not yet. Hopefully some time before Christmas."

"Thomas, trust me, you will," complimented Stephanie.

"Thanks."

She looked at him awkwardly. "Can I…?" She stopped.

"Can you read my next novel?" asked Thomas.

She smiled. "Yes."

"I'll send you a copy once it's ready to be mailed out," replied Thomas. "Probably be in a few weeks."

"Thank you," she replied.

The bell rang to remind patrons that the intermission ended in five minutes. Stephanie excused herself and went to the bathroom.

"And to think I used to have you all to myself," said Rachel.

"Hello Rachel, come here," he kissed her on the cheek. "You look amazing tonight! That dress fits you in all the right places."

"You always know the right things to say. When will I get a man like you?" she asked.

"I thought you had one," replied Thomas.

She smiled at Thomas and drank her champagne.

"I'm looking forward to Aruba," said Thomas.

"I hoped you would be," she replied.

"Hi Thomas," said Jessica and kissed him on the cheek. "Rachel I'll meet you back at the seats. I'm going back with Jack and Henri."

"Okay, I'll be along in a minute." She watched her mother leave and turned to Thomas. "I have my itinerary for my shoot, maybe next break I can tell you about it."

"I'd like that; it's all new to me."

They finished their champagne and she put her arm through Thomas's and they walked back to their seats.

Rebecca danced magnificently and the crowd applauded loudly as the curtain fell for the second intermission.

"Thomas, I have never been so proud in all my life," said Henri as he walked with Thomas to the lounge. "I will be leaving at lunch time tomorrow. I was hoping you and Rebecca would join me for a light breakfast and let me know about your wedding plans. Say around nine o'clock."

"Of course, I'll come to Rebecca's a few minutes before," replied Thomas.

"Let me tell you again how happy I am for the both of you. I'm hoping you will both come and see me soon, perhaps in December?"

"I would like that. Maybe tomorrow we can come up with a date," suggested Thomas. "Will we be seeing you over Christmas?"

"I'm surprising Rebecca tomorrow. I booked my tickets for the twenty-third till the twenty-seventh," said Henri happily.

"She will be thrilled."

"I would like to buy the next round of drinks, please excuse me so that I can intercept Jack at the bar," he said, and departed.

Thomas talked to Eileen and Kate. Henri and Jack returned with a tray of drinks.

"Thomas why don't we step outside and get some fresh air?" asked Rachel.

"That's a good idea," said Thomas. He excused himself and escorted Rachel out to the patio.

"Being outside reminds me of the first night we met. Remember at the hotel in that garden under the gazebo."

"I remember. I said I liked your freckles and you got all embarrassed."

"I know." She looked out in the distance and was thinking hard about something.

"Is everything alright?" asked Thomas.

"Uh-huh," she replied and looked at him.

"Tell me about Aruba?"

"Well, it seems as if the shoots will be all day Thursday and Friday morning. So I'll have quite a bit of free time to spend with you and the others."

"What happens during the shoots?"

"Well they are going to be taking pictures around the hotel pool, on Palm Beach and some sunset shots. The next day they want some more on the beach and in the water with the sunrise."

"They keep you busy?"

"It's a lot of work. I guess the worst part is the waiting around, for the sun to come from behind the clouds or for a rain shower to pass. Then there's hair and make-up and the heat." She smiled. "But it's a lot of fun."

"And you love it?"

"I do," she said as her eyes lit up. She hesitated and spoke quietly as if she didn't want anyone to hear her. "I was hoping you would come and watch. You don't have to, but you can if you want?"

"Is it okay?"

"Of course, the hotel will set up a tent and umbrellas inside a roped off perimeter and you can watch from there. I'm going to ask the others as well but I really want you to be there."

"I think that would be great. I'm interested to see what goes on."

Rachel smiled and continued. "They're only looking for five pictures, that's one for each bikini," explained Rachel. "But they will take hundreds. The team that they have going are excellent, I've worked with each of them on a few different shoots and they're very professional. The only person I haven't worked with is the lady that designed the swimsuits but she's not considered part of the team. Jim, that's the photographer, says she's really easy to get along with."

Thomas tried to imagine what it would be like having three or four people working on you.

"It's not easy having someone matching your hair and makeup with a bathing suit and a photographer hurrying you up before the sun goes behind the clouds."

"I was just thinking about that," replied Thomas. "It sounds exciting; I'm looking forward to it." Thomas drank his champagne and as he did he couldn't help thinking that there was something on Rachel's mind.

"We should go back with the others," said Rachel.

"Rachel, are you sure you are okay?"

She looked into Thomas's eyes, "Thomas," she thought about it and changed her mind. "I'm fine, really."

Thomas wasn't convinced. He took her arm and walked her back to the others. He excused himself and walked in the direction of the bathroom. On the way he thought he recognized someone and followed at a distance and waited to see if they would turn around. The person stood at the back of the theater waiting for the last act to start. The person looked around and over in Thomas's direction. Thomas realized he was right. He left and went to the bathroom and back to his seat.

The curtain fell to end the ballet. The audience was on their feet and the applause was deafening. There were shouts of 'Bravo!' from all around the theater. The curtain rose and fell eight times. Each time Rebecca looked over at Thomas and smiled. Finally Rebecca and Frank appeared from behind the curtain. Rebecca looked over at Thomas and blew him a kiss. Henri, Eileen, Jack and Jessica went to the right side of the stage and threw bouquets of roses. Frank picked them up and passed them to Rebecca. Thomas was behind them and was about to throw his roses and a small pink ballet teddy bear on the stage when Rebecca whispered to Frank who signaled Thomas to the side. Frank escorted Rebecca. She handed Frank the flowers and met Thomas at the stairs and put her arms around him and kissed him on the cheek. She was crying.

"I love you," she said. "Tonight was for you."

"I love you," he handed her the flowers and gave her the teddy bear. She took a rose out and kissed its petals and handed it back to him.

Thomas headed for his seat. Rebecca and Frank walked back to the middle of the stage. She looked over at Thomas and smiled.

THE WAITERS WALKED AROUND WITH TRAYS OF glasses filled with champagne and the waitress held trays of hors d'oeuvres. Suddenly there was a commotion over at the doorway. The low applause increased in volume as the hundred guests looked towards the entrance and the air echoed with the cries of 'Bravo!' Rebecca had arrived and she was with Frank, Eric and Penny.

They slowly made their way through the crowd to an area where there was a microphone. The crowd stood around the quartet. Thomas was with the rest of the group at the back and could see her face. She was desperately looking around the room for him.

"Ladies and gentlemen, please," said Eric signaling with his hands to stop the clapping. "Thank you. Can I please have a waiter bring up four glasses of champagne?" He waited for the waiter to arrive and hand out the champagne and leave. "Tonight you witnessed one of the brightest young stars to grace the stage as a member of the First National Ballet. Her grace, elegance, style and techniques can be compared to that of the late, great and sensational Margaret Carlyle. I think you will all agree that tonight she kept her audience captive from start to finish."

The crowd cheered and clapped.

Eric waited patiently till they stopped. "Never have I heard eight curtain calls at that theater. I believe if we had not turned on the lights we may have been there all night."

The crowd laughed.

"Please let me hear your loud applause for a ballerina who is destined for greatness and is one of the future stars of the not only the First National Ballet but the world stage, Ms. Rebecca La Croix."

Eric turned and kissed Rebecca and motioned her to the microphone. The applause continued for ten minutes. Eventually Eric had to come back to the microphone and ask them to stop.

"Ladies, gentlemen, friends and family thank you for being a part of this very special night. There are several people I would like to thank so please bear with me." Rebecca stopped and composed herself. "I would like to thank my first teacher and mentor Mrs. Margaret Carlyle. Not only were her technique and style second to none, but also her patience, caring and understanding. She was without fault. She is sadly missed and may she rest in peace. I know she was looking down at me tonight. I would like to thank my second teacher, mentor and very good friend Ms. Penelope Daily, who not only took me on as a student but as a daughter. She taught me not only the expression of dance but how to let that expression evolve with my techniques and make me a complete dancer," she turned and walked to Penny and gave her a kiss and a hug. Rebecca came back to the microphone. "The third person I would like to thank is my artistic director Eric Smythe who taught me how to marry my dance with the music and the movement of the ballet. His interpretation is second-to-none," she turned to him and kissed him on the cheek. "The fourth person is my partner Frank Gray, whose technique and timing make my routine seem effortless, he is in his own right an accomplished dancer whom I respect dearly. His knowledge, patience and experience have made my rehearsing and my performing for you a joy. I could not ask for a better partner. I am also very fortunate to be able to call him my friend," she turned around and kissed Frank on the cheek. She turned back to the audience. "I would like to thank you all for tonight and for supporting me over the years. I thank you and I applaud you." Rebecca clapped her hands. "There are two additional people I would like to thank. The first is my father, Henri, who took me to the Nutcracker; it was there that I fell in love with ballet. Upon my request he enrolled me in ballet classes and then the First National Ballet School. I thank him for his love and kindness and his on going support. I thank him for opening up this door of opportunity. Where is my father?" Rebecca looked around the room. Her father made his way up to the front. She kissed him and hugged him tightly. "The last person I would like to thank is a very, very special man in my life. Outside of ballet he has shown me how to trust, believe, need, care and most importantly, love. He has helped me grow as a person and mature as a ballerina. Those of you who know who I am talking about have been touched by him one way or another and know the kind of person he is. To me he is my world, my life, my love, my soul mate, my friend and now my fiancée. He is the kind of man who will stand in the back and let me have my spotlight and allow you, the audience the time with me. But I ask him to walk up here and share this moment with me. I love you with all my heart Thomas, please come forward." Rebecca looked around the room.

Thomas was close to tears.

"Rebecca he's over here," shouted Jack. Jack pointed at Thomas. The crowd turned and Jack pushed Thomas forward. Thomas started walking toward Rebecca. Rebecca walked toward Thomas. They met in the middle.

"I love you," she said.

"I love you," he replied.

She kissed him on the lips and hugged him tightly. She let go and grabbed his hand and walked back with him to the microphone. The crowd watched in silence.

"Ladies and gentlemen, friends and family I would like to thank you all once again. I will try to come by and meet each of you before the end of the evening. Thank you." The crowd applauded. Thomas tried to let go of her hand but she held on tightly. He took one step back; Rebecca stood back next to him. Eric came to the microphone and asked the guests to enjoy themselves. He signaled to the trio in the corner and they began play. The crowd turned away into smaller groups and talked amongst themselves.

Rebecca turned to Thomas. She was radiant. "Why didn't you come backstage after the show? I was waiting for you."

"I don't belong back there."

"We'll see about that," she said and smiled. "How do I look?"

"You look beautiful. And you danced angelically."

"You are too kind sir," she jested.

"Thanks for what you said you almost had me in tears."

"I meant every word."

"I know you did."

"When you win your literary awards you can praise me."

"I'm not so sure about that."

"Why you," she said, and playfully punched him in the stomach.

"There are a lot of people waiting to see you. So give me a kiss and I'll see you later. You know I'll be the last one here."

"I know you will," she kissed him. "I love you more than dancing, in fact, more than anything in this world."

CHAPTER 17

Time

THEY SAT AND WATCHED THE WAITRESS POUR the coffee and waited for her to leave. "Rebecca I have a surprise!" said Henri.

"What is it?"

"I've booked a trip to come on the twenty-third of December to the twenty-seventh," said Henri.

"You have!" cried Rebecca, "I thought you said you couldn't get the time off."

"I worked some things out, moved some plans around and made the time," he replied.

"That's great. You've made me so happy," said Rebecca standing and giving her father a hug. She sat back down, "this means so much to me, having you here for Christmas."

"I know and it means a lot to me," he replied. "Tell me how are the wedding plans going."

"They're going well. I'm going with Kate, Rachel and Penny to pick out my wedding and bridesmaid dresses a week Sunday." She went through her memorized list, "we booked the church, the restaurant, the limousines, and the disc jockey. We picked out the wedding cake. The invitations have been sent. We still have to pick out the meal, which we are doing next week."

"Seems like everything is under control?"

"Everything is going fine." She held Henri's hand and looked at Thomas.

"I was thinking that on the twenty-fourth or the twenty-seventh we could get fitted for the tuxedos. I thought it would look smart if you, Jack, Frank and I all had on the same style and color. If that's okay?" asked Thomas.

"Not a problem, whatever you want." He stopped and looked at them both. "You're still letting me pay for all this?" he asked.

"Yes," replied Rebecca. "We have an itemized list and have been putting down the cost next to each item, after the dresses and the restaurant; we'll have an approximate figure."

"Thomas, are you okay with me paying?"

"Henri, I think it's very decent of you to do this for Rebecca. Hopefully I will be able to do it for Kate one day. I know my father would have wanted it that way."

"I'm glad," said Henri, "I would hate to be looked upon as someone interfering."

"You're not," said Rebecca.

"You must make me one promise then. That is, that you spare no expense when it comes to making your plans. I would be very upset if they are not serving the best wine and champagne."

"I promise," replied Rebecca.

Henri put his hand into his pocket and pulled out two, hand-size gift-wrapped boxes. "This one is for you Rebecca and this if for you Thomas."

"What are these?" asked Rebecca.

"An engagement present," he replied.

Rebecca and Thomas opened their gifts. They looked at his and her matching gold watches. They looked at each other and then at Henri.

"Just reminders to make sure that you both always have time for each other. If you look at the back I had them put on an inscription."

Rebecca read it out loud, "'Time is Love', and underneath it has our wedding date." She looked at Henri. "Dad, these are beautiful."

"These are," said Thomas.

"Try them on for me?" he asked.

They put them on.

"They look good on you," he complimented. "Now I have something here for Rebecca." He went into one of his bags and pulled out a small shoebox.

Rebecca took it off of him and opened it. "These are my first pair of ballet slippers. You had them all this time."

"I have all of them," he smiled. "I left the other ones on your bed."

"So that's why you had to go into my room," said Rebecca giving him a mischievous look. "You've been hanging around this one too long," she said pointing her thumb at Thomas.

"I thought you might want to keep them for sentimental reasons or to show your children or maybe a daughter who might wear them.

You know some of the smaller ones are like new. I also have all your old costumes. I thought you could take them back with you next time you come to visit."

Rebecca looked at Thomas and back at her father. "These are great. I can't believe you kept all this stuff."

"Thomas, I even have eight millimeter films of her. I had them copied to DVD. I've been waiting for an excuse to watch them again. Maybe when you come and visit?" he asked.

"Maybe we can come early December? The second weekend," suggested Rebecca looking back at Thomas.

"That would be fine," said Thomas.

"The second weekend it is." He stopped and looked in his bag, "before I forget, this is for you Thomas." He handed Thomas an envelope.

Thomas opened it and pulled out an engagement card and read it out. "It says, 'Love, Happiness and Health' on the front page and inside he removed a folded piece of paper and continued to read the card. 'To Thomas and Rebecca, Congratulations on your engagement all our love the First Baptist Church of Harlem Choir'." Thomas passed the card to Rebecca and opened up the note and read:

> *Dear Thomas, Rebecca and Kate,*
> *The children are putting on a Christmas Show on Sunday December eleventh; they will be reenacting the Nativity, as well as singing Christmas hymns and songs. There will be food and beverages after the show and a visit from Santa Claus. If you could make it would make the children's day. Please say you will. If not we understand. Thank you, Ms. Brown.*

Thomas looked at Rebecca and Henri. Henri spoke. "Ms. Brown asked me to pass this on to you. The children are raising money for repairs. Ms. Brown and the children don't know it yet but the Opera House is donating five thousand dollars and some gifts for the children. Several of the cast will be attending the show, they know about me and Rufus, but there are six others that they are unaware of."

"We should stop off at the store and pick up a card," said Rebecca, "and write a note and let them know we will be attending."

"We'll stop on the way to the airport," said Thomas.

"You will be making their Christmas," said Henri.

THOMAS AND REBECCA STOOD WITH FRANK ON the sidelines. At half time Eileen and Stephanie came from the other side to say hello then went back for the second half to sit with John. John had refused to come over. They watched Ted's team beat the opposition to win the championship. Ted was presented with the games most valuable player trophy for leading the team to victory with five sacks, one fumble recovery and one interception for a touchdown. After the presentation he came over and gave Frank a big hug and invited him back to the bar for the celebration. Frank accepted. He thanked Thomas and Rebecca for coming and extended the invite to them.

"Thanks Ted but I promised Kate we would go to her place for dinner tonight," replied Thomas.

"Thanks for the invite," said Rebecca.

"I understand," replied Ted as he looked over at his dad. "I wish he would snap out of this." He looked at Frank, "it's not right."

"I think he's going to be like this for the rest of his life," said Frank. "We might as well get used to it."

"I'm starting to believe that myself," agreed Ted. "He can be as stubborn as a mule." Ted looked over at Thomas. "I don't think time is going to heal him."

"I wouldn't say that," replied Thomas.

"You wouldn't?" asked Frank.

"I wasn't going to say anything but maybe I should."

"Say what?" said Frank and Ted.

Rebecca looked on.

"I saw your father last Wednesday night at the ballet. He was standing at the back of the theater," said Thomas.

"That's impossible," said Ted. "He was out with one of his friends at a poker game he said he won fifty dollars."

"I was going to the bathroom after the second intermission and I thought I recognized him but he was quite a distance away, so I followed him and saw him standing at the back of the theater. He looked in my direction. I don't think he saw me but it was him."

Frank and Ted looked at each other. "Well I'll be…"

Thomas interrupted. "I guess he doesn't want you to know. I'm telling you two so you don't fly off the handle and say something you might regret later. You need to give him some more time." Thomas looked over at John. "Besides if you tell him that someone saw him what would he say?" asked Thomas.

"That he wasn't there," replied Frank.

"Maybe we should give him some more time," suggested Ted.

"I think you're right Ted," said Frank

"How's the manuscript?" asked Rebecca standing in the doorway of the den.

"I'll be finished tomorrow," replied Thomas. "You can read it then."

"Great! Do you still have to do more today?"

"No, I'm finished. I was going to tidy up. How was shopping?"

"Come into the kitchen and I'll make some coffee and I'll tell you," she said.

Thomas sat down as she put the cups of coffee on the table. "Well," she said with a big smile, "I've picked out the wedding dress and the maid of honor and bridesmaids dresses."

"How do they look?"

"Sorry Thomas, you will have to wait till the wedding day," she replied. "I also picked out, shall I say, the lingerie for the wedding night." She caught Thomas's eyes widen. "No, I won't show you." She smiled and moved closer to him and whispered. "But I will tell you its very sexy, see through and small," she kissed him on the cheek and neck.

"Anything else?" he asked.

She continued to whisper. "Actually yes, I picked up a couple more bikinis, another dress and a few other odds and ends for Aruba. They're all very sexy but you will have to wait till we're there to see them." She sat back and sipped her coffee.

"I guess," said Thomas, and playfully pouted.

She kissed his pouting lips.

"Did you have a good time shopping?"

"I had a lot of fun today, especially with Rachel, she was joking and laughing all the time, she was really enjoying herself. I think we're becoming closer, better friends. Kate and Penny they tell me loads of personal things but not Rachel, I think she would like to, maybe over time she will." She took a sip of her coffee. "When are you going shopping? I thought you wanted to get a couple of pairs of pants."

"I'm going Tuesday. Do you want to come with me?" he asked.

"You just reminded me of something strange. Jack and Penny are leaving for Aruba tomorrow. Penny said her and Jack wanted some time alone before everyone got there."

"What's wrong with that?"

"Two things, first, Penny and Jack would have wanted to travel with all of us, that's the type of people they are. Second, Penny has asked me to teach her classes for Monday and Tuesday. She's never missed teaching, ever!"

"Really!" said Thomas, "I guess that is strange. What classes are you teaching?"

Rebecca looked at him. "Children between the ages of six and eleven. There's one class for each age group and I have two private lessons. I've never taught children so at first I said no. Then Penny showed me the outline and what was to be taught at each class. She said she didn't feel comfortable asking anyone else and if I didn't do it she would have to cancel and leave Wednesday."

"What is she doing for Wednesday, Thursday, and Friday?" asked Thomas.

"She has someone to fill in, apparently this person is unavailable Monday and Tuesday," replied Rebecca. "The more I think about it the more I don't mind. I'm actually looking forward to it. Why don't you come by and watch? Come Tuesday! Please come! Then we could go shopping right after."

"Tuesday it is," replied Thomas.

THOMAS STOOD AND LOOKED THROUGH THE VIEWING room window and watched Rebecca instruct the seven-year-old girls. She was on the bar and was showing the five positions; six sets of eager eyes watched her patiently. Thomas sat down next to a couple of the girl's mothers.

"Good morning," said Thomas.

"Morning," replied the two mothers.

"Okay girls, why don't you each take a place at the bar," said Rebecca as she placed them safely one behind the other facing the same direction. She walked to an area on the bar and faced them. "Here we go. Watch me now. Position one and two and three and four and five, don't forget to extend your free hand. That's it. Good. Keep on going on your own." Rebecca walked up and down the line helping them with their posture and positioning. Fifteen minutes later a buzzer signaled the final two minutes of the lesson. "Girls in a straight line behind me and let's float around the room like butterflies." She took the line of girls around the floor several times, weaving back and forth. She ran ahead and stopped and turned and crouched. The girls ran to her screaming. They all hugged her.

"The girl with the red hair is mine. Which little girl is your one?" asked one of the women.

Thomas looked over at her and realized she was asking him. "I'm Rebecca's fiancée," he replied.

"She's very good with the children. They all took to her straight away. I think it's because she makes the lessons a fun, learning experience. I had my ten-year old daughter in here yesterday and she couldn't stop talking about her. She must have been doing this for some time?" she asked.

"She loves being around children," replied Thomas.

"Let her know I'll be putting in a good word with Penny," she said. "They should have her back."

"Maybe you could tell her," suggested Thomas.

"You're right I will."

The door opened and two of the girls ran to their mothers. A mother and a father had just arrived and one of the girls ran over. Rebecca noticed Thomas through the doorway and called him over.

"When did you get here?" asked Rebecca.

"Fifteen minutes ago," he replied.

She kissed him on the lips. "I'm glad you came I have the eight year olds next. Take off your coat." She motioned to the girls waiting outside to come into the room. She turned to Thomas, "Want a juice?"

"I wouldn't mind one," replied Thomas taking off his coat and placing it on a bench.

"They're in the refrigerator in the kitchen. Follow me," she said. "I only have a couple of minutes before the next class."

"Ms. La Croix."

Rebecca turned around to look at the lady with the young girl with red hair.

"You go over, I'll meet you in the kitchen," said Thomas. Thomas picked out a couple of cartons of orange juice and placed them on the table. He watched Rebecca listening to the lady. Rebecca turned to look at Thomas for a brief moment then turned back around. They said goodbye and Rebecca walked into the kitchen. Thomas handed her an orange juice.

"What was that all about?" asked Thomas.

Rebecca smiled. "She thought that I was excellent with the children and should consider instructing them more often. She said I was very patient and that all the children take to me."

"That was very nice of her."

She looked at Thomas and smiled.

"You look very sexy in your leotard and tights."

"I do? Well maybe I should wear these around the condo more often if it turns you on," she said in a sexy voice.

"Maybe," he replied with a grin.

She took a drink of her juice and looked at Thomas. "Don't read too much into this, but I love it, the children have so much energy and excitement. They want to learn and have fun. They're like sponges. Do you know what they call me?"

Thomas shook his head.

"Ms. Rebecca. Isn't that adorable," she said excitedly. "I have to get back out there and meet the rest of the children as they're getting dropped off."

Thomas sat alone in the viewing room and watched the eight year olds. The six year olds were next and a mother with a four month old in a stroller sat down next to him.

"I hope she sleeps through this," she said. "She's not due for another feed till about twelve-thirty."

Thomas looked into the stroller. "She's beautiful. What's her name?"

"Victoria, we call her Vicky."

"What about the other girl?"

"Her name is Christine and we call her Chrissie. She's the one with the dark hair and ponytail. I also have a boy three and a half, he's with his grandmother."

"Busy," stated Thomas.

"Busy but enjoyable, I wouldn't trade it in for the world. Do you have a little girl out there?" she asked.

"Actually I do. See the tallest one in the black leotard with her brown hair in a ponytail."

"Which one?" She noticed the tallest girl was a blonde and was confused.

Thomas smiled. "The teacher is my fiancée," said Thomas.

"Oh I see and you came out to watch her. How thoughtful," she replied.

They talked about children as they watched Rebecca teach the class. Ten minutes before the end the baby woke and started to cry. The lady, who's name was Joyce, started to worry about her crying disrupting the class. Thomas helped her to the kitchen were she closed the door.

After the class Thomas and Rebecca walked with Chrissie to the kitchen and went inside. Rebecca offered Chrissie a juice. Thomas and Rebecca realized that the baby was being breast-feeding under the blanket.

"I'm sorry," said Thomas, "I'll come back in a few minutes."

"Don't get all embarrassed. She's just fallen asleep. Turn around and I'll sort myself out."

Thomas turned around.

"Here Rebecca take hold of Vicky for me while I do this up. Almost done. Done. Thomas I'm decent you can turn back around."

Thomas turned around. Joyce was sitting in the chair and Rebecca was standing holding the baby. "I guess Penelope never told you that she let's me feed in the kitchen at lunch time?" asked Joyce.

Rebecca shook her head.

"Usually, Penny comes in and has a talk with me while I feed. She's a lovely lady."

"She is," replied Rebecca.

"You both know her?" asked Joyce.

"We do," replied Thomas.

"You don't mind holding little Vicky for a while?" asked Joyce of Rebecca. "My arm is a little tired." Joyce looked over at Chrissie. "Chrissie bring that seat around for Rebecca to sit on."

Rebecca sat down and looked at the baby. Thomas made a cup of coffee for Joyce and they sat and talked about Chrissie.

"I almost lost her," said Joyce pointing to Chrissie who was busy reading a book. "The umbilical cord was caught around her neck while I was delivering. The doctor said a few more minutes and she may not have made it. Look at her now."

"How many are you planning for?" asked Thomas.

"Six."

"Did you come from a big family?" asked Thomas.

"Actually the opposite, I had no sisters and brothers. I always wish I had at least one, you know, someone to play with at night when you were called into the house before dark, or watch movies with or talk to. I never liked being alone and I said that the man I marry better be prepared to have a big family. I met Phil and we are on our way. I look back now and I can't remember a life without the children. I mean at your age, I was the same, you want to spend some time together and experience each other." The baby started to cry. "She's got some wind. Here let me help you out." Joyce put a cloth over Rebecca's shoulder and helped Rebecca put the baby over it. "Now just pat and rub her back gently. A slight rocking motion sometimes helps."

Thomas looked at Rebecca who looked up at Thomas. The baby cried louder.

"Keep on patting," said Joyce.

The baby let out a big burp and a little bit of milk came up and onto the cloth. Rebecca continued to pat and rock the baby till she fell back asleep. Rebecca turned the baby and cradled her in her lap.

"It's as easy as that," said Joyce. "You're a natural."

Rebecca looked up at Thomas and smiled proudly.

Thomas smiled back.

Chapter 18

Aruba

Rebecca and Kate sat opposite each other next to the window. Thomas sat next to Rebecca in the aisle seat. The next row over was Frank and Stephanie and opposite them, Rachel and Jessica. Veronica and Buddy where sitting behind them. Thomas remembered the plush comfortable seats and stretched out his legs. The plane taxied and took off into the cool November afternoon. Once in the air they had full meal service, drinks and music; it was a party in the sky. Over the Caribbean Sea they could see small islands with white sandy beaches and palm trees, most looked uninhabited. The larger ones had houses, roads and hotels.

After four hours on the plane the captain came over the speaker. "Ladies and Gentlemen we will be approaching Aruba in approximately twenty minutes. For those of you seated off to the west, the right of the plane, you will see Venezuela in the distance. I have asked for permission to circle the island of Aruba before our approach, I will let you know once I have the okay. In the meantime please finish all drinks and food and make sure your seat belt is buckled. The flight attendant will be around momentarily. We will be starting our descent shortly. Thank you."

The flight attendant came around and cleaned off the tables and checked seat belts. She cleaned up the cabin and eventually took her seat. Five minutes later the captain came over the speaker. "Ladies and Gentlemen due to low traffic in the area we have had the tower's permission to circle the island before taking up our landing path. We will be coming across the northwest tip of Aruba from the southwest, flying over Eagle Beach and Palm Beach. They are considered to be in the top ten most beautiful beaches in the world. We will then turn southeast and follow Aruba's north coastline; the coast is rugged with large waves. Look out for the Divi-divi trees. Then we will come around the most southern tip of the island and pass over San Nicolas and make our approach to Oranjestad. We will be passing over the beaches in ten minutes. Enjoy the view."

Thomas and Rebecca held hands and looked out the window and enjoyed the aerial tour. It was paradise. As they approached the airport Rebecca turned to Thomas and smiled. "We are going to have so much fun. I can't wait," she kissed him. "I'm looking forward to every moment with you. Just think our first trip together." She leaned over and whispered. "Our next trip to the Caribbean we will be alone and I will be Mrs. Rebecca Carlyle." She smiled and rubbed her nose against his.

"I love you," said Thomas softly and gently squeezed her hand.

They landed, picked up their luggage and went through customs. In the airport Stephanie noticed two men holding up signs reading 'Rachel's Party'. They followed them to the two minibuses waiting outside. It was almost five thirty and the weather was hot; Thomas looked up at the cloudless sky. The drivers loaded the bags and the group separated into the minibuses. The driver pointed out the local sights along the way. A cool breeze came through the open windows. Twenty minutes later they pulled up in front of the deluxe hotel.

In the middle of the lobby was an island with palm trees, chirping exotic birds, a waterfall and a pond. Jessica and Rachel walked to the reception desk to check-in; everyone else looked at the birds and fish in the pond.

"This is quite something," said Kate.

"It is," replied Stephanie.

"It's lovely," added Rebecca.

"So what are we going to do first?" asked Thomas.

"Pool," the three girls answered.

"Each of you needs to go to the receptionist. She will have you sign the guest cards and give you your room keys. We are all spread over the tenth floor," said Rachel. "What I suggest is that we stay in the same groups as in the bus and that way we can follow our luggage."

They each filled in a guest card and were given a room key that gave them signing privileges at the hotel and casino. They were taken up to the tenth floor; the suites for Rebecca, Thomas, Frank and Rachel were to the right of the elevator and the rest of the group to the left. They all agreed to meet at the pool in half an hour. Thomas walked into his corner suite and was speechless.

The hotel's assistant showed Thomas around. "We have four suites like this on the floor. These are the best this hotel and that Aruba have to offer, with the exception of our penthouse suite. In here you will find your bedroom with its own balcony and en suite, the walk in closet, the television with satellite channels and a DVD player." The assistant opened the balcony doors. "The trade winds will keep you cool and the sounds of the waves are very relaxing. If we go back outside here and through this door you will find a den with a desk, phone and printer. If you require a computer we have several, top of the line, available. This window also opens." He walked out the room. "In through here is the main bathroom with a sunken tub for two and shower." He turned and walked out to the main room. "As you see you have a sunken living area with an entertainment system. There is also an entrance to another balcony that is much larger." He walked across the floor. "Here is the wet bar and refrigerator. It's fully stocked with some of our finest beer, liquor, wine, and champagne." He walked back towards the front door. "The room has fresh fruit daily," he pointed to a fruit bowl on the glass dining room table. "Fresh flowers throughout, which will be replaced as required. If you need anything to make your stay more pleasant please do not hesitate to call the front desk and ask for me, my name is Andrew. Any one of the other assistant managers that are on duty can also help you. Enjoy your stay."

Thomas pulled out his wallet to give him a tip.

"Sorry sir, all gratuities have been covered by your hostess. Thank you," replied Andrew and closed the door behind him.

The phone rang, "Hello,"

"Hi Rebecca," said Thomas and listened. "Okay, come down to my room as soon as you are ready." He listened again. "Okay, I'll see you then, love you, bye." He hung up the phone and went to the bathroom and unpacked his bathing suit and got undressed and put it on. There was a knock on the door.

"That was fast," he thought.

He opened the door. "How do you like it?" asked Rachel. She was wearing a yellow bikini and a wrap that covered her waist and thighs.

"Wow!" said Thomas, "You look great."

She blushed and smiled. "I'm right across the hall," she pointed. "I have the exact same suite as you. Kate and my mother have the other two at the far end." She walked in, "these are luxurious. Have you seen the view?" asked Rachel.

"Not yet," replied Thomas.

"Come on I'll show you," she grabbed his hand and led him down the sunken living room and opened the balcony doors and they went outside. They looked down at the blue water and sandy white beaches. They could see the large pool surrounded by lush palm trees. People were sitting in lounge chairs and swimming in the water.

There was a knock at the door. Thomas went inside and opened it. "For you sir" said a hotel employee and handed Thomas an envelope. Thomas thanked him and watched the man go across the hall.

"Rachel Carter?" asked Thomas.

"Yes sir," he answered.

"She's in here on the balcony. Would you like me to get her?"

"That will not be necessary. If you could hand this to her I would appreciate it. Thank you."

"Have you read the note yet?" asked Rebecca who was walking down the hallway to Thomas.

"I've just got it," replied Thomas.

Rebecca was wearing a floral bikini with bright yellow and light blues. Her waist was covered with a short light blue wrap that matched her bikini. The wrap was short and sheer and revealed her long shapely legs. "You look good enough to eat," said Thomas.

"I'll take that as a compliment," she smiled.

He put his arms on her waist and could feel her soft skin, "I'll be more direct. You look sexy and beautiful."

"That's more like it." Her eyes smiled.

They kissed. Then they joined Rachel on the balcony.

"Here you go," said Thomas handing Rachel the envelope.

"What's this?" she asked looking at Thomas and then Rebecca. "Did you get one?"

"I read mine back in my suite," replied Rebecca.

"What is it?" asked Thomas.

"I'm not sure?" replied Rebecca.

They opened the envelopes and read. Thomas looked at them both. "Dinner at the penthouse suite at eight tonight. Any ideas?"

"It must be Jack and Penny hosting a 'Welcome Party'," said Rebecca.

"That sounds like Jack alright," said Rachel.

They went down to the lobby and out to the pool area. There were cascading waterfalls, palms trees and several swim up bars. They walked around till Rebecca spotted Kate, Jessica and Stephanie.

"Hello," they said.

"We've just got our drinks," said Jessica, "I'm drinking a pina colada, Kate is drinking a banana daiquiri, and Stephanie is drinking a strawberry margarita. We've all been trying each other's, they are all delicious. What are you three going to have?" she asked.

"I want one of those drinks that come in a coconut," said Rachel.

"Me too," said Rebecca.

"Make it three," said Thomas.

Thomas sat down in the shade in a chair next to Jessica; Rebecca laid next to him on a chaise lounge and Rachel on the next one over. Rebecca and Rachel each took off their wrap and revealed high cut bikini bottoms. They put suntan lotion over the front of their bodies. Thomas noticed the men looking as they walked by.

"You stay in the shade with me," said Jessica to Thomas, "and get used to this heat."

"Kate you're not sunbathing?" asked Thomas.

"Tomorrow, Stephanie and I want to go swimming? Frank's already in the pool."

"Where is he?" asked Thomas as he looked around.

Stephanie pointed him out and they both waved.

"Buddy and Veronica did go in for a swim but they've ended up at the swim-up pool bar," said Jessica.

The waiter brought the coconut drinks and placed one next to each of the recipients. "Okay," said Thomas. "I'm going to pass this around tell me what you think."

"Jessica first."

She took a couple of sips, "um, that's good."

"Kate."

Kate sipped, "wow, strong."

"Stephanie."

Stephanie took a long sip, "it's good and strong."

Thomas drank. "Perfect," he said, "Perfect."

They drank and talked for a while as they watched Kate, Stephanie and Frank swimming.

Fifteen minutes later Thomas stood. "Rebecca? Rachel? Going in?" asked Thomas.

"The sun will be setting in a little while," informed Rebecca, "and I want to take full advantage of the sunshine."

"Me too," agreed Rachel.

"I guess it's just you and me," said Thomas to Jessica.

They all watched Thomas remove his t-shirt and shorts and reveal a blue Speedo.

Rebecca and Rachel discreetly watched him as he went into the pool. Rebecca loved his broad shoulder and muscular build and the way he filled his Speedo. "And that butt," she thought.

Thomas and Jessica swam up to Kate and Stephanie.

"What are you two up to?" asked Jessica.

"We are checking out the sights," replied Kate diplomatically.

"What she's really saying Jessica is the studs around the pool," clarified Thomas.

"And there are lots of them," she said and smiled. "We figure this corner here is the best place. See those four over there? Well tanned, well built and cute," said Kate.

"Yes, I do," said Jessica.

Thomas hid behind Kate and lifted up her arm and yelled in a girlish voice, "over here!" He let go of her hand and went under water and swam away, well out of sight. What the four men witnessed was Kate waving over to them and saying, "Over here."

Thomas surfaced at the pool bar and ordered a drink. He sat and talked to Buddy, Veronica and Frank for a while. He finished his drink and swam around the bar. Out of the corner of his eye he saw a figure waving to him. It was Jack and he was calling him over. He swam to the side of the pool.

"Hello Thomas, get out of the pool and come with me for a minute," said Jack.

"Hi, to you too." Thomas lifted himself out of the water and onto the deck.

"Follow me," said Jack. As he walked by a pool assistant he grabbed a couple of towels from her and threw them to Thomas. They walked to the poolside bar and sat in the shade. They were far from the pool area and out of sight.

"Two."

"Sure Jack," said the bartender.

"What's up Jack?"

"What do you mean?"

"Well, you look nervous." Thomas looked around, "and you brought me to the secluded area of the bar and away from the pool. Everyone else is out there. Which tells me, you don't want us to be seen talking or you don't want to be seen?"

"Easy Sherlock Holmes, I am nervous," confided Jack. He hesitated. "I brought you over here so I could talk to you in private. If I went out there and called you to one side they would think I was up to something."

"Are you?" asked Thomas slyly.

"Of course I am," smiled Jack. "I've been trying to wave you down for the last ten minutes. I looked like a bird flapping my arms. Everyone must think I'm mad."

"Jack, with that red and yellow Hawaiian shirt, that straw hat, those sandals and dress socks, I don't think anyone thinks it."

"Okay, okay, enough with the jokes. I haven't been myself lately. I need your help?"

"Sure Jack," said Thomas in a more serious tone.

"Did everyone make it?" asked Jack.

"Everyone," replied Thomas.

"Good," said Jack. He pulled out a small bag with something in it. "I need you to hold on to this for me and bring it tonight. It's a small gift for Penny and I don't want her to find it."

"Not a problem Jack."

"You have to promise me that you won't look at it or let anyone know you have it. If Jessica sees you with it she'll hound you till you open it."

"Don't worry about it Jack. No one will see it," said Thomas. He looked at Jack. "Jack I've never seen you this unsettled."

"I know, I know. I have a special night for Penny tonight and I want to make sure everything goes right."

"I understand," said Thomas. "One problem. Where am I supposed to hide this?"

Jack looked down at his Speedo and laughed.

The bartender dropped off the drinks.

"I have to drink this quickly and get back or Penny will get suspicious."

Thomas looked at the two glasses. "Whiskey Jack? We're in Aruba."

"What did you expect me to order?" asked Jack with a puzzled look.

Thomas looked at him, "True."

They drank their drinks and Jack thought about how Thomas was going to conceal the gift.

"Come with me?" asked Jack. "Actually no, you will have to wait here while I go inside, you can't go in wearing just that." He stood up. "Order two more drinks and I'll be back in a minute."

Thomas ordered two whiskies and was half way done when Jack came back.

"Here you go put this on, I put the gift in the pocket," said Jack. "They won't notice it if you leave the shirt unbuttoned."

Thomas looked at the bright yellow Hawaiian shirt with green pineapples, "Jack you have to be kidding?"

"What?"

"They had nothing more stylish."

"This is style and it cost me eighty dollars, put it on." He picked up his drink and downed it. "I have to go."

"What am I supposed to say when I go back wearing this?" asked Thomas.

Jack smiled. "You'll think of something Sherlock. Besides, it's like you said, they'll think you're mad." Jack left.

Thomas walked back wearing his shirt thinking it couldn't get any worse, and it did, everyone was there. He stood while they laughed.

"Thomas, where have you been? What are you wearing? Did you go shopping?" asked Rebecca as she walked over to him.

Thomas looked at them. "Nobody ask, it's a long story, I'll tell you later."

"I can't wait to hear this one," said Kate.

"Thomas, I like it. I think it suits you!" said Jessica. She looked at the group. "Did you hear what he did to Kate in the pool?"

"What happened to Kate?" asked those who weren't involved.

Jessica told them. They all laughed.

"I was so embarrassed. I'm going to get you for this," said Kate smiling. "Be on your best guard."

"Well, I'll be wearing this shirt so you won't get me confused with someone else."

"Oh, I wont!" replied Kate.

"Want to go for that swim?" asked Rebecca.

Thomas wanted to get the gift into one of his short pockets. "Let me have a drink first."

"I ordered one for you a few minutes ago, it's by your chair," said Rebecca. She reached over and passed it to him. "I'll wait for you."

Rachel stood up. "I'm going for a swim. Who's coming?"

Everyone except Rebecca and Thomas went in.

Rebecca looked at Thomas, "What's going on? I went in the water five minutes later looking for you. I even walked around the pool. Where have you been? I was worried."

Thomas pulled out the gift and put it into his pocket.

"What's that?" she asked.

Thomas told her about Jack.

"Did you look at it?"

"I promised him we wouldn't."

Thomas took off the shirt and had some of his drink. "Let's go for a swim."

They swam together in the water, kissing once in a while. Rebecca wrapped her legs and arms around him. "I love this," said Rebecca.

They swam for another fifteen minutes and went up to their rooms to get ready. Thomas put on a pair of cotton pants and a white shirt and was about to leave when he noticed a door by the dining room table. It was locked. He unlocked it and fastened it open. There was another door behind it that was locked. He went into the hall and knocked on the door to Rebecca's suite. She opened it wearing a sky blue spandex dress that had thin shoulder straps and stopped above the knee. It clung to her shapely body. She had her hair in a French braid and was wearing light blue lipstick.

"Wow!" said Thomas. "You look incredible."

"Thank you," she replied, "you look very handsome." She kissed him on the cheek.

"I need to get my shoes and bag. I'll be a minute." She left and went to the bedroom.

Thomas walked over to the side door, unlocked it and was looking into his suite. He leveraged it open. He went and sat down on the sofa.

Rebecca came out of the room wearing matching shoes and handbag. She had a white cotton cardigan draped over her arm. "You know there is only one problem with these suites, the front doors, at the condominium we have no locked doors between us."

"I was thinking the same thing," replied Thomas. "How about I knock down the wall?"

She laughed. "Very funny. If you can get me access to your suite and vice a versa I will give you…"

Thomas looked at her, "What?"

"Whatever you want?"

"Anything?" he asked.

"Anything! I promise."

Thomas walked her over to the adjoining doors.

"This is great!" Then she realized. "You knew all along. That's unfair. The bet is off," said Rebecca pushing him playfully into the door. She kissed him.

Thomas stopped and looked at her. "A bet is a bet. I'll let you know."

"Oh you will," she replied curiously.

They left the room and walked to the elevators. Andrew was standing next to one that he had reserved. They waited a couple of minutes for Kate and Stephanie and then got in. The doors closed and Andrew put in the elevator card and pressed the penthouse button. Andrew informed them that there was only one penthouse suite and it took up half the floor. It had its own swimming pool and mentioned several famous people who had stayed there. As they exited Jack and Penny greeted them and showed them into the living room. A bartender made cocktails and two waitresses served hot hors d'oeuvres.

"Did you bring the gift?" whispered Jack.

"I did," replied Thomas.

"Do me a favor and hold onto it till I need it."

"Sure thing Jack."

They stood and talked and waited for everyone to arrive. Once they did they were invited into the dining room for dinner. They sat down to a five-course meal accompanied with white and red wine, champagne, liqueur and coffees. After they finished they were invited onto a large patio by the swimming pool. The bartender opened bottles of champagne and poured them into flutes and the waitresses passed them around.

Jack spoke. "This is a very special evening for Penny and me, and I am glad you are all here to share it with us. As you know Penny and I have known each other for many years; what some of you may not know is that we have been in a relationship for the last several." Jack stopped and asked Thomas for the bag. He opened the bag and pulled out the small blue velvet box and opened it and went down on one knee and held her hand. "Make me the happiest man in the world and say you will marry me this Saturday?"

Penny looked down at him with a big smile. She placed her free hand over her mouth and said in a quivering voice, "I will," and cried. Jack placed her mother's engagement ring on her finger. "My mother's ring. Oh, Jack!" Tears rolled down her face.

"My only regret," said Jack," is that I didn't ask you sooner." They both kissed and everyone clapped. "I would like you to raise your glass and toast with me to the most beautiful woman in the world and who I love dearly. To the future Mrs. Collins."

Everyone raised their glasses and drank.

"The wedding plans will be made available tomorrow night, as soon as Penny finalizes a few arrangements with the wedding coordinator. I promise you a wedding you will never forget."

Penny pulled Jack close and whispered in his ear. Jack nodded in agreement.

"Thomas and Rebecca, can you join us up here?" asked Jack. He waited as they stood next to him. He turned to Thomas and Rebecca, "Come in between us. Go ahead Penny."

"Rebecca would you be my Maid of Honor?" asked Penny.

"It would be my pleasure," answered Rebecca and hugged her.

"Thomas," said Jack, "I want you to be my best man?"

"Yes Jack, of course, I'm flattered." They shook hands and hugged.

Everyone gathered around to congratulate them.

THE FOLLOWING MORNING THOMAS WOKE EARLY AND went into Rebecca's room and lay next to her. He put his arm around her and kissed the back of her head. He lay there for several minutes.

"Rebecca," he sang, "Rebecca."

She turned around and smiled. "Hold me," she said.

He put his arms around her and she put her head on his chest. "Rebecca, are you coming down to watch Rachel."

"What time is it?"

"Six."

"Six! We only got to bed at two," she reminded him.

"Do you want to sleep for a while longer? I can come back later and get you?"

"No. I'll come with you."

They got dressed and went down to the lobby and picked up two coffees.

"That was a surprise last night," stated Thomas.

"It was," replied Rebecca. "Penny told me that last week she said to Jack that she wanted to get married."

"Well Jack didn't take long. He said he was waiting for them to go public about their relationship. I guess if you're going to go public, you do it in style." Thomas looked at Rebecca. "Did she say why she wanted to get married, now?"

"She loves him and I think it was when he surprised her with the house and..." Rebecca faded.

"And?" asked Thomas.

"Jack asked her about adopting children."

"Really? Wow. Why not! I think they should."

"Which is what she thought but she wanted to be married first." Rebecca moved closer to Thomas.

"Good for them," said Thomas.

They went out to the pool and walked over to the canvas tent. Rachel noticed them and waved them over. She was sitting in a chair, with her blonde hair curled and wearing one of the hotel's robes.

"Good morning," she said.

"Good morning," they replied.

"They're just finishing my make up. They'll be taking pictures around the pool and waterfalls. I had them set up some chairs in the shade for you," said Rachel.

"You're full of life this morning," said Rebecca.

"That's because you two didn't see me leave at ten last night. In bed by ten, last night and tonight; then Friday and Saturday, party, party, party," she said and smiled. "You two look pretty beat. You can go back to bed if you like?"

"No," said Rebecca. "We'll be fine once we get the coffee down us."

"There's some food on the table over there, help yourself."

The make up lady came back with the other shade of lipstick.

"We'll let you get ready," said Thomas. "Good luck," and was going to kiss her on the cheek but caught the makeup woman's look and opted for the hand. They walked away to the chairs.

"Thomas, Rebecca," Rachel said. They both turned around. "Thanks."

They smiled and sat down. Four hours they watched Rachel pose in front of the camera. They took pictures of her around the pool area; using the pool, beach and palm trees for the background. She posed standing, lying on her side, on her back and on her stomach. They had her go in the water and stand on the ladder, then lie on the pool steps. They took pictures of her standing in front of the waterfall, then sitting on the rocks by the waterfall, and then underneath the waterfall. She changed four times into the different bikinis and for each change they applied a different shade of make-up and hairstyle. They followed the exact same sequence for each bikini.

Throughout the morning Jessica, Veronica, Kate and Stephanie joined them. The shooting stopped at eleven and they had lunch inside at the restaurant. They started shooting again at three at the north end of the beach. This time they shot her on the sand, standing and sitting on rocks, walking into the water and walking out. They finished at six and were reconvening at eight for sunset pictures. This time they had a light dinner on the beach under a tent. Rebecca and Thomas had slipped away several times throughout the day to cool off in the sea, but the majority of time was spent watching her pose. Most of the others, with the exception of Jessica, had spent their time at the pool, each periodically coming over to watch. At eight, everyone was there and watched Rachel posing for her final pictures, which were of her walking on the beach with the sun setting and waves crashing in the background. At nine they wrapped up.

As they walked back to the hotel everyone agreed to meet the next morning at ten in the lobby. Jessica, Penny and Jack went out for drink. Kate, Frank, Stephanie, Veronica and Buddy went to a nightclub. Rachel, Thomas and Rebecca decided to have a walk on the beach.

"I didn't realize modeling swimsuits was so much work. I was exhausted watching," said Rebecca.

"It can be repetitive at times," replied Rachel. "But I love it!"

"You have a lot of patience," said Rebecca.

"I couldn't have all those people fussing around me, changing in and out of bathing suits and having all those people watching me," said Thomas.

"You get used to it," said Rachel. "I want to thank you both again for staying with me all day."

"We'll be there tomorrow," said Rebecca.

"It's only for a few hours tomorrow. I'll be finished at nine. They want to take some pictures on the east coast with the sun rising. They have a mini bus picking us up at six, you two can come with us or take a taxi, its only fifteen minutes away," suggested Rachel.

"If we're not there at six leave without us and we'll get a taxi," said Thomas.

They walked down the beach and talked about how beautiful Aruba was, about the wedding, and some of the activities that they wanted to do. They went back to the hotel and walked Rachel to her suite. Rebecca followed Thomas into his and they sat down.

"I could do with a bath," said Rebecca.

"You go and get undressed, put on your robe and get a nightgown and I'll run a bubble bath for you."

She looked at him and smiled. "That sounds wonderful! You always take care of me." She stood up. "After, can we sit on the balcony and listen to the waves and the sounds of the island?"

He stood up and kissed her.

"Can you order us something to eat?"

"What would you like?" asked Thomas.

"Surprise me," she said and left.

Thomas ordered room service and ran the bath. He went outside and looked over the balcony and down at the beach below. He listened to the waves, the hum of people, and the beat of the nightclub and thought about his third novel.

After her bath Rebecca came out onto the balcony wearing a short silk nightgown. She walked up behind Thomas and put her arms around him and rested her head on his back. Thomas could feel her hard nipples press up against him. Her soft hands caressed his chest. He turned and looked into her eyes.

"I am so in love with you," she said and kissed him on the lips. "I'm so happy you're in my life."

"No one on this earth can ever keep me away from you; you have me for as long as I shall live," he said.

"I will only ever love you. You are my soul mate."

"And you are mine."

Thomas lifted her up and she put her legs around his waist and he placed her on the chaise lounge and lay on top of her. They kissed.

He stopped and gently touched her cheek with his hand. "I am the luckiest man in the world."

She smiled at him.

There was a knock at the door.

"Hope you're hungry?" he asked.

"I am."

"You wait here and I'll bring the food out."

She smiled. "You are definitely the last romantic!"

He came back and put the food on the table and sat on the patio chair next to her and they ate.

"Thomas this food is perfect. It tastes so good." She looked over at him. "Is there anything you want to do while we are here?" she asked.

"I thought we could rent some jeeps and tour the island; stop off at some beaches, have some lunch and see some of the towns."

"That's a great idea. Hold on a minute." She stood up and walked toward the balcony doors and the balcony light caught her silhouette; he noticed she wasn't wearing anything underneath. She returned a few minutes later. "I talked to the assistant manager and he is going to take care of it. I think it'll be a lot of fun."

They sat on the balcony for another hour and looked up at the stars in the sky. Rebecca was starting to fall asleep. "I think I'm ready for bed," she said.

Thomas helped her up. They went inside and she started for her suite.

"Rebecca," Thomas said softly. "Why don't you sleep with me in my bed tonight?"

She looked at him. "I thought you would never ask. Let me go and brush my teeth."

Thomas watched her walk away. He closed the doors and turned off the lights and went into his bedroom and opened the balcony doors. He went into the en suite and changed into his pajama bottoms. When he came out Rebecca was already in bed. He pulled away the covers and lay next to her on his back. She put her head on his chest and he put his arm around her and kissed the top of her head. She kissed his chest. The full moon's light fell on them.

"The breeze is lovely and the sound of the waves is so relaxing. If I'm dreaming don't wake me," said Rebecca and fell asleep.

"That was an adventurous day," said Kate.

"That was a lot of fun," replied Stephanie.

"Except the bats in the caves," said Rachel.

"What did they call those caves?" asked Thomas.

"I marked them on the map," said Rebecca opening it out, "The Quadiriki Caves! We also went to the California Lighthouse, De Olde Molen, Bushiribana, and Hooiberg."

"I like the De Olde Molen," said Thomas.

"No, no. Lunch in San Nicolas was the highlight," said Jack.

"Men! Shopping in Oranjestad," said Jessica knocking Jack's hat off. "That was the best!"

Jack picked his hat off the ground and the pool waitress placed the drinks on the table. Jack fixed his hat and sipped on his whiskey. "What should we do tonight?" he asked.

"Let's go for dinner at a nice, local restaurant?" asked Penny.

Jack looked over at Thomas. "And after that?"

"Well Jack," said Thomas, "since it's both your last night as single people I suggest we go out and have some fun."

"What did you have in mind?" asked Jack.

"I say we go for that meal, hit the casinos, and then a dance floor," interrupted Rachel.

Jack smiled. "Sounds like a plan."

"Penny, it's your night too," said Thomas.

"I don't like the casinos that much," replied Penny with a disapproving look.

Jack laughed. "Don't you believe her for one second? She loves them. In Vegas I went to bed before her. I'm surprised she still wants to go for the meal."

"I do love them," said Penny with a laugh. "Let's meet in the lobby for seven and go for an early dinner, that way we will be on the tables by nine, just when they're getting hot!"

"I have my shirt picked out," said Thomas.

"You're not," said Rebecca.

Thomas smiled.

"Me too," said Jack.

They both laughed and touched glasses and said, "Cheers!" and drank.

"Rebecca, what are we going to do with them?" asked Penny.

THOMAS AND REBECCA PUT JACK'S CARD IN the elevator and went up to the penthouse suite.

"Did he say why he wanted us to drop by?" asked Rebecca.

"No, he gave me his card and said come up at six thirty. They wanted to talk to us, probably about the wedding."

"Probably," said Rebecca.

"I like your outfit," said Thomas as he tickled her bare mid section.

"Hands off pal or I'll give you one of these," she said clenching her fist and grinning. She opened it up and caressed his clean-shaven face and kissed his nose. She looked at his shirt, "My little Pineapple Boy."

"If you look closely at this Pineapple you can see Spongebob Squarepants coming out of it."

She laughed. "Very Funny!"

The door opened and Jack was standing there with his Hawaiian shirt on.

Rebecca laughed. "You two have to be kidding."

"Aloha Thomas," said Jack.

"Book'em Jack-o," said Thomas.

They both laughed.

"You are as bad as one another," said Rebecca. She turned and noticed Penny walking toward her. "Finally, someone sane. Hello Penny."

"Hello dear," said Penny and looked at Thomas, "Hello Don Ho." She took Rebecca's hand. "Come into the living room." Jack and Thomas followed behind. "Rebecca, I was wondering if I could ask a favor from you?"

"Of course!"

"Can I stay with you tonight?"

"Of course you can!" she replied.

"It may sound foolish after all this time but a part of me would like Jack to see me for the first time tomorrow at the ceremony walking down to his side," explained Penny.

"Penny that's not foolish, that's the way it should be."

"Thomas maybe you could stay here. There's an extra bedroom and we could leave together tomorrow," said Jack.

"Love to Jack!"

Jack passed them both a gift. "This is a small token of our appreciation."

Thomas watched Rebecca open up a small box containing a pair of dangling diamond earrings. Penny put them on. "They are beautiful," said Rebecca. "You shouldn't have."

"I wanted to," said Penny.

"Are these diamonds?"

"There are five carats in each one," said Penny. "They look beautiful on you and will go lovely with your dress."

"My dress?"

"It's hidden in the spare room closet next to mine. We'll take them down with us and we can lay them on the bed," replied Penny. She was about to take her to the room and realized Thomas hadn't opened his gift; "I'm sorry Thomas you haven't opened yours."

Thomas opened the box and inside was a pair of gold cufflinks and a gold money clip, each had a setting of diamonds in the shape of the letter 'T'.

"Jack, Penny, these are beautiful. Thank you," replied Thomas.

"Our pleasure," said Jack. He turned to Penny and Rebecca, "you two should go drop off your clothes and we'll meet you downstairs."

Penny went to the room with Rebecca and they came out with the two dress bags, two shoe boxes, and Penny's over night bag.

"I should come down with you and grab my stuff," said Thomas and started to follow them.

Jack grabbed his arm, "no need, you're all set, follow me."

Thomas followed him into the spare room and hanging in the closet was a summer suit. "It's an Armani. There's your shirt and slip on shoes. You can wear the cufflinks with the shirt," commented Jack. "There is some underwear in the bag; after seeing you in the Speedo I wasn't sure what you wear so I got you a couple of different style. There's also some stuff to go golfing in tomorrow morning."

Thomas laughed. "This is great Jack."

"Let's have dinner and hit the tables."

They went to a restaurant that specialized in Aruban specialties and ordered scavechi, sopi di jambo, keshi yena and for dessert bread pudding with rum sauce. It was delicious. The local band added to the energetic atmosphere. After the meal they hit the casinos and played blackjack, roulette, and the slot machines. Then they went to the nightclub. Rebecca, Penny and Jessica went up before twelve. Thomas and Jack made it to bed just before two. Rachel, Kate and the rest stayed out till dawn.

Early the next morning Jack got Thomas out of bed and took him to the golf course for nine holes while Rebecca and Penny went to the salon and got their hair, nails and make up done.

At two thirty Jack and Thomas arrived at a small church in the countryside. They waited in a small room off to the side of the altar. Thomas pulled out a flask of whiskey and passed it to Jack, he smiled and took a long shot and passed it back to Thomas who took a gulp. Jack gave Thomas the ring. They waited twenty minutes then went inside and stood in front of the altar. Five minutes later the music started and Rebecca walked down the aisle holding a bouquet of bright colorful flowers and wearing a pretty lilac dress. She looked beautiful. Behind her was Penny who was being walked down the aisle by Frank. She was in a white dress, similar in style to Rebecca's, except hers passed over her knees. The bridal bouquet contained white lilies. She let go of Frank's arm and she stood next to Jack. Throughout the thirty-minute ceremony Rebecca and Thomas looked at each other, both wishing it was their day.

Outside the photographer took some more pictures; his last one was of the group outside the church.

Jack and Penny went off in a horse drawn carriage and at a distance the group followed behind them in a mini van. They took a long windy road and eventually arrived at a small, quaint restaurant that overlooked the sea. Jack had hired the restaurant for the day. Several hours later, after the drinks, a delectable meal, speeches, and the catching of the bouquet by Rachel, they followed the carriage to the harbor and boarded a yacht. The yacht left port, the music began and everyone danced. As the sun started to set the disc jockey put on some background music and the group watched the sun fade. Thomas put his arm around Rebecca and looked into her eyes and kissed her with all his heart and soul. That night Thomas would sleep in Rebecca's bed but they would wait till their wedding night to make love.

The last day they spent on the beach. Rebecca and Thomas made sandcastles with some of the children, played volleyball, swam and went for a walk. At three o'clock they headed for the airport, boarded the plane. Jack and Penny had decided to stay on for an extra couple of days. By eleven o'clock, Rebecca, Thomas and Kate were back in their condominiums. Rebecca went into her room and collapsed on the bed. Thomas lay next to her.

She sat up and looked at him. "I've only just realized that I never read your manuscript."

"I never brought it with me. I figured we would relax and take it easy," said Thomas.

They both laughed at the word relax. "I need a week to recover," said Rebecca.

"More like two. I thought it was nice of Stephanie to come with Frank."

"I thought so too," replied Rebecca.

"I meant to ask. How did Jack and Penny get married in Aruba? I thought you couldn't get married unless one of you was Aruban?" asked Thomas.

"Penny is."

"She is?"

"Her great-grandparents were from the Netherlands and moved to Aruba. Her mother was Aruban. Her father was with the British government and was stationed in Aruba for several years. Her parents married and had her there. They moved when his contract ended, she was two or three. That's why her name is very British, Penelope Daily."

"I never knew. That's interesting."

They both looked at the ceiling.

"Thomas," she said. "I can't wait till we're married."

"How many more weeks?"

"Six, yesterday."

"Well, we have New York next week, then Christmas, then New Years and then are wedding. Then we will be married and have the rest of our lives together." He looked over at Rebecca's sad face. "It will go quick," he said reassuringly.

"I know."

"We have asked our wedding party."

"I know," she replied. She was a little sad.

"Come on, I'll run you a bath. When you get out I'll have a nice cup of tea waiting for you. That'll make you feel better." He stood and walked into the bathroom and ran the water. He passed her on the way out and she gave him a kiss. He went to his room and got a copy of his manuscript and left it on her bed. He heard her in the tub singing 'You're the Best Thing' and listened to her for a couple of minutes. He smiled and went into the kitchen and made some tea.

CHAPTER 19

Memories

THEY ARRIVED IN NEW YORK AND WENT straight to the Opera House and watched Henri perform Scarpia in 'Tosca'. After the show they went backstage and waited for him.

"Rebecca," said Henri. He hugged and kissed her. He looked over at Thomas, "Thomas. How are you?" he asked as he put his arms around him.

"I'm doing fine," replied Thomas.

"You two must be hungry? I have reservations at a lovely Italian restaurant. This way." He put his arm through Rebecca's and Thomas followed behind. They went out the stage doors and into the night air. There was a crowd of people waiting outside and as soon as they recognized him they called his name. He waved to them as the limousine pulled up. Rebecca and Thomas sat inside. Henri stuck his head in and asked if it were okay for him to spend a few minutes signing autographs and meeting some of the people. They told him to go ahead and to take his time. He closed the door.

Rebecca looked at Thomas and gave him a kiss. "Five weeks tomorrow."

Thomas looked at her, "Do you have to remind me?" he asked.

"Why you rotten scoundr…"

Before she could finish her sentence he kissed her. "The more I see you the more I realize there is nothing you could wear that will ever look bad on you. Everything fits you perfectly, especially this black gown."

She smiled at him and whispered in his ear. "You should see the black underwear set I have on underneath," and licked his ear.

The door opened and Henri waved to the crowd and got in. The chauffeur drove to the restaurant. On the way they talked about Aruba. Henri told them that he had been invited but he had commitments that he couldn't change. After the meal they went to Henri's place in the heart of Manhattan. Out of his window you could see the lights of Broadway and Times Square.

"This is a beautiful view," said Thomas.

"It is," said Henri walking up and standing beside him.

He turned to Rebecca. "Tomorrow I have a full day planned. Is there anything you want to do in particular?"

"No, whatever you have planned is great."

"Good. Tomorrow wear some comfortable shoes and dress warm. These December mornings are cool."

Henri took them on a tour of New York. In the morning they went up the Statue of Liberty. They walked down Wall Street. As they crossed the road to the Empire State Building Thomas grabbed hold of Rebecca's arm and told her to hang on tightly, "Remember what happened in 'An Affair to Remember'?" She smiled and held him. They ate lunch in Times Square and took a ride in a horse drawn carriage in Central park. They finished off the late afternoon with a coffee in a small diner in Manhattan. After, they went back to Henri's apartment and all helped make dinner and drink a couple bottles of wine.

"That was a great meal," said Rebecca.

"It was a great day. Thank you Henri," said Thomas.

"It was my pleasure." He looked at Rebecca, "let me get the suitcase for you." He came back with a large suitcase and opened it up. "I had these in a box. I bought the suitcase for you, so that you could take them back. Remember I was telling you I had all your old ballet slippers, leotards and dance costumes. Here's the fairy costume, the princess, the kitten, they're all in here."

Rebecca went on her knees and looked through them. "Here's the lioness. These bring back memories."

"You know your mother made all these," said Henri.

Rebecca looked at him surprised.

"She made them until you were eight. She was very good with her hands. She used to be up early hours in the morning, sewing. I remember especially the embroidery taking a lot of time. You made her so proud when she watched you dance in them," recalled Henri.

"I never knew or maybe I have just forgotten," said Rebecca.

"Your mother was not one to brag. She was quietly content and very humble. She loved being involved with you and your dancing," said Henri. "Your mother loved being around children."

Rebecca looked at her father. "Why did you only have me?"

The question was unexpected but Henri realized there was no better time to answer than now. "Your mother and I tried to have more children. She miscarried once before you and twice after. The doctor's had to watch her constantly during your pregnancy. They had her in the hospital for her last trimester. When she had you I remember how we cried with joy. We knew God had blessed us. She would have kept trying but the doctors told her to stop for her health." Henri looked at Rebecca and continued, "You can't blame your mother for everything that happened between us. I was on the road all the time and when I was in town I was working late. Many people saw me walking you to your classes and watching you but they didn't realize that your mother was up late nights making your costumes and going into work the next morning. I worked at night and was off in the daytime. Don't get me wrong I loved taking you to your classes and watching you and being party of your life but your mother was just as involved as I was, just in a different way. She never missed any of your competitions. As you got older she wasn't allowed to make you dresses; we had to buy them through a costume designer, and so she stopped. I wasn't around as much as I should have been or at least I should have made up for it when I was there. She felt empty and grew lonely and I was somewhat to blame." He sipped his red wine. "Rebecca, always remember your mother loves you. You may not see her or talk to her as much as you used to, I'm not too sure why not. Maybe you remind her of the life she, we, once had. Maybe it's too much pain. Whenever I speak to her she always asks after you. I don't know if this helps you or makes much sense." He looked at the wine. "The wine has loosened my lips but the words that come out are true."

She went over to her father and put her arms around him and sat on his knee and held him. "I love you." She held him for a little while longer and asked him "Daddy, why did you keep on trying to have children after the first miscarriage?"

"We loved each other and we wanted to have a family," he looked at her. "Look at you. You've grown into a fine young woman. You are an angelic dancer and you make me so proud. When you have children you will understand. Here, sit next to me on the sofa I want you to see the home movies. Thomas you'll get a laugh out of these."

Henri put on two DVDs, mostly just the three of them, Rebecca, Henri and her mother. Thomas had never seen her mother before and because they were taken when she was younger her resemblance to Rebecca was uncanny. It could have been Rebecca he was watching on the television.

Henri had filmed Rebecca from the time she was born until she was sixteen. There was lots of footage of Rebecca dancing at competitions, walking in the park with her parents, playing in the backyard, having birthday parties. Her mother was always there. It had several shots of her mother up till two and three in the morning making her costume and asleep the next morning in the chair. Henri looked a lot younger and he had long hairy sideburns. Thomas smiled to himself when he saw them. They both looked very happily. Thomas assumed that the separation must have been devastating. The scene ended and the television went black. Suddenly a scene of Rebecca's mother showing her swollen stomach came on. She looked different to the way she looked in earlier footage when she was carrying Rebecca. Henri scrambled to turn it off.

"Dad, what was that?"

"Nothing" replied Henri turning off the set. He hadn't realized that was there.

"Dad?" asked Rebecca.

Henri sat down next to Rebecca. "The first and last miscarriages had been in the first four weeks, the second was in the third month. It was very difficult on us both." He stopped and gained his composure. "I had filmed your mother up until the last week. That was your mother the week before the miscarriage. I had thought I had taped over it."

"Why didn't you want me to know about the miscarriages?"

Henri held her hand. "That miscarriage in particular hit us both very hard. We had seen the baby on the ultrasound a week earlier and everything was normal and the baby seemed healthy. We were devastated when we lost her at such a stage." He stopped and collected his thoughts. "Rebecca when you are married, you'll understand that as man and wife you have a life to live, and it's your life to share. You two will want to have your own private secrets and your own reasons for keeping them so. The decisions you make are yours and no one should alter them. Your mother and I agreed not to tell you the particulars of the miscarriages. The main reason was the memory was so painful." He had tears rolling down his cheeks. "We always wanted you to have brothers and sisters." Rebecca pulled his head toward him and he cried. Thomas left and went to the kitchen to make some coffee. He looked out the window and thought about Rebecca and having children. Fifteen minutes later she came in to the kitchen.

"He's gone to bed. He's upset. I shouldn't have pushed him," she said with a sad look on her face.

"Don't feel bad. You had some questions you wanted answers to," said Thomas comforting her.

Henri came into the kitchen. "Rebecca I don't want you to be upset. I'm relieved we talked about it and that you know. I'll see you in the morning." He kissed her and ruffled Thomas's hair. "Goodnight." He turned and walked away and stopped and looked back. "Rebecca, Thomas, no matter how painful it was going through the miscarriages with Margot, if the doctors would have let us we would have kept on trying." He smiled and looked at Rebecca. "Imagine having two or three delicate creatures with us today, just like Rebecca." He smiled and turned and left the kitchen.

Rebecca held Thomas closely and closed her eyes and cried.

Early the next morning Thomas felt Rebecca get under the covers and hold him. He fell back asleep and woke a few hours later. Rebecca was awake and looking at him.

"Good morning," said Thomas.

She smiled.

"Did you sleep okay?"

"No," she whispered.

"Are you okay?"

"I'm fine. I was up most of the night thinking."

"Do you want to talk about it?" he asked.

"Not now," she replied and smiled. "Maybe later."

THE AFTERNOON WAS SPENT WATCHING THE BOYS and girls of the First Baptist Church of Harlem Choir perform. Thomas and Rebecca were their special guests and were given the best seats. The audience consisted of parents, family, friends and several members of the opera company. They watched them perform the Nativity and sing Christmas Hymns. When they had finished members of the opera company were invited to sing with the children. It made their dreams come true and gave them a lifetime memory. After the show they had a sit down lunch of sandwiches, coffee and Christmas cake, which the children served. Thomas and Rebecca got to meet the parents of the children and were thanked for giving them a chance to see the operas. After the meal Rufus made a speech and gave them a check for five thousand dollars and the gifts.

When Rufus finished, Thomas stood and spoke. "After reading the letter from Ms. Brown, Rebecca and I, went around to our family, friends and co-workers and asked them to donate to the Harlem Choir Building Fund. I am pleased to announce that we were able to match the opera company's contribution of five thousand dollars. We plan on making this an annual donation and we hope we can better the money raised from this year."

Rebecca handed Ms. Brown the check. She broke down and cried. The audience clapped and the children swarmed Rebecca, Thomas and Rufus.

Rebecca, Thomas and Henri stayed as late as they could and left in time to catch their flight. They said goodbye to Henri who looked much happier, as if a big weight had been lifted off his shoulders.

On the plane Rebecca read Thomas's manuscript, she had another fifty pages left and said she would be finished by the weekend, she told him it was better than the first.

CHAPTER 20

My Little Girl

THOMAS HUNG UP THE PHONE AND WENT into his room and put on his jacket. He went back into the kitchen and picked up the piece of paper that he had written the information on and went out the door smiling. It was almost twelve and he could catch Rebecca for lunch and tell her the exciting news. He went down the elevator, said good morning to Rob the doorman and went outside. The weather was cloudy and the wind was brisk, he did up his jacket and looked up at the sky, they were calling for snow over the next few days and were predicting that it would be a white Christmas. "Christmas day," thought Thomas, "only five days away." He started walking down the street.

Rebecca had performed yesterday in the Friday matinee of the Nutcracker. When they came home they decorated the condominium and put up the Christmas tree. They were going Christmas shopping tomorrow and Monday and had arranged to visit Henri for New Years in Times Square. Kate, Jack, Penny, Rachel and Jessica were also going to go.

Thomas looked around at the people and thought about the holidays. There was definitely a feeling of Christmas in the air and he was looking forward to spending the holidays with Rebecca. He was happy and smiled to himself.

"My little girl," screamed a woman who was standing to Thomas's far left. He turned and looked at her dropping her bags of Christmas gifts and pointing over Thomas's shoulder. The woman started in his direction. Thomas turned around to see a little girl on the road picking something off the ground. Everything was happening in slow motion. He looked at the approaching car and the driver talking on the cell phone. He wasn't paying attention to the road and Thomas realized he wouldn't see her till it was too late. Thomas could push her out of the way but he would be pushing her into the oncoming traffic approaching from the other direction. They would both be hit. He could grab her and throw her off the road onto the sidewalk, there was no guarantee she would make it, definitely not if the car tried to swerve out of the way. As these options ran through his head he was already moving toward the girl and picking her up. He covered himself around her and pulled her close to his body. His hands protected her head. He waited for the impact. The driver slammed on the brakes, too late, he hit Thomas hard. Thomas felt a tremendous pain in his legs as he was lifted off the ground and into the air, he tightly held the girl. He hit the windshield with his right shoulder and right side of his back. Thomas could hear the windshield shattering and the cracking of the bones in his collarbone and arm. He bounced off the windshield and turned in the air landing on the trunk of the car on his back, there was a loud thump as his head banged off the metal. He bounced off the trunk and landed on his side still on the road, still cradling the girl's head and body. Blood poured out onto the road. Thomas saw a light then everything went black.

CHAPTER 21

Light and Sound

Saturday

THOMAS WAS IN DARKNESS BUT NOT IN total obscurity for there was a small bright light very far off in the distance; it looked like a star in the evening sky. He was not of body and could not speak, taste or touch. He wasn't sure if he was seeing through his eyes or his mind and if what he was hearing was through his ears. Was he in his subconscious or his soul? For some reason he knew that the light was life; he didn't know how, he knew, he just did. He knew he was in hospital and he knew he had been in an accident. Someone had told him. Suddenly he experienced a great sensation, Rebecca. He knew he wasn't alone.

"Oh no! No! Thomas!" she cried, "Thomas, Thomas." She ran to his side and stroked his bruised face and cried.

"I'll get the doctor," said the nurse and left the room.

Moments later Kate arrived. "Rebecca?" she noticed Thomas, "Thomas! Thomas!" screamed Kate. She ran to the other side of the bed and held his hand and looked at him. "Thomas, oh no, Thomas. I didn't realize it was this bad." She cried.

The doctor walked into the room and addressed them, "Hello my name is Doctor Moore. May I ask who you are?"

"I am his sister and she is his fiancée," sobbed Kate. Rebecca was still too emotional to respond.

"Are your parents coming?" asked the doctor.

"My parents are dead. I am the only living relative," replied Kate and realizing this cried even more.

"Please, please I understand this is a very difficult time for you both but I would like to talk to you about his condition." He stopped and looked at the two sobbing women. "Perhaps I will come back later, when you've had some time." He went to leave.

"No," said Rebecca looking at him with tears streaming down her face. "Is he going to die?"

"Please, if you could both have a seat over here?" asked the doctor pointing to two chairs in the corner.

They both sat down.

He waited till they were settled. "Unfortunately your question is not that easy to answer. When Thomas took on the force of the car, his body was very rigid and the contact was very hard. Normally individuals who get hit by cars are not expecting the impact and either get hit and thrown away from the car or over the car. They are somewhat relaxed and they go with the impact. From what I understand Thomas was aware he was going to get hit by the car and was even more rigid as he protected the little girl."

Rebecca cut off the doctor and asked with a puzzled look. "Little girl?"

"You don't know what happened?" asked the doctor.

"The police said that he had been hit by a car and I phoned Rebecca," replied Kate.

"I guess they were waiting for me to tell you in person." The doctor took a deep breath and told them what he had heard from the mother and the police.

Rebecca and Kate looked at each other.

"You're telling me that Thomas jumped out on the street and picked up the little girl and took the force of the car to protect her?" asked Rebecca.

"Yes," he replied.

There was silence for a few moments.

"And the little girl?" asked Kate.

"She had scrapes and bruises on her legs, a broken arm, a couple of bruised ribs and a bruised jaw. We are keeping her in the critical ward overnight to keep an eye on her, just as a precaution. Tomorrow we will move her to the children's ward and the following day she will probably be released. Right now her condition is stable. She is sleeping, we gave her a sedative." He paused. "If Thomas had not done what he did she would have been killed. He without a doubt saved that little girl's life. Her mother has been asking me about Thomas all day."

Rebecca stood up and walked over to Thomas and looked at him. "I don't want him to die!" she said, "I want you to promise me you will do everything you can to save his life like he did for that little girl," she cried. "Promise me."

The doctor walked over to Rebecca and put his arm around her and promised he would do all he could. He walked her back to the chair and sat her down. "I need to tell you about Thomas's condition." He looked at them both. "The car hit his legs, mostly his right, his right leg is broken and his hip is badly bruised. He hit the windshield with his right side of his upper body; he has a broken collarbone, arm and three ribs. He landed on his back on the trunk, luckily, with no injury to his spine. But unfortunately he landed square on his back causing his head to whiplash against the trunk of the car with a tremendous force." He sadly looked at them both. "This is very serious; the force of the impact on his head has caused severe bruising and a swelling. When he landed on the road the right side of his head was cut above the ear and his jaw was badly bruised. He has scrapes and bruises over his face and body." He looked over at Thomas. "I have to be honest with you he's very lucky to be alive."

"Is he going to be okay?" asked Kate.

The doctor delivered the worst news. "He's not in the clear yet, in fact he is far from it, he hasn't gained consciousness and is in a coma. We had to operate to remove the blood trapped between his brain and skull. Before the operation he had less than a twenty percent chance of pulling through, after having the operation we give him a thirty percent chance. As each day goes by the odds improve and that percentage will increase but there is no guarantee. I have to be truthful with you he may never regain consciousness and there is a high probability that he will never recover and will die. He needs to come out of his coma."

Rebecca and Kate looked at the doctor. He had seen their reaction too many times in his career. It was the worst part of his job telling bad news to a patient's family and friends. He reemphasized, "I'm sorry."

Rebecca and Kate cried.

Over their sobbing he spoke. "I suggest when you are with Thomas you talk to him and touch him and let him know you are here and how much you want to see him." He looked at them both. "I'm very sorry. I will do everything I can to help him. Once he's stable we will move him downstairs to the ward. The machines that you see are monitoring his vitals and he is being fed intravenously. All we can do is wait. The faster he comes out of this the better his chances are."

The doctor left and shortly after the nurse came in and comforted the two crying girls. She sat with them until a hospital volunteer came in and took over.

They cried for hours.

Jack and Penny arrived at the hospital. They walked into the room expecting the worst but nothing they imagined would come close to what they witnessed. Penny cried and Jack looked away in pain. They both cried after Kate explained what the doctor had told them. Jack left the room and demanded to talk to the head nurse and the doctor. He could be heard in the hallway yelling and demanding that Thomas get the best treatment and care. The doctor and nurse responded that all patients receive the best treatment and that they were giving him the best possible care. He walked back in the room and told Penny he was off to find Mackenzie the director of the hospital.

"To think I donated a wing to this place," said Jack as he walked out shaking his head.

Penny, Kate and Rebecca stood in silence and looked at Thomas. Rebecca broke down and cried and Penny and Kate comforted her.

Jessica arrived an hour later. "How is he?" she asked as she walked in the room. "What happened?" She saw Thomas's state and almost fainted. They helped her into a chair and gave her some water. "Poor Thomas," she said. Penny explained to her what had happened.

Rachel was the next to walk in. She looked at her mother, Penny, Kate, and Rebecca standing in front of her and asked them, "He's okay? Tell me he's okay?"

"He's in a coma," replied Jessica.

Rachel walked around them and looked at Thomas. She left the room crying with her hand over her mouth. Jessica went out to comfort her and tell her what had happened. They came back in the room thirty minutes later.

They stood around the room and said nothing.

One would start crying and stop, then another. One would start crying and then they all would. Then all would be silent again.

A nurse came in and looked around the room at the distant faces. As she checked Thomas's vitals she started to talk to him. "Hello Thomas, I'm your nurse Sarah. How are you doing this evening? Okay! Good. I'm the night nurse tonight and I'll be here in case you need me. Well everything looks stable. Now you get yourself all better and wake up soon. You have a lot of visitors here tonight. There's a pretty young girl with blonde hair her name is?" she looked over.

Rachel looked up. "Rachel," she replied.

"Rachel," said the nurse to Thomas, and there is a beautiful girl behind me who hasn't left your side since I've been here and her name is?"

"Rebecca."

"Rebecca," said the nurse. "There's another attractive lady at the end of the bed."

"Kate."

"Named Kate and sitting in the chairs are?" she looked over.

"Penny."

"Jessica."

"Penny and Jessica. The big man standing at the door is," she looked over at Jack.

"My name is Jack," he replied.

"Jack," she said. "Thomas, all these people are here because they care about you and want to let you know that you have company while you're sleeping and that you're not alone." She looked around at them and back at Thomas, "They are very upset right now but once they've gotten over that they'll start talking to you, I promise. So you hang on dear, good. I'll be back in a couple of hours." She walked toward the door and turned around. "He can hear you, he can. He can hear you crying but I think talking to him is better." She walked out the room.

They were silent for a few minutes.

Rebecca couldn't wait any longer. "Thomas, it's me Rebecca. I wanted you to know I love you and I'm going to be here day and night. I want you to get better. You know Christmas Eve is in four days and we still have to do our shopping." She was starting to cry.

"It's Kate, Thomas. I'm here too and I want you to know that I love you. I wanted to let you know that the little girl is fine and that you saved her life. We are all very proud of you but it's time to come back." Kate couldn't help herself and quietly cried.

One by one they told Thomas that they loved him and that they wanted him back. They all cried after talking to him but each felt better.

It was getting late and Rebecca and Kate said thanks to Jack, who had arranged for them to stay for as long as they wanted, the rest had to leave and said they would be back in the morning. Jack told Thomas before he left that he spoke to Mackenzie and that he was going to get top rate service and support from his staff.

Sunday

THE SMALL BRIGHT LIGHT IN THE DISTANCE had increased to the size of a quarter. Thomas didn't know if he was moving toward it or it was moving toward him. He heard vibrations coming and going and they were soothing.

"Thomas, it's me Rebecca. It's almost three and I can't sleep. I wanted you to know that I was still here. Kate and I have been talking to each other hoping that you can hear us." She looked at Kate. "I went and got some water and Kate's just fallen asleep. I thought I would spend some time and talk to you alone. I've been thinking about this and I was wondering why you were out. You said to me that you weren't going anywhere. I wondered if you were going to surprise me and meet me for lunch or were you going out to buy me a secret present? Maybe both. I guess when you wake up you can tell me all about it." She looked at him. "Thomas I know what you did and why you did it and I love you for that but a little piece inside me wishes you hadn't, actually more than a little. I know I shouldn't think that way but I can't help it. Today her mother has her and I don't have you. Thomas, you must have known when you picked her up that the car was going to hurt you and possibly kill you and yet you still did it. I'm so angry, not with you, but that little girl and her mother. I want to tell them what you are going through and what I'm going through. I know you wouldn't want me to do that so I won't but that's how I feel. I love you and I miss you and I'm scared."

"THOMAS IF YOU ARE FEELING SOMETHING NEXT to your left leg that's Rebecca's head lying on the bed next to you, she's fallen asleep. It's almost four thirty. How are you?" She tried to force a smile. "You have a lot of people hoping and praying you will get better. You take your time but don't stay away too long. You promised me you would always be here for me and I know you never break your promises. Please don't leave me." Kate cried.

"WHAT'S IT LIKE? TO KNOW THAT THIS is the person you want and no one else?" asked Kate.

"It's difficult to explain. It's like he is the piece of me that was missing. He makes me whole. My soul mate!" Rebecca looked away from Thomas and at Kate. "I remember the first time I met him I thought he was the handsomest man I had ever seen; I fell in love with him straight away. And after meeting him and being with him, I fell deeper in love with him. I knew there was no one else," said Rebecca.

Kate looked at her. "How did you feel when he saw you with Frank that time?"

"I was so upset! I thought that was it and that he was gone forever. It was my own fault. I should have told him about Frank before that. But I wouldn't have given up until he knew the truth," Rebecca looked down at her ring. "When he didn't want to talk to me I thought he didn't care for me the same way that I did for him. It was only after what he did for my father I knew that he did and that I had a chance."

"Did he tell you that he cried that night? The day he saw you with Frank."

Rebecca looked at her in disbelief.

"It's true."

She looked at Thomas. "He never told me."

"I knew he was hurt. So I decided to go to his room and talk to him. I listened at the door and could hear him crying." Kate looked at Thomas. "I had actually talked him into going to the fundraiser half hoping he would meet someone who was in the publishing business, someone he could talk to about his novel. I thought it might open a door of opportunity." She stopped and looked back at Rebecca. "I guess it did. He met you and fell in love and you pushed him to send his novel off. I am so grateful he met you." She reached over and squeezed Rebecca's hand.

"Thank you," replied Rebecca and smiled. "I feel so bad, he hasn't heard back from anyone and we had set Christmas as the deadline. We were going to follow up after the New Year. His story was excellent I can't believe none of them were interested?" asked Rebecca.

"There's still time."

"Have you read his second novel?"

"I started it this week."

"It's better than the first. He was going to send it out in the New Year." She looked at Thomas and corrected herself. "He is going to send it out in the New Year."

"Good morning," said the nurse. "How are you doing?"

"Okay," they both replied.

The nurse took his vitals. "He's doing better today."

"Really?" asked Rebecca excitedly.

"Slightly and believe me that's a milestone in the right direction. The doctor will be making his rounds within the hour and will be giving him a full examination. You won't be allowed to watch and it will take him about thirty minutes. Enough time to get some breakfast and a wash and change of clothes," said the nurse, and smiled as she left.

They smiled back.

When the doctor arrived they told him they were going to get some breakfast and would be back in thirty minutes. He said he would wait for them to return so he could let them know how Thomas was doing.

The doctor examined him and talked him through the examination. He told him he was doing fine. He pulled the curtain back and saw the girls standing outside in the hallway and called them in.

"Looks good!" said the doctor looking at the food.

"Would you like a juice or muffin?" asked Kate.

"No thanks. I'll get a juice later."

"Here," Kate gave him an apple juice.

He smiled and said thanks.

"How is he?" asked Rebecca.

"He is doing better, better than I expected. This evening Doctor Peterson will be in to take a look at him; he's the doctor that operated and an expert in head traumas. If he confirms what I believe, that Thomas is stable, then tomorrow we will move him downstairs into a private room. Thomas is still listed as critical and in danger but there is nothing we can do for him up here. It's a waiting game and we have to see how he reacts to his injuries." The doctor looked down at Thomas and back at the girls. "He needs to come out of the coma, the sooner the better."

They thanked the doctor and watched him leave. They sat down and started to eat. Kate shouted over to Thomas. "We're back, we went and got some juices, muffins, bagels and cream cheese and a cup of tea." Kate looked at Rebecca. "You look tired?"

"I didn't sleep very well last night," replied Rebecca.

"Me either."

"We just put up the Christmas decorations a few days ago and we were going to go shopping. This should be a happy time of the year." She couldn't help crying.

Kate held her.

Rebecca composed herself. "I'm sorry. I'll be okay in a minute. I want him to be okay, that's all."

"I do too," said Kate and smiled. "Have something to eat."

Rebecca ate a bagel and drank her tea.

Kate walked over to Thomas. "How are you doing today?" She kept expecting him to wake up and answer her.

"Kate how is he?" asked Rachel walking toward her. She was carrying a gym bag.

"The doctor said he's doing better. The doctor who performed the operation is coming in this afternoon to check on him and make sure everything is okay. They're probably going to move him into a private room downstairs. He says that Thomas needs to come out of the coma."

Rachel kissed Thomas on the cheek and said, "Good morning Thomas" and walked over to Rebecca and sat next to her and held her hand. "Hello Rebecca, how are you holding up?"

"Fine," she replied forcing a smile.

"I brought track pants and shirts for you both and some toiletries. I thought you might like a change of clothes. Help yourself they're in the bag." She placed the bag on the table.

"Thanks Rachel," said Rebecca.

Kate walked over to Rachel. "I think I'll take you up on that offer. I need to get out of this skirt and blouse." She picked up the bag and went out the room.

"Why don't we put these two chairs closer? You can put your feet up and close your eyes. I'll watch Thomas for a while." Rachel stood and put the two chairs together and helped Rebecca put her feet up. Rebecca closed her eyes and was a sleep in minutes.

Rachel walked over to Thomas and looked at him. "Thomas, it's Rachel, you're looking better and the doctor says you're going to continue to get better." She smiled at him and her face crumbled and she started to cry. She quickly regained her composure. "Thomas, remember the last time you were in hospital and you told that nurse that your eyesight was okay." She laughed. "That was pretty funny. Remember the time we went riding and we had the picnic. That was nice. Aruba, that was a lot of fun!"

Penny walked in the room and noticed Rebecca sleeping in the chair and walked over to Rachel and whispered. "Hello, Rachel. How is he?"

Rachel repeated what Kate had told her earlier.

"Good," said Penny. "Jack is talking with Mackenzie and setting Thomas up. Where's Kate?"

"She's getting changed. I brought them some clothes."

"Good girl," replied Penny. "Your mother?"

"She'll be here soon she wanted to get some flowers to brighten up the room. She didn't like the ones they had in the gift shop."

"I know, me either. I bought some at the florist."

Jack walked in with a bouquet of flowers in a vase and put them on the side table next to Thomas. He looked at Thomas and asked him how he was doing. Jack looked over at Rachel, "The snow is starting to fall."

"Is it?" asked Kate walking into the room.

"It's going to fall all day," continued Jack. "They reckon ten inches and it's going to fall on and off over the next five days."

"A white Christmas," said Rachel. "He was wishing for a white Christmas."

They all looked at Thomas.

"It's really coming down out there," said Jessica walking into the room. "How is everyone? Kate you look tired?"

"I'm okay," replied Kate.

"Rebecca?"

"She's sleeping," said Kate pointing behind Jack and Penny.

"Poor girl," said Jessica. "I brought some flowers," she placed them on the table, "and some fruit, croissants and juices for you girls." She placed the bag next to the flowers. She looked at Thomas and couldn't stop herself from crying. Rachel comforted her and she began to cry. They all cried.

"Can I come in?"

"Frank," said Rebecca, "of course come on over."

Frank looked at Thomas and his heart went out to him. "How are you doing Kate?" he asked.

"I keep waiting for him to sit up in that bed and say something."

"He will," comforted Frank. "Rebecca how are you doing?"

"I'm okay. If I only knew he was going to be all right. This waiting is eating me up inside," replied Rebecca.

"He'll be fine," reassured Frank. "I brought a portable CD player. The nurse said it was okay as long as it was low. I brought some CDs that I think he would like and a few books and magazines that you may want to read to him. I'll put them on the table." He moved over and put them down.

"Thanks," said Kate.

They sat and talked to Thomas as if he were involved in the conversation. Once in a while one of them would answer on his behalf.

Doctor Peterson came early that evening to check on him and told them he had recovered as well as could be expected from the surgery, he said he was very worried about his comatose state but they would have to take it one day at a time. He said he would be back tomorrow morning with Dr. Moore and if everything remained stable they would move him down to a private room.

After he left Jack informed them that Thomas had an extra large private room waiting for him. They were going to put in a couple of cots and extra chairs and a television with a DVD player. A private nurse had been hired to take care of him full time; Mackenzie had assured him the nurse was one of the best. Rebecca and Kate thanked him.

"HI THOMAS, IT'S ME RACHEL. EVERYONE HAS gone downstairs for dinner. I said I would stay with you. You know I've wanted to talk to you for the longest time about something and I've been quiet up until know. Remember the night of my party and we where in the hot tub looking at the stars and I asked you to be my best friend? You said you would and I said I was glad. That was a lie. I really didn't want you to just be my friend I really wanted to hear you to tell me that you liked me more than a friend and that you found me interesting, attractive and sexy and wanted to be with me. Because that's the way I felt about you. Thinking back I realized how stupid I was." She looked down and held his hand. "I have a confession to make, I only dated Mathew to get a response from you…something… some sign that you liked me or were jealous. What a fool I have been. I should have told you how I felt at least you would have known; maybe things may have worked out differently." She smiled at him. "I always looked forward to you coming over. I will always remember the time we went riding and we had the picnic. I often lie in bed and think about us that day. I even thought about us making love, right there on the side of the valley. Remember looking at the night sky and seeing who could spot the first star and we saw the shooting star. Do you know what I wished for? You." She stopped and thought for a moment. "I also wished we had gone horseback riding the day after my party. I would have told you then how I felt about you." She wiped the tears from her eyes. "I am so in love with you. I fell in love with you the night we met at the fundraiser." She stopped for a moment and caressed his hair. "Aruba! Now that was fun. I brought the pictures. I haven't seen them yet. I'll show them later when everyone is here and we'll describe them to you. I was so happy when you watched me; you were with me the whole time. It was then I realized you and Rebecca were my best friends and it was at that point I decided I would never come between you and Rebecca or let you know how I felt." She leaned over and kissed him on the lips. "Thomas, I love you, I loved you from the first day I met you. You will never hear me tell you this again. It will be my secret."

They returned from dinner and had brought something back for Rachel. She sat quietly in the corner and ate. The redness in her eyes gave away the fact that she had been crying for a very long time. They left her alone. They talked about the weather, celebrities and sports. Jack read out loud a gossip magazine in which everyone gave their input as to whether it was true or not. The nurse came in and checked on Thomas and said everything was the same.

Eric stopped by and dropped off chocolates and a get-well card signed by the First National Ballet. He told Rebecca and Penny, that under Penny's request, Rebecca has been excused from any classes and performances of the Nutcracker.

He squeezed her hand as he spoke. "Myself, and the First National Ballet are praying for you both. Take whatever time is needed."

Rebecca was grateful for his kindness and understanding, "Thank you and please thank my fellow dancers."

"I will," replied Eric as he kissed her and gave Thomas's hand a squeeze, "I'll keep him in my prayers."

Eileen, Stephanie and Ted walked in the room as Eric was leaving. Stephanie cried. Eileen put her hand over her mouth and tears welled up in her eyes. Frank comforted them. Ted spoke for them when he asked, "Is he going to be okay?"

Kate explained the waiting period.

"Why does this always happen to the nice guys?" asked Ted.

"Why does it?" said a voice from behind. It was John.

"I thought you were going to wait in the car?" asked Eileen.

"I changed my mind." He walked by them and stood in front of Thomas. He looked down at Thomas and over at Frank and Rebecca. "After the three of you left my house that evening I despised you all. There you were telling me how I should love and treat my son. Then my wife and daughter turn against me, then Ted. You know what Ted said to me, I'm sure you will all get a kick out of this; he said I was a bastard. Actually a self-pitying, loveless bastard who was forcing his sons to live his life and didn't know what he had. I started thinking about that and what Frank said. I realized I was being pointed out as the bad man and they were ganging up on me." He looked directly at Frank. "You know Frank when you guys were younger, I never wanted you to be bigots. I always said to love everyone no matter what race, creed, color, sex, or religion. You did, you all did. I took a long look at myself in the mirror and wondered why I had changed. I realized I hadn't changed toward the people at work or with my neighbors or people I meet on the street. I accepted them for who they were. Yet my own son, my own flesh and blood asks me to accept him, not for being gay or for being a ballet dancer, but just as a son, to be happy for him and be proud of him. I realized that my children have all turned out pretty good. They don't do drugs, they aren't criminals and they respect us and our house." He looked at his family. "I knew I was wrong I was just too pig headed to admit it. So, I went and stood in the back of the theater and watched Frank dance. The next day at work I spoke to the mechanics at my shop, my neighbors and my friends and told them that I went to watch Frank dance in a ballet and that he is one hell of a dancer." He looked at Thomas on the bed. "Do you know on Christmas Eve, my wife, my daughter and my son are going out and leaving me in the house on my own and meeting Frank for a drink at the pub." He stopped for a moment and collected his thoughts. "You see I was going to surprise them and show up and have a drink with them. Then I heard about your accident and I felt this pang of pain in my chest because I thought to myself what if this was Frank? He would never know how sorry I was. How proud of him I am and how much I love him." John broke down and cried and walked to Frank and put his arms around him. "I'm so sorry my son, please forgive me."

Frank cried. "I love you dad there's nothing to forgive." He took his dad outside and his family followed.

Rebecca looked at Thomas and leaned over and whispered. "You're right I should have had more faith in families." She kissed his cheek.

They came back in and John spoke. "Rebecca and Kate, I'm sorry for what happened to Thomas, I hope he recovers quickly." He leaned over Thomas. "Get well soon and thank you for being Frank's friend."

RACHEL OPENED THE ENVELOPE AND TOOK THE pictures out one by one. Kate and Rebecca leaned over her shoulder. As she looked at them she described them out loud for Thomas, putting them in front of his face before she passed them on. "Here we are all sitting on the plane waiting to take off for Aruba. This is the four of us in the van going to the hotel. These are pictures of the beach and sea and pool and from the room. Here's one of my mom. Thomas and Rebecca. Me, Rebecca, and Kate. Buddy and Veronica. Kate, Stephanie and my mom in the pool."

"Remember when Thomas called out to those guys and went under water and they thought it was Kate," said Jessica.

"That was funny I'll have to get him back for that," said Kate. She started to get upset.

"Kate, tell them the time with my father and you, you know, the singing?" asked Rebecca.

"Oh, okay," said Kate. She told them about her singing to Rebecca's father in front of the people at the lounge. "…And here I was singing a song to Henri La Croix, one of the greatest opera singers, and right after he'd just finished singing, I was so embarrassed. Your father was looking at me a little confused. That's Thomas for you." Kate let out a laugh and felt a little better.

Rachel continued going through the photographs.

Rebecca looked at the one of her and Thomas outside the church. She looked at him in his suit and her in her dress. She remembered thinking at the time that it wouldn't be long before they would be getting pictures taken for their wedding. He looked so handsome. There was another picture of Rebecca talking with Jack and Thomas was looking at her unaware he was being photographed. She could tell he was thinking about something and she wondered what it was. She liked the pictures of her and Thomas making sand castles with the children and the one of them walking back from their sunset walk on the beach.

They all laughed at the picture with Thomas and Jack in their Hawaiian shirts and talked about them at great length. Jack fought back the tears.

"You know he has that hanging up in his closet. He says he was going to wear it to his bachelor party," said Rebecca. She corrected herself again. "Is going to wear it." She broke down and cried.

"THOMAS IT'S ME REBECCA. KATE HAS GONE downstairs to walk Rachel and Jessica out. She wanted to get some fresh air." Rebecca looked at Thomas and played with his hair. She had never felt so lonely in all her life. She quietly sang, "You're the Best Thing," then cried with all her heart.

Monday

THE LIGHT HAD NOW GROWN INTO THE size of a basketball. It was brighter than any light he had ever seen. It didn't hurt and it wasn't warm. He realized that he was moving closer. The vibrating had changed to a hum and it made him feel better.

The doctors told Rebecca and Kate they were moving Thomas downstairs and re-emphasized that they were still concerned about his unconscious state. As promised by Jack, he was moved into a large private room. Rebecca and Kate met the hired nurse Anne; she was very well spoken and gentle. She explained her qualifications, talked about her husband and children; they took an immediate liking to her.

"Hello, may I come in?" asked a woman in her early thirties wearing an overcoat.

No one knew her.

"I was there when Thomas was struck by the car," she explained.

"Come in and have a seat," said Jack standing.

"No thank you I prefer to stand," she said nervously. "Are you all family?" she asked.

Jessica replied. "The girl on this side of the bed is Thomas's sister Kate and on the other side is Thomas's fiancée Rebecca. Me and my daughter with the blonde hair," Rachel put up her hand, "are very close friends, as our Jack and Penny."

They all looked at the nervous woman.

"My name is Elizabeth Jones," she looked at them and wondered where to begin and how to explain. "I am the reason Thomas was hit by the car." They looked at each other. "My little girl Jenny and I were coming back from doing some Christmas shopping at the mall. You see she had received a letter from Santa Claus and I took her to the mall because she wanted to see Santa and let him know she got his letter and wanted to show it to him. On the way home she was walking next to me and I was carrying these heavy bags, so I put them down for a moment. She had been holding onto this letter all day and I told her it was windy outside and it would blow away and she should put it in her pocket. You know how seven year old children are. She wanted to hold it all the way home and put it straight under the Christmas tree. As I rested the wind blew the letter out of her hand and it was right there next to her so I told her to pick it up. I leaned down and picked up the bags and I looked over and she had gone. The letter had blown onto the road and she had chased after it and was trying to pick it up. I shouted and Thomas heard me and saw her. He ran and picked Jenny up….then the car hit him hard….his body and his head hit so hard…..and that sound and the blood." She began to shake and cry. "I wanted you to know that I am the reason Thomas was struck by the car and that I am sorry. I wanted to come sooner but I knew you would need some time alone and I was scared to come. I'm having a difficult time sleeping and I've been waking up screaming. I needed to talk to you and ask you to forgive me, please." She cried and fell to the ground.

Rebecca, stood up, walked over and helped her off the floor and held her. Kate came over and hugged them both. They both reassured her it wasn't her fault.

They sat the lady down and Rebecca and Kate sat next to her. "I have something I want to read to you." She opened an envelope and pulled out a letter written in red crayon. "I'll read it as she wrote it on the paper." She read:

> *Dear Santa Claus,*
>
> *I wrote you a letter telling you what toys to bring me. I don't want them anymore. I don't want my dollies any more. I don't want my teddies any more. I don't want any candy. None of them. I want you to make my Christmas Angel better for Christmas Day. He's very sick in hospital and his name is Thomas. Thank you. I've been a very, very, very, very good girl, maybe one dolly, Jenny.*

"She wrote it last night and asked me to take it to Santa straight away. I told her I would go and see him. She wants him to sign it and make her a promise," said Elizabeth.

"How is she?" asked Kate.

"She's fine. They are releasing her tomorrow. Her father is in the army and he'll be home Christmas Eve. She doesn't know yet and he doesn't know about this."

"Why don't you bring her in tomorrow before you leave?" asked Rebecca.

"Are you sure?" she asked.

"I'd like to meet her," said Rebecca.

The lady stood up. "Thank you for your kindness. I've been praying for Thomas." She started for the door. "I almost forgot. Thomas had this crumpled in his jacket it almost blew away but I picked it up and wanted to give it to one of you." She opened her bag and took out the piece of paper and gave it to Rebecca.

"Thank you," replied Rebecca and watched Elizabeth leave. She opened up the crumpled paper and read aloud what Thomas had written:

> *Elliott & Davis*
> *Janice Jacobs*
> *Wants me to meet with her first week in January at Manhattan*
> *Office.*
> *Will email information.*
> *Very interested in reading full manuscript and buying rights to*
> *novel.*

Rebecca looked at them. "Elliott and Davis had called and told him they were interested in his novel and wanted to meet him in Manhattan."

"That's where their head office is," said Jack.

"He was on his way over to tell me," said Rebecca and looked at Kate, "that they wanted to publish his novel."

Frank dropped in that evening and read some poetry and short stories to Thomas. The Valley Choir stopped in at seven.

"Okay Thomas," said Greg, "we practiced this song, we were told how much you like it so we got the CD and the lyrics, here goes." They harmonized Genesis's, 'Dancing With the Moonlit Knight'. They were incredible. When they finished Kate, Rebecca and Frank clapped and asked for an encore. They graciously accepted and sang Billy Idol's 'Rebel Yell'. One by one they stood over Thomas and wished him well.

Blair gave Rebecca a poem in a frame. "It's a poem that Thomas recited for Greg and me at our anniversary. It is so beautiful. I typed out the poem and framed it on my wall at home and I made one for you. I believe it also applies to you two."

Rebecca thanked him.

Miguel put a leather coat at the end of the bed, "For when he wakes up it's a present from us all."

Rebecca and Kate thanked them.

"We'll stop in on Christmas Eve and sing some carols," said Greg.

"That would be nice," said Frank as he walked them to the door.

Rebecca looked at the framed poem and read what Blair had written on it, "To Thomas and Rebecca, For Love that is Perfectly Mixed." She read the poem out loud and imagined Thomas reading it to her.

"Thomas it's me Rebecca, Kate just left to get some coffee. While we are alone I wanted to remind you that we only have three and a half weeks till our wedding. I've been wondering about the special dance you were going to do for me on our wedding night. I was so turned on when you did that dance in those leather pants. You were so lucky Kate was there." She hesitated momentarily. "Do you remember at The Duke? When you described what you were going to do to me and stopped halfway through and said I would have to wait for our wedding night for the ending, well, since that time I've imagined several different steamy endings, all with us making love all night." She started to sob. "So don't you deny me my ending Thomas? I need you. I would give up dancing forever to have you wake up and be with me. I wish we had made love and were married. I want you back Thomas. Please come back to me. I love you so much and I can't go on without you. I can't go on like this. I don't know how much longer I can last before I go out of my mind." She cried and cried, and cried herself to sleep.

"I WAS GONE A WHILE SO THAT Rebecca can have some time to talk to you. I have a cup of coffee for her but she's fallen asleep. Her head is resting on the end of the bed." She sipped her coffee. "I wanted to let you know that I'm really proud of what you did for that little girl, her name is Jenny. I miss you and want you to wake up and be with us. We need you here." She started to get upset. "If you leave I'll be here all alone and I don't know if I can live with that. I will have no one." She cried for a few moments and stopped. "I dreamed about me getting married one day and you walking me down the aisle and giving me away. Nothing would make me prouder. You've been the best brother a sister could have. You've always taken care of me and always put me first. You helped me have a normal teenage life." She remembered something. "Remember when Mom and Dad were away and I got my first period and you explained what it was? Then you went out and bought me tampons but also came back with fifty dollars worth of other items from the drugstore because you were embarrassed to buy them on their own. You had toothpaste, toothbrushes, soap, and magazines." She laughed to herself. "And you weren't too sure what kind to buy so you picked up several different brands and types. It wasn't till I got older I realized how much courage that must have took," she held his hand, "and how much you loved me." She sipped her coffee. "You helped me through school, to get a part time job that I love, you bought the new car for me instead of yourself, and you got me the condominium so I could be close to you. You always take care of me." She stopped and thought for a moment. "We had a great time in New York, I laugh when I think about the time you made me sing, that was one of your best practical jokes and then having them put my picture on the wall, that was pretty good too but I got you back for that. We had a lot of fun in Aruba." She looked down at Rebecca. "You know I really like Rebecca. If I could have picked out someone for you to marry it would have been her. Rachel's nice too and she would have been a very close second choice." She looked back at Thomas. "Rebecca really loves you and misses you, so do I, Thomas please hurry up and get well." She kissed him on the forehead and the tears fell from her face onto his cheek. She wiped them away but the tears were falling faster.

Tuesday

THE LIGHT HAD TAKEN UP HALF THE space and it was a void like the darkness. The light was quickly eating away at the darkness and Thomas could now feel pain and realized as the light grew so did the pain. The hum has changed to a murmur and it made him feel, happy.

"Hello Thomas its Henri. I brought some coffees and doughnuts for Rebecca and Kate but they are sleeping. Kate is on the cot and I'm going to put Rebecca on the other one," he stood up and picked up Rebecca and lay her down; he threw a blanket over each of them and came back and sat in a chair next to Thomas. "I talked to Anne outside and she told me about your condition and that everyone has been talking to you and that you can hear them. So I will sit here and talk with you and drink my coffee and eat my doughnut. First of all the choir have been renovating their practice hall and they said to say hello and Merry Christmas, that was last week, they didn't know about your condition. Rufus is going to call them today and tell them. I have some pictures showing them painting and fixing and such and will show them later. I was looking forward to us going out to get fitted for the tuxedos so that we could spend some time together. I wanted to tell you how fond I am of you and that Rebecca couldn't have met a finer man." Henri was finding it difficult to speak, he tried to keep up the conversation but when he looked at Thomas his heart was in his mouth, he put his head down and cried.

"Daddy?" asked Rebecca. "Daddy!" She jumped out of bed and ran to him. They held each other. "Daddy, I'm so glad you are here."

THERE WAS A KNOCK ON THE DOOR and a young girl with blonde hair and big eyes came in. She had a cast on her arm and the right side of her jaw was green and purplish. "May I come in?" she asked.

Rebecca and Kate walked over to her. "You must be Jenny?" asked Rebecca.

"Yes Miss."

"My name is Rebecca."

"Hi Rebecca."

"My name is Kate."

"Hi Kate."

"Come on in," said Rebecca. "This is Jessica, Rachel, Penny, Jack, and Henri."

"Hi." She said.

"Hello Jenny," they replied.

"Does your arm hurt?" asked Penny.

Elizabeth walked in behind her.

"Not too much. It gets itchy," she replied. "My mom will be here in a minute."

"I'm right behind you honey."

"I bought some candies for Thomas. I saved them for him."

"You can put them on the table next to his bed," said Kate.

She walked over and reached up and put them down. She struggled to look up and see Thomas.

"Dad, why don't you put her on the bed?" asked Rebecca.

Henri stood up and placed the little girl on the end of the bed. Rebecca walked up to her.

"Is he sleeping?"

"Yes he is Jenny," replied Rebecca.

"Can we wake him up?"

"Not now honey. He needs his rest," replied Rebecca.

"Soon?"

"A day or so."

"He looks sore."

"He's a little sore but he'll get better just like your arm and chin. See, he has a cast on his leg and a bruise on his face too."

"I made this for Thomas, it's a Christmas card."

"Let's see," she looked over at Kate. "Come have a look Kate." Kate walked next to Rebecca.

Rebecca looked at the drawing on the cover.

"It's my Christmas Angel," said Jenny.

Rebecca and Kate looked at a round head with eyes and a smile, wearing a triangular gown with two stick legs and feet. The angel had a halo above its head.

"That's Thomas, he's my Christmas Angel and he's floating over the earth and taking care of me," said Jenny. She took the card off of Rebecca and opened it up. "I wrote something inside. Would you like to hear it?"

Rebecca and Kate nodded and smiled and said "Yes".

"My mommy helped me." She read:

> *Dear Thomas, My Christmas Angel,*
> *Santa is going to make you all better for Christmas.*
> *I did ask Santa for one dolly, I hope that's okay?*
> *Merry Christmas, Love Jenny.*

"That's beautiful," said Rebecca.

"Would you like me to put it on the table next to his candy?" asked Kate.

"Yes please," she looked up at Thomas, "I'm going home today."

"You are? Just in time for Christmas Eve and Santa," said Rebecca.

The girl looked over at her mother, "Mommy can we come here tomorrow evening before I go to sleep?"

"Well I don't know?" questioned the mother.

"Of course you can. Do you like singing Christmas Carols?" Rebecca asked.

"Yes I do."

"Good, because we have some singers coming around dinner time and you can sing with them."

"I want to."

"Maybe we should ask your mommy first."

"Mommy, can we?"

"Of course we can."

The little girl looked at Rebecca and Kate. "I'm sorry I was a naughty girl and got Thomas hurt."

Rebecca and Kate's eyes filled with tears. "It's not your fault and you don't worry about that, ever."

The little girl hugged Rebecca and Kate and asked, "Can I give him a kiss bye?"

"I think Thomas would like that," said Kate moving her up the bed.

Jenny leaned over and kissed Thomas on the cheek. Kate put her on the floor and she walked over to her mother. "Bye. I'll be back tomorrow." She waved.

Her mother said, "Bye," and they left the room.

A few minutes later a priest came in and asked how everyone was. He said a quick mass, blessed Thomas, and gave out communion to those that wanted it. "I'm here Tuesdays and Thursdays. I'll be in Christmas Day in the afternoon. I'll drop in and see you. We'll mention his name at the church masses and offer our prayers." He walked toward the door and turned around. "I'll see you then." They thanked him as he walked out the room.

REBECCA AND KATE LOOKED OVER AT HENRI snoring. Rebecca turned her attention to Kate and spoke gently. "I was so excited about Thomas and me spending our first Christmas together. We had everything organized. We were going to go shopping for gifts on Sunday and Monday. Monday evening I was performing in the Nutcracker and after we were going to The Duke for a drink and something to eat, Thomas loves those fish and chips. Today he was going to go with my dad and Frank and get fitted for the tuxedos. I was going to pick up his gift." She tried desperately to hold back the tears. "This evening Thomas, my dad, you and I were going out to buy the turkey, the groceries, the beer and wine. And when we got back we were going to have some apple cider and eggnog and watch the fireplace and listen to Christmas music. Christmas Eve Penny, Jack, Jessica and Rachel were all going to meet us in the afternoon and go to the outdoor rink and skate to the music and drink hot chocolate with marshmallows. Then we would drop in and have a drink with Frank. The four of us would go back to our place and put on the gas fireplace and watch Christmas movies." The tears started to roll down her cheek. "On Christmas day I would watch Thomas open his gift and see the surprise look on his face. I would smile because I would be so happy. Then he would give me mine and make me guess at what he had bought me. Everyone would come by in the afternoon and we would have a beautiful dinner and we would play silly games and laugh and have fun. Then on Boxing Day we would all go up to Jack's cabin and go for a sleigh ride and tobogganing. Then we would go to Manhattan and visit my dad and go for a horse drawn carriage ride around the city. On New Year's Eve we would watch the ball fall at Times Square and sing Auld Lang Syne and I would turn to Thomas and kiss him and tell him I loved him and in two weeks we would be married." She looked at Thomas and broke down and cried very hard. Kate walked over to her and held her and cried with her.

Christmas Eve

THOMAS WAS NOW SURROUNDED BY LIGHT. THE darkness was a basketball shape off in the distance and it was shrinking at a much greater rate than the light had expanded. He knew that once the darkness disappeared something would happen. The pain was becoming unbearable and the murmur had become fragmented sounds.

"Hello Thomas, its Jack and Penny," said Penny.

"Hello Thomas. The girls have gone to get a shower and change their clothes. I wanted to let you know that we are both hoping that you get better soon. I was looking forward to taking you and Rebecca up to the cabin and watching you two skiing. You know I got you a membership at the golf club for a Christmas gift. I know you probably would have objected but it was something I wanted to do. Beside, I would feel a lot better if you beat me there as a member. I'm looking forward to playing you in the summer." Jack laughed a little. "You've been more than a good friend to me. When I look at you, I think if I had a son and he was you, I would be the proudest father alive. So you take your rest and get better and when you're ready you come back to us soon." Jack had so much more to say but the tears streamed down his face and he started to sob and walked away.

Penny spoke. "We all miss you and want you back. I want to see you and Rebecca married and growing as a couple and having a family. Don't disappoint us now. We are all praying for you. You know it would be the most wonderful gift if you were to open those eyes and smile. Rebecca is like a daughter to me and I'm so proud of her, and of you, and I'm so excited about the two of you. Your grandmother liked Rebecca immensely. When you two were younger we always hoped you two might end up together. We all love you. Come back soon." Penny stopped and started to cry. She walked over to Jack and they held each other. Jessica came in and they left the room and gave her some time with Thomas.

"Thomas, Rachel and I have your Christmas present under our tree, now I'm not going to tell you what it is because it will ruin the surprise. I know that you'll be waking up soon and I'll be able to give it to you in person and see your reaction." Jessica thought she was going to be able to handle this better but tears were already starting to form. "Oh why did this have to happen to you? Thomas we all love you and miss you. We are all waiting for you. We need you here with us, Heaven can wait." She cried.

THROUGHOUT THE DAY PEOPLE CAME AND STAYED: there was Rebecca, Kate, Henri, Penny, Jack, Rachel, Jessica, and Frank. They decorated the room and played Christmas music. They watched the Christmas specials on television and they sat and talked about Christmas and the snow outside and skiing. At five o'clock Jenny and her mother and father joined them. Jenny's dad, Chet, dressed in his sergeant's uniform, thanked Thomas for saving his little girls' life and placed a rosary inside his hand. He told them that his wife had given him the rosary to make sure he came back safe from the Middle East. They wanted Thomas to have it. He saluted Thomas.

At six, Frank, his family and the Village Choir came. They sang Christmas Carols and told Christmas stories. Eileen had brought sandwiches from home and served them. Penny served apple cider and eggnog; some spiced it up with rum. At eight o'clock Chet, at his daughter's request, recited 'Twas the Night Before Christmas'. At ten everyone left except Rebecca, Kate and Henri.

The three of then talked about how special the day had been and how nice it was having them around. Rebecca looked over at Thomas and wished he would open his eyes.

"Thomas, I'm going to put on some movies. Penny picked them up for me. The first is 'It's a Wonderful Life' with James Stewart, I know that's one of your favorites and the second is one is 'A Christmas Carol' with Alastair Sim. Rebecca put on the movie and sat next to Thomas and held his hand. She watched them both and made comments throughout them to Thomas. Henri had fallen asleep in the chair just after the second movie had started. Kate, lying on the cot, fell asleep halfway through the second.

The movie ended and Rebecca turned off the television. There was an unnerving silence. "Thomas, we have so many wonderful memories. When we met in May during the intermission of Giselle…the fundraiser…at the cathedral the next day, we walked and talked and laughed. Remember when you came to my house for dinner and we danced to our song and watched those old romantic movies and the following day we went shopping, that was so much fun. Then at Jack's cabin, where we confessed our love for each other, and we had dinner and went on the picnic and I danced for you and you read poetry to me. Remember?" She stopped for moment. "I love singing and dancing for you. Remember me singing with the guy in the park and dancing on the stage for you. Remember Aruba and Manhattan, and when you watched me dance in my debut and I got to kiss you right after my performance. Did you know I got in trouble for that? I told them I didn't care and if they wanted to, fire me! They asked me not to do it again but I will if I want to." She laughed then smiled at him. "I have so many wonderful memories. I remember every single one of them. You've made me so very happy, I've never been happier in my life. I'm so in love with you and knowing that you love me just as much makes it so special and so perfect. I'm looking forward to being Mrs. Rebecca Carlyle." She looked at her engagement ring, "And being married to the world famous writer Thomas Carlyle. You still have to read me your novel. Thomas, we still have so much life to live, so much still to do, and so many memories to make." She paused, "and love to make." Rebecca stopped and whispered, "My angel." She smiled at Thomas and touched his face and his hair. She stood and kissed him on the mouth and sat back down. She looked at her watch. "Since it's three o'clock and it's Christmas Day I guess I can tell you what your gifts are, there are three. Now if you wake up today and you remember them, pretend you don't and act surprised. The first one, well, I was supposed to go to the store yesterday and pick it up but as you know I was here. So I'll have to tell you. I've booked us on a trip in August for three weeks. Guess where? Okay, I'll tell you. The first stop is in London for three days; I thought we could visit Buckingham Palace, Trafalgar Square, and Piccadilly Circus and see some shows. We then take a train through the Chunnel to Paris and stay there for three nights, they say Paris is for lovers and is very romantic, I thought we could take a boat ride on the Seine, visit the Eiffel Tower and have a glass of wine at some quaint sidewalk café. Then we take a train down to Nice and have fun in the sun for two whole weeks. I know how much you wanted to go there. We can have delectable meals, play the casinos, and dance the night away. In the day we can lie on the beach or go for a swim in the Mediterranean. Guess what hotel I booked in Nice? That's right, The Carlton! The one they used in 'To Catch a Thief'. You always wanted to stay there. Doesn't it sound wonderful and exciting?" She looked at Thomas and waited and hoped for a response. But none came. It was too much she cried for a little while and stopped and wiped her eyes. "The second gift is more personal, I was going to take you to the theater one morning, like last time, and dance for you on the stage. You don't know this but in my spare time I choreographed a routine for the Genesis song 'Firth of Fifth', remember I borrowed your CD to practice to, well, I know how much you like them and you know how much I love that song, so I choreographed a special ballet for you. When it was finished I had Penny watch me and she said it was amazing. It was a great compliment. I can't wait to perform it for you. I know you will love it. My last gift is something very personal and very special. I want you to know I want to have children, not immediately, but sooner rather than later. I knew you would be ecstatic. When we were in Manhattan, that morning in bed, I was going to tell you then but I changed my mind and decided I would surprise you on Christmas Day." She became upset. "If only I knew then what I know now I would have told you that morning. But how was I to know." She fought back the tears. "You're probably wondering why I changed my mind. Maybe it was the little girl on the bicycle in the park? Teaching the children ballet? Holding the baby? Making sandcastles in Aruba? What my father told me? Maybe all those events contributed. But the main reason is that I love you. I want us to share that love with one another and have children and share our love with them. I want to see our children grow and have children and be grandparents and have everyone over for Christmas dinner. I want a family, a family of our own. And want us to grow old together." She began to cry. "Thomas I love you, I need you. Come to me! Come to me! I miss you! Please come back to me! I love you." She cried and put her head on the bed for several minutes. She wiped her eyes and looked up at him. "Thomas, if you can hear me. Come back to me, please. I can't live without you." She wiped her eyes and softly sang 'You're the Best Thing'. She struggled with the last few words, 'so don't go, don't go, don't you go away,' and broke down and cried. She cried herself to sleep.

CHAPTER 22

4 am

THE DARKNESS WAS FADING QUICKLY IN THE distance and the faster it faded the more excruciating the pain. The darkness disappeared and all around him was the bright light. The pain was unbearable. The fragments of sound had now become words and Thomas could hear Rebecca's voice. She had found him and he knew she needed him. He needed her and wanted to go to her. He slowly started moving towards her voice. She had started singing and he recognized the song and started moving very quickly through the white light. Her singing became louder and the white light around him started to break up and shatter. He felt as if he was falling at an incredible speed. Rebecca's singing became clearer and he could distinctly hear the words. The bright light disappeared and he stopped suddenly, everything was blue. The blue light slowly dissipated and objects came into view. He was hovering high above himself in the hospital room and he could see and hear Rebecca crying at his side. Suddenly he was turned around and thrown with great force to the bed. He was back in his body. The pain was tremendous and it was killing him. He fought desperately to open his eyes but his eyelids were heavy. Rebecca's crying had stopped. He needed to see her. He needed to be with her. He fought to be with her. He fought for his life.

At four AM Thomas opened his eyes slowly. The room was out of focus and he waited till his eyes adjusted. He looked down at Rebecca asleep on the bed. She looked so beautiful. Her head was resting on his hand and with all his strength he moved his fingers. She started to wake. He moved them again. She quickly realized what was happening and looked up at Thomas. "Thomas," she whispered.

"Rebecca," he replied.

She moved closer to him. "I thought I had lost you."

"No," he said. "You found me."

"I did?" she replied. The tears started to form. "I love you, Thomas."

"I love you, Rebecca."

They kissed and tears of joy ran down her face.

About the Author

KEVIN MCGANN HAS A UNIQUE STYLE OF developing a romantic love story around relationships, families, modern day issues and universal themes. His well rounded characters and flowing, lighthearted, and sometimes humorous storylyline, makes you believe that you are a character in the unfolding story.

Kevin McGann was born in Liverpool, England and immigrated with his family to North America at the age of ten. At university he studied English, History and Psychology.

For more information visit: www.kevinmcgann.com

LaVergne, TN USA
11 February 2010
172865LV00001B/23/P